ALSO BY ELLE KENNEDY

The
DIXON
RULE

ELLE KENNEDY

Bloom *books*

Published by Bloom Books, an imprint of Sourcebooks
P.O. Box 4410, Naperville, Illinois 60567-4410
(630) 961-3900
sourcebooks.com

Cataloging-in-Publication data is on file with the Library of Congress.

Printed and bound in the United States of America.
LSC 10 9 8 7 6 5 4 3 2

RED BIRCH
BUILDING LAYOUT

GROUND FLOOR

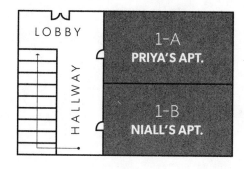

SECOND FLOOR

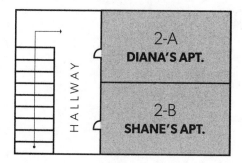

MEADOW HILL
APARTMENTS

CHAPTER ONE
DIANA

Satan strikes again

JULY

TWO BEADS OF WATER FORM AT THE TOP OF MY MIRROR AND THEN slowly begin to race each other down to the bottom. I make a bet with myself that bead number two will be the winner, since it's marginally bigger. Go big or go home, right? But while it picks up speed, there's a quick veer to the left. Bead one stays the course and drips onto my bathroom vanity.

This is why I refuse to gamble.

I grab a washcloth and wipe the rest of the condensation away to reveal my reflection. A pink flush covers my chest and shoulders, evidence of the scalding water temperature. There's something wrong with my shower, but I'm too broke to bring in a plumber, and my dad said he can't drive down to my neck of the woods until later this week. Which means I need to deal with my lava water for a few more days, if my skin doesn't burn off first.

Maybe after Dad fixes the shower, I muse, he can tackle the drawer of the kitchen cabinet that suddenly refuses to open. And then figure out why the refrigerator ice dispenser stopped working for no discernable reason.

Being a homeowner is exhausting. Especially when you're totally incompetent. Did I mention the original issue with my showerhead was that it wouldn't stop dripping? I attempted to fix the drip myself by watching an online tutorial, and that's how the shower spray turned into a volcano. DIY plumbing is not my friend.

I turn away from the mirror and pull a fluffy, pink towel off the door hook, exiting the steam-filled bathroom to inhale the normal air in the hallway.

"I almost died in there," I inform Skip when I enter the living room, tucking the towel around me. I glance across the roomy, loftlike space toward the twenty-gallon fish tank against the far wall of the living area.

The fat goldfish glances back at me with that deathly, unnerving stare.

"I don't like that you can't blink," I tell him. "It freaks me the fuck out."

He stares again, then swishes his fins and swims to the other end of the tank. A second later, he's not so covertly hiding behind a gold-painted treasure chest. When I showed the guy at the fish store a picture of Skip, he told me he'd never seen a goldfish that large. Apparently my fish is obese. Not to mention too silent for my peace of mind. I don't trust pets that don't make noise.

"You know what, Skip? One of these days you're going to be upset about something and instead of comforting you, I'm going to swim away too. So put that in your stupid pirate's chest and choke on it."

I hate fish. If I had the choice, I would not be a fish owner. This horrible task was foisted on me by my dead aunt, who bequeathed her prized, unhelpful goldfish to me in her last will and testament. The executor looked like he was trying not to laugh when he read that part out loud to our family. My younger brother, Thomas, didn't make the effort—he busted out in laughter until Dad gave him the look.

On the upside, the fishbowl came with Aunt Jennifer's apartment, which makes me a twenty-one-year-old homeowner. So you win some, you lose some.

The shower was so scorching it left me parched. I want to chug a bottle of water before I get dressed. I walk barefoot to the fridge, but my step stutters when the cell phone on the granite counter suddenly chimes, startling me. I pivot and check the screen, then stifle a groan. It's a message from my ex.

PERCY:

> Hey, want to get together tonight and catch up? I'm free after 8.

Nope. Not interested. But I can't be that blunt, obviously. I might have a temper, but I'm not needlessly rude. I'll have to find a nice way of letting him down.

This isn't the first time he's reached out to "catch up." I suppose it's my fault, since I said we could remain friends after the breakup. Here's some advice: *never* offer to stay friends if you don't mean it. It's a recipe for disaster.

I abandon my phone on the counter and grab a water bottle from the fridge. I'll deal with this Percy text after I get dressed.

I'm tossing the empty bottle in the trash can under the sink when the familiar sound of meowing permeates the hall. The paper-thin walls of my condo do nothing to block out the noise outside my door. I hear every footstep, and the pitter-patter of Lucy's tiny paws is no exception. Plus the damn thing wears a bell on her collar, advertising her every move.

I stifle a curse as the sense of obligation sinks in. I love my downstairs neighbor, Priya, but her escape-artist cat drives me nuts. At least once a week, Lucy manages to break out of her apartment unseen.

Opening the door pulls a gust of cold air into my entryway. I try to shake off the goose bumps forming on my arms as I step onto the smooth tile outside my door.

"Lucy?" I ring out in a singsong voice.

I know better than to allow any hint of frustration to show in my tone when I call her name. At the slightest sign of anger, that gray ball of fluff will shoot downstairs for the lobby door like a meteor hurtling toward Earth.

Meadow Hill, our apartment complex, isn't like other buildings. It's not some fifty-story monstrosity stuffed with hundreds of condos. Instead, the architect who designed it fashioned it after a beach resort, so the grounds consist of fifteen two-story buildings each housing four condos. Winding paths connect all the buildings, many of which overlook the lush lawn, tennis courts, and swimming pool. The last time Lucy snuck out, my other downstairs neighbor, Niall, was just coming home from work. Lucy took advantage of the opening lobby door and flew past him in the search for eternal freedom.

"Lucy?" I call again.

The jingling of a bell beckons me from the staircase. With a hoarse meow, the gray, striped cat appears on the top step. She sits down, all prim and proper, and stares at me defiantly.

Yeah, I'm here, she's taunting. *What are you gonna do about it, bitch?*

I slowly lower myself to my knees so we're closer to eye level. "You are the devil's cat," I inform her.

She studies me for a moment, then lifts one paw, giving it a demure lick before setting it back on the tile.

"I mean it. You were brought here from hell, personally delivered by the cold hands of Satan. Be honest—did he send you up here to torment me?"

"*Meow*," she says smugly. Unblinking.

My jaw drops. Bitch basically just confirmed it!

I shuffle forward on my knees, gripping the top of my towel. I'm two feet away when, without warning, voices echo in the lobby and footsteps thunder from the bottom of the stairs.

Lucy bolts, literally jumping over my shoulder like she's a tiny hurdler in the feline Olympics. She flies through the open crack in my door, leaving me so startled that I stumble forward. My hands instinctively splay out in front of me to catch myself, causing me to lose my grip on my towel.

It hits the floor just as a shadow falls over me.

I screech in surprise. The next thing I know, three hockey players are staring down at me.

At *naked* me. Because I'm naked.

Did I mention that I'm naked?

"You okay there, Dixon?" drawls a deep, mocking voice.

My hands rush to hide my nudity, but I only have two of them and there are at least three zones I'd prefer obscured.

"Oh my God, look away," I command, snatching the towel off the floor.

To their credit, the guys do avert their gazes. I shoot to my feet, hastily securing the terrycloth in place. Of *all* the people who could've found me in this predicament, it just *had* to be Shane Lindley and his friends. And what are they even doing here—

Understanding dawns. Oh no.

Dread forms in the pit of my stomach at the sight of Shane's amused dark eyes. "*No.* It's today?"

He flashes a broad smile, showing off a set of perfect white teeth. "Oh, it's today."

Satan strikes again.

Shane is moving in.

Luckily, not with me. Because that would be doubly appalling. I could never share an apartment with such a cocky jackass. It's bad enough that we'll be sharing a floor. Shane's parents—because they're rich and apparently believe that excessively spoiling their children is conducive to raising humble adults—bought their not-at-all-humble son the unit next to mine. It's been sitting vacant since my last neighbor, Chandra, retired and moved to Maine to be closer to family.

My best friend, Gigi, is married to Shane's best friend, Ryder, so she warned me the move would be happening sometime this week. I would've appreciated a more specific day and time, however. Or at least a heads-up text today. Then I could've been prepared and maybe *not* in a towel. I'm definitely yelling at her about this at dinner tonight.

"Don't worry, we didn't see a thing." The reassurance comes from the boy-next-door face of Will Larsen.

"I saw your tits and one butt cheek," Beckett Dunne says helpfully.

I don't know whether to laugh or groan. With his perfect face, faint Australian accent, and wavy blond hair, Beckett is too sexy for his own good. Anything that exits his mouth simply comes off as charming, whereas from anyone else it would be sleazy.

"Erase them from your memory," I warn.

"Impossible," he replies, winking at me.

I glance back at Shane, my good humor fading. "It's not too late to sell," I say in a hopeful tone.

But I know that's just a beautiful dream. He's not going anywhere, not after his parents probably spent a fortune renovating the place for him. There've been nonstop construction noises coming out of his condo this past month. Poor Niall from downstairs was having daily power drill–induced nervous breakdowns. That man is violently allergic to noise.

I wonder what changes Shane made to the apartment. I bet he turned it into a stereotypical man cave to suit his fuckboy tastes.

And trust me, I'm well aware of those tastes. They include (as of now, but I'm still counting) two and a half of my cheerleading teammates—half because he only made out with the third one. Still, the guy's plowing through them like a farmer after harvest season. Gigi told me he got his heart broken last year and this is his first time being single in forever. She says he's making up for lost time. But that sounds like a whole bunch of excuses, and I don't think you need to make excuses for fuckboys. They're just born with that gene.

"You don't have to put on this tough-girl act in front of the guys," Shane tells me. "Everyone knows about your crush."

I snort. "I think the only one who has a crush on you is *you*."

Honestly, I wouldn't be surprised if the guy spent his free time off the ice ogling himself in the mirror. Hockey players are notoriously obsessed with two things: hockey and themselves. And Shane Lindley is no exception.

I'm not sucked in by how handsome he is, though he's unarguably gorgeous. Tall and handsome. Wide, sensual mouth and black hair in a buzz cut. A jacked athlete's body and dimples that dig little grooves into his cheeks whenever he tries to lure you in with a brash smile. This afternoon, that ripped body is clad in basketball shorts and a red T-shirt that complements his darker skin tone.

When I notice Beckett's gray eyes give my towel-wrapped body another scan, I aim a frown his way. "You can stare as long as you want, but I promise, the towel isn't slipping down again."

"Well, if it does, I'd prefer not to miss it." His teeth practically gleam from the fluorescent lights when he gives that fuck-me smile.

"Is that your apartment?" Will asks, gesturing to the door behind me.

"Unfortunately."

"Damn. When Gigi said you two were going to be neighbors, I didn't realize you were *neighbors*," he remarks, his gaze shifting from my door to the one down the hall.

"Please don't rub it in," I grumble. To Shane, I say, "If you're expecting a welcome parade, you're shit out of luck. My new goal is to find a way to live my life without ever bumping into you."

"Good luck with that." Shane's dark-brown eyes flicker with humor. "Because *my* new goal is for us to become best friends and spend every waking hour together. Oh, hey, actually. I'm throwing a party this weekend. We should cohost. Keep both our doors open and—"

"*No.*" I stab my index finger in the air. "Nope. That is not happening. In fact, you two"—I shoot a glare at Will and Beckett—"go wait for him in his apartment. Lindley and I need to discuss the rules of engagement."

CHAPTER TWO
SHANE

The summer of Shane

I'M LAUGHING TO MYSELF AS I FOLLOW THE ANGRY BLOND INTO HER apartment. The moment we emerge from the entryway into the main room, I have to blink a couple of times because it's not at all what I expected. The living area contains mismatched furniture and a burgundy area rug that clashes with the pale-blue floral-pattered sofa. The kind of sofa you might find in your dead grandma's house when you're going there to clean out her stuff. Like, nobody in the family is going to be fighting over that couch unless it's to argue about who has to drive it to Goodwill.

"This place has a real cat-lady vibe," I remark.

"*Meow,*" something whines from the kitchen.

"Holy shit. You actually have a cat." My jaw drops as a gray tabby appears from behind the narrow island and eyes me like I murdered her kittens.

Diana's expression mirrors the cat's. "That's Lucy. She likes to sneak out when our downstairs neighbor is seeing one of her therapy clients."

"S'up?" I tell the cat, nodding in greeting.

"Don't bother. She's a demon from the pits of hell," Diana says at the exact moment Lucy wanders over and rubs up against my leg.

The cat gives a happy purr, snaking her furry body between my shins.

Diana glowers at us. "Why am I not surprised you two get along? Go away, Lucy. Lindley and I need to talk."

Lucy just sits at my feet, still purring.

"She has great taste in people," I say, while continuing to examine my bizarre surroundings.

There's an antique cabinet full of glassware that's completely out of place next to the super-modern bookcase beside it. And is that...

"Oh my God. You have a fish? Who has a pet fish? Have some self-respect, Dixon."

Her emerald-green eyes shoot fireballs at me. I can practically feel the heat. "Leave my fish out of this. He's not perfect, but he's mine."

I bite back a laugh. It doesn't escape me that she's still in nothing but a towel. And...well, I'm not going to lie...she looks really fucking good. Diana's gorgeous, with wide-set eyes, platinum-blond hair, and a sassy mouth. She's a little shorter than I usually like, barely over five feet, five-two if we're being generous. A pint-sized hottie with a big personality. Although it seems like a major part of that personality involves busting the balls of yours truly.

"I'm going to change. But we need to talk, so don't go anywhere."

"I can help you get dressed," I offer innocently.

"Ew. Never."

I smother a laugh. Diana and I have a love-hate relationship. As in, she hates me, and I love to annoy her.

As she flounces off, I admire the way the towel rides up the backs of her toned thighs. I swear I glimpse the bottom curve of her ass cheeks. Her fair skin boasts a deep summer tan, which tells me she must be making good use of the pool outside. Fuck, I've got a *pool* now. This place is so sick.

I don't even care that my friends and teammates keep ragging me about the fact that my "rich daddy" bought me a condo. Sure, my family has money, but I'm not some spoiled, entitled dickhead. I didn't ask Dad to buy me an apartment. It's an investment for him—once I graduate from Briar University and head to Chicago to play in the NHL, he'll just rent this place out, the way he does with his hordes of other properties in Vermont and northern Massachusetts.

In the meantime, I get to enjoy my own space after sharing a house with Ryder and Beckett for the past three years. Two of those years were spent at Eastwood, our former college. After the Eastwood and Briar men's hockey teams merged, we moved to Hastings, the small town closest to the Briar campus.

Diana returns in a pair of tiny cutoff shorts and a baggy T-shirt. She's not wearing a bra, and my eyes dip involuntarily toward the tight buds of her nipples, which are poking against the thin material.

"Stop looking at my boobs."

I don't deny that's what I was doing. Shrugging, I shift my gaze and sweep my hand to gesture at the loftlike space. "Terrible interior design aside, this place is really nice. Looks a little bigger than mine too. How much is your rent?"

"I don't rent. And I'm not telling you how much my mortgage is. Nosy much?"

My eyebrows fly up. "You own it? That's badass."

She pauses, as if she doesn't want to engage with me, then says, "My aunt left it to me in her will. She only lived here a year before she died."

I glance around. I don't want to ask, but...

"Oh my God, she didn't die in this room. She had a heart attack in her office in Boston."

"Damn. That sucks. I'm sorry."

"Anyway. Let's get this out of the way. The rules." Diana crosses her arms. "Just because you're in Meadow Hill now, doesn't mean you'll have the run of the place."

"I think that's exactly what it means." Highly amused, I mimic her pose by crossing my own arms. "I live here."

"No, you live *there*." She points to the wall behind her to indicate my apartment beyond it. "You don't live *here*." She waves her hand around her living room. "So don't go around offering to throw parties in my house."

"I didn't offer. I simply made a suggestion."

She ignores me. "Because I'm not cohosting any parties with you. This is my sanctuary. I don't know what Gigi's told you about me—"

"She said you're a pain in the ass."

Diana gasps. "She did not."

"And she said you're high-maintenance."

"She didn't say that either."

"Actually, that part she did."

That narrows her eyes, and I know she'll be texting Gigi after this for verification. My best friend's wife—Christ, that's still strange to say—warned me away from Diana, advising me to leave her best friend alone if I didn't want daily tongue-lashings. It's not in my nature, though. Some people might shy away from confrontation. Some might lose sleep over the notion that someone might not like them—and I know for a fact Diana doesn't like me. But I'm not averse to confrontation, and for some reason, her dislike only makes me want to bother her even more. It's the preschooler in me. All men regress to their kindergarten days every now and then.

"Are you listening to me?" she grumbles.

I lift my head. Oh, she's still lecturing. Totally spaced out. "Sure. No parties in your apartment."

"And no parties in the pool."

I raise a brow. "Now you're speaking for the whole building?"

"No. The building is speaking for the building. Did you not read your homeowner's packet?"

"Babe, I just walked in here."

"Don't call me babe."

"I didn't even reach my front door before you dragged me in here."

"Well, read your HOA package. We take this stuff very seriously, okay? The association meets twice a month on Sunday morning."

"Yeah, I'm not doing that."

"I didn't expect you to. And frankly, don't want you there. Okay—" She claps her hands as if she's leading one of her cheerleading practices. Diana's the cheer captain at Briar. "Let's summarize the rules. Go easy on the parties. Wipe the equipment down after you use the gym. Don't have sex in the pool."

"What about blowjobs in the pool?"

"Look, I don't care who you want to suck off, Lindley. Just don't do it in the pool."

I grin at her. "I meant I would be on the receiving end."

"Oh. Did you?" Diana smiles sweetly. "I think the most important thing for you to remember is, we are not friends."

"Lovers, then?" I wink at her.

"We are neither friends nor lovers. We are floor mates. We are quiet, respectful residents of the Red Birch building in Meadow Hill. We don't annoy each other—"

"I mean, you're kind of annoying me right now."

"—we don't cause trouble, and, preferably, we don't speak."

"Isn't this considered speaking?"

"No. This is the conversation leading up to the future conversations we won't be having. In conclusion, we're not friends. No shenanigans. Oh, and stop screwing my teammates."

Ah, so that's what all this is about. She's still salty because I messed around with a few of her cheerleaders last semester. Apparently one of them, Audrey, caught feelings and was so distracted at practice she fell off the pyramid and sprained her ankle. But how is that on me? When I'm on the ice, I'm able to push everything out and focus on hockey. Banish all distractions and excel at my sport. If Audrey couldn't block out a dude she hooked up with *once*, that sounds like a her-problem.

"All right," I say impatiently. "Are there any more Dixon rules, or may I please be excused? My furniture isn't gonna assemble itself."

"That's all. Although, really, there's only one Dixon rule that matters. No Shanes allowed."

"Allowed where?"

"Anywhere and everywhere. But mostly just in my vicinity." She smiles again, but it lacks any trace of humor. "Okay, we're done here." She points to the entryway. "You can go now."

"So it's going to be like that, huh?"

"Yes, I literally just *told* you it was going to be like that. Happy housewarming, Lindley."

I dutifully leave her apartment and return to mine, where Will and Beckett are tackling the assembly of my new sectional couch. Will's using a knife to slice open the plastic that the big cushions come in, while Beckett crouches on the hardwood floor, trying to figure out how to lock the main section to the chaise. I opted for a dark-gray color because it'll be easier to clean. Not that I'll ever get the chance—my mother insists on sending a cleaner to my house every two weeks. She did the same for the townhouse I shared with the boys. According to her, my cleaning abilities will never be anything other than subpar. I disagree. I think I could at least make par. Gotta aim high in the cleaning world.

"Sorry about that," I tell the guys. "Dixon needed to chew me out for a while. It's how she shows her love for me."

Will snorts.

Beckett glances up with a grin. "Yeah, sorry, mate, but that is one bird you're not gonna win over with those dimples."

He's probably right about that.

"Dude, she really doesn't like you," Will adds, hammering the point home. "I grabbed dinner with her and Gigi last week, and when your name came up, Diana rolled her eyes so hard, it looked like they were gonna pop out of her face."

"Aw, thank you. Hearing that makes me feel *so* good about myself."

"Uh-huh, I'm sure your massive ego took a real hit."

I walk over to help Will with the cushions and then the three of us drag the couch to a new spot after Beck decides it can't be under the window because it'll get too cold in the winter. We position the sectional so it now faces the exposed red brick that makes up the far wall of living room. I step back to examine the layout. It's perfect.

"We should mount the TV there," I say, pointing to the brick. "Can we drill into that?"

"Yeah, should be fine," Beckett answers, walking over to study the wall. He shoves a few messy strands of blond hair out of his face. "Larsen, grab the drill?"

"Look at you," I mock. "Mr. Handyman."

Beckett winks. "Are you seriously surprised to hear I'm good with my hands?"

Good point.

Once we've got the couch and TV squared away, we head for the bedroom to put the bed together. It's a queen, although I probably could've fit a king in here. Will unpacks the hardware. Beckett and I organize the various pieces of sleek dark-cherry wood. While we work, Beck rambles on about everything he plans to do when he's home this summer. Technically speaking, his home is in Indianapolis, which is where his family moved when Beckett was ten, but he was born and half raised in Australia. He's leaving for Sydney on Sunday.

"Sucks neither of you are coming," he says glumly. "I get why Ryder can't. But seriously? Neither of you could get away?"

I shrug. "Yeah, sorry. I can't fuck off to Australia. Summer's really the only time I get to hang out with my family." It's the truth. For the rest of the year, I'm laser-focused on hockey and, to a lesser extent, the schoolwork required in order to remain eligible to play.

Beckett nods. "I feel you. Family's important." I know he's tight with his parents and with his cousins in Australia. He's an only child, so they're the closest things to siblings he has.

"I'm surprised you're not going," I say, glancing at Will.

He shrugs. "I'm working this summer. I want to do a backpacking trip through Europe after graduation. Maybe spend six months to a year over there."

"Nice. Sounds awesome."

Beckett snickers at me. "Coming from the guy who would never be caught dead backpacking."

"That's not true. I would totally do it."

"Really," Beck says dubiously.

"Sure. I'd wear a backpack while we explored some cool part of the city and then take it off when I returned to my five-star hotel."

"Bougie prick."

I grin. In all honesty, I don't mind roughing it. Camping is great. And backpacking around Europe does sound like a blast. But why travel on a budget when you don't have a budget?

"You've got a landscaping gig or something, right?" I ask Will.

"Pool company."

My jaw drops. "You're a pool boy?"

As Will nods, Beckett heaves a loud sigh.

I glance over in amusement. "Do you have something to add?"

"Just…don't get your hopes up. You find out your mate is a pool boy and you create a whole narrative in your head and then *bam*, he shoots down your bubble and your dreams float away like a feather on the wind."

"Those were a lot of weird metaphors just to say I don't fuck the clients." Will rolls his eyes and reiterates that point to me. "I don't fuck the clients."

"Why the hell not?" I'm picturing neglected MILFs in tiny bikinis sashaying over to bring Will glasses of lemonade, and then, *oops, my bikini top fell off. Would you like to bang?*

"Because I'd get fired, for one." His tone is dry.

"Fair. But what's life without the risk of getting fired?"

"Says the rich boy."

"Isn't your dad a congressman? I feel like you're probably richer than I am. AKA the last person who needs to work as a pool boy all summer."

"Nah. I don't ever want to be beholden to my dad. I'd rather make my own way."

I guess that's admirable. With that said, I'm not about to complain about the fact that my folks are still paying my way. I'm twenty-one years old and blissfully unemployed. It's the summer before senior year and I want to enjoy every second of it. My plan is to really focus on strength and conditioning ahead of this hockey season. Hit the gym every morning. Try to incorporate swimming into my cardio regimen. I also got a membership to a golf club near here, so I'll be on the green at least a few times a week.

Let the Summer of Shane commence.

After the boys and I finish assembling the bed and clean up, Beck and Will ask if I want to grab dinner with them in town, but I beg off. I want to do some unpacking and organize my shit.

For this afternoon's services, I'm repaying them in the form of beer and a party on Saturday night, which Beckett reminds me of as I walk them to the front hall.

"Don't forget about my goodbye party," he drawls.

"Yes, of course, the goodbye party you're throwing for yourself."

"And?"

"And that's stupid. But I'm looking forward to christening the pool, so I guess a my-dumbass-friend-is-going-on-vacation gathering is as good a reason as any."

He chuckles. "What did your new neighbor say about the party?"

"Dixon? Oh, she's excited. Can't wait for it."

"Tread carefully," Will warns. "Diana can be vicious. And she's not above playing dirty."

"Is that supposed to deter me?" I ask with a grin. "The dirtier the better."

After my buddies leave, I wander toward the kitchen island to examine all the documents my mom left on the counter. My parents were here yesterday making some final preparations ahead of my move-in date. Meaning that Mom stocked the fridge and made sure all the important paperwork was in one place, while Dad squared up with his contractor.

I settle on a tall, black-leather stool and sigh as I sift through the large stack of paper. The information is about as lame as I expect it to be.

I flip pages until one catches my eye. It's an illustrated map of the Meadow Hill property, and I lean forward on my forearms to study it. Why is every building named after trees? Mine is Red Birch. Next door is Silver Pine. White Ash, Weeping Willow, Sugar Maple. The main building is called the Sycamore, which is where our mailboxes are located. It also offers a round-the-clock security guard at the front desk. That's good.

I set the map aside and try to focus on the next page, but it's tedious reading. Like Diana said, the homeowners' association meets every two weeks, and I'm invited to join. Twice a month, though? What kind of HOA needs to meet that often? And on a Sunday? Yeah, I won't be caught dead at some stuffy board meeting where soccer moms and their sex-starved husbands can argue about pool regulations and when to start your lawn mowers. I'll never be that mundane.

The noise ordinances make zero sense. It says no noise after nine p.m. on weekdays, except for Fridays, when it's eleven p.m. No noise after midnight on weekends, except on Sunday, when you're only allowed to be noisy until ten p.m. So basically, Friday doesn't count as the weekend, neither does Sunday, and the only night you can have fun is Saturday. Okay then.

I get about halfway through the stack before I give up. I'll finish the rest later. My brain isn't equipped for this much boredom.

I head to my new bedroom. My approach to packing up my room in the old townhouse was very utilitarian. Much to my mother's dismay, I shoved most of my clothes and linens into garbage bags.

Not pretty, but efficient. I rummage through the linens bag and find a new set of sheets and pillowcases. Another garbage bag houses a duvet and cover. After I make the bed, I sit at the foot of it, wriggle my phone out of my pocket, and dial my mom's number.

"Hello!" she answers happily. "Are you all done?"

"Yup, the guys just left. Couch, TV, and bed are all set up."

"Good. What about the condo in general? Do you like it? Are you happy with the paint colors we chose for the kitchen? And the backsplash? I thought the white tile was more tasteful."

"It all looks great," I assure her. "I mean it. Thanks again for everything you did. I couldn't have decorated it more perfectly myself."

Mom literally chose it all: the paint swatches, the artwork for the walls. The random shit I probably wouldn't have even thought about, like dish racks and coat hangers.

"Of course," she says. "Anything for my kid. Have you—Maryanne! No! Give me that baking soda!" Her voice grows muffled as she reprimands my little sister. Then she's back, and I hear her clearly again. "Sorry. Your sister is driving me up the wall. She's trying to build a modified bottle rocket."

"I'm sorry, what?"

"They learned how to make mini bottle rockets at camp last week and she found a way to modify it so it's more powerful." Mom curses under her breath. "This is what we get for sending her to space camp."

"I thought she was doing geology camp."

"No, that's in August."

Only my little sister would be attending not one but two science camps in the span of a summer. Luckily, this doesn't make her a nerd because she's legitimately the coolest ten-year-old I've ever met in my life. Maryanne is awesome. So are my parents, for that matter. We've always been super tight.

"Anyway, what else did I want to ask you?" she says thoughtfully.

"Oh right. The three other condos in Red Birch. What about your neighbors? Have you met any of them?"

"Just one. She was outside her apartment buck naked when we got here."

"What? You're joking?" Mom gasps.

"Nope. She was chasing after a cat and dropped her towel. Best accident I've ever witnessed."

"Don't be gross, Shane."

I laugh to myself. "Sorry. Anyway, don't worry. She hates my guts, so we're all good."

"What? That isn't good at all. Why doesn't she like you?"

"Oh, I know her from Briar—she's a friend of a friend. It's fine. I don't consider her a real neighbor. I'm sure the other ones are awesome and not at all obnoxious."

We chat for a bit longer, and I make plans to come home to Vermont at the end of the week for a couple days. After I end the call, I wonder who else might be in town this week. If any old high school friends are visiting for the summer and—

Is this what we're doing now? a voice in my head mocks. *Lying to ourselves?*

Oh fuck. Fine. I wonder if Lynsey will be there. And I know I shouldn't wonder. Or care. Because we broke up a little over a year ago, and that's a fuckin' long time to still be thinking about someone.

Fortunately, my phone buzzes with an incoming text before I can dwell on how pathetic I am for still being hung up on my ex-girlfriend.

CRYSTAL:

Are you all moved in?

I ran into her in town earlier when the boys and I grabbed coffee from Starbucks before heading over here. She's cute. Dark, shiny hair. Great smile. Even greater rack. We exchanged numbers while standing in line, much to the amusement of Beckett and Will.

Since I need to redirect my brain ASAP, I waste no time composing a response to Crystal. The last thing I want to do tonight is sit here obsessing over my ex. I'm better than that. And hornier.

ME:

Wanna chill tonight?

CRYSTAL:

Yeah, I could hang. I don't have cheer camp tomorrow.

I guess I should also mention that Crystal is a cheerleader at Briar. Yup. Another one of Diana's teammates.

Look at me, breaking all the Dixon rules.

ME:

I'll text you the address.

CHAPTER THREE
DIANA

Who taught you life?

"OH MY GOD, I'M GOING TO PEE MY PANTS. MOVE! MOVE, DIANA! GET out of my way!"

Gigi Graham barrels through my door and practically knocks me into the hall closet. We have dinner plans tonight, but instead of waiting for me in the driveway outside the Sycamore building like she was supposed to, she used her spare key to access the lobby and showed up at my door in a pee panic.

Her sandals slap the hardwood on her mad race to the bathroom. She's in too much of a hurry to close the door, and seconds later I hear the faint tinkle hitting the porcelain.

"Where are your manners?" I call out.

"They left me after the third iced coffee. I made the mistake of chugging another one right before I left Boston to come get you."

"Iced coffee, huh? Are you sure you're not…you know…"

"What?"

"Pregnant, Gigi."

There's a loud strangled noise. "What! God no! Just because I got married doesn't mean I'm ready for a kid. I drank too much in the car and didn't feel like stopping. Trust me, you'd be the first person I called if I got pregnant. Because I'd be freaking the fuck out."

The toilet flushes. I hear her washing her hands and then she returns to the kitchen, much more relaxed.

Her gaze drifts to my coffee table and stops there. "Did you get a cat?"

Thanks to the chaos of Shane moving in next door, I forgot about Lucy. She's cowering under the table, her tail flicking in agitation. I texted Priya I'd bring her back when I left for dinner.

When Lucy sees me looking, she gives a whiny meow.

"Oh, you're annoyed at me? Really? I get caught naked in front of my fuckboy neighbor because you decide to body-check me and *I'm* the bad guy?" I turn to Gigi, answering her question. "She's my neighbor's cat and she's a demon. We need to drop her off downstairs on our way out."

"Wait, were you talking about Shane?" Gigi bursts out laughing. "Shane saw you naked?"

"I fell when Lucy bolted and lost my towel just as Shane was coming up the stairs." I growl. "I *hate* giving Lindley the upper hand. Seeing me naked is totally upper hand ammunition." I raise my eyes upward in exasperation. "Why is this my life?"

"Why are you talking to the ceiling?"

"I'm not talking to the ceiling. I'm talking to the universe."

"Why is the universe up there? It's all around us."

"Fine, I'm talking to the gods, then. All fifty of them."

"You're so fucking weird." She steps away from the counter. "Okay, shall we head out?"

The click of her sandals on the kitchen tile is no louder than the drop of a pen to my ears, but to my neighbor Niall, our steps might as well have been an avalanche of pots and pans raining down from the ceiling.

"Keep it down!" I hear his muffled voice shout from below us.

"And I repeat, why is this my life?" I give the floor a quick stomp. "If you don't like basic walking, Niall," I shout, "then you're really not going to like all the dancing I'm going to do tomorrow!"

"I take it Kenji's coming over?" Gigi says in amusement.

"Yup."

Kenji is a friend from school and, more importantly, my dance partner. This marks our third year as aspiring ballroom dance champions, and we're not entering just any competition either. Only *the* biggest amateur dance event in the country, held annually in Boston.

Yes, people. I'm talking about the National Upper Amateur Ballroom Championships.

It used to be the NABC, minus the U, but too many beginners were treating it like a fun event. God forbid! So now we're UPPER amateurs, thank you very much. Meaning that no Joe and Sally off the street brandishing a check for the entry amount can just pay their way to compete. The ballroom dance gatekeepers don't mess around. In fact, you can't even qualify for an NUABC slot without passing a preliminary round. All potential entrants are required to send a two-minute video featuring a routine from the list of approved dances. A panel of three judges reviews every audition tape and green-lights who gets to compete.

Which means I'm training for something that might not even result in me competing. Kenji and I qualified last year, though, so I have high hopes we'll do it again.

"You always have so many things going on," Gigi marvels. "Cheerleading, this dance stuff…"

"That's two things."

"Fine, but you're always throwing yourself headfirst into these side gigs. Your cheer schedule is already hectic enough as it is, and then you go adding ballroom dancing to the mix and somehow manage to give it an equal amount of attention. If I had to concentrate on something other than hockey and put the same effort into it, I'd be a zombie." She shakes her head as another thing occurs to her. "And you have two jobs! What the hell. Are you a superhuman?"

I shrug. "Life's too short to not do all the things I want to do."

"Life is also exhausting." She snorts. "To everyone but you, apparently."

I do possess a scary amount of energy. I'll give her that.

Grabbing my purse off the plaid-upholstered armchair next to the couch, I throw the strap over my shoulder, then kneel in front of the coffee table. "Come on, demon. Time to go home."

Lucy tries to back away, but I pick her up despite her mewled protest.

"No," I order. "I've had enough of your attitude."

I manage to keep a firm grip on the tabby while I lock up, and then Gigi and I descend the one flight of stairs to the main floor. Lucy wails in annoyance when I pass her off to a very relieved Priya.

"Thanks for keeping her," Priya says, her dark eyes shining with gratitude. "I would've run upstairs to grab her earlier, but I couldn't leave my client alone in the apartment."

"It's no problem. Although I'm sure Niall didn't enjoy hearing her meows bouncing off the walls as she prowled the building."

The man with the keenest sense of hearing on the planet voices a confirmation. "It was intolerable!" comes the muffled complaint behind the door of 1B.

"Oh, get over it, Niall!" Priya calls back.

My best friend shakes her head at me as we exit the tiny lobby and step onto the wide path in front of Red Birch.

"What?" I ask.

"You know, your mom may have a point about this condo. You can't even walk in your own kitchen without being yelled at. It's ridiculous."

After Aunt Jennifer's estate was settled, my mother wanted me to sell the condo and take the cash like my younger brother did with her Boston apartment. But Thomas and I are very different creatures. Despite what most people think when they meet me, I'm somewhat of a homebody. I love going out, sure, but I'm also perfectly content, and often prefer, staying home.

Thomas, on the other hand, is always on the go. His dream is to work for an international organization like Doctors Without Borders after med school. He graduated high school this spring, and now he's taking a gap year to explore the world and volunteer with a couple of different charities. The money from the sale of Aunt Jennifer's apartment will not only fund his travels but cover his college and medical school tuition.

I got a full scholarship to Briar, which means I don't need to pay for school, and I'm not too interested in global exploration. So really, I don't need the liquid cash. Except maybe to pay for a real handyman. But I'd never tell my mother that. I don't want to give her the satisfaction of knowing my domestic situation is anything other than blissful.

She's always had low expectations of me. But I'm used to it. It annoys me, sure, but there's nothing I can do to change the way she views me. And, truthfully, I harbor no ill will toward my mom. We just aren't close. After my parents divorced when I was twelve, I chose to live with my father because he's less regimented. Mom had a laundry list of rules that I had to adhere to. Living away from her created a barrier in our relationship that we couldn't shake. A distance we couldn't bridge.

It also doesn't help that she thinks I'm an idiot. Truly. In my mother's eyes, anyone with an IQ below 150 is beneath her.

Gigi and I grab dinner at a burger place in Hastings, where we chat about our summer plans while we wait for our food.

"No chance you can make it to Tahoe?" She can't hide her disappointment.

Gigi's family spends every August in Lake Tahoe, but this year they're only there for two weeks because Gigi is getting married at the end of the month. Seems redundant, considering she and Ryder already eloped in April. But her parents—well, her dad mostly—guilted Gigi into having a proper wedding.

"I really can't," I say regretfully. "I have to work."

It's nearly impossible finding a job in Hastings, especially during the school year. Anyone who wants solid work usually has to make the hour commute to Boston, which takes even longer when you don't have a car, like me. When I snagged this waitressing gig at the diner in town, I didn't think twice. It's a necessary sacrifice—I work at Della's during the summer and secure myself a job for the fall. I'm also coaching at a youth cheer camp in July and August, so either way I wouldn't have been able to gallivant off to Tahoe.

"I'll have some free weekends and a lot of weeknights," I tell Gigi. "So I'll definitely be able to come see you in Boston or help with wedding stuff. Attend dress fittings and all that."

"Oh, don't worry. My aunt Summer is handling it all." She sighs. "So you can expect at least two emails a day."

She doesn't know the half of it. It's already started. I'm planning Gigi's bachelorette with my co–maid of honor, Mya, Gigi's former roommate. And Aunt Summer has already unleashed herself on us. She insists on being involved in our plans, despite not even being in the wedding party. The woman is a chaos tornado in designer threads.

"I can't believe I won't have a plus-one for your wedding," I realize.

"You could go with Shane."

I laugh so loudly that the couple in the next booth glances over.

"Got it. No Shane." She looks ill at ease now. "I'd suggest asking Percy, since you insist on staying friends with him, but honestly, I'd rather he didn't come. I'd also rather you ditched this friend idea."

"You don't have to worry. I was just being nice when I told him that." I hesitate. "And now I'm regretting it. He texted me earlier asking to hang out."

"I hope you said no."

"I didn't answer."

"Good. Don't."

I crack a smile. "You really didn't like him, huh?"

"No. He was kind of a dick," she admits, and it's not the first time she's said that.

We frequently hashed and rehashed Gigi's thoughts toward my ex-boyfriend during my six-month relationship with Percy. Her biggest beef was with our age difference, although if I'm honest, that was part of his appeal and a major factor in why I stuck it out for so long when it was obvious after only a few months that we were incompatible.

Percy's twenty-six, and while five years isn't a massive gap in the grand scheme of things, it does make a difference in your twenties. So many guys I know who are twenty or twenty-one seem like little boys compared to those I've met who are twenty-five or twenty-six.

Percy's maturity drew me to him. I can't deny it was exciting being with someone older. He was confident, so grounded in his opinions, his goals. He was sweet and attentive. He treated me like a valued partner, rather than a glorified sex doll like a lot of guys I've had the displeasure of encountering. He was a perfect gentleman.

For a while.

Once I got to know him better, I realized he's not confident but thin-skinned. He's opinionated, yes, but in a condescending way. And that sweet, attentive man had a habit of sulking when something didn't go his way.

"He was so possessive when we all went out that one time," Gigi reminds me. She makes a face. "Oh, and he said he loved you during *sex*. That's so cringey."

I don't disagree. Percy could be...intense when it came to sharing his feelings. The first time he dropped the L-Bomb was mid-ejaculation. I didn't say it back, and I could tell by the displeased flash in his eyes that he didn't love *that*. I jokingly told him I-love-yous during sex can't be taken seriously because of all the endorphins. So a few weeks later he took me out to dinner and, over dessert he insisted we share using *one* fork, said it for real that time.

Again, I didn't say it back.

I'm more of a slow burner. I've only told one boyfriend I loved him, and that was after six months of dating. But when Percy and I hit the six-month mark and I still didn't feel anything deeper than "I guess I like him," it was a sure sign we weren't a match.

That, and he threw a glass against the wall.

Yeah.

I never told Gigi about this. Didn't want to give her any more ammo in her dislike for my boyfriend. But after a phone argument with his older brother, Percy hurled a full wineglass at his living room wall while I sat on the couch in stunned silence, watching shards of glass explode and bloodred drops soak into the rug.

Not gonna lie—it was a massive turnoff. I know some people need an outlet for their anger. I mean, I've heard about those "rage rooms" where people pay actual money to smash old TVs and vases with baseball bats. And while I have a temper myself, I've never broken anything out of anger. Seeing Percy lose his temper like that over a silly fight about his brother bailing on Thanksgiving had given me a serious case of the ick. I broke up with him three days later.

My ex's ears must be burning because he chooses that moment to text again. Uh-oh, he's double texting.

I know I should respond, but I don't know how to act around him. Every time I give him an inch, he tries to win me back.

"Man, he really wants to come over tonight," I say, glancing at my phone.

"He can suck a dick."

I grin and polish off the last bite of my burger. After dinner, we take a walk along Main Street, popping into some shops to browse handcrafted knickknacks and one-of-a-kind clothing, and then Gigi drives me home. She still has to get back to Boston tonight; she's staying with her parents until she and Ryder move into their own place in September.

"I wish you were in the dorms this summer, so you wouldn't have to drive more than an hour to hang out with me." I pout.

"Honestly, I'm barely going to be around these next couple months. I've got wedding-planning shit. Then Arizona next week, so Ryder is super stressed. Then Tahoe with the fam, Italy with the husband, and the wedding itself."

I whistle. "Jeez. World traveler over here. And stop doing things backward, will you? Elopement, Italian honeymoon, and *then* wedding? Who taught you life?"

She snorts.

I don't comment on the Arizona trip because it's an awkward subject. They're going out there for Ryder's dad's parole hearing. It's tragic, really. Ryder's dad killed his mother when Ryder was little. He took a plea deal and is up for parole after only fifteen years, but the prosecutors don't think he stands a chance of getting out. Still, I can see how it would be stressful for Gigi's new husband.

She slows down at the massive white sign that reads MEADOW HILL and pulls into the circular driveway in front of the Sycamore building.

Gigi puts the car in park. "I'll see you this weekend?" We have dinner plans again.

"Definitely. And if you're able to get away from your fam before that, let me know. Come over and swim. You might have to watch a dance rehearsal depending on the day, but Kenji and I only practice for about an hour."

"I'll let you know. Love you."

"Love you."

I give her a side hug and slide out of the SUV, tucking my purse over my shoulder. Gigi drives away just as another vehicle pulls up. I'm naturally curious—fine, nosy—so I glance over in time to see a familiar face emerge from the back seat.

I narrow my eyes. It's Crystal Haller, one of my fellow cheerleaders.

Oh, come on.

That fucking asshole. Why!?! We *just* had a talk about this.

"Diana. Hey." Crystal approaches with an awkward smile.

We're not close. As captain of the team, I make an effort to try to bond with every squad member, but I can't be expected to become best friends with dozens of people with different personalities. Crystal and I have never clicked. She's a bit snooty, to be honest. We're both counselors at cheer camp this summer, and she's dropped several comments since camp began about how she doesn't *really* need the money, but it's nice to have a little "pocket change."

For me, this isn't "pocket change." It's what pays my mortgage.

We approach the main doors of the Sycamore, pausing out front. "I forgot you lived here," Crystal says. "I'm here to see—"

"Yeah, I know. Lindley."

She's startled. "How did you know that?"

"He's my new neighbor. I assumed it was only a matter of time before the girl parade started."

That gets me a deep frown.

"Sorry," I hedge. "I didn't mean it like that." I pause. "Actually. I did. You do know he's a player, right?"

She rolls her eyes. "Yes, Di. I am fully aware that he's a player."

I relax at her use of my nickname. Means she can't be that mad about the girl-parade remark.

"Okay, good. Just, you know, temper your expectations. Audrey sprained her ankle because of the guy."

"That's unfair. *He* didn't sprain her ankle."

"No," I grudgingly admit, "not personally. But she fell because she was so distracted by her will-he-or-won't-he-call obsession. And then spoiler alert—he didn't call." I purse my lips. "Okay, he *did* call. But that was to tell her he wouldn't be calling anymore." I give Crystal a firm look. "He is a very dangerous man."

"It's all right," she answers, clearly amused. "You don't have to worry about me. I'm a big girl."

"You've been warned," I say as I use my key fob to buzz myself in. She trails after me into the well-lit lobby.

"Evening, Diana."

Richard, the guard who works the night shift, greets me with a smile. He's in his fifties, with pale skin that always holds a reddish tinge to it as if he's perpetually sunburned.

"Hey, Richard." I approach the desk. "This is Crystal. She's here to see Shane Lindley. Red Birch, apartment 2B."

He nods and jots it down in his ledger.

"Come on," I tell her. "It's this way."

We leave through the double doors at the back and emerge onto the winding, paved path. Red Birch is the third building from the Sycamore. We pass Cherry Blossom and Silver Pine before I lead her into our own mini lobby.

"We're up here," I say, heading for the staircase.

"Oh, you weren't kidding. You really are neighbors."

"Ugh. Yeah."

"Don't sound so thrilled about it."

"I don't like hockey players," I mutter.

Well, that's not true. My best friend is a hockey player.

So is her husband, and I like *him*.

And I like Beckett.

And Will.

Huh. I guess the only one I don't like is Shane. You learn something new every day.

We reach the top of the stairs. I walk toward my door, which displays a small silver plate that reads 2A. Directing Crystal, I point toward 2B. "He's over there."

"Thanks."

I let myself in and lock the door behind me. From the hall, I hear the murmur of voices. A deep rumble of laughter—Shane's. Then the faint sound of his door closing.

In my kitchen, I shoot Gigi a quick text.

> What's Shane's number? I need it.

I brew myself a cup of herbal tea while I chat with Skip, who's swimming laps around his tank. My plan for the rest of the night is to tune in to TRN, the reality show network I'm obsessed with. They're airing a meet-the-cast special tonight for my favorite show, and I'm dying to see who's going to be in the hacienda this season.

I'm making myself cozy on the couch when my phone dings. It's Percy again.

PERCY:

> I only ask because I thought it would be nice to see each other and catch up. I totally get it if you don't want to, but we agreed to be friends, so...

He punctuates that with a shrugging emoji.

I stifle a sigh. I *did* tell him we could be friends, but it was a way to soften the blow. Except now I look like a total ass if I take it back.

ME:

> Hey, sorry for not getting back to you sooner. I was out with Gigi. If you want to watch some reality TV with me, you can come by for a bit, but I warn you I'm planning to go to bed early. I'm working the breakfast shift tomorrow.

PERCY:

> I'll stay an hour, tops. See you soon.

I can practically feel the excitement pouring off his words. And I see that same enthusiasm in his smile when I swing the door open less than twenty minutes later.

"How've you been?" I ask after I let him in.

"Good. I was just at Malone's meeting with a realtor."

"At eight thirty at night?"

"Yeah, he met up with me after work. I told you my landlords are selling the house, right? This real estate agent is trying to help me track down another place, but there's really nothing available. I might be screwed."

Percy's been renting a townhouse in town, but just like how jobs in Hastings are scarce, so is housing. Although Briar is only a ten-minute drive, Hastings is not technically a college town, which means we're not set up to house thousands of students. Only in the last couple of years did the Hastings town council even agree to allow buildings taller than three stories.

"Oh my God, will you have to live in the graduate dorms?" I ask sympathetically.

Percy sighs and runs a hand through his hair. He has such great hair. A sweep of thick, brown strands that are perpetually wind-tousled even when it's not windy. He also has chiseled cheekbones and pale skin, a combo that gives off Victorian prince vibes. He's always seemed so much older to me and not simply because he is. I would honestly buy it if you'd told me he was some immortal creature who's been alive for centuries.

Groaning, he kicks off his loafers and follows me into the living area. "I can't live in the dorms. Some of the singles are nice, but the only ones left have a communal bathroom. Christ. I'm a total germa-phobe. You know I need my own bathroom."

"I don't blame you. So do I."

I offer him some tea and we chat more about his living arrange-ments while waiting for the kettle to boil. It isn't until we're seated on opposite ends of the couch that he inquires about me.

"So how are you doing?" he asks awkwardly.

"I'm good. It's shaping out to be a busy summer." I wrap both hands around my mug. "Juggling two jobs is going to be rough. I'm basically working every day of the week."

"I love your work ethic. Reminds me of myself. I worked three jobs when I was doing my undergrad."

"Right, I remember you telling me that."

We both sip our tea. I notice him watching me over the rim of his mug and know he wants to ask me something else. Probably if I'm seeing someone. Fortunately, he squashes that impulse.

"So, are you ready for this?" With my free hand, I grab the remote off the coffee table. "The new season of *Fling or Forever* starts next week."

He grimaces. "Can't believe you made me watch a whole season of that junk."

"Three episodes, Percival. You only watched *three*."

"That's three too many." Humor dances in his moss-green eyes.

Okay, this isn't too bad. Maybe we *can* be friends.

I find TRN and curl up against the arm of the couch with my tea as *Fling or Forever*'s "Meet the Cast" special flashes on the screen. For the next thirty minutes, Percy and I watch the show, offering running commentary about this season's first ten contestants.

"Holy shit, that's Steven Price," I exclaim.

"Who?" Percy asks blankly.

"NFL player. Well, former player. He was injured a few seasons ago, tried to make a comeback, and then got hurt again. So now he's officially retired."

"Christ. Here I am toiling away to earn my master's and this guy is my age and already retired." Percy's tone is wry.

I study the next contestant. Zoey, a gorgeous brunette with big eyes and incredible lips. "She's a cellist," I remark, reading the bio that overlays the screen.

"Poor girl. What the hell is she doing on a show like this?"

"Oh my God. Okay—him. That's my guy." I grin at the next contestant who slides onto a stool and introduces himself to the camera. "That's who I'm rooting for."

"He goes by 'The Connor,' Diana. And he talks like a

douchebag." Distaste drips from Percy's tone, which makes me laugh.

"Don't judge a radio DJ by his cover," I chide. "I bet you he's a secret softie. Oh, hold on. Getting a text."

It's from Gigi. She's sent me Shane's contact info.

GIGI:

> Please be nice to him. He's basically my
> brother-in-law now.

Nice? Has she met me?

I open a new message thread and start typing. For some reason Shane strikes me as the type of guy who would check his texts in the middle of sex, so just to annoy him, I send my message one line at a time.

The tally is up to ten when I'm done.

"Who are you texting?"

"Oh, sorry. Just my new neighbor. He's so cocky and obnoxious. And this whole year he's been fucking up my life."

There's a slight narrowing of Percy's eyes. "What do you mean?"

"He's the one that keeps sleeping with all my cheerleaders. I told you about him, remember? The hockey player?"

"I don't think you ever mentioned him." His mouth is a bit tight.

"Oh, I thought I had. Anyway, he plays for Briar and he's a total fuckboy. I just caught my teammate Crystal going to his apartment tonight after I specifically told him to leave the cheer team alone."

"How do you know this guy?" Percy's displeasure is now perfectly outlined in every crease of his face. "Are you dating him?"

"What? No." I stare at him. "I hate him."

"Really? Because you seem very invested in the sex life of a complete stranger."

"He's not a complete stranger. I just told you, he's a hockey player. I know him through Gigi."

"And you're trying to, what, sabotage his date?" Percy curses softly. "Is that why I'm here right now?"

"What the hell are you talking about?"

"Why am I here?"

"Because you wanted to hang out. As friends," I say pointedly.

"Right. You made that very clear."

"Of course I made that clear. Because we broke up." My teeth grind against each other. I clear my throat to hide any agitation. "Actually, *this* is why we broke up."

"Why? Because I don't understand why you're texting this guy? Why do you even have his phone number?"

"I don't have his phone number."

"You texted him!"

"No, I know, but I didn't have it before. I literally just got it from Gigi."

Percy looks doubtful.

"Are you serious right now?" I open Gigi's text and hold the phone in front of his face. "See? I texted her asking for his number. I never had it before tonight."

And *why* am I even explaining myself?

I take a breath and rise from the couch. "Okay. It's time for you to go."

Immediately, a note of panic enters his voice. "Diana, come on."

"No, this is why we broke up, Percy. Because we're not compatible. Because you're so distrustful of me when I never give you any reason not to trust me. I didn't even *look* at another guy when we were together, and I've never cheated on anyone in my life, yet you interrogate me about every single guy I talk to, including this jerk." I gesture at my phone. "I don't even like him. So yes, clearly we're mismatched in what we need from a relationship."

"Because I need reassurance every now and then?" he says bitterly.

"Yes," I admit. "And there's nothing wrong with that. I'm sure you'll find a woman who will be happy to offer tons of reassurance. Whereas I need to find a man who trusts me completely."

"I do," he insists.

I ignore that. "I mean it. It's time to go. I want to go to bed."

Something flashes in his eyes. It gets my back up. But then he inhales deeply. "All right. Sorry. I'll get out of your way."

At the door, he tries to hug me goodbye. I step away from it.

"No," I say. "I'm really not in the mood. Please."

"I'm sorry." His expression conveys defeat. "I'll text you tomorrow."

Please don't, I want to shout, but he's already gone.

When I return to the living room, I find a message from Shane on my phone. A response to my lengthy and not-so-nice *Leave my cheerleaders alone.*

SHANE:

> Aww, sounds like someone's feeling left out. Come join us.

I glare at the phone before responding.

ME:

> Never.

Meet the Cast of *Fling* or *Forever* Season 2!

Keep It Real.com
Byline: Trina Banner
Original Publication Date: July 5

It's that time of year again, gals and guys!

Summer. Beautiful, splendid summer.

And you know what that means…

Five new guys and five new gals will be arriving at the hacienda to flirt the summer away in a brand-new season of TRN's *Fling or Forever*.

The drama! The spice! The Sugar Suite! Get ready for eight weeks of nonstop action, in every sense of the word. Ten OG boys and girls will be joined by other singles throughout the summer, each determined to find love and create chaos.

Keep scrolling to meet this season's contestants…

ZOEY, 21

New york native Zoey is a cello prodigy with dreams of playing in the London Symphony Orchestra one day. She also rocks a mean bikini. Be warned: you need to level up to win this talented hottie's heart.

LENI, 24

Swimsuit model, part-time salesgirl, and avid hiker, Leni has all the boys in LA wrapped around her little finger. A self-proclaimed girl's girl, Leni hopes to find both friendship and love at the hacienda.

CONNOR, 24

THE CONNOR! Yes, folks. Love him or hate him, shock-jock Connor is coming to the hacienda. There's a reason he has the women in Nashville glued to their earbuds. He's loud, brash, and ready to smash!

STEVEN, 26

You're not hallucinating. Yes, that is former NFL fullback Steven Price, and yes, those abs are delicious. After years of playing the field (literally), this secret softie is finally ready to find love.

ZEKE, 22

Miami-based model and personal trainer Zeke is no stranger to reality shows. You might recognize him from his stint on TRN's *Friend Zone*, where he made it to Proposal Day only for Christa to shatter his heart and send him to the F-zone. Now he's back, looking to get a second chance at love. And a tan.

TODD, 22

Club promoter Todd spends most of his time enjoying the Manhattan nightlife. He's cheated on every girlfriend he's ever had but is hoping he'll find someone in the hacienda that he doesn't want to stray from.

KY, 21

LA-based, aspiring actress Ky is ready to meet her Prince Charming. But only if that prince has a bit of a wild streak. She's too young and too hot to be bored in a relationship. Don't excite her? Thank you, next.

DONOVAN, 20

British accent, anyone? International student Donovan studies fine arts during the day, and the fine art of fuc*boying at night. He says it will take a very special girl to make him change his wild-man ways.

JAS, 22

NYU law student Jasmine AKA Jas is not afraid to speak her mind. One strike and you're out with her. She's got a short temper and she doesn't give second chances. With that ass, why should she?

FAITH, 27

"Office supply sales from Georgia"?? Boring! Don't worry, Faith moonlights as an Instagram model with over 2M followers. The self-proclaimed queen of thirst traps, Faith isn't interested in boys.She wants a MAN.

CHAPTER FOUR

SHANE

I don't want a relationship...with you.

I HAVE A CONFESSION TO MAKE.

I'm not a fuckboy.

This sad, incontrovertible truth continues to hit me like a freight train after every single hookup. Before last night, I was able to squash these blasphemous thoughts. Banish them to the backburner of my brain and pretend the hollow feeling in my chest doesn't exist.

Today, I'm staring at this stomach-dropping text from Crystal and finally forcing myself to accept my pathetic reality.

I want a relationship.

CRYSTAL:

> This is really embarrassing, but last night was the best date I've ever had. It was so low-key, but it was like perfect.

It wasn't supposed to be a date.

But I accidentally turned it into one when I didn't have sex with her.

I had her in my lap, her tongue in my mouth, her hands roaming, and I just...couldn't do it. I wasn't in it. If I'm honest with myself, I haven't been in it for a long time now. Sure, it was fun at first. Fresh off a breakup from a long-term relationship, my dick eager and raring to go. It was exciting, those first few encounters, the newness of it all. Kissing someone other than my ex. Seeing a naked body that didn't belong to her.

But the novelty has worn off. Yesterday with Crystal is proof of that.

CRYSTAL:

> I can't wait to see you again.

I sit at the kitchen counter and drop my head in my hands, my breakfast forgotten, appetite gone. This is my fault. I invited her over because I thought she was hot and because I wanted to get laid. No part of that scenario involved getting into a relationship with her. Crystal's great, but we don't click on a deeper level. I'm not interested in taking it any further than a sloppy, aborted make-out session on my couch.

Meanwhile, *she* left with stars in her eyes, riding the high from "the best date she's ever had."

Fuck me.

Feeling like a total shithead, I force myself to craft a response before Crystal decides to tell me she loves me and can't wait to have my babies. I compose my standard *I don't want anything serious, I thought we were on the same page* text.

The chat thread stays dormant, my message still the last one in the scroll. I stare at it for nearly a minute before I see Crystal begin to type. Shit. It was too much to hope that she'd let it be.

I slide off the stool, carry my half-eaten cereal bowl to the sink, and shove the mushy remains down the garbage disposal. When I come back, she's still typing, so I go take a shower and pray her reply won't be too bad.

I dunk my head under the spray and bemoan my fate.

I'm not meant for hookups.

Yes, I realize that's ironic, considering I've been indulging in nothing *but* hookups since my breakup with Lynsey last spring. I've slept with more women this month alone than in all the years I've been sexually active. There was one girl before Lynsey, and then Lynsey and I were together for four years, dating from junior year of high school until we broke up my sophomore year at Eastwood College.

To my friends, I insist that our parting was mutual.

By mutual, I mean I nodded numbly and said *if that's how you feel, then I can't stop you.*

I drag my hands over my scalp, shampoo suds sliding down my face and over my chest. I rinse off and then proceed to stand under the hot spray for another five minutes.

Wallowing.

I like having a girlfriend. I don't care if that makes me a total sap. Deep down, I've always been a relationship guy. Always had this clear vision for my life, one that really solidified when I started dating Lynsey. There's a reason I haven't ragged on Ryder that much about his elopement with Gigi Graham. To me, it's not an unfathomable move. I always saw myself marrying young. Hell, I wouldn't even be against having a kid in my early twenties. I can visualize my entire future laid out in front of me. NHL super stardom, a wife, a couple of kids.

I don't want to fuck random girls anymore. I want to fuck *the* girl.

I step out of the shower, dry off, and stroll naked into my bedroom. My phone still lies on the patterned bedspread where I'd tossed it. I check it, and sure enough, there's an essay from Crystal.

As I read it, I alternate between annoyance and guilt. The thesis statement is basically *you led me on, you fucking asshole.*

I didn't, though. And I make that clear in my response.

ME:

I'm really sorry. I didn't mean to upset you. But I told you within five minutes of you getting here that I wasn't looking for anything serious, and you fully agreed. You said it was cool.

CRYSTAL:

Right, but then we hooked up. Hooking up changes the rules, and now it's NOT cool.

ME:

All we did was kiss, Crystal.

CRYSTAL:

Kissing is even more intimate than sex.

Is she for real? If I kiss a girl, that means I'm now obligated to propose marriage? If we'd had sex, sure, maybe I'd entertain that line of reasoning, but we made out for ten minutes, I told her I was tired, and then she left. How can that be considered anything deep?

ME:

I'm sorry. But I was completely up front with you. I'm not really over my breakup.

I cringe even typing those words. Sounds so pathetic. If this was any of my friends, I'd be like, *get the fuck over it already.*

ME:

> I told you last night, I'm not emotionally equipped for anything serious right now.

CRYSTAL:

> It's not like I'm asking you to get serious RIGHT AWAY. Relationships need time to develop.

ME:

> I don't want a relationship.

…with you.

That's always the unspoken caveat, and sometimes I wish social etiquette didn't require us to pretend that's *not* what we mean. If someone wants to be in a relationship with you, they will. They won't string you along. They won't hit you up in the middle of the night for sex. They won't feed you endless excuses about how they're "not cut out for relationships" or how "you deserve so much better." They would be with you, plain and simple.

And despite the reputation we get for being clueless or fickle or not being able to keep our dicks in our pants, a man usually knows pretty fast, often within minutes, if he considers someone girlfriend material.

CRYSTAL:

> I don't get it. I thought we had fun. Were you faking the whole time?

ME:

> Of course not. I did have fun last night. But I don't want a relationship.

CRYSTAL:

> OMG I'm not asking you for one!!

Then what the hell are we fighting about? I want to gouge my eyes out. Instead, I apologize once again, and we go back and forth for a while. Normally I'm good at keeping my cool, but Crystal's next message really gets my goddamn goat, as my dad always says.

CRYSTAL:

> Fuck you. You're such a selfish prick. I'm going to warn every girl I meet to stay away from you and make sure she knows you'll just be using her.

My jaw tightens. Okay, then. We're done here.

ME:

> Yeah, so... I wasn't interested in a relationship with you last night, and I'm even less interested in one now. Again, I'm sorry you're hurt. But I've entertained about as much of this conversation as I'm willing to.

I send a final text to punctuate that.

ME:

> I'm not interested in seeing you again. Best of luck.

Then I block her.

Fucking hell. All we did was make out. How is this even a thing? And why do I still feel like a total asshole?

As I throw on a pair of black basketball shorts and a Bruins T-shirt, I reread the entire conversation to determine whether I deserved to be yelled at. But my brain truly can't comprehend what

I did wrong. The level of Crystal's vitriol is completely dispropor-
tional to what actually occurred.

I jump when the phone vibrates in my hand. For a moment I'm
afraid Crystal found a way to get around the blocking, but it's my
dad asking when they should expect me tomorrow. I'm heading to
my hometown, which boasts the very cheesy name of Heartsong,
Vermont, to visit my family.

As for today, I was *planning* on golfing, but now I'm too
annoyed to golf. Maybe I'll swim laps instead. That'll require less
concentration.

Fuck. Why are women so exhausting? Even Lynsey was exhausting, and I *liked* our relationship.

My heart clenches as her face flashes in my mind. Her big dark
eyes. The cute little smirk she wears when she's proven right about
something. Before I can stop myself, I sit on the foot of my bed and
creep her social media, yet another thing that makes me feel like a
chump. She unfollowed me after we broke up, but I still follow her. Just
haven't been able to press that stupid button to click her out of my life.
Besides, she has a private account, so if I did unfollow and then felt the
pitiful need to cyberstalk her again, I'd have to send a request, which is
even more embarrassing than the fact that I'm still following her.

I'm a stray dog begging for scraps, dying to see what she's up
to. I eagerly scroll through new shots of her at the dance studio. A
black leotard is plastered to her lithe body, pale pink tights hugging
her shapely legs. Lynsey is constantly lamenting that she wishes she
were shorter. She's 5'6", which is tiny compared to me, but apparently the average height for a ballerina is like 5'4" or something.

Lynsey is beyond talented, though. She attends the Liberty
Conservatory of Fine Arts in Connecticut, one of the top performing
arts colleges in the country. Like Juilliard, the Liberty Conservatory
offers a highly sought-after dance program and accepts a shockingly
small number of students. I took Lynsey for a steak dinner when she
received her acceptance letter.

I keep scrolling, until I reach a photo that raises my hackles. It's of her and some guy. Their hands all over each other. I can't see his face, but my fist itches to punch it.

I relax when I read the caption.

DAY 1 OF REHEARSALS FOR #NUABC.

She tagged Sergei, her best friend, who did the competition with her last year too. He also happens to be gay, so not a threat.

Guilt tugs at my gut. She'd always wanted *me* to be her partner. Thought it would be fun to do it as a couple. Which, frankly, always surprised me because there are far better dancers than I am, and Lynsey is incredibly ambitious. To her, winning an amateur ballroom dance competition is equivalent to securing an Olympic gold medal. I suspect she was secretly relieved whenever I would balk and say absolutely not.

Now I'm wondering if my resistance is yet another reason she dumped me.

Yeah, bro, you got dumped because you didn't want to do the damn salsa with her.

Who knows. Maybe that *is* the reason.

I've had a lot of time for self-reflection since the breakup, and I'm honestly questioning if maybe I'm just a shit boyfriend. I'm too focused on hockey and I've never been willing to compromise about that. My game schedule was and is nonnegotiable. But, damn it, I did make an effort. I went to all her dance recitals, sitting front-row center. I attended all her family events, often picking them over my own. I did my best to put her first.

Guess it wasn't good enough.

I let out a breath, staring at her picture. My fingers slide across the cool surface of my phone.

I should call her.

No, you shouldn't.

No, I should. We're still friends. Friends call each other.

You shouldn't call her, and you're not friends. You're still in love with her.

Friends can be in love with each other.

They can't.

The inner debate goes on for a while. Until my fingers make the decision for me and dial her number. One ring in and I regret it, but it's too late. She'll see the missed call. Maybe she won't pick up, though. Maybe—

"Hey," she answers, sounding surprised. "What's up?"

"Hey." My vocal cords sound like they're wrapped in two bags of gravel. I clear my throat. "I was just scrolling Insta and saw the post of you and Sergei. I realized we hadn't spoken in a while, so I wanted to check in and say hi."

"Oh. Yeah. No, you're right. It has been a while." She doesn't sound put off that I called. "Actually, I ran into your mom last night at the pancake house."

"You're home?" My heart speeds up, then stutters for a beat, because Lynsey saw my mother and didn't even text me about it? I guess that shows where her head is at. "I'll be there tomorrow until Friday. How long is your visit?"

"I'm leaving this afternoon. Going up north to Monique's family's cabin for a week."

"Nice." Last July, I went with her on her best friend's annual lake trip.

Do not bring that up—

"We had the best time there last year."

Fucking tool.

"We did, didn't we?"

I chuckle to myself. "Remember night swimming?"

"Oh, you mean when you almost got your dick bitten off by a snapping turtle?"

"It did not almost bite my dick off. It just brushed my thigh."

"That's mighty close to your dick, Lindy."

The nickname makes my heart clench. And it reminds me of all those times we laughed about what would happen if we got married. She'd be Lynsey Lindley. Very firmly, she'd declared it was too much of a tongue twister and vowed to never take my name. Eventually we compromised and decided she'd hyphenate.

Not that it matters anymore.

"You're right, it did get a bit too close for comfort," I relent, still chuckling. "Man, that was a fun trip."

"It was."

A short silence falls.

Don't tell her you miss her.

"I miss you."

There's a pause.

"As a friend," I add, fighting a grin. "I miss our friendship."

"Yeah, I can hear you smiling right now."

She knows me too well. "I'm not."

Another pause.

"I miss our friendship too," she admits. "But I still think distance is the right move."

She's not wrong. I can't imagine the agony of talking to her regularly while not being together.

I want to ask her if she's seeing anybody, but I know I shouldn't. Fortunately, this time my mouth is able to curb the impulse.

"How about you?" Lynsey asks. "Everything's good?"

"Yeah. Hockey's great. New apartment is sick. Oh—my best friend got married."

"What?! Who? Beckett?"

"Seriously? That's your guess?" I sputter with laughter. "Try again."

She gasps. "No. *Ryder?*"

"Yep."

"When did this happen?" she demands.

"Three months ago."

"And you didn't tell me?"

"Distance, remember?"

She sighs grudgingly. "Fine. That's fair. But I think when it comes to friends getting married, you have an obligation to make that call. Deal?"

"Deal. I'll call you when Beck gets married."

"Thank you." This time I can hear *her* smiling, and it sends another ache to my heart. "Did you guys enjoy your first season at Briar?"

"Definitely. We got off to a rocky start, but we won the Frozen Four, so I can't complain."

"What's the campus like?"

"Great. Why? Want to transfer?" I joke.

She hesitates. "Actually..."

My pulse starts racing again. "Are you kidding me? You're really thinking of transferring?"

"I've been considering it. I might want to take on another major, and Liberty doesn't offer many academic options. I heard Briar has an excellent psych program. And I already spoke to my advisor—she said it would be easy to transfer. I have all the credits I need and won't have to retake anything. But...I don't know. It's kind of far, and..."

And you're there is the rest of that sentence.

"Come on, Linz. Briar is big enough for the both of us. We could probably go years without crossing paths."

"No, that's not it."

I snort.

"It's not entirely it," she amends. "But yes, I might come and do a tour."

"Nice. If you do, you're welcome to crash here. I have a very comfortable couch."

"Oh, I wouldn't want to impose."

"It's not an imposition. You know you're always welcome here.

Same goes for Monique and the rest of the old crew. Just because you and I aren't together, doesn't mean we're not all still friends, right?"

Her voice softens. "Well, thanks, Lindy. I appreciate that."

I'm wired after we end the call. My skin's buzzing, pulse still off-kilter. I head for the living room and step onto my balcony, which overlooks the landscaped grounds. I can't quite see the pool, but I have a clear view of the flower-lined path leading to it. I feel like I'm at a Caribbean resort. It's fucking amazing.

I breathe in the warm summer air. It's a gorgeous morning. Maybe I'll play golf after all. But that swim sounds nice too. So why not both?

Like the man of leisure I am, I change into swim trunks and shove my feet into flip-flops. With an oversized towel over my arm, I grab my sunglasses and keys from the hall credenza.

Outside, the scent of freshly cut grass hits my face. I inhale deeply. I need fresh air to process that phone call.

I arrive on the pool deck in time to see Diana gliding through the air.

Literally.

A guy with jet-black hair and bronzed skin is lifting her up by her calves, twirling them both around while Diana's arms are stretched high above her in a V pose. It's like some weird form of water dancing.

When Diana notices me, she makes a face and jumps out of the guy's arms, landing in the water with a splash.

"No," she growls as she heaves herself out of the pool. Her wet ponytail hangs over one shoulder. She's in a red two-piece, the top resembling a sports bra and the bottoms tiny booty shorts.

Je-sus. Her body is ridiculous. Toned to high heaven, without an ounce of fat on her. Female athletes are so hot.

"Tuesdays are *my* pool day," Diana declares.

"That's not a rule," I answer cheerfully.

"It is now."

"You can't invent new Dixon rules whenever you want." I suddenly notice the tripod and smartphone set up in front of the pool. "What the hell's going on here?"

As if remembering the camera, she stomps over to turn it off, dripping water all over the concrete.

"We're rehearsing," she says haughtily, "and Shanes aren't allowed. Especially on Tuesdays, which are my pool days."

I turn toward the guy in the water, who's watching us in amusement. I wave. "I'm Shane."

"Kenji," he calls back.

"Don't befriend my partner," Diana orders.

Grinning, I drop my towel and keys on a nearby lounge chair. Everything about this apartment complex is lit, but the pool area tops everything. Rows of loungers, a gathering area with tables and chairs, a frickin' pizza oven. And these red-and-white-striped umbrellas are bomb.

I slide my shades on. "So what are we rehearsing for?"

"None of your business."

Once again, I seek out Kenji because he seems more level-headed. "NUABC," he supplies.

"What the fuck's New Absey?"

Diana huffs in annoyance. "It's the National Upper Amateur Ballroom Championships."

"You say that like I'm supposed to know what it is—" I stop. "Wait, actually I do know what that is."

"Bullshit."

"Seriously. My ex competes."

She eyes me suspiciously. "Who's your ex?"

"Lynsey Whitcomb."

"Oh, I remember her," Kenji tells Diana as he does a lazy backstroke. "She and her partner placed third in the American Nine last year."

Diana glares at me as if I'm personally responsible for Lynsey's dance prowess. "Did you come all the way down here to flaunt that your ex-girlfriend is some ballroom prodigy?"

"No." I roll my eyes. "I came down to swim laps. So chill out and go back to your water dancing. I'll stay out of your way if you stay out of mine."

"But we're filming," she complains.

"Great. Then your viewers can feast their eyes on the beautiful, godlike man in the pool."

She stares at me. "Oh, you're referring to yourself."

I snicker. Arguing with Diana has succeeded in easing the lingering tension from my call with Lynsey. I was in low spirits before, but my chest feels lighter.

I saunter past the irritable blond and descend the steps in the shallow end. With the late morning sun beating down on us, the water feels like heaven against my skin.

"Do you go to Briar too?" I ask Kenji as I swim by him.

He opens his mouth, but Diana silences him with her hand. "You don't have to answer that, Kenji."

I chuckle and wait for him to speak for himself, but he simply gives me an apologetic shrug. Wimp.

Grinning, I slice through the cool water to start the first lap. It brings me deep enjoyment knowing Dixon doesn't want me here.

I'm in a terrific mood now.

WATER LIFTS DAY 3 FT. ASS***E NEIGHBOR

👍 6K   248 comments. 29 shares

@candykaaane
omg asshole neighbor is 🔥

@haileyhoran345
Who is THAT??

@btg345
Um. More of asshole neighbor please and thank u

@lorabora
@candykaane RIGHT???

@mikemarnes
need me some hot neighbor🔥🔥🔥

@user2934593342
scuse me moving to your building

CHAPTER FIVE
DIANA

A good old-fashioned shunning

I'M RUNNING LATE ON WEDNESDAY, SO I TAKE A SHORTCUT TO THE bus stop, cutting across the small parkette in front of Meadow Hill. The ground is still wet with morning dew, and a light mist of water sprays my ankles as my white tennis shoes drag against the grass.

I could walk, but I prefer the bus because it gives me time to edit my videos for Ride or Dance, the social media account I created for me and Kenji a couple of years ago. I use it mostly to post videos of our dance rehearsals, and then last year at NUABC, we posted a bunch of behind-the-scenes type segments. Somehow, we've amassed almost a hundred thousand followers. No idea how that happened, but I'm certainly not complaining. Unlike what Crystal thinks about our paychecks, the ad revenue from this account *can* be considered pocket change. Sometimes I even make enough to buy groceries for the month.

This morning, I find an exasperating number of comments about Shane under my latest rehearsal video, which makes me want to delete the whole account and then burn my phone.

At my stop, I hop off and walk the remaining hundred yards to the high school, where for three days a week, I mold the minds, bodies, and spirits of young athletes, guiding them along the path to achieving their dreams.

In other words, I teach cheerleading and basic gymnastics to eight- to twelve-year-olds.

This morning's group of campers are ages eleven and twelve, their uniforms consisting of white shorts and yellow tees emblazoned with the camp logo. They'll don their pleated cheer uniforms at the final event in August when each group performs two routines for the entire camp, one dance heavy, and one stunt based.

Our camp days are split into morning and afternoon sessions. Since my group is stunting for the first session, we gather on one side of the gymnasium, congregating on a sea of blue mats.

"All right, my little bunny rabbits," I greet the girls. "Let's get in position."

Tatiana, the ringleader of the 11–12s, sticks up her hand. "Diana," she announces. "We all took a vote and decided we don't want to be called bunny rabbits anymore."

I bite my lip to keep from laughing. "I see. Any particular reason?"

"Because they poop everywhere."

The laugh slips out. From the corner of my eye, I glimpse my co-counselor, Fatima, grinning.

"I mean, that's a fair point," I acknowledge. "But the poop thing only occurred to you now?"

"My little brother got a pet rabbit this weekend," Avery explains, her face glum. "I hate that thing with all my heart."

"All right, then." I mull it over. "How about…let's get in position, my majestic eagles."

"Love it," Tatiana says emphatically. The other girls are nodding. "Excellent."

Fatima and I share an amused glance before splitting the campers into groups of three. I've choreographed four routines this year, two for my 8–10s group, and two for the 11–12s, who are my favorite by far.

Since these are children, we keep all the stunts fairly simple. The 8–10s are doing mostly doggy sits and knee sits. Cartwheels and roundoffs for the beginner tumblers. With this group, we've been working on double thigh stands, which is what we start with this morning. Fatima and I act as spotters, keeping a close eye from the back and front.

"Chloe, your lunge needs to be deeper," I tell the freckled redhead. "Otherwise Harper doesn't have a stable base."

"Why can't I be a flyer?" she whines.

"Because right now you're a base," I answer with a patient smile. "We talked about this—everyone will have a chance to be a flyer in the final routine. Right now, we need you as a base."

She nods sullenly. Some kids are such brats, holding a sense of entitlement that *they* should be the star. Others are terrible at stunts but so darn happy to be here; they possess the necessary spirit, which is the most important part of cheer.

I help the two bases get into position. The flyer, Kerry, climbs onto her teammate's thighs.

"Step, lock, tighten!" I remind them.

The bases hold the flyer's legs. Fatima steps in to lightly support Kerry's waist as the young girl extends her arms in a V pose.

"Perfect!" I exclaim. "Careful on the dismount. Feet together, Kerry."

She flawlessly lands in front of the stunt, feet closed, face beaming.

"Excellent. Next group!"

At noon, we break for lunch. We usually eat outdoors, under the covered pavilion near the football field. I join my 11–12s at one of the long picnic tables and pry off the lid of my Greek salad. The girls are giggling to one another, casting peeks at one of the other tables.

"Share with the class," I chide.

Tatiana smirks. "Crystal has a hickey."

I smother a laugh. Lindley leaving his mark, I see.

I glance over, but while I can't spot this alleged hickey, I do notice Crystal seems subdued. She's completely zoned out as fellow counselor Natalia babbles obliviously.

"It's rude to stare at people's hickeys," I inform Tatiana. "We only stare at their pimples."

Everyone breaks out laughing.

"Kidding. I'm just kidding. You should never zit-shame. Also, fun fact—those things never really go away. My mom is in her forties, and she *still* gets zits. The rumor that they leave you after your teen years is an urban legend."

The girls are horrified. They should be. Puberty hasn't done its damage yet, so all of them still boast that smooth, unblemished skin I use hundreds of dollars' worth of products to achieve.

After lunch, the campers have fifteen minutes of free time before the afternoon session starts, so I wander over to Crystal who now stands alone, engrossed with her phone.

Her head lifts when I walk up.

"You okay?" I ask. "You seem down."

"I'm fine." Then her jaw hardens bitterly. "Actually, no. I'm not fine. You were right about that jerk."

I sigh. "Lindley?"

"Yeah. He's *such* a dick." Her body language is stiff as she lowers herself onto the top of the picnic table with her feet planted on the bench. "And no, I don't particularly want an I-told-you-so."

"I wasn't going to give one."

"Good. Because I feel shitty enough as it is. I'm *so* angry, Di. He totally used me. And, like, he was so blatant about it."

"What do you mean?"

"Like, I get that he only wanted a hookup, but he didn't have to be so rude about it. He was basically, like, *I never want to see you again, best of luck.*"

A crease digs into my forehead. I might find Shane annoying, but I can't imagine him being so disrespectful toward a woman.

"What, you don't believe me?" When Crystal notices my dubious face, her own darkens.

"No, I do. I'm just surprised. I don't think he behaved that way with Audrey."

Audrey is our teammate from Briar, the one who hooked up with Shane last fall and then sprained her ankle. Yes, she was upset he broke it off, but she didn't say a word about Shane doing it in a malicious way.

"Well, maybe he's become more of a dick since Audrey." Crystal's fingers travel over her screen for a moment. "Like, look at this. This is what he sent yesterday."

She hands me the phone, and I wince when I read Shane's text.

SHANE:

> I'm not interested in seeing you again. Best of luck.

"That's what he sent the day after you had sex?" I say in disbelief.
"Yup."

"Wow. That is beyond rude." Because I'm nosy, I try to scroll up to see the rest of the thread. But this is the only message on it. "You guys never texted before this?"

"Only on Insta."

I reread the message. I can't imagine sleeping with someone and then receiving this the next morning. Brutal.

"I honestly don't blame you for being upset." I give the phone back. "Do you want me to yell at him when I get home?"

"Please do. He deserves it."

He sure does.

On the bus ride home later, I'm still thinking about the way Shane shot Crystal down. *Best of luck.* I'm surprised she didn't completely unload on him after that message. If any guy ever treated me this way, I'd lose my shit. But I also have a temper, and confrontation doesn't faze me. Maybe it fazes Crystal.

When I enter the lobby of the Sycamore, I smile in greeting at Harry, who works the day shift. He doesn't smile back. Harry is notoriously grumpy and hates everyone, so I don't take it personally.

I head for the shiny silver grid of condominium mailboxes, pleasantly surprised to find Priya in the vestibule, flipping through a pile of envelopes.

"Hey," I say as I stick my key in the mailbox lock. "Why aren't you working?" She usually sees clients until six, and it's only four.

"I took the afternoon off. Lucy had a vet appointment."

"Oh no, is she okay?"

"Annual shots. Nothing to worry about. You just missed our neighbor."

"Niall?"

"No. 2B. The hockey player. I heard him tell Harry he's heading out of town to see his parents for a few days."

"Good riddance," I mutter.

Her eyes narrow. "Do we not like him?"

"We certainly don't." I peer into my mailbox. I find a few pieces of junk mail that I stuff into my gym bag. "He gives new meaning to the word fuckboy."

Priya grins. "You realize being promiscuous doesn't make one a bad person, right?"

"Of course not. But *one* should also handle their hookups with tact, and that is something Shane is lacking."

I quickly tell her about the way he treated Crystal, reciting his morning-after message verbatim. Yes, I memorized it.

Priya's jaw drops. "No."

"Yes."

"He didn't even say, *I had a good time? You're an amazing person, but… It was fun but…*" She lists all the polite platitudes Shane could've offered Crystal and didn't.

"Nope."

"And I was thinking of inviting him to the neighbors group chat!"

"Oh, bad idea. We don't want that kind of energy in the group chat."

"You're right. We don't," she says firmly. "In fact, I'll spread the word. Make sure everybody knows to steer clear of this creep."

"Good call," I say, turning my cheek so she doesn't see my grin.

"Ugh." Priya nudges my shoulder with her own. "Don't look now, but here comes Broomstick Niall."

I hear his loud footfalls from the entryway behind us. For someone who lodges so many noise complaints, you'd think he'd work on moving with a lighter step.

Niall's mailbox is next to mine, so there's no avoiding him. "Hey, Niall."

He yanks out his mail, ignoring my greeting. "Have you *heard* what's going on in 2B? I swear, that hockey boy must be throwing pucks around his living room."

Priya and I exchange an eye roll behind his head. We've both learned to brush off Niall when he claims another neighbor is too loud.

"Forget about the noise, Niall," Priya advises. "We have other things to dislike him for."

"I'll dislike him for the noise, thank you," he says tightly.

Jeez. Get over it, man. Life is noisy.

"Priya is putting out the call for everyone to not roll out the welcome wagon," I tell Niall.

For the first time ever, a genuine smile spreads across his lips. "Outstanding. A good old-fashioned shunning."

"So we completely ignore him?" Priya asks with an evil look.

"Exactly," he replies. "Don't talk to him in the hall. Don't invite him to any of the summer barbecues. Really drill it in that we have no interest in getting to know someone who doesn't respect the noise ordinances."

"Well, that's not why we're shunning him, but sure," I say.

Priya grins at me. "You in?"

"Oh, definitely." Nothing would give me greater pleasure than tormenting Shane Lindley.

"Then it's settled, we'll make a pact to shun him." Niall beams proudly.

I can't believe Broomstick Niall is now my ally. Before Shane moved in, Niall was the person Priya and I disliked most in the building, and now here the three of us are, organizing a shunning.

Nothing like hate to bring people together, I guess.

CHAPTER SIX
SHANE

Five gold stars for women's liberation

"AND THEN WE GOT TO SEND *ACTUAL* MESSAGES TO THE *ACTUAL* astronauts in the International Space Station! Can you believe it! And tomorrow we get to see their responses. Can you believe that!"

If she weren't ten years old, I would question whether Maryanne snorted a pound of cocaine before I got here. She's pacing the living room, talking a mile a minute, wearing a look that can only be described as euphoric.

Sadly, all this ecstasy is a result not of coke but space camp.

"Firstly, I need you to chill," I advise her. "You're making me dizzy. Secondly, what was your message?"

She offers a broad smile. "I asked whether farts smell differently in zero gravity."

I gape at her. "*That?* That was your question? We're talking about a real astronaut in outer space, and that's what you choose to ask them?"

She shrugs. "I must know."

"Also, I heard this camp's got you making bottle rockets. What if you mix all the ingredients wrong and accidentally create a biological weapon?"

Maryanne thinks it over for a beat. "Then I guess we kill every-one at camp."

"Wow. Kid. That's dark." Laughing, I shake off the fact that my little sister might be a psychopath. "All right, go change out of that uniform. Mini golf ain't going to play itself."

"Eeee! I love it when you're home!"

Next thing I know, she throws her skinny arms around me. I lift her off her feet in a big hug, making her laugh in delight.

I love being home too. I love my family, and I especially love this geeky girl in my arms. Some kids might resent their parents for giving them a sibling after eleven years of being an only child, but Maryanne's had me wrapped around her little finger since she was an hour old and I was a preteen. I used to race home from hockey practice and demand to feed her. At night, I would sing her lullabies until my parents sat me down one day, informed me that I can't sing, and said they would prefer, for the sake of their ears, not to hear my singing voice ever again. Merciless, those two.

I can hear them chatting in the kitchen, so I drift down the hall toward the doorway.

Mom just got home from a meeting, and she leans against the white granite counter in her trademark business getup—fitted slacks and a silk blouse—with her curly black hair pulled into a tight bun at her nape. She always looks like she stepped off the cover of a corporate magazine.

Dad, meanwhile, is a perpetual bum. Even before he started working from home, he'd wear jeans and a T-shirt to the office. Now the jeans have been replaced with baggy sweatpants.

They make such an odd couple. They met in high school when Mom was the type-A class president and Dad was the laid-back hockey star. Now he's the laid-back entrepreneur who sort of fell into a super-successful business after his NHL dreams didn't pan out. And she's the type-A town manager of Heartsong, Vermont, a position that works functionally as a mayor. She's the first Black woman to ever hold the position, so it was a big deal when she was elected by the city council. Heartsong has gotten a lot more progressive over the past ten years. The townspeople adore my mom.

My parents glance over at my entrance, halting their conversation.

"Sorry to interrupt," I say.

"Oh, you're not interrupting," Mom answers quickly. "Just discussing work stuff. Where's your sister?"

"Changing out of her camp uniform. I'm taking her mini golfing." I gesture to my dad's bare arms and ask, "You been hitting the course this summer? Your arms are looking less pudgy from the last time I saw them."

He glares in indignation. "Pudgy? How dare you?"

"The truth hurts, bro. You've definitely been working out or something, though. You look great." He must've lost a solid fifteen pounds these past few months.

"Trying to."

"I probably shouldn't have brought so much sausage, then," I say with a grin. I might've gone a little overboard when I paid a visit to my favorite butcher in Boston on my way to Heartsong.

"Wait, there's sausage?" His eyes light up. "Please tell me it's from Gustav."

"No, I went to some generic grocery store butcher. Of course it's from Gustav."

Mom glances from me to Dad. "I will never understand this obsession."

"Some people just can't see the big picture," Dad says, nodding at me.

I nod back. "Exactly."

She's exasperated. "What does sausage have to do with the big picture? What big picture are we even talking about? You know what—forget it! I don't care. I'm just happy you're home," Mom says, wrapping her arms around my waist.

Her head barely grazes my chin. At six one, I inherited Dad's height and the perfect blend of their skin tones. I gotta say, I'm really fucking good-looking.

"I wish you could stay longer," she clucks.

"Me too, but I'm hosting a goodbye party for Beck on Saturday night."

Her eyes widen. "Is he moving?"

"No. He's going to Australia on vacation. This dude demands a goodbye party for a monthlong vacay."

"I've always liked that guy," Dad remarks, because everyone likes Beckett Dunne. He oozes charm, that asshole.

"I'll come back again next week," I promise my folks. "I want to try to be here every weekend for the rest of the summer."

Mom is pleased. "Your sister is going to love that." She pauses. "Are you going to see Lynsey while you're here? We ran into her the other night at the pancake house."

"Yeah, I know. She told me."

"Oh, so you're still talking." Mom speaks in a careful tone.

I honestly can't gauge if my parents are upset or thrilled that Lynsey and I are broken up. Sometimes, they really seemed to like her. And then other times, I'd catch them exchanging looks, as they do now.

"You'd be happy if we got back together, right?" I ask them.

Mom blinks in surprise. "I didn't realize you two were discussing getting back together."

"We're not. Just hypothetically, you'd be happy with it if we did?"

"We will always support whatever you do," she says, and Dad nods in agreement.

It's not quite an answer. But I'm also not going to push a hypothetical, given that Lynsey has shown zero desire to rekindle our relationship.

"All right, I'm going to track down the squirt and head out. Let her expend some energy on the putt-putt course and then fill her up with junk food and sugar so she crashes hard when we get home."

"Thanks for taking her out. We're excited to have a quiet night in." Dad winks at Mom.

"Seriously, gross. I don't want to think about the activities you have planned while we're gone."

Dad offers a wolfish look. "Probably a good idea."

"I literally just said I don't want to know," I growl.

I hear them laughing at me as I stomp out of the kitchen.

The following night, Dad and I indulge in a Stanley Cup marathon where we watch old footage featuring some of our favorite championship wins. He's been recording every single game for the last twenty-five years, so we have plenty to choose from. When we get to the game Garrett Graham won with the Bruins, sweeping that series 4–0, Dad says, "I can't believe Luke married into that family."

"Right? I mean, I can't believe he's married, period. But that's a serious family to join." I marvel. "Hockey royalty doesn't even do it justice."

I note the way Dad's eyes shine when Graham scores one of the most beautiful goals I've ever seen to secure the Cup for the team. Fuck, I can't wait for the opportunity to chase that trophy. I want to hold the Stanley Cup in my hands. I want to see the cool silver shimmer under stadium lights.

"Do you miss it?" I ask my father. "Playing?"

"Every day." He speaks without hesitation, and it brings a clench to my chest.

I can't imagine how devastating it would be to skate onto the ice for your very first NHL game and suffer a career-ending injury on your very first shift. In one tragic play, Dad tore both his ACL *and* MCL, and his knee was collateral damage. There was no way he could ever play at the same level again. His joint stability was shot, and the doctors warned him he could do permanent damage if he kept playing.

Hockey was his entire life, and it was stolen from him. When I was drafted by Chicago, I broke down and cried. Seeing the pride on my dad's face, knowing I was going to play for the same team he had, albeit fleetingly—it had triggered a wave of sheer, throat-closing emotion. All I've ever wanted was to make him proud. To make both of them proud. I don't care how sappy it makes me, but they're legit the best parents anyone could ever have. Maryanne and I are beyond lucky.

Speaking of Maryanne, she chooses that moment to wander into the family room and flop on the couch between us, chattering on about tomorrow's itinerary. They're going to the planetarium.

"Man, space camp actually sounds dope," I remark.

"It's fun," she acknowledges. "But! Geology camp is even *better.*"

"Uh-huh. Is it now?" I play along. From the corner of my eye, I see Dad fighting a smile.

"Absolutely!" Maryanne proceeds to tell us about geology camp, explaining how there are three whole days dedicated to archaeology, when they do a mock excavation. "And! We get to make our own magnetic fields. And! We go on rock hunts. The brochure says there's tons of agate around here."

"A what?" I ask.

"Agate. It's a gemstone." She huffs at me. "Don't you know anything about Vermont geology?"

"Nope. And I'm insulted that you think I would. I was popular in school."

"I'm very popular," Maryanne says haughtily, then continues spitting out geology camp stats. "Oh! And we get to dig for serpentine!"

"Like snakes?" I wrinkle my forehead.

"No. It's a rock. Serpentine. And it's *so* pretty. It's greenish and black and super smooth. The brochure says they give us these little pickaxes we can use to dig."

"I'm sorry, what? They're giving children pickaxes?"

"So?" Maryanne challenges.

"So that seems aggressively irresponsible."

Dad howls with laughter.

The rest of the visit flies by, and I'm bummed to say goodbye when Friday rolls around. I leave Heartsong after the morning rush, making it back to Hastings in the early afternoon.

Almost immediately, I realize something has happened to the residents of my apartment complex.

They've been replaced by pod people.

Pod people who, for some reason, have it out for me.

Not that everyone was overly friendly before, but at least I got smiles and introductions when I wandered around Meadow Hill.

Suddenly everyone is borderline hostile.

Like that dude, Niall, who lives downstairs. When I bump into him in the outdoor visitors' lot where I park my Mercedes, he points his finger at me and snaps, "Your music's too loud." Then he clicks the key fob to lock his little Toyota hatchback and stalks off.

Harry, who mans the lobby in the Sycamore building, scowls when I give him a heads-up that I'm having people over on Saturday. I'm not even obligated to tell him. It was a *courtesy*.

Then, on the path, I pass one of the married couples who live in Weeping Willow, and the wife gives me a look that could freeze water.

When I say hello, she responds with, "Yeah, okay."

Now, I'm checking my mail after two days away, and the woman who lives next door to Niall—I think her name is Priya?—cautiously approaches the mailboxes as if she's entering a lion's cage.

I greet her with a smile and realize, no, that's not wariness. Her expression conveys deep contempt, as if she's entering the cage of a lion she wants to murder.

"Hello," I say, my smile faltering.

"Sure."

I don't know if "sure" is better than "yeah, okay," but it sort of feels like it's a rung lower on the greeting ladder.

"Priya, right?" I reintroduce myself. "Shane."

"I remember your name. I don't forget names."

"Right, you must be good at that. Keeping track of all those clients. Diana mentioned you were a counselor or something?"

"I'm a psychotherapist."

"That's really cool. Did you go to school for that?" It's the dumbest question I could have asked, but she's making me uncomfortable with those sullen eyes and the frown marring her lips.

"I chose to go the psychotherapy route, but I have both an MD in psychiatry and a PhD in psychology." She spares me a disparaging look before turning to unlock her mailbox. "From Harvard."

"Wow." I'm suitably impressed.

"I know, right? Isn't it astonishing that women can be doctors in the twenty-first century? That our worth is no longer tied to the way men treat us?"

I blink.

She's smiling sweetly at me.

I have no idea what the fuck is going on.

So I keep a pleasant expression plastered on my face and say, "Definitely. Five gold stars for women's liberation."

Her eyes narrow. Jesus. Those eyes. Dark as coal. "Are you mocking the feminist movement?"

"Not at all. I think it's great." I hastily tuck my mail under my arm. "Okay, I have to go now."

I hurry out of the vestibule, feeling Priya's gaze piercing into my back.

What the hell is the matter with these people? None of them threw a welcome parade for me, but I assumed that's because they didn't like the idea of a college guy moving into a complex full of couples and families. But there's a large number of singles in Meadow

Hill too, and nearly all the ones I've run into today have acted like total dickheads.

It isn't until I go outside for a swim a couple of hours later that I finally encounter a friendly face, belonging to a woman in her early fifties who's leaving the pool area as I'm entering. I've seen her hanging out at the pool before, but this is the first time she's stopped to chat. Before now, she seemed content to ogle me from behind her book while I pretended not to notice.

"Hello! It's Shane, right?" She has dyed-red hair, very tanned skin, and, unlike everyone else in this goddamn place today, is sporting an actual smile.

"Yup. That's me." I extend a hand to her. "Nice to meet you."

"I'm Veronika. Cherry Blossom, 1A."

Her hand lingers a little too long, until I'm forced to wrench mine away. I use the pretense of needing to pull my phone out of my pocket, but that simply draws her attention to the phone and gives her the wrong idea.

"Yes, good call, we should exchange numbers!" Veronika sounds delighted. She has one of those raspy voices that tells me she probably smoked two packs a day in her youth. Maybe still does. "It's always smart to have a neighbor's contact info. Would you like me to add you to our Meadow Hill group chat?"

There's a group chat?

Fuckin' Dixon. I bet she's been scheming to keep me off it.

"I'd love that," I tell Veronika, flashing her my dimples.

She giggles like a schoolgirl. We exchange numbers, and she saunters off with the exaggerated sway of her hips.

I'm pretty sure that lady wants to bone me.

I stretch my towel over one of the loungers and settle on top of it, deciding to scroll on my phone for a while before swimming laps. I just completed an hour workout in the Meadow Hill gym, and I think maybe I overdid it. It's arm day, so the thought of using my arms again to propel myself through water makes every muscle in my body weep.

I take my off-season training seriously, but this summer I'm kicking it into a whole new gear. I plan to be in the best shape of my life when hockey season starts. There's no room for slacking off anymore. This time next year, I'll be reporting to training camp. The last thing I want to do is show up for my first NHL training camp huffing and puffing like a fifty-year-old smoker because I let myself get out of shape.

I find some new messages in our guys' group chat. THE BOYS ALL CAPS, as Beckett named it. And yes, ALL CAPS is part of it. I truly don't know why women fawn all over that guy. He's not funny.

BECKETT:

Anyone feel like hitting up a club tonight?

WILL:

Pass. I'm too sunburnt to move.

Originally the group chat was only for me, Beckett, and Ryder, but Beck added Will after they became joined at the hip. I've never met two dudes more obsessed with time-travel movies. And group sex. They do a lot of that too. But I don't judge.

BECKETT:

You should have asked one of the milfs to rub sunscreen all over your dick.

WILL:

I don't fuck the clients. Gonna keep saying that until you're forced to accept it.

BECKETT:

Never. Ryder, you down?

RYDER:

> Me personally? Fuck no. But lemme ask the wife. If she wants to go, I'll go.

BECKETT:

> Wow.

RYDER:

> Wow what?

BECKETT:

> That woman owns you now. You realize that, right, mate?

RYDER:

> Yes and?

I raise a brow at the screen. Lord, what's happened to my buddy Ryder? Dude's gone from avoiding girlfriends like the plague to getting married and happily handing over his balls on a silver platter.

Although I suppose if my wife were Gigi Graham, I'd gladly let her handle my balls.

I heard her come once. I still think about that sometimes. Jerked off to it a few times too, though I'd never tell Ryder that. He'd rip my throat out.

Or maybe he wouldn't?

I mean…he was fully aware I was standing outside the door of that study room when he and Gigi fooled around in the library last fall. And I'm sure he knows I would've had to be painfully hard listening to her soft moans. Part of me thinks he might've let me watch if Gigi had wanted it. He'd give that woman anything she asked her. Man's smitten.

Watching isn't my kink, though.

Being watched, on the other hand…I could get on board with that. But that's not something I'd ever suggest to a girlfriend. The one time I mentioned this kink to Lynsey, she was so disgusted that I never brought it up again. She accused me of watching too much pornography. Which is laughably not the case because I very rarely use porn to jack off. I prefer the real thing.

Well, not so much these days. Now that random hookups are off the table thanks to the Crystal fiasco, the only way I'm getting laid is if I 1) have a girlfriend or 2) find myself a friends-with-benefits arrangement. Someone I spend an extended amount of time with. Someone to have regular sex with instead of impersonal and hollow one-night stands.

I'm sending a message to the group chat saying I don't feel like going out tonight when the phone vibrates in my hand. I brighten when I see the notification.

VERONIKA PINLO HAS ADDED YOU TO THE GROUP
NEIGHBORS.

Hell yeah. Progress! I may have been spurned by everyone else today, but at least I won over Veronika. And now maybe the rest of them will be wowed by my stellar personality via my hilarious messages and start warming up to me.

No sooner does the optimism take root than another notification pops up.

DIANA DIXON HAS REMOVED YOU FROM THE GROUP
NEIGHBORS.

THE DIXON
LIST

- [ ] <u>Nail prelim audition</u>
- [ ] <u>Win NUABC competition</u>
- [ ] <u>Turn entire building</u>
  <u>against Shane Lindley**</u>
- [ ] _____
  _____
- [ ] _____
- [ ] _____

**he deserves it

CHAPTER SEVEN
DIANA

Kenji has betrayed me

DAD COMES OVER SATURDAY MORNING TO FIX MY SHOWER. I OFFER TO help him, but he waves me off and says he works better alone, so I cook up some omelets for us while I wait. He lumbers out of the bathroom literally ten minutes after he entered it and announces, "We're good."

I stare at him incredulously. "Do you realize I watched hours' worth of how-to videos to try to fix that stupid thing and you did it in *minutes*?"

He shrugs. "Just had to adjust the control valve."

"I hate that after all those online tutorials, I still don't know what you're talking about. I feel completely useless right now."

Dad grins at me. "It's okay, kiddo. I'll never ask you to fix my shower temperature, but you're still the first person I'd want by my side in a fight."

"Obviously. Thomas would never have your back."

"Nah, he would. He'd throw down. But then he'd feel guilty and start patching up the enemy's wounds. You, on the other hand…"

"I'd crush their skulls to dust," I say solemnly.

"That's my girl."

"Here." I slide a plate toward him. "Let me butter your toast."

We eat our breakfast side by side at the kitchen counter, chatting about what we've been up to lately. Dad is a SWAT team leader on the Boston PD, so his updates are always way more interesting than mine. He tells me about a meth lab his squad raided last week, shaking his head when he gets to the part about finding three little kids at the house, cowering in a closet. I don't know how he's able to do this job. Kicking in doors of drug houses. Executing high-risk searches. Dealing with hostage crises. All that adrenaline would put me into cardiac arrest. But Dad thrives on it. He's honestly the toughest man I know.

"How about you?" he asks. "How're the dance rehearsals going?"

"Really well! I have high hopes for this year's competition. I think Kenji and I might be able to crack the top ten."

"Of course you can. You're unstoppable."

"So is everyone else who's competing," I grumble. "This will definitely be an uphill battle."

"You got this." He leans closer and nudges my shoulder with his. "You've never shied away from a challenge your entire life. Never met an obstacle you haven't been able to overcome."

My dad is my biggest champion, and that's pretty damn great.

It's not until after he leaves me with a hug and a promise to stop by next week that I realize the battle I'm facing is beyond uphill—it's a vertical line shooting straight up into the heavens.

Kenji calls as I'm getting ready for my shift at the diner and drops the bomb of all bombs.

"What do you mean you can't do the competition?" I shriek into the phone. "Why not?"

"I need you to brace yourself."

"It's too late! I'm already keeled over in horror." Anxiety flutters through me. He can't be bailing on me. He *can't*. We're supposed to film our audition video soon.

"I got a job on a superyacht," Kenji reveals. "I leave tomorrow for six months."

"What are you even saying to me right now?"

"I'm going to be working as a private bartender on a superyacht owned by an eccentric billionaire whose name I'm not allowed to divulge because of the nondisclosure agreement I signed, but let's just say he's in tech and may or may not be a bigamist."

I gasp. "Oh my God, you're working for Constantine Zayn?"

Zayn is the third richest man in the world. It recently came out that the dude is legally married to two women, one in Greece and the other in America, and now both wives are trying to divorce him and coming after half of his considerable fortune.

"I can neither confirm nor deny," Kenji says innocently.

"Okay, first, we will discuss this in detail later. I have faith we can find loopholes in the NDA. Second—how could you!"

He groans loudly in my ear. "I know. I'm sorry. Like, really, really sorry. I know how important this is to you. But…a *superyacht*, Di."

"What about school?" He's about to go into his junior year at Briar. "You can't just disappear for six months."

"I'll come back in January for winter semester, then make up the rest of my courses next summer. This is the opportunity of a lifetime."

"How did you even land this job?"

"Get this! My mother does the mistress's hair."

"This dude has two wives *and* a mistress? That feels like overkill."

"So the mistress is sitting in my mom's salon, complaining how they lost half the yacht's waitstaff because they were all busted for running a human trafficking ring."

"I'm sorry. *What?*" My head is spinning.

"Trust me, this story is a labyrinth that would take years to navigate. So Mom goes, hey, my son tends bar to pay for college, he'd be perfect for this job. Next day? I get a call from Cons—my new unnamed employer," he corrects quickly. "I spoke to a billionaire, Diana."

"I'm happy for you. I truly am. But…goddamn it, Kenji. This is NUABC!"

"I know. I'm sure you'll be able to find someone else, though."

"Yes, I'll have my pick of all those ballroom dance enthusiasts wandering the streets of Hastings hoping to compete one day."

"Post an SOS video on Ride or Dance. See if anyone in the Boston area wants to audition to be your partner."

"Okay, that's not a terrible idea. But I'm still mad at you."

"I'm sorry. I was having fun at rehearsals. But let's be honest—we're never going to place."

"That's not true," I protest. "We might make the top ten. That's like two grand in winnings."

He snorts loudly. "We both know we're not winning any money. We came in fifteenth in our category last year. Out of twenty."

He's right. It's unlikely. But I don't like seeing my dream balloon burst like this. It's nicer when it's floating around signifying hope and glory. Like maybe this year we'll nail the Viennese waltz, and the judges will sit there in awe, weeping from the sheer beauty of our bodies in motion. Maybe all the other competitors will break their legs in a tragic summer skiing accident the night before. I really don't understand why Kenji is being so pessimistic. The dream balloon is full of endless possibilities!

"Please don't go. Please?" I make a last-ditch begging effort, but Kenji was lost to me from the word *billionaire*.

As I change into my waitressing uniform, I'm grumbling under my breath the entire time. I don't handle disappointment well, especially when it's due to something that isn't in my control. It'd be one thing if I backed out myself, but the choice was taken from me, damn it.

I'm officially adding Constantine Zayn to my list of archenemies, under my old gymnastics coach and Shane Lindley.

My mood only worsens when I start my shift at Della's Diner. Each customer I serve is worse than the last. One man makes me return his pie three times because he doesn't like the way the crust looks. I'm finally forced to get my manager, who informs the picky patron that he has to pay for two out of the three pieces because despite the offensive crust, he still ate nearly half of each slice.

After work, I duck into the bathroom to change out of my uniform and into denim shorts and a striped T-shirt. I'm meeting Gigi for dinner at Malone's down the street.

My white tennis shoes slap the pavement as I hurry down the sidewalk toward the sports bar at the corner of Main Street. Gigi texted to say she'd already arrived and grabbed us a booth.

"Kenji has betrayed me," I announce as I slide across from her.

She lifts her eyes from the menu. Her lips are twitching with humor. "That's a pity."

I glare at her. "It's not funny."

"What happened?"

"He bailed on the competition."

"No! Okay, that is pretty bad."

"See? I told you."

"Can you find another partner?"

I moan. "Who, Gigi? Who is going to spend their summer learning the tango well enough to execute a routine good enough to qualify for the most important dance competition of all time?"

"I don't think it's the most important of all time—"

"All time for eternity," I say stubbornly.

I can tell she's trying not to laugh at me again. To her credit, she spends the next ten minutes brainstorming where I can find a new partner, but I'm not feeling hopeful. The dream balloon is completely deflated. Doesn't seem like NUABC is in the cards this year, and I'm bummed.

We spend the rest of dinner chatting about the wedding, for which Gigi has very little involvement. Her aunt is running the show and we're all just along for the ride. We have a fitting scheduled for next week, and I'm looking forward to seeing my dress. Mya complained via text the other day how we weren't allowed to pick our own dress styles, but I had to remind her that Summer Di Laurentis is a highly-in-demand fashion designer. No way she's going to steer us wrong. Plus, the bridal party is wearing sage. I rock a mean sage.

"Oh, I actually wanted to talk to you about that," Gigi says when I mention that Mya and I have a video call scheduled tomorrow to discuss all things bachelorette. "Would you guys be super offended if we don't have one?"

"Are you serious?"

"Fuck, I guess that means yes."

"No, it means no!" Relief washes over me. "You have no idea what a logistical nightmare this has been. Everyone on your hockey team is scattered all over the country, you have five thousand aunts and cousins, everyone has jobs or are away on summer trips. No joke—Mya and I have been struggling here, and you *know* the two of us can normally plan the hell out of a girls' trip. We can still make something happen, but—"

"Oh my God, let's skip it, then," Gigi cuts in, equally relieved. "There are way too many things going on this summer. We leave for Arizona tomorrow and I'm not even packed. That's why we have to bail on the party tonight."

"What party?"

"The party at your apartment complex? Beckett's goodbye thing."

"What! Is he moving? Why didn't I know about this?"

She grins. "He's not moving. He's going on vacation."

"Oh. Wow. That's extra."

"Beyond extra."

I purse my lips for a moment. "Eh. I'd still suck his dick."

She bursts out laughing.

"Ugh. Stupid Shane, though. Why is he throwing a party? I just wanted one quiet night to catch up on *Fling or Forever*."

"Holy shit, we didn't even get to talk about that!" Her gray eyes become animated. "Did you *see* that Leni and Donovan date? I've never heard so much bullshit escape a man's mouth."

I nod my agreement. "Donovan is as shady as they come. He's not there for the right reasons. He's only pretending to like Leni, and I feel so bad for her because she's so sweet and she genuinely likes him."

"That relationship is a dumpster fire waiting to happen," Gigi sighs.

Speaking of dumpster fires, Shane's about to invite the wrath of the Meadow Hill HOA, judging by the amount of noise I hear coming from the pool when I get home. Granted, it's only nine o'clock. Technically Niall can't start complaining until midnight.

On the other hand, I assume after the pool lights automatically turn off, Shane will move the party to Red Birch, which will give Niall a nervous breakdown.

I let myself into my apartment, kick off my sneakers, and go to feed Skip. As I sprinkle fish food into his tank, he stares up at me with those lifeless eyes and I stare back until he feels self-conscious and swims away. That's right, Skip. You're not the boss.

Even with the balcony door shut, noise drifts in from the pool area. Muffled laughter, music, and the drone of voices. Curious to see who Shane paid to attend his party (because nobody would willingly be his friend), I slide the glass door open and step up to the white railing.

It's a decent-sized gathering. Maybe two dozen people, half of them in the pool, the others draped over lounge chairs or sitting around the white tables on the deck. An outdoor speaker plays a chill pop song on low volume, which tells me Shane is trying to be mindful of our neighbors so they don't hate him. Joke's on him. All the neighbors already hate him.

I'm trying to back away when Shane spots me, his dark head swinging toward my balcony. He's standing in the middle of the pool in waist-level water, wearing red swim trunks and holding a beer. The sun has already set, but the moon is nearly full and sits high in the sky, illuminating every chiseled feature of Shane's face.

When our gazes lock, he raises the beer bottle. "Dixon," he calls. "Come join."

"Sorry, can't hear you over the music." I point to my ears, feigning cluelessness.

Effortlessly, he hoists himself out of the pool. Water drips from his hair and runs down his body in twisting lines. His ab muscles glisten as the moonlight shines off the droplets. I try to peel my eyes away, but I can't even blink as I watch him move toward me.

Then I realize what's happening and almost gag in revulsion.

Oh my God. I was admiring Shane Lindley's body.

I need an intervention.

"I said come join us," he repeats, walking barefoot across the grass. He stops about ten yards from the balcony. "It's a good time."

"No, thank you."

"Why not?"

"Because that would be breaking a Dixon rule. You and I don't fraternize."

"What about us? Do we fraternize?" Beckett Dunne sidles up to Shane, also barefoot and shirtless. His blond hair is wet and nearly reaches his shoulders.

Lord, he's an Australian god, so delicious I can't help but ogle him. At least *him* I'm allowed to ogle.

"I'm lonely, Juliet," Beckett drawls up to the balcony. "Come keep me company."

I flash him a sweet smile. "Hard pass, Romeo."

"C'mon, one drink."

"Di!" someone shouts.

I peer past the guys' broad shoulders and spot Fatima from cheer camp. She's wearing a sleek black one-piece and waving at me from one of the lounge chairs. Damn it, they lured *her* into this? And is that Lily and Gia in the pool? Lily is another counselor, while Gia is on the Briar squad with me. The two bikini-clad young women are in the shallow end, laughing with Will Larsen and a couple guys I don't recognize.

Why are all my friends here?

My gaze flicks back to Shane's and Beckett's muscular bare chests.

I mean. That's why.

"Fine," I relent, although I make a point to grimace at Shane. "I'll be right down."

CHAPTER EIGHT

SHANE

I win

MOST PEOPLE ARE AWAY FOR THE SUMMER, SO TONIGHT'S GATHERING isn't a banger. It's just Will, Beck, a few other guys from the team. A few cheerleaders. Some local girls Beckett met in Hastings, and some guys we played pool with at Malone's. All in all, twenty, twenty-five people. Certainly can't be enough to piss off the homeowners' association, but I do feel a bit like a hall monitor as I wander around cautioning everyone to keep it down and making sure nothing gets too out of hand.

Like this pool game of chicken that somehow just became topless.

"Hey, tops on," I reprimand the redhead whose bikini top is suddenly at her waist. "This is a family establishment."

Winking, she covers up a pair of very nice tits and reties the strings of her bikini. "Sorry, daddy."

Damned if my dick doesn't perk up at that.

I don't *think* I have a daddy kink, but I do enjoy being the boss in the bedroom. Not in an aggressively dominant way; I'd never ask a woman to crawl on the floor toward me or some shit. But calling the shots does get me off.

"I can't believe Kenji bailed on the competition," Fatima is saying when I join the small group. She's standing with Will, Beck, and Dixon, who I'm shocked decided to grace us with her presence.

"Kenji ditched you?" I ask Diana, raising a brow. "He finally saw the light? Good for him."

She gives me the finger. "Had nothing to do with me and how wonderful I am. He got a new job." She dismisses me from her gaze, those green eyes shifting hopefully to Will. "Any chance you want to be my ballroom dance partner?"

He almost spits out his beer laughing. "No. Never."

"Please? I'll split half the prize money if we win."

"Wait, were you not going to split it with my man Kenji?" I demand.

That earns me a scowl. "Of course I was. I'm just trying to make it sound like I'm sweetening the deal."

"Yeah, not happening," Will tells her. "There is nothing I enjoy less than dancing."

At his steadfast refusal, she turns her attention to Beckett, batting her eyelashes.

"Nope. I'm going to Australia." He shudders. "Thank God for that because I can't say no to hot women. I would've done it if I were here."

"Cancel the trip," she begs.

"No."

Diana pouts and takes a sip of the nauseatingly pink liquid in her glass. When she saw we only had beer in the cooler and a few bottles of whiskey for shots, she ran back upstairs and returned with a bottle of the pink stuff. That's literally what the brand is called— the Pink Stuff. According to the girls, it's *the* hot new wine cooler on the block, but I haven't tried it and don't intend to. I don't feel like hurling tonight.

While she drinks, I eye her expectantly.

"What?" she says over the rim of her glass.

"You're not going to ask me to be your partner?"

Rather than answer, Diana starts to laugh.

"What's so funny?"

"You thought I would actually ask you." She's still giggling as she takes another sip. "That's cute."

Man, my ego is usually rock-solid, but Diana's damn good at poking holes in it.

Which reminds me of the stunt she pulled yesterday.

"By the way, that wasn't cool," I grumble. "Banishing me from the group chat."

"That wasn't me," she lies, then smiles smugly and takes Fatima's hand. "Babe, let's go dance."

"I *saw* it was you!" I growl at her retreating back. "Stop gaslighting me!"

I ignore Will's and Beckett's laughter at my expense and decide to go mingle with people who aren't traitors.

It's the perfect summer night. Hardly any breeze. No humidity. Just warm air, a bright moon, and good people. Well, mostly good people. Diana doesn't count.

As it nears midnight, I turn down the music again, but none of the couples dancing on the grass seem to notice. Diana's body moves sensually against Beckett, whose hands are all over her. I watch in amusement. She's into the dancing, and he's into her.

I guess I see the appeal. Sure, she might have the devil's tongue and a vendetta against me that isn't at all justified, but she's irrefutably beautiful. Her baggy, striped tee has slid down, exposing her bare shoulder. Pale hair falls between her shoulder blades as she throws her head back, lost in the sultry R&B track quietly playing in the night air.

My gaze fixes on Dixon's little denim shorts that reveal the bottom of her ass cheeks, then travel south, over her tanned legs, defined calves, and bare feet. Her toenails are painted pink. It's cute.

Will, who's next to me shoving half a slice of pizza in his mouth, follows my gaze. Appreciation flickers across his face as he watches

Diana and Beckett. His eyes track the sinful path of Beck's hands as they curve over Dixon's ass.

I smirk at him. "Aw, did you guys just find the meat in your sandwich tonight?"

He balks. "Jesus. Of course not."

"Right. I guess you can't really go there. Gigi would kill you."

"One hundred percent." He polishes off the rest of the slice and reaches for the beer on the table.

Joey and Ray, a couple local guys we met at Malone's, come up to tell me they're heading out. They clap my back and bump my fist before disappearing toward the path. I hope they don't get lost on their way off the property. Last thing I need is for one of my neighbors to find a pair of dudes passed out in the bushes tomorrow morning.

At midnight, the party dwindles even further. The only people remaining are Will, Beck, Dixon, and two of her friends—Lily and Gia. The pool lights switch off, bathing us in darkness, but we're not deterred. The girls chat on a pair of lounge chairs, while the guys and I sit on the pool deck, feet in the water. We're talking about our Frozen Four win in the spring, reliving the winning shot courtesy of Case Colson.

"Damn, when he released that bullet." Beckett shudders. "I almost came in my jock."

"Fucking beauty," Will agrees.

"Do you think we have a shot at back-to-back championship wins?" muses Beck.

"With me, Ryder, and Colson on the team?" I retort. "Of course."

"Gee, thanks," Will says dryly. "Don't I feel valuable."

I reach over to pat his shoulder. "Don't sell yourself short. You're almost as good as us."

He gives me the finger.

It's true, though. Will and Beck are great players, but neither one is headed for the NHL. Going pro isn't their life plan like it is with me or Ryder or even Colson.

"With his parents in the next bed!"

"Ew. *No.*"

Diana and Lily's conversation has the three of us exchanging grins.

"Yup. And I'm not talking about a suite with adjoining rooms. I'm talking *same room.* Two double beds. Mom and Dad in one bed. Todd and his girlfriend, full-on sex in the other bed."

"I think I'm going to throw up."

I twist around to stare at the girls. "What the hell kind of weird-ass shit are you discussing?"

"You wouldn't understand," Dixon replies, dismissing me in typical Diana fashion.

"I don't think I want to," Beckett says frankly.

"It's one of the secrets someone revealed on *Fling or Forever* last night," Gia explains. "The craziest shit comes out during their drinking games."

"Did you see they put that drinking game on the app?" Gia tells her friends, her expression shining with enthusiasm. I swear, women get excited about the wildest things.

"Really?" Lily is equally elated as she snatches her phone from the table between the loungers. She and Gia proceed to huddle over the screen happily.

"Okay, we *have* to play this," Gia declares. "We can split into two teams like they do on *FoF.*"

Lily brightens. "Oooh, boys against girls."

And that's how the guys and I are coerced into playing a party game. It's super simple. A command pops up on the screen, and the player who's up has sixty seconds to complete the task, which is either a truth or a dare. If they do it successfully, they win the point. If they fail, the other team gets the point.

"So...we're playing truth or dare," Will says, amused.

"There's no time limit in truth or dare." Gia's tone is haughty.

"You're right," Beckett says solemnly. "This is completely different."

We're seated around one of the tables, the girls on the opposite side of us. I'm surprised Dixon is allowing this. I half expected her to say something dramatic, like how she'd rather eat glass while bathing in a tub of spiders than play a party game with me. But there she is, sitting carelessly in her chair, blond hair swept over one shoulder, green eyes dancing.

Lily is up first. She stands and waits for Gia to flash the phone screen at her. The first command is written in big, bold letters, and the timer starts the moment it appears. Sixty seconds begin to count down.

ACT OUT YOUR FAVORITE SEXUAL POSITION WITH SOMEONE ON THE OPPOSITE TEAM

"Easy," she says, grinning as she yanks Beckett out of his chair. "Doggy-style."

We're all laughing as she bends over the table and Beck steps up behind her, hands clasping around her hips.

"Girl, you finished that in four seconds." Gia sounds impressed.

Lily shrugs. "I know what I like."

I snicker.

The app keeps score, and the girls' team now has one point on us. I'm not worried about falling behind, seeing as how this game doesn't require much effort or concentration. Most of the commands are similar to the first one. Act out something naughty. Reveal something sexy. Do something wild. Beckett is tasked with pouring whiskey over one of Gia's ass cheeks and licking it off. Diana and Will have to jump into the pool fully clothed, the first one in getting the point. I win a point against Diana when I swallow a whiskey shot before she does, while she gags because apparently she can't stomach the taste of whiskey.

Beckett then has to tell his best joke to our opponents and get at least one laugh for the point. His contribution is solid. "What do you call a pool boy that doesn't fuck the lady of the house?"

"What?" Diana says warily.

"Will."

"That's not a joke! It's a statement of fact!" Diana sputters, but Gia ruins it for the women by guffawing.

"Traitor," Diana accuses her.

"It was funny," protests Gia.

Lily's next command pops up.

DRINK IF YOU'VE EVER KISSED SOMEONE OF THE SAME SEX.

TEAM WITH MOST DRINKERS WINS THE POINT.

For the women, Lily and Gia both drink. For us, Beckett lifts his bottle to his lips. When Diana raises a brow at him, he simply winks. He's got Lily on his lap now, while he runs a hand over her bare thigh. Still in nothing but her bikini, she claimed she was cold and required his body heat.

I note that Will didn't drink. Which means he's either lying or all his illicit extracurriculars with Beckett involve a hands-off approach.

"Your turn," Gia tells me, and I refocus my attention on the phone.

TELL A PLAYER OF THE OPPOSING TEAM'S CHOICE THEIR SEXIEST FEATURE.

"Do Diana," Lily says with a chortle.

The countdown starts, and I make a big show of studying Diana's face. Tilting my head, squinting, taking a good, hard look.

"Oh, fuck off," she grumbles. "We all know you're going to say something sleazy, like my—"

"Your smile."

Her suspicion is palpable. "Are you serious?"

"You have a really pretty smile." My voice suddenly sounds a little gruff to my ears.

"The prompt was *sexiest* feature, not prettiest," Gia gloats. "You guys don't score the point."

"Oh, in that case, I love her ass."

"And there he is," Diana says, sighing.

After a few more rounds, the game is tied. There's only one turn left: Dixon's. And the determined gleam in her eyes makes me smother a laugh. Of course she's insanely competitive. I wouldn't expect anything less.

"Ready?" Gia says.

"Give it to me." Diana turns her attention toward the screen.

KISS A PLAYER OF THE OPPOSING TEAM'S CHOICE FOR AT LEAST 20 SECONDS.

"Shane!" Will and Beckett say in unison, then exchange grins.

Diana stares at them in horror. "How could you?"

The countdown on the screen reads fifty-six seconds.

"Ticktock," I taunt, tapping the imaginary watch on my wrist.

"Just go and kiss him," Lily urges Diana. "He's hot."

"I'd rather eat crushed seashells."

See? Drama queen.

"That's oddly specific," Will remarks, staring at her.

"Forty-five seconds..." Beckett says in a singsong voice.

As Diana remains frozen in her seat, I glance at the other two girls, smirking. "Go ahead and give us the W already. She ain't gonna do it. It goes against everything she believes in."

"I can't believe *Fling or Forever* has turned on me," Diana declares. So melodramatic, this one.

The countdown is at thirty-eight seconds.

"Told you," I brag. "She won't do it. She knows she'll enjoy it too much."

Her eyes flare. "Oh, you wish. If my tongue was in your mouth, only one of us would be enjoying it."

"Yeah. You."

At that, I unleash the dragon. Diana jumps out of her chair and marches over to mine. I blink, and suddenly she's straddling me.

She makes herself comfortable on my lap, and my hands instinctively cup her ass to steady her. A tingle runs down my spine the moment I make contact.

Licking her lips, Diana brings her mouth to mine and kisses me. When our lips touch, a jolt rolls through my body. And then her tongue slides out to touch mine, and fire rushes up and burns in my blood. My heartbeat pounds in my fingertips as I drag them beneath her shirt and run them over the smooth skin of her lower back. She moans softly in response. Her tongue lightly swirls over mine, teasing me, until I make a hoarse sound of desperation.

I don't know what the hell is going on right now, but I want more. I want to know how every inch of her tastes.

But more doesn't happen.

"And time!" Lily declares, and she and Gia start cheering that the girls scored their point.

Me, I'm too busy trying to comprehend how one kiss with Diana Dixon got me this hard.

"Lindley," she whispers, her palm stroking up my bare arm.

I pull back, my head a little foggy. I can't take my gaze off her. Her green eyes are like a drug.

I swallow. I can't find my voice. My dick is a hard spike, and there's no disguising it. I know she feels it pressing against her thigh.

"Yeah?" My throat is hoarse.

She brings her mouth close to my ear. "I win."

CHAPTER NINE

DIANA

Hey, can my best friend fuck you?

THE PARTY IS WINDING DOWN, BUT MY HEARTBEAT IS STILL COMPLETELY out of control.

I kissed Shane Lindley.

It was out of spite and to win a game, but still.

What I did was unacceptable. It was egregious. It was—

The hottest kiss ever?

Oh my God, fuck off, I order my traitorous inner voice. How can my own subconscious betray me like this?

And yet the thought persists. Maybe I did feel a teeny, tiny tingle of arousal from that kiss. How could I not when his erection was pressing against me? And it was...substantial. A generous penis, as my friend Brooke described a boyfriend's package once.

Unfortunately, that generous penis belongs to the cocky, insufferable Shane Lindley. Therefore, I will not be partaking in that penis, thank you very much.

Will Larsen pulls me aside as I'm dumping empty beer bottles into a garbage bag. I'm not sure how I got roped into cleanup duty considering this wasn't my party.

"Hey, can I crash at your place tonight?" he asks in a low voice.

I give him a strange look. "Why? You live so close. And you don't seem too drunk to walk a few blocks."

"Yeah, I'm not even buzzed." He glances over his shoulder.

I follow his gaze and spot Beckett and Lily. I heard her agree to go home with him tonight, and she's draped over him like a cashmere scarf.

"C'mon, Di. Let me crash. And, uh, maybe act like we're gonna hook up?"

I snort.

"I'm serious," Will says. "Just...you know...make it look like I have a reason to go upstairs with you."

The pleading flash in his brown eyes is cause for alarm. He only recently moved in with Beck and Ryder, right after Shane moved to Meadow Hill. So why doesn't he want to go home? It's been a week. They can't already be having roommate issues.

But I'm unable to ignore a man in distress, so when Shane joins us, I shove the garbage bag at him and reach for his teammate's hand.

With a wink, Will laces his fingers through mine and calls out to Beckett. "Hey, go on without me. I'm gonna crash here."

Beckett seems startled for a moment. Then he notices our intertwined hands, and the corners of his mouth tick up. "Got it. See you tomorrow."

Once Beckett and Lily are gone, I tug on Will's hand. "Come on, let's go."

Shane's jaw drops. "Really? You assholes aren't gonna help?" He points to the tables still laden with pizza boxes and empties.

I smirk at him. "Not my party, not my responsibility."

Will merely shrugs. "Sorry, bro. I've got other plans."

Shane glares at his teammate. "Don't do this, man. She's going to eat you alive. There's still time to make the right decision."

"He's just jealous," I assure Will. "I swear, this guy is obsessed with me."

"You wish," Shane growls. "And don't forget who kissed who."

"Don't forget whose penis got hard and whose vagina got dry."

"You were wetter than the Atlantic," he shoots back.

"Dryer than the Sahara. But it's okay. I'm positive you'll be able to turn on a woman someday. Just keep practicing on your sex doll."

Fluttering my free hand in a careless wave, I pull Will away from the pool area toward the path home. A glance over my shoulder reveals a sullen Shane, broad shoulders hunched, clearing up the rest of the mess.

"You could be nicer to him," Will tells me. The full moon clearly reveals the amused curve of his mouth.

"I could," I agree. "But I won't."

I'll also never give him the satisfaction of knowing how much I enjoyed kissing him. Why are the arrogant jerks always the best kissers?

Once we're safely inside Red Birch and I've closed my apartment door behind us, Will offers a sincere look and says, "Thanks for doing this."

"Are you really staying over?"

He nods. "It's still cool, right?"

"I mean, yes, but…"

"Don't worry, I'm not expecting anything to happen."

"Well, good. Because nothing's happening. But I do require an explanation in exchange for room and board."

"You have like an extra sheet and blanket or something I can throw on the couch?"

"Don't be silly. You're going to sleep in my bed. It's big enough for both of us. You'll have to endure my beauty routine, though. I refuse to go to bed without taking care of my skin." I study him. "Actually, you could use some face TLC too. You have a bit of a sunburn."

"I worked outside all week."

"All right. Come into my office."

He smiles, drawing my attention to his boy-next-door looks. He's just that classic all-American guy, the one who wears his letterman jacket in high school, graduates college with a very practical degree, and marries a woman who'll give him 2.5 kids and bake cookies on the weekends. Then in the fall, they go to pumpkin patches together and take family pictures, posing in matching orange sweaters.

"You okay there?"

I snap out of my reverie. "Sorry. I was picturing you at a pumpkin patch."

"Was I naked?"

"Of course not. That would scare the other families."

He's puzzled. "I was there with family?"

"Long story."

Will chuckles. "Okay."

We walk into the bathroom, where I pull out the exfoliant I use once a week. I twist off the lid on the tub of pinkish-white substance.

"First, we exfoliate," I explain.

To his credit, he doesn't complain at all. He follows my instructions, and we're both laughing our asses off as I rub the grainy substance all over his face. After we wash off the exfoliant, I reach for the next product.

"Now we mask up. This needs to stay on for fifteen minutes."

He balks as he watches me squeeze a glob of black goo onto my fingers. "What the hell is that? Charcoal?"

"There's charcoal in it. Trust me, your eye bags will thank me in the morning."

After I apply the mask onto our faces, we walk into my bedroom to wait it out.

Will glances down at his swim trunks, then at the bed. "These are still damp. What are the chances you have some men's boxers lying around?"

"Actually." I brighten. "I do."

He narrows his eyes. "Please tell me they're clean."

"They are. My younger brother has a drawer for when he stays over," I say, going to the dresser. In the bottom drawer, I find a pair of plaid boxers. I hold them up by the waistband and study Will's hips. "He's around your size, so these should fit. Might be a little tight, but that just means I get to stare at your bulge."

He grins and catches the bundle of plaid when I toss it at him. I grab my own pj's and change in the bathroom, returning to my room to find Will has made himself comfortable on the bed. His bare legs, dusted with light brown hair, stretch out in front of him. He's got some hair on his chest too, but not a lot, and of course, he possesses the six-pack abs of a hockey player.

"So what's the deal? Are you not enjoying living with Ryder and Beckett? Too crowded or something? Because Ryder's moving out after the wedding," I remind him. Gigi and her husband signed a lease for an apartment that becomes available in September.

"No, I love it there. It's a million times better than the dorms. And Ryder's never even home."

"Got it. So it's Beckett we're avoiding."

"We're not avoiding anybody."

"Then why didn't you want to go home tonight?"

"Didn't feel like walking."

"Is that what we do now, we lie to each other? We're supposed to be best friends, William."

He snickers. "No we're not."

"Fine. Best friend adjacent. You and Gigi are close. Therefore, you and I are close." I flop down beside him on the mattress. "Spill the tea."

"Nah. I'd much rather discuss how you made out with Lindley tonight. I think he enjoyed it."

"Oh, definitely. Things were poking out of his swim trunks for sure."

"Things?"

"Well, only one thing. His dick," I say helpfully.

Will snorts out a laugh. "Yeah, I got that."

"Anyway, stop deflecting. Why are we avoiding Beckett?"

"It's...complicated."

He releases a heavy breath that piques my interest.

"Wait. Are you two...?" I raise a brow suggestively.

"No."

"You sure? Sometimes I get some bi vibes from him. Not from you, though." I shrug. "Either way, I'm not judging."

"Nah, it's not like that."

"What's it like, then?"

Will bites his lip, visibly uncomfortable. But I can tell from his expression that he wants to talk about it.

"I won't tell anyone," I assure him. "Not even Gigi."

"I don't believe you."

"I'm serious. I'm an excellent secret-keeper. Ask me what Brooke Sato did in Mexico last winter."

"What did she do?"

"I'm not telling you. It's a secret."

That gets me another bark of laughter. "All right, you pass the first test."

"I won't breathe a word, I promise."

Will runs both hands through his hair before rubbing the back of his neck. "Beckett and I have been doing this, uh, thing lately. Well, really, we've been doing it since we became friends."

"What thing?"

"Like..." He offers an awkward shrug. "Threesomes."

I attempt to keep an impartial face. "Okay..."

I *may* have already known, thanks to the rumor mill, AKA Gigi, that Will and Beck had hooked up with the same girl a few times. But that information was given to me in confidence, so I pretend this is the first I'm hearing of it.

"Threesomes can be fun," I say neutrally.

"They're hot," he admits.

"Okay."

"Really hot."

"Okay." I keep my tone encouraging, hoping it will get him talking in more than two-word sentences. "Then what's the problem?"

He responds with a frustrated groan. "The problem is, I'm not supposed to think they're hot."

I bite my lip to stop from laughing. He sounds so tormented. "You're allowed to enjoy group sex, Will. It doesn't make you gay or anything, if that's what you're worried about."

"I'm not worried about that at all. I just…" He trails off, and before I can push him to finish, he points to his face and says, "Shouldn't this come off?"

"Oh crap. Yes." I scramble off the bed. "We need to wash now, or it'll dry out our skin."

We return to the bathroom to scrub our respective faces. Afterward, I take a small silver tube out of my moisturizer drawer.

"This is our finishing move. The best moisturizer you'll ever experience. It has collagen in it, but that's basically the only confirmed ingredient. The manufacturer keeps the exact recipe a mystery, so for all I know it's made from zebra tears and alligator semen—"

Will keels over with a howl.

"—but whatever it is, it's life-changing. Trust me, you'll love it. Give me your face."

He obediently lowers his head so he's not towering over me, and I rub the collagen gel into his freshly exfoliated skin. His stubble abrades my fingertips as I drag them over his cheeks and along the line of chin. His jaw is chiseled out of stone. I can see why women are equally eager to jump him as they are Beckett.

"Anyway," I say, studying his reflection in the mirror as I moisturize my own face. "Back to these threesomes you're having with Beckett that you don't want to enjoy."

"It's more than that. It's…like, I've been having sex my whole life, right?"

"Your whole life? When did you start?"

He rolls his eyes. "You know what I mean. I'm not some virgin who's new to the scene. I've slept with enough women to know I love sex."

"Understood. We've established you love sex."

"So last weekend, I went to see my cousin in Boston, and we met these girls at a bar. Chilled with them all night. They were roommates and invited us back to their place, so we went, obviously. My cousin and one of the girls disappeared into her bedroom. I hung out with her roommate. She was gorgeous and funny and exactly my type. One thing led to another…and it was good. Don't get me wrong, it was not bad. But…" He mumbles something under his breath.

"What?"

His cheeks are red now, and I don't think it has to do with the skincare routine. "It took me a while to finish."

I dig around in my arsenal and find some tact. "Oh. Okay. Well. That's completely normal. What, did she expect you to come on command or something? Ejaculate the second she snapped her fingers?"

"No, she wasn't complaining. This was entirely a me issue. I know it can take some men a long time, but I've never had that problem." He smiles ruefully. "In fact, I probably *could* come on command." He meets my gaze in the mirror. "The reason it took longer is because I couldn't stop thinking how much hotter it would be if Beckett was there."

I blink at our reflections. "Oh."

"Yeah."

"Oh," I say again, trailing after him as he leaves the bathroom.

"Yeah."

"Hotter how?" I can't help but ask.

He doesn't answer until we're sitting on my bed again. "I kept thinking how much more she would enjoy it if he was, you know, playing with her tits. Or kissing her while I fucked her. Or if she had his dick in her mouth…" An embarrassed Will averts his eyes.

"Seriously, it just messed with my head. Distracted me. Then I lost my hard-on, and it took a while to get it back."

He buries his newly moisturized face in his palms and groans into them.

"Aww." I scoot closer to him. Linking our arms, I rest my head against his shoulder. "You're right. That sounds stressful."

"Fuckin' understatement. I couldn't sleep that night because my mind kept questioning what happened. And that's when I came to the conclusion that I think I prefer sex when it's…"

"More interactive?" I supply.

Despite his chuckle, his expression is pained. "That's not normal, Diana. That's like deviant shit."

"Says who?"

"I don't know. Society." He groans again. "Anyway, I need to take a break from all that. I knew exactly what would happen if I went home with Beck and Lily tonight. Like, she's a rocket."

"Stunning," I agree.

"And she flat-out said she was interested in both of us. If I left with them, the three of us would've wound up in bed together and…I don't want to go there anymore."

"But you just said you enjoy it."

"It can't become a habit." His tone remains firm. "I want a girlfriend at some point. If I'm with someone, I can't exactly be like, *hey, can my best friend fuck you?*"

"Good point. If my boyfriend said that to me, it'd be a huge turnoff."

"See?"

"I get where you're coming from, I really do. And while I don't know if you need to stop the threeways entirely, maybe it wouldn't hurt to take a pause. Sprinkle some one-on-one sex in between them."

He looks relieved by my agreement. "That's what I'm thinking. Beck's leaving tomorrow night and he'll be gone for a month. That'll be a nice breather. Maybe I'll meet someone in Boston when I'm working—" He yawns abruptly. "Fuck, I just got stupid tired all of a sudden."

The yawn is contagious. "Me too." I slide away from him and lift the corner of the duvet. "Stay on your side of the bed or you'll lose sleepover privileges forever."

"I won't even breathe in your direction," he promises.

I hop up to turn off the lights, then crawl into bed and make myself cozy under the duvet. Will stays true to his word, settling on the opposite side and falling asleep instantly. I lie there for a while, a part of me wishing I'd told him we could cuddle. Platonically, of course. I miss snuggling under the covers with a man. For all his faults, Percy was a solid cuddler.

Oddly enough, not only do I fall asleep thinking about Percy, but I also wake up hearing his voice.

It isn't until the wispy cobwebs of sleep disperse that I realize I'm not dreaming it. Someone is knocking on my front door, and that is absolutely Percy's voice saying, "Diana, are you home?"

I shoot into a sitting position, rubbing my eyes. The alarm clock tells me it's nine o'clock. Not obscenely early by any means, but it's Sunday morning and he's here unannounced.

What in the actual fuck?

"Diana?" Percy again, his voice muffled from the hall.

Another knock.

I glance at Will, who's beginning to stir.

Shit.

"What is it?" he mumbles sleepily.

I climb out of bed and comb my fingers through my sleep-mussed hair, tucking it behind my ears. "Don't say a word," I warn. "I need to go deal with this."

CHAPTER TEN

DIANA

Takes one to know one

I CAREFULLY OPEN THE FRONT DOOR, MAKING SURE IT REMAINS PARTIALLY closed so Percy understands I'm not inviting him inside. I greet him with a question rather than a hello.

"What are you doing here?"

But the answer is in his hands. The brown bag he's holding bears the Della's Diner logo, and the splotch of grease on the bottom tells me the breakfast sandwiches I like are in there.

It's a sweet gesture, but I didn't ask for it, and I don't particularly want it.

"I brought you breakfast," my ex says with a strained smile.

"Thank you. That's nice. But I literally just woke up and I'm not hungry." I frown as something occurs to me. "How did you get into the building?"

"Louis buzzed me in. I told him you wouldn't mind."

I grit my teeth because I *do* mind and now I need to talk with Louis. He works the weekend day shift at the Sycamore front desk, and he knows better than to let anyone onto the property without buzzing the owner first. Yes, Percy had been a constant weekend visitor for the six months we were dating, but I never once told Louis he could let Percy in willy-nilly.

In fact, I might have to lodge a complaint at this morning's HOA meeting. Which starts soon, I realize. Brenda strikes her gavel promptly at ten.

Crap, I almost slept through it. This is unacceptable. I don't miss HOA meetings if I can help it. Maybe I should be thanking Percy for the wake-up call.

…No. I'm still irritated.

"Look, I appreciate the gesture, but you shouldn't have come."

He's unable to shutter his frustration in time. "You're still mad at me," he says flatly.

"I'm not mad. I was never mad."

"When I came over this week, you seemed mad."

"No, I was simply pointing out why we're not a good match."

I hear a rustling behind me, turning to glimpse a shadow moving past the kitchen. Will is walking to the bathroom.

Shit. I close the gap another inch, so the door is pressed against my shoulder. Percy doesn't miss my response.

"Is someone in there?" he demands.

"No," I lie.

"You can tell me if there is."

No, I can't. Because then you're going to lose your shit like you always do.

But I don't say any of that out loud. It's apparent that a friendship with Percy is not sustainable. And it's time he knew it.

Unlike most people, I'm not averse to confrontation. I know my boundaries, I've always been confident in myself, and I always follow words with actions.

I speak in a firm tone. "I don't think we can be friends."

He rears as if I've struck him. Then his shoulders deflate, and his Adam's apple bobs in a panicked gulp. "So you *are* still angry."

"I already told you, I'm not angry. But I've had a lot of time to reflect since we broke up, and I truly believe this is not a healthy situation anymore. We should both be trying to move on. You shouldn't be bringing me breakfast." I nod toward the greasy Della's bag. "We're not getting back together, and no amount of fried egg sandwiches is going to change that."

"This is a friendship gesture," he insists.

"If it was a friendship gesture, you wouldn't care if there was someone in my apartment."

"So there is." His eyes flash, and the hairs on my neck stand at attention.

I curl my fingers over the edge of the door. "There isn't."

"I think you're lying. I think you have a man in there." Accusation drips from his tone. "Is it your neighbor? The hockey player?"

"Percy." Frustration gathers inside me, tensing my muscles. "Every word you're saying right now is the reason we can't be friends. I'm sorry things ended and that you didn't want them to, but we're not together anymore. So, please, I need you to respect that. I need you respect my boundaries and go."

He stands perfectly motionless for a moment. A second ticks by. Two. Then three. His already sharp cheekbones become even more prominent as his cheeks seems to hollow. He's grinding his teeth. Dead silent and chalk still.

Finally, he shakes his head and mutters, "I'm disappointed in you. I thought you were different."

I don't care! Just leave!

Out loud, I say, "I'm sorry you feel that way."

With one last disparaging look, he turns on his heel and marches away. He takes the breakfast bag with him, as if I'm unworthy of it now.

Percy's footfalls echo in the staircase, but I don't budge from my doorway until I hear the telltale buzzing from downstairs. The noise the front door makes whenever anyone exits or enters Red Birch.

Once there's nothing but blessed silence, I release a long exhalation. God. This is why I'm fifty-fifty on relationships. Sometimes I adore them. Other times—when they explode like a grenade in your face, for example—they're a fucking hassle and I tell myself I should be having a lot more casual sex.

The door of apartment 2B suddenly creaks open. I catch movement from the corner of my eye as Shane pokes his head out.

"Damn, Dixon. You're a stone-cold bitch. Poor guy."

"That 'poor guy' has been bothering me for months," I retort. "And don't eavesdrop. It's not an attractive quality in a person."

"I wasn't eavesdropping. Everyone can hear everything in this building. Seriously. We need to speak to whoever did the drywall because they skimped on the good stuff. Poor Niall is probably so pissed at you right now."

A muffled shout comes from below us. "Don't speak for me!" There's a pause. "But I am pissed. And it's at you, 2B! Your gathering last night was the last straw."

"Yeah, 2B," I mock. "The last straw."

Shane has murder in his eyes. "What did you do to them?"

"To whom?"

"The whole building. And not only Red Birch. I know you've been trash-talking me all over Meadow Hill."

"Sorry to break it to you, but you've earned your own reputation."

"Bullshit."

I hear footsteps behind me and jump when a fully dressed Will appears.

"Everything okay here?" He smiles wryly. "It's been a very chaotic morning."

"It's been a pain in the ass, that's what it is."

"Is Will still here?" Shane asks, craning his nosy neck toward my door.

"None of your business."

I step back into my apartment and slam the door.

"I hate that he lives here," I say darkly. "I hate it with all of my heart."

Will laughs. "I kinda like it."

"Enjoying my misery, huh?"

"I prefer his misery, actually. It's fun watching you bust his balls. I bet he stays up all night stewing about it, wondering how he can get the last word in."

There's a very loud knock on the door.

Will grins. "See?"

Sure enough, when I open the door, Shane stomps past me and walks into my apartment like he lives here.

"I was thinking about it last night and decided that if I'm not allowed to sleep with cheerleaders, then you can't sleep with hockey players. New rule. The Lindley rule. You can't screw my teammates."

"Why not?" I counter, even though absolutely nothing happened between me and Will.

"Spite," Shane retorts. "And vengeance. This is purely retaliatory."

"You're such a child."

"Takes one to know one."

"Oh my God, that's literally what a child would say."

"Oh, and another rule. You're not allowed to turn the building against me."

"Too late," I say smugly.

"So you did say something to them!"

Will's gaze swings between us like a Ping-Pong ball. "Are you flirting?"

"No," I say in horror.

"What did you do to the neighbors?" Shane presses.

"Nothing, I swear."

He scowls. "Are you lying?"

"Of course."

Will starts to laugh. He claps Shane on the arm, then glances at me. "Um. I think I'll leave you guys to it. Thanks for letting me crash here."

"Please don't leave me with him," I plead, but Will is already heading for the door. I turn back to Shane. "See what you did? You drive everyone away with your personality. I have no friends because of you."

His lips twitch. "You're such a fucking drama queen."

"Takes one to know one," I mimic. "With that said, go away. I need to get ready for the HOA meeting. We can finish this conversation...let me check my schedule...never."

"Don't worry, we can finish it at the homeowners' meeting," Shane says with a smirk. "I'm planning to attend."

"Don't you dare."

"Oh, I dare. I have some matters to raise with the council."

"There is no council."

"There will be when I'm done with them."

"What does that even mean!" I wail, but Shane pulls a Will and marches to the door.

"I'll be back in twenty minutes to escort you to the meeting," he calls over his shoulder.

"Don't you dare," I growl after him.

"Oh, I fucking dare" is all I hear as the door shuts.

Oh my God. I hate him. I can't believe my lips touched his last night. And his tongue was in my mouth. And I *liked* it.

The memory only exacerbates the morning from hell. I grumble curses under my breath as I get ready. Brushing my teeth angrily and then throwing on a blue sundress with little white flowers on it. While I wait for the coffeemaker to do its thing, I check my phone and find a few messages from my brother and one from Gigi.

Thomas is checking in from Peru, where he's volunteering with a humanitarian aid organization. He assures me he's alive and still planning on coming home at the end of the summer for Dad's annual potluck. Good. I miss him.

Gigi's message is only twenty minutes old. She sent it from the airport, claiming they're waiting at their gate and she's bored because Ryder is reading a book instead of talking to her.

I text her back first since it's obvious she needs the attention more than Thomas.

ME:

> I kissed Shane last night as a dare in a game. It was the worst experience of my life and I ask for privacy during this time of great shame and suffering.

GIGI:

> LOL Did you actually kiss him?

ME:

> Unfortunately.

GIGI:

> Is he a good kisser?

ME:

> Like a 5/10?

I'm lying. It was a solid eight. Might've even been a nine if we didn't have an audience. Or maybe the audience is what upped it from seven to eight. It was weirdly hot having eyes on us.

GIGI:

> Did he try to feel you up?

ME:

> No. But I felt something.

GIGI:

OMG Like you caught feelings?

ME:

No, I literally FELT something. He was rocking a boner, and it was...impressive.

GIGI:

Oh, I know. I bumped into him in the middle of the night once on my way to the bathroom and he was naked.

ME:

And HARD?

GIGI:

No, no. He was flaccid. But even flaccid it was eye-catching.

ME:

I don't know why, but I'm weirdly affronted by the word flaccid.

GIGI:

Agreed. It's so unpleasant. Let's switch to "not hard."

ME:

Okay, so he was big even while not hard?

GIGI:

Oh yeah. Comparable to a not-hard Ryder, and Ryder's massive.

This is the first time she's alluded to Ryder having a large package, and my curiosity is naturally sparked.

ME:

How massive?

GIGI:

None of your business.

ME:

Come on. Share with the class. I won't ever bring it up to him. Define massive.

There's a long delay. Then:

GIGI:

10 inches.

I almost choke on my coffee. Oh my fucking God. Look at this guy. Six-foot-five king walking around with a ten-inch cock.

I'm never going to be able to look him in the dick again.

I'm still marveling over Ryder's downstairs situation when Gigi says it's time to board and promises to message me from Arizona. I finish my coffee, carrying it to the sink just as, for the thousandth time this morning, a knock sounds from the entryway.

Awesome. Shane is following through on his threat to crash our meeting.

He smirks when I open the door. "Ready?"

"No," I answer sourly.

"Great. Let's go."

CHAPTER ELEVEN
DIANA

The Sugar Suite

"Diana, do you have a record of the minutes of the last meeting?" asks Brenda, the head of the board.

"Right here." I lift the notebook in my lap.

"Great."

The conference room is packed, as it always is for HOA meetings. At the front of the room is a long table where the board members sit. Brenda runs the show, while tight-lipped Jackson and perpetually mute Tracey follow Brenda's lead or risk death. Brenda is a human dragon who will burn them to ash if they go against her.

The rest of the room comprises of rows of metal chairs. I'm seated in the front, with Shane to my left. When we first walked in, Veronika waved him over, patting the empty chair next to her. He either didn't see or pretended not to and sat directly beside me instead, forcing his presence upon me.

"Why are there so many people here?" he whispers. "Aren't these things supposed to be boring?"

"Give it ten minutes and you'll understand why the word *boring* has no place in this room," I whisper back, before realizing what I'm doing.

No. Absolutely not. I can't be whispering with him like coconspirators. We are enemies.

Brenda stands to address the room. "Hello, everyone. Let's get started. First and foremost, I see a new face among us." She gives Shane a pointed look.

In response, he flashes his usual cocky grin. "Busted. I'm Shane Lindley. I live in—"

"We know who you are," she says coldly.

Shane's mouth slams shut in surprise.

"We prefer that newcomers watch and listen for their first meeting." Her expression suggests his mere existence is an insult to her. "Participation is not encouraged."

Priya is on my right, biting her lip to keep from laughing. This is not an actual HOA rule, so obviously the shunning now extends to the leader of our board. Last I heard, the Meadow Hill rumor mill had spun some pretty ludicrous stories about our newest resident. Marnie and Dave from Weeping Willow told me they heard Shane was escorted off an airplane last year for bullying the flight staff. I legit have no clue how that rumor even got started.

"Moving on," Brenda says. "Are there any concerns that need to be brought up?"

Niall's hand shoots up, as it does every meeting. "Yes. I have seen no change in the noise level since last month. I think it's necessary to institute an eight p.m. noise ordinance."

Ray, a stout man who always attends the meetings with his quiet wife, speaks up.

"That is absolutely ridiculous. Some of us have lives, we have kids. How am I going to get my kids to stay silent after eight p.m.?"

"I don't know, maybe put your kids to sleep at seven. Isn't that a usual bedtime for children?" Niall asks.

"Are you trying to tell me how to parent?" Ray's voice grows louder.

"I am trying to tell you how to be a considerate neighbor."

Ray is standing now, and Niall's crossed his arms, barely making eye contact behind his thick black glasses. Ray's meek wife, Lisa, is tugging on his shirt to get him to settle down.

"Damn," Shane murmurs to me, "is it always this dramatic?"

"Just wait," I murmur back, "the main item on the agenda is hiring a new pool boy because Veronika got caught fucking the last one in the bathroom by the barbecues."

He chuckles at that, and I can't help but smile myself. Despite all my resistance, there is an innate ease when I talk to Shane. Even when we're fighting or snapping at each other, there's just this…flow.

And now that I've acknowledged it, I find the realization incredibly disconcerting.

"That's enough!" Brenda nearly shouts. "Both of you, stop this. The board has heard Niall's suggestion and will take it under consideration." She takes a calming breath. "Next on the agenda—Carla's motion to deny Liam and Celeste Garrison's request to list their condo online as a short-term vacation rental. Jackson?" she says, glancing at the bushy-bearded man next to her.

Jackson half rises from his chair, frowns at the bossy, uptight woman we all try to avoid, and mutters, "Motion denied."

Carla shoots to her feet. "You have no right to do that!"

"Actually, we do," Brenda replies. "We voted last meeting about it. The majority agreed that the Garrisons could list the unit for the six weeks they'll be in Atlanta."

"I voted against it!" Carla huffs. "Why doesn't the minority have a say?"

"Because that's not how majority-and-minority votes work," Brenda says coldly.

"Sit down, Carla," Jackson rumbles from the head table. "Or I'll make you."

"I'd like to see you try!"

From the corner of my eye, I see Shane shaking with laughter. Damn it. He's enjoying this far too much. What if he regularly starts attending? I can't allow that to happen. These meetings are literally all I live for.

"I have a motion," I announce, sticking up my hand.

Brenda acknowledges me with a nod. "Yes?"

"Motion to ban all parties on the premises."

"I second," Niall says instantly.

"Absolutely not," Veronika pipes up angrily.

"I can't believe I'm saying this, but I agree with Veronika," says Elaine, a high-powered attorney at a law practice in Boston. "'All parties' is too broad a term. Let's narrow down the scope. Does this include children's birthday parties? What about the monthly community barbecues?"

Brenda bangs her gavel. "Diana's motion is denied. No vote required."

Shane beams at me.

"Worth a shot," I say with a shrug.

"Speaking of the upcoming barbecue." This comes from Carla. "I'd like to discuss the dietary requirements. My son cannot get within fifty feet of watermelon. He will die."

Shane speaks, sounding curious. "Sorry, can we back up? When is this barbecue?"

Everyone immediately clams up.

Brenda ignores his question. "We can save any barbecue discussions for the group chat. Next item—"

"About this group chat," Shane interrupts, focusing on Jackson. "You in the Bruins shirt—I'll give you two tickets to their season opener if you add me to this thing. I think I was accidentally removed."

I whip up my hand. "Motion to evict Shane Lindley from Meadow Hill for attempting to bribe a board member."

"I second," Priya chimes in. Because she's always got my back.

"Motion denied," Jackson harrumphs. "I would like those tickets."

Shane gleefully pokes me in the side. "Ha."

Brenda taps her gavel again. "Let's tackle the most important item on the agenda. We need to decide on a pool cleaning company."

"*Yes*," I mumble under my breath. "Here we go."

"I don't understand the issue with the old cleaning company," Veronika says shamelessly.

"Are you serious right now?" Priya asks her, twisting her head to glare at our resident cougar. "We're all wasting our time with pool services because of you, and you're going to waste it further?"

"Because of me?" Veronika questions with an exaggerated gasp. "But what did I do?"

Carla joins in on the attack. "You made poor Niall witness your indiscretion next to a urinal, of all places!"

"I still don't see the issue."

"Diana, can you please read the minutes from last meeting so we might remember what exactly transpired between Veronika and the pool boy? Since she is unclear as to why we have to hire a new one." Brenda doesn't bother to hide her exasperation.

I flip a page in my notebook and clear my throat.

"Well, Niall detailed that he walked into the men's bathroom during our community barbecue to find Arvin, the pool boy, hoisting Veronika up between two urinals. She yelled out, and I'm quoting, 'Clean up this dirty hoe like you clean up our pool.'"

This sends Shane over the edge. He bends toward me, his head practically glued to my arm as he shudders with silent laughter. His T-shirt-clad chest heaves while he tries to catch his breath. His response is contagious, and I have to swallow my own wave of hysterical giggles.

"Are you clear now, Veronika, on why it would be inappropriate to continue with our old pool company?" Brenda asks coolly.

"Not really," she answers in a sultry voice. "Can you read it again?"

"Quit it!" Jackson snaps at her. "Diego, do you have the price quotes from the other pool companies?"

"I do. Let me pull them up." In the second row, Diego from Silver Pine fidgets on his phone.

The rest of the meeting goes off without a hitch, except for the moment when Veronika blows Shane a kiss and I can't control my laughter again. When Brenda dismisses us, I walk out of the conference room with Priya and Niall, leaving Shane at the board's mercy. Brenda has cornered him at the door.

"Good job in there," I tell my fellow Red Birchers. "I know Lindley's entertaining, but don't get lured in."

"I haven't been lured," Niall says firmly.

"Good, Niall. Stay strong."

He holds out his fist expectantly. I stare at it. Then I sigh and bump it with my fist. So that's what we do now, Niall and I. We fist bump.

Shane catches up to us as we exit through the back doors of the Sycamore.

"That was the greatest thing I've ever experienced," he crows. "Dixon! Why didn't you tell me how lit these meetings are? I'm never missing one. Oh God, what if I have some Sunday games this season? What do I do? Can you film them for me?"

"Brenda doesn't allow cameras in the conference room," Niall says curtly.

Shane heaves a sigh. "Yeah, of course she doesn't. That's so Brenda."

I swallow my own sigh, but it hisses out of my lungs when a notification buzzes on my phone.

JACKSON DELUTE HAS ADDED SHANE LINDLEY TO THE
GROUP NEIGHBORS.

Traitor!

Shane checks his phone and whoops. "Guess who scored a second chance at the group chat."

Priya gives him a cool look. "Congratulations. Try not to send any highly insensitive breakup messages to it."

He narrows his eyes at her, but she and Niall are already walking ahead of us.

"What does *that* mean?" Shane asks me.

"Oh, sorry, hold on."

I'm busy fiddling on my phone.

ME:

> Guys, Shane has requested to be removed from the group chat. He's overwhelmed by human interaction. Don't re-add him, please. He finds group situations super stressful and was too embarrassed to say anything in the meeting.

YOU HAVE REMOVED SHANE LINDLEY FROM THE GROUP NEIGHBORS.

An alert pops up on his phone. Shane's jaw drops in outrage.

I smile at him. "That's right. This girl is not afraid to abuse her admin powers."

Later that night, there's a rap against my door. I answer it to find Shane's scowling face. His expression is as dark as the black T-shirt hugging his muscular chest.

"I'm sorry, I don't do solicitors," I say sweetly.

He brushes past me to step through the doorway. "What was Priya's comment about?"

"What?"

Shane stalks into the living room, his eyebrows drawn together in consternation. "That comment Priya made after the meeting about insensitive breakup texts. I've been thinking about it all day and I can't make sense of it. I know I've joked about you turning the neighbors against me, but have you been talking shit about me? Like actual trash talk?"

"Trash talk? No. The truth? Yes."

"What the hell's that supposed to mean?"

"It means the way you handled the situation with Crystal was insensitive. And, frankly, really mean."

He stares at me in confusion. "Crystal? This is about Crystal?"

I head for the kitchen to continue the task I was undertaking before Shane showed up at my door. I grab a bottle of tequila from the cabinet next to the sink and place it next to the blender.

Shane storms after me, his anger intensifying. I see it in the tight set of his shoulders. The way he curls the fingers of one hand over the edge of the white granite counter.

"How exactly did I handle that situation poorly?" Irritation and disbelief mingle in his expression.

"Are you kidding? I read your text, Lindley. It was harsh as fuck."

"Are *you* kidding? Literally *this morning* I heard you telling your ex you're not interested. How is what you did any different?"

"What I said to Percy came after months of him showing up and texting. I was harsh because he wasn't getting the message. The first time I broke up with him, I didn't just say, *sorry, get lost, take care.*"

Rolling my eyes, I pour strawberry margarita mix, tequila, and ice into the blender, and hit the power button. The ingredients crash into the blade, cubes flying around in the pitcher like tiny pieces of glass from a broken window. I hold the button for longer than necessary. It's my passive-aggressive way of sticking it to Niall.

When the noise stops, Shane speaks again, a frown twisting his mouth. "That's not what I said to her at all."

"Bullshit. I read your message."

He shakes his head, appearing even more annoyed. "So what you're saying is, you read that entire message thread, but you're only judging me based on the last one? Which, yes, admittedly, it was harsh, but she was saying some pretty nasty shit before that."

"The last one?" I echo, wrinkling my forehead. I think back to the text exchange Crystal showed me. "There was only one message on that thread, Shane."

"No, there were about twenty messages. Maybe more."

Suspicion flickers through me. I don't know who I'm feeling mistrustful of, Crystal or Shane. Noticing my expression, he curls his lips and pulls his phone from the pocket of his navy-blue sweatpants.

"What, you don't believe me? Here. Read the damn thing for yourself."

I see him scrolling up an alarming wall of text before he finally hands me his phone.

"It starts here," he mutters. "Where she says it was the best date she's ever had."

As I start reading, a needle of guilt pricks at me. The more I read, the guiltier I feel.

Shane is actually nice in most of the messages. He lets her down easy. Even when she accuses him of leading her on, he handles it with tact and kindness.

In response, she... Oh boy. Crystal comes off a bit unhinged here. But who am I kidding? I can't say I've never done the same. I think most women have a mortifying, borderline-stalker, pleading-text session in their romantic histories, and if not, I commend them for never succumbing to insecurity or desperation.

I can totally understand why Crystal deleted everything leading up to Shane's final message. Her own messages go from sappy to pathetic to bitterly unattractive.

By the time Shane wrote, I'm not interested in seeing you again. Best of luck it's clear he'd had enough of Crystal's verbal abuse.

Also...

I look up from the screen. "You didn't have sex?"

"No." Indignation flashes in his expression. "Did she say we did?"

I try to recall her exact words. I think she used the phrase "hook-up," but when I said I couldn't believe he would treat her like that after having sex, she didn't correct me.

"She implied it," I admit.

Now that I know it was just a kiss, I feel even worse for Shane that Crystal exploded on him. She'd *threatened* to tell every girl she met that he was a user.

That would rightly piss me off too. I don't blame him for snapping. Same way I snapped at Percy today. When someone can't see reason or refuses to hear you out, sometimes you end up losing it. I'm not excusing the behavior, but I understand it.

I return the phone without another word. Shane folds his arms against his chest. His biceps flex, drawing my gaze to his smooth, brown skin. I sort of like that he doesn't have tattoos. The lack of ink only emphasizes every vein and muscle when he crosses his arms tighter.

"I'm waiting," he says.

I grit my teeth. "I'm sorry."

His lips tick up with humor. "For what?" he prompts.

"For jumping to conclusions and thinking you were a dick to Crystal. In my defense, you're an obnoxious ass most of the time, so I assumed you were being consistent."

"How is this a good apology?"

Ugh. Fine. I know when to be the bigger person when I need to be.

"I'm sorry. I think you handled that entire conversation nearly flawlessly." Curiosity tugs at me. "Did you mean what you said to Crystal about not being over your ex?"

Discomfort puckers his brow. "It's complicated."

"That means yes."

Shane shrugs, the fingers of one hand ambling along the shiny surface of the counter. This subject clearly makes him uneasy.

"We were together four years. That's not something you can get over with the snap of your fingers."

"Dude, it's fine. You don't have to justify why you're still mooning over your ex." I grab a tall plastic cup out of the dishwasher and walk back to the blender. "On that note, you can leave now. I have a margarita to drink and four episodes of *Fling or Forever* to catch up on."

"Cool. Wanna order a pizza? I'll grab some beer from my apartment."

I stare at him. "I didn't invite you."

"Oh, I invited myself. Was that not clear?"

And that's how Shane and I end up on my couch, with drinks in our hands and an open box of pepperoni pizza on the coffee table, while I give him the rundown on the current couples in the hacienda.

"So Leni is my favorite girl. But we *hate* Donovan. He's not good enough for her. And Zoey and the Connor are my favorite couple at the moment."

"The Connor?"

"I know. It's obnoxious, but luckily, he doesn't make her call him that. He's a radio DJ in Nashville. Total frat-boy type. Very douchey."

"What's our girl Zoey doing with him, then?"

"I think it's an opposites-attract situation."

Shane reaches for another slice, chewing slowly as we watch the exchange unfolding on the screen. As always, I'm riveted.

"All I'm saying is, I would be open to it." Zoey's voice is soft but firm. "I'm not completely closed off."

Connor is upset. He runs a hand through his dark curls, leaning forward on the edge of the daybed. "What the hell, Zoey? You'd seriously be cool if Ben picked you?"

"Who's Ben?" demands Shane.

I pause the show to explain. "Ben's the new guy. Every week, a new boy and girl arrive, and each one has to break up an existing couple."

"Damn. What happens to the people who get dumped?"

"Okay, so *they*—" I'm starting to become animated. "They go to the Sugar Shack."

Shane snorts. "Who makes up this shit?"

"The greatest producers of all time."

I unpause.

"The Sugar Shack sounds like a place where people go to fuck," he remarks.

I hit pause again. "No, that's the Sugar Suite."

He breaks out in a deep rumble of laughter.

"Every few episodes, the public votes on which couple gets an overnight in the Sugar Suite. I think this is why the Connor is so upset right now, because Zoey and Connor *just* had the overnight. And! They did stuff."

"What kind of stuff?" Shane sounds intrigued.

"I don't know. They can't show it. But it looked like his hand was moving under the blanket. People get very attached after they go to the Sugar Suite."

"Well, especially someone like Zoey," Shane agrees. "She's so sensitive."

I try to gauge if he's mocking me.

"What?" he says sheepishly. "You can just tell. Did you see how upset she got when Jas made fun of Todd's chest hair? She pulled Todd aside and told him it looked nice."

"If she's so sensitive, why is she open to Ben?" I counter. "We both know if Ben picks her, the Connor may end up alone because Erica is for sure not picking the Connor."

"No, he's not alpha enough for Erica."

"I'm unpausing now. Hush."

Shane chuckles as he reaches for his beer. "You're so fucking bossy."

By the time the episode ends, we've demolished the pizza and consumed a drink each.

"Let me grab another beer before you put the next one on," Shane says, rising from the couch. "Want a top-up?" He nods at my nearly empty glass.

I hand it to him. "Yes please."

Rather than walk off, he peers down at me, thoughtful.

"What?" I say.

Shane gestures toward the pizza box, the beer, the TV. "This is a truce, right?"

"No." I snicker. "And you're naive for even asking that."

"I know. I felt stupid the moment I said it." He lets out a sigh. "Let me grab those refills."

CHAPTER TWELVE
SHANE

*Don't turn me on this early
in the morning*

I SPEND MOST OF THE WEEK GOLFING AND WORKING OUT, THE TWO CORE tenets of the Summer of Shane. So far, life is pretty phenomenal. I feel sorry for the pool-boy Wills and construction-laborer Ryders of the world. I grabbed drinks with Will last night at Malone's, and he was so tired and sunburned from work, he almost passed out in our booth.

On Thursday night, when I return to my apartment from the Meadow Hill gym, I receive a text that sends my pulse racing.

LYNSEY:

> Is that offer to crash on your couch still open?

I stare at the message for an eternity. I don't want to sound too eager. Can't be responding with a "Hell yeah. Get your sweet ass to Hastings." Because we're supposed to be friends, and I shouldn't be commenting on her sweet ass. I also can't respond too fast, so rather than test my willpower, I leave my phone on the couch and go take a shower.

My sweaty T-shirt is still plastered to my chest. I would've stayed longer at the gym and done a few more reps of deadlifts, but by the end of my workout, I had some company in the form of two middle-aged female residents whose blatant ogling was beginning to freak me out. I swear, all the women in this complex are sex starved.

After my shower, I slip into a pair of basketball shorts and return to the living room. It's been seventeen minutes. That seems long enough.

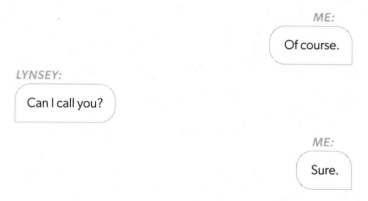

ME:

Of course.

LYNSEY:

Can I call you?

ME:

Sure.

A moment later, her throaty voice fills my ears. It's so familiar, it feels like coming home.

"I arranged for a Briar tour on Saturday morning. One of the summer students is going to show me around campus, and then I have a meeting with the head of the Performing Arts department."

"Wow. This transfer thing is for real, huh?" My pulse quickens at the notion of having her here all the time. I mean, it's a big campus and we'll probably never see each other, but just knowing she's here…

But I can't get ahead of myself.

"I think so, yeah. I'd like to talk to the department heads and some of the faculty before I make any decisions, though. There's a summer course in progress right now. Advanced ballet. They're going to let me join the class for the afternoon."

"That's great. I hope it works out," I say casually, trying to pretend there isn't a hockey stadium full of fans cheering inside me.

"I'll probably leave Connecticut around dinner time tomorrow and be at your place around seven or eight? Does that work?"

"Sure. I'll text you the address."

"Thank you. Oh, I might be bringing a friend, if that's okay. Not sure yet, though."

"That's fine." I push away the resulting pang of disappointment because I can't exactly ask her not to bring Monique or one of the old crew. One, it would sound sketchy, and two, they were my friends too all throughout high school. It'll be good to see them, anyway.

"I'll text you tomorrow when I'm heading out," she says. "And thanks again, Lindy. This'll be so much easier than grabbing a hotel in Boston, since you're only ten minutes from campus."

"Of course. Like I said, anytime."

My heart is thrashing in my chest as I end the call. Buzzing with energy, I quickly examine my surroundings. My apartment's clean, but Lynsey is sort of a neat freak. In high school she used to drag her finger through the layer of dust on my bedroom window ledge and say, "Is this how you want to live, Shane?" It was cute. Well, most of the time. I can't deny sometimes it could get annoying.

During my cleaning mission, it comes to my attention that I don't own a vacuum. I have no idea how my mother allowed this atrocity to happen. Probably because she pays for a cleaner and assumed I would never even attempt to tidy up between appointments.

There are no chain stores in Hastings, only small boutiques, but the hardware store probably sells vacuums. I could go tomorrow morning when it opens.

A mocking voice in my head points out I'm going to a lot of effort for Lynsey, who might not even come, but I inform that voice that everyone needs a vacuum, so fuck off, please.

The next morning, I'm awake bright and early, leaving my apartment at the same time Diana's door swings open.

"Morning," she says when our gazes collide.

"Morning."

She's wearing white shorts and a yellow T-shirt with the words SPIRIT ACADEMY stenciled on in a blue scribble. Her platinum-blond hair is tied in a high ponytail.

"Heading to work?" I ask as we fall into step together.

Holding a travel mug, she practically races down the stairs. "Yeah, and I'm late. I overslept, and I'm pretty sure I missed the bus."

"Where's this spirit camp? I'll give you a ride."

Her expression is full of distrust.

"C'mon. Where do you need to be?"

"The high school in Hastings. And I'm only saying yes because I'm desperate."

"I appreciate you allowing me the honor."

In the parking lot, Diana rolls her eyes at my shiny silver Mercedes. "God, you are such a spoiled brat. Did your mommy and daddy buy you that?"

"Of course." I unlock the doors and slide in, waiting for her to settle in the passenger side. Once she's seated, I tip my head and ask, "If your parents bought you an expensive car for high school graduation, are you honestly saying you wouldn't accept it?"

She purses her lips. Then sighs. "Fuck no. I'd snatch the keys out of their hands before they changed their minds."

"Exactly," I say, and start the engine.

The school is only a five-minute drive. I steer through the automatic gates at the side of the apartment complex and turn onto the street. Mature trees line both sides of the road, residential gardens in full bloom. Everything we drive past is green and colorful. I love summer.

"Why'd you oversleep?" I ask. "Go to bed late?"

"I stayed up watching commentary videos about *Fling or Forever*. The internet is shook that Ben chose Jasmine."

"I knew he would."

"I thought he'd pick Zoey for sure."

"Nah. It was obvious Zoey's set on Connor because he made

her come in the Sugar Suite. Plus, that fight with Ben and Jas was fucking epic. The producers know what they're doing—of course they steered Ben toward the girl that's going to bring them the most drama. Zoey's too sweet."

"I still can't tell if you're making fun of me."

Neither can I anymore. Kind of started off that way, but after four consecutive episodes, I'm strangely invested in Zoey and the Connor's relationship.

"Where are you going this morning?" Diana asks with a sidelong look. "You're not wearing your dorky golf clothes."

"My golf clothes aren't dorky. And I'm going to buy a vacuum. I need to clean up for a houseguest."

She snorts. "It's Niall's day off. Can you film his reaction for me?"

"He doesn't like the vacuum—Wait, why am I even asking? Dude doesn't like anything that's over point two decibels."

Our short drive comes to an end as I pull up in front of the school, a sprawling gray stucco building with white window trims.

I put the car in park so she can get out. "Later, Dixon."

"Thanks for the ride, Daddy."

"Don't turn me on this early in the morning, please."

She's laughing as she runs out. We might not have called an official truce, but she seems a lot less hostile ever since I debunked Crystal's lies. It still smarts that Crystal led Diana to believe not only did we have sex but that I sent her a one-line brush-off afterward. I would never treat a woman like that.

After I drop Diana off, I purchase a vacuum I'll likely only use once, then spend the next couple hours cleaning and hoping it's not in vain.

When I finally turn off the vacuum, I hear an aggravated cry from downstairs.

"*Finally.*"

"Let it go, Niall!" I shout, giving the finger to the door. Fuckin' Niall.

At around three, Lynsey texts to say she's heading out. Or rather, she says *we're* heading out. I guess that means Monique is coming too. But maybe that's a good thing. It's been more than a year since Lynsey and I were alone together. We've seen each other since the breakup, but only with other people around.

It suddenly occurs to me that maybe she's intentionally bringing a buffer along. We're supposedly friends now, though. Friends shouldn't require a buffer. Which tells me she's afraid to be alone with me. And the only reason that would scare her is because…she still has feelings for me too.

Or maybe I'm reaching.

I spend the rest of the afternoon grabbing groceries in town, then squeeze in a quick workout at the complex's gym. At around seven, Lynsey texts that they've reached Boston. That gives me an hour to shower and get dressed. I make an effort not to look like a slob. No basketball shorts, no threadbare tee. I put on jeans and a clean shirt and shove a baseball cap on my head. The hat has the logo of the Warriors, our old high school football team. Maybe it'll tickle her nostalgia bone.

Just past eight, Richard from the Sycamore buzzes to say my guests have arrived and that he gave them the overnight parking pass I requested so their car isn't towed. Shortly after, there's another call to my phone, a buzz-in request from the Red Birch doors.

"It's me." Lynsey's staticky voice fills my ear.

"Come on up."

My palms are a bit damp, so I wipe them on my jeans. Fuck, I was with this girl for four years. I know her better than I know myself. I shouldn't be this nervous.

Through the thin walls, I hear footsteps on the staircase.

I open the front door and there she is. Stunning, of course. A white flowered sundress hugs her toned body, revealing a pair of shapely legs honed by years of ballet. She's straightened her sleek, black hair and wears it loose around her shoulders, rather than tied back in a low ponytail, which she usually prefers.

A hesitant smile plays on her lips. I instantly understand her hesitation when my gaze moves to the guy standing beside her.

I recover fast, forcing an easy smile. "Hey. Glad you made it in one piece." After a beat, I lean in to give her a brief hug. "You look great."

Maybe he's just a friend.

I mean, she did call him a friend.

But I saw the possessive hand he kept on her hip before she hugged me back.

Ignoring the awkward tension hanging in the air, I stick my hand out to the dude. "Hey, man. I'm Shane."

Lynsey visibly swallows. "Oh, sorry, I'm bad at introductions. Shane, this is Tyreek. My boyfriend."

CHAPTER THIRTEEN
DIANA

The rich tapestry of our love

I GET HOME FROM WORK ON FRIDAY NIGHT WANTING NOTHING MORE than to put on comfy clothes, order Chinese takeout, and watch *FoF*. I rarely get to watch it live, so I'm stoked. That means tonight I get to vote for someone in the Sugar Shack to return to the hacienda.

I meet the delivery guy in the Red Birch lobby, accept the plastic bag he hands me, and cart it back upstairs. I'm pulling out and placing small cardboard containers on the counter when my phone rings. I crane my neck at the screen, swallowing a sigh at my mother's name. Conversations with Mom are either painful or *very* painful.

I put her on speaker, continuing to unpack my food. "Hey, Mom."

"Hello, sweetheart. I realized I hadn't heard from you in a while, so I called to see how you were."

"I'm okay. Busy with work. How are you?"

"Good. I just got off the phone with your brother." Of course she called Thomas first. He's the favorite. "I'm thinking of joining him in Lima for a week or two next month. He said he's thoroughly enjoying his work down there."

She proceeds to gush about my little brother for the next five minutes. How proud she is of him for getting into his first-choice college. How he's going to make a brilliant doctor. How she hopes he considers getting a PhD along with an MD, because what's better than one doctoral degrees? Two doctoral degrees!

Finally, as an afterthought, she inquires, "What are your plans for tonight?"

"Chinese takeout and bad reality TV," I answer. That's right, Mom. Thomas isn't the only one in the family with lofty ambitions!

"I don't know how you watch that garbage." Disapproval rolls off her tongue. "You could be doing something so much more productive with your time."

"Well, I've been rehearsing hard this past month, but Kenji just left me in the lurch."

"Kenji?" she says blankly.

"My dance partner."

"Dance partner?"

"For the ballroom dance competition, remember?"

"Oh yes. Right. You competed last year. You came in…?" She lets the question hang.

"Fifteenth," I supply with some embarrassment. To an overachiever like my mother, fifteenth place is a disgrace. A stain on our family name. "We were up against some incredibly talented pairs, but it was still super fun. Dad, Thomas, and Larissa were there to cheer us on."

And you weren't is my unspoken reminder. Even my stepmother, Larissa, cares more about my interests.

But Mom is too intelligent not to pick up on it and too no-nonsense not to address it. My mother doesn't tolerate passive-aggressive.

"Sweetheart, I think we can both agree that my time is better spent on more meaningful pursuits."

Yes. I forgot. Dance is a useless, pedestrian pursuit. Pardon me. I remember when I first showed an interest in it as a kid. I begged my parents for lessons, and Mom put her foot down and said, "I'm not going to be a dance mom, Diana." Like it was so beneath her. Dad convinced her to let me take dance and gymnastics, but he was the one driving me to and from practice, and the only one who attended my meets and recitals.

The ironic part is, when I caught the ballroom bug a few years ago, I thought it was the kind of thing that would finally attract Mom's approval. Ballroom is viewed as "serious," not as pedestrian as the modern and hip-hop dancing I enjoyed as a kid. But my mother's approval doesn't seem to be in the cards for me. If anything, ballroom dancing only makes me even more frivolous in her super-serious professor eyes.

Look, don't get me wrong. Academia is a respectable field. I truly believe that. But it also breeds some very pretentious people, and my mother happens to be one of them. It seems like she's gotten even more insufferable since she left MIT to lecture at Columbia. Although I suppose the upside to that is she's no longer in the same state as me.

Sensing I'm two seconds from hanging up on her, Mom changes the subject to one that's even less appealing.

"Have you spoken to Percival?"

"Nope." I don't mention that he tried to bring me breakfast last week and I essentially told him to get lost.

"I don't know why you broke up with him." The disapproving tone returns.

"Because we weren't compatible."

There's a long pause.

"What?" I say, my irritation rising.

When she speaks again, it's cautiously. "Diana, I know dating intellectuals can be challenging—"

Intellectuals? Oh my God. That's *such* bullshit. Sure, Percy could teach an advanced physics class in his sleep, but when it comes to emotional intelligence or interpersonal skills, he was completely lacking. I tried bringing him out with my friends once, and he spoke in monosyllabic responses the entire time.

I, personally, think there are different kinds of intelligence.

My mother, however, subscribes to the theory that there's only one measure of intellect, and it's determined by an IQ test.

"—believe he was a good match for you."

Oh, she's still talking.

I force myself to pay attention, cutting her off before she can continue extolling Percy's big-brained virtues. "We didn't communicate well, Mom. And he was too insecure. That's like the least attractive quality in a man."

To my astonishment, she voices her agreement. Then again, even a broken clock is right twice a day.

"Yes, I can see how that might be grating. Building confidence is key for human development."

Fortunately, the conversation ends not long after that, and I'm able to refocus my attention on tonight's more simple-minded, plebeian agenda.

Dinner and the hacienda, baby.

As always, the episode is rife with drama and dripping with sweat and sexual tension. When voting comes up, I have a big decision to make. The two Sugar Shack singles with the most votes are allowed to return but aren't permitted to break up a couple or reunite with their former partner. They become a couple themselves, so sometimes you have to vote strategically. This show is very stupid.

When my votes are locked in, my phone rings again and this time it's Shane.

"What do you want?" I ask in lieu of hello.

"Hey, I need your help." His voice is oddly hushed.

"No."

"You don't even know what I need."

"Yeah, I don't think I'm gonna like it."

"I think you're gonna love it. Seems like the kind of game-playing you'll enjoy."

"All right, I'm intrigued."

He mumbles something.

"Sorry, what? I can't hear you."

He mumbles again.

"Shane! I can't hear you."

"I'm trying to be quiet. They're in the other room."

"Who's in the other room?"

"My ex-girlfriend and her new boyfriend," he mutters as if speaking through clenched teeth. I hear a hiss of air.

"Oh. Oh no."

"I can hear you smiling, Dixon."

"I mean, you cleaned the house for her."

"No, apparently, I cleaned the house for *them*. It's cool, though. I did some damage control."

"What kind of damage control?"

"I told them I had a girlfriend."

I start to laugh. "This is the greatest day of my life."

"Oh, it gets better, Dixon. I told them it was you."

My jaw falls open. I'm stunned speechless for a moment. *"Me?"*

"Yes. I said you lived next door but that you went out tonight with your girls." He groans softly. "I don't think they believed me."

"Of course they didn't. It's clearly a lie."

"Yeah. And now I look like an even bigger tool. So, please, I need your help. Can you come over, but, like, get dolled up beforehand? I told them you were going to the club."

"Uh-huh. Cool. You want me to put on clubbing clothes, come over, and...do what?"

"Be my girlfriend, Diana!" he growls. "Please."

He called me Diana. And he said *please*.

This must be dire.

"Like, this is fucking embarrassing."

A lot of men might be too proud to admit that. Shane sounds so distressed that I find myself softening toward his plight.

"What are the rules?" I ask slowly. "How did we meet?"

"I don't care. You can make up whatever stories you want. Just do me the solid."

"Why am I not at the club?"

"I don't know. Tell them Gigi got food poisoning or something."

"Gigi was coming to the club with me?"

"I don't fucking *care* who—" He abruptly lowers his voice again, his next words barely above a whisper. "I don't care what story you come up with."

"Where are you right now?"

"I'm in my bedroom. Pretending to hunt for an old high school yearbook so we can show her boyfriend."

"Ouch."

"Yeah."

"Okay, so to recap, I'm your pretend girlfriend and I have free rein in what I say? I can create a rich tapestry of our love?"

"If you come and help me, you can do whatever the hell you want."

I can't stop smiling. "Give me an hour."

CHAPTER FOURTEEN
DIANA

Top ten reasons why you should date me

PRECISELY SIXTY MINUTES LATER, I FLOUNCE INTO SHANE'S APARTMENT and heave the most dramatic of sighs.

"I am *so* pissed off right now, babe! Like, it's one thing if she got food poisoning or something, but to blow me off for a guy? We had this planned for weeks. I haven't been to Boston in *ages*. I was looking forward to it and I wanted to dance and—" I pretend to suddenly notice the couple sitting on Shane's sectional couch. "Oh. Sorry." I glance back at Shane. "This was tonight?"

I am a phenomenal actress.

"Yup." He's fighting a smile. "I told you that when we spoke on the phone earlier."

"Right, sorry. I was only half listening. Too busy making myself look like *this*."

I fling my hands up and down to gesture at my skin-tight black dress. It's completely backless and sexy as hell. So is the rest of me, if I do say so myself. My hair is up in a top knot. Lips are bloodred. Dangly earrings hang from my earlobes, and crisscross strappy shoes accentuate my tanned legs, the heels not too high that I can't dance in them. Although really, I could probably dance in anything.

I scope out Shane's ex-girlfriend, not surprised to find that she's absolutely gorgeous. She has glossy, dark hair that's stick straight but has some volume. Her features are flawless, and so is her skin. She's got pouty lips and brown eyes that flicker with curiosity when they meet mine. And maybe I'm imagining it, but I swear I glimpse a glimmer of annoyance too.

"Hi," I say brightly, smiling at the couple. "I'm Diana. Sorry to barge in."

She smiles back. Whatever I saw in her eyes is gone, replaced by a friendly expression. "I'm Lynsey. This is Tyreek."

"Nice to meet you guys." I turn to Shane. "Please tell me you have some alcohol here because I really need a drink."

"What are you in the mood for?"

"You know what I like," I say coyly, then sit on the chaise part of the sectional. As I bend over to start undoing my shoes, I glance at the other couple. "Zero loyalty," I tell them.

"What?" Tyreek asks, looking amused. He's an attractive guy with a shaved head and a nice smile but definitely not as hot as Shane.

"My best friend," I clarify. "She has no loyalty. Ditched me tonight for a man." I sigh. "She's in the honeymoon phase. Literally, because they just got married."

"Oh, right." Lynsey surprises me by nodding. "Luke."

I falter for a second before realizing that of course she must know Shane's friends. I need to be careful about what I say regarding Ryder.

"Yeah, my best friend Gigi married him," I reply. "Which, you know, romantic and all. But now they're joined at the hip, and this is the second time she's canceled girls' night in three weeks."

"What club were you going to?" Tyreek asks.

"Mist. Ladies get in free on Friday nights."

Yes, I did my research before I walked over here. I'm not an amateur.

Shane returns, smirking slightly. I realize why when I notice what he's holding. I have to bite my tongue not to growl at him.

"Whiskey. Neat. Just how you like it." He arches a brow.

Oh, so that's how it's going to be? He *knows* I can't stand the taste of whiskey. Asshole. The only reason I gave him beverage carte blanche was because I figured he'd do something cute to make Lynsey jealous. Like bring me a wine cooler with a little umbrella sticking out of the can.

His evil look makes me resist a glare. "Thank you, Boyfriend."

I accept the very full lowball glass. With a big smile, I take a teeny sip and try not to gag.

Room temperature whiskey is vile.

"That's your drink of choice?" Tyreek sounds impressed. "Never met a woman who drank straight whiskey."

"Oh, sure. It's my thing. I love it." My stomach is on fire. This is what I get for doing Shane Lindley a favor.

"Here, let me help you with this, baby."

Next thing I know, Shane is on his knees undoing the straps of my other heel.

Despite myself, a shiver travels up my leg and tingles between my thighs.

"Thanks," I say, my throat a bit husky.

His hand lingers on my ankle. He gives it a light stroke before getting up to join me on the couch. He sits with his legs splayed and pulls me close to him, throwing a muscular arm around me. He smells good. Like soap and sandalwood, and a hint of spicy aftershave.

"I know you're upset about the club, but I'm not exactly complaining that it didn't pan out." He brings his lips close to my ear. "You look so fucking good." He whispers those words but loud enough that I know Lynsey and Tyreek can hear him.

"Aw, thanks, babe." I turn my head slightly and our lips are suddenly millimeters apart.

My heart flips as, for a second, I think he's going to kiss me. But he merely smiles and winks. His hand absently moves down my bare arm in a lazy caress.

I swallow. "So, what were you guys doing before I showed up?"

"Nothing really. Just chatting, catching up," Shane answers.

"You two attended high school together, right?" I say, glancing from Shane to Lynsey. "What about you?" I ask Tyreek. "Are you also from Vermont?"

Tyreek shakes his head. "I'm from Boston. I go to BU."

"Nice. What's your major?"

"Kinesiology."

"Really? Me too," I exclaim.

"No shit. Are you an athlete?" Tyreek asks.

"Cheerleader."

Lynsey joins the conversation with a polite smile. "Oh, that's cool. I'm at a performing arts college. We don't have any NCAA teams, so I'm not too knowledgeable about that stuff, but is cheerleading recognized as a sport now?"

"No, it's not." I don't know if she meant to be bitchy, but it comes off that way. Still, I return her smile. "It should be, though. We work our butts off."

But she's not the first person to imply, whether intentionally or not, that cheerleading isn't an official "sport." The NCAA still doesn't recognize it, which is total bullshit, because can anyone really say with a straight face that cheerleaders aren't athletes? We train hard. We're flexible as fuck. Hell, I can knock out tumbling routines that a hockey player like Shane wouldn't even begin to know how to execute. Which isn't to say cheerleading is more demanding than hockey. Only that we're athletes and deserve the recognition.

The Briar cheer program is very competitive. The moment the school year starts, we're off and running. Killing ourselves and pushing our bodies to the limits to prepare for regionals in November. Then, if we're lucky enough to move on, it's off to nationals in the spring.

Surprisingly, Lynsey's boyfriend has my back. "Yo, for real. Our squad is nuts."

"Do you play BU football?" I ask him.

"Basketball. And, bro, the routines those women bust out during halftime? It's incredible."

"Trust me, I know. BU has a solid squad. They almost edged us out at regionals last year." I glance at Lynsey. "How about you? Shane says you're a ballet dancer?"

She nods. "I train at the Liberty Conservatory in Connecticut."

"Oh, that's amazing. They have an excellent program." I reach for my glass again until I remember what's in it. So it remains on the coffee table and I discreetly pull back my hand. "I actually studied ballet until I was fourteen."

"Really?" She seems interested now. "Why did you stop?"

"It was too—" I halt, because I nearly said *pretentious*. "Rigid," I finish. "I like to think I have discipline, but ballet required more than I was willing to give. Same for gymnastics. When I was a kid, I dreamed of going to the Olympics. Until I realized that you literally don't get to have a life. You have to live and breathe gymnastics. To be honest, I prefer teaching to doing. I'm coaching at a youth cheer camp this summer and it's so rewarding."

Lynsey wrinkles her nose. "I could never teach. I don't have that kind of patience, especially with children. I get annoyed when I see them doing something wrong."

Her remark doesn't surprise me. I'm rapidly forming an opinion about Shane's ex, and it's not entirely positive.

"I don't mind it," I say. "Sure, children make lots of mistakes— because they're *kids*. They're so eager to learn, though. There's nothing I love more than seeing them master a skill."

She shrugs. "I get more satisfaction mastering my own skills."

I'm very aware of Shane's fingers still stroking my arm. When I finish speaking, he leans in and nuzzles my neck before giving my cheek a quick peck. He's being so affectionate. It's disconcerting. I also can't handle how good he smells.

"I bet you miss having this guy around to dance with," I tease, grinning at Lynsey while patting Shane's thigh. "I can't keep him off the dance floor."

Her eyebrows shoot up. "Really?"

"Oh yeah. That's how we met, actually. He cleared out the whole floor and tried to woo me with dance. Performed a solo and everything. Babe, tell her about it."

Shane twists his head slightly to peer down at me. He looks like he wants to murder me, but when he turns his face back to them, he's grinning sheepishly. "Yeah, I basically made a complete ass of myself."

"No, you were so cute." I lean forward to pick up my whiskey, this time forcing myself to take a confident sip.

Mind over matter. Just pretend it's not burning my throat and churning like lava in my stomach. I've drunk about a quarter of the glass now, and I'm already feeling a buzz.

I hold it out to Shane. "Want some?"

"Nah, I'll stick to my beer."

Asshole.

"I want to hear the rest of this story," Lynsey says.

Tyreek chuckles. "Bro, me too. Did you legit bust out some crazy dance routine to win over a girl?"

"He sure did," I answer for Shane. "We were at this Latin club in Boston. I can't remember what it was called, but it was right after the Frozen Four win, and we all went there to celebrate. By that point, Shane had been trying to get with me for months."

"It wasn't that long. I only asked you out once."

"Sure, once a week since September. He was smitten," I say, grinning at Lynsey and Tyreek. "I kept turning him down, and he was getting more and more desperate."

"Not desperate. Determined," Shane cuts in. He's mock-glaring at me, but only I know there's nothing mock about it.

"He would send me these text messages—they were so cheesy. It was, like, *top ten reasons why you should date me.*"

Tyreek snorts mid-sip of his beer. "What were the reasons?"

"I can't remember all of them." I pretend to search my memory. "Some were so ridiculous. Like...*I can last twenty whole minutes in bed.*"

That gets Tyreek doubling over in laughter. Lynsey barely cracks a smile.

I notice she's not super funny. Not that it's a bad thing. Not everyone has a stellar sense of humor like yours truly. But serious people make me uncomfortable sometimes. It reminds me too much of my mother, who doesn't know the meaning of the word *joke.*

"There were romantic reasons too," Shane objects before I can drop another ego-crushing tidbit. "I said I was kind and compassionate, remember?"

"True. You did. I'll give you that one."

"I said I knew how to treat a woman right, that I was very chivalrous."

"Also true." I shrug. "But the number one reason was what a great dancer he was, and I called his bluff that night. Told him to wow me. So Shane here goes up to the DJ and asks him to play this ridiculous track, a really awful Vizza Billity rap-pop remix. And he gets in the middle of the dance floor and starts doing his, like, 'moves.'" I use air quotes. Tyreek and Lynsey are both laughing now. "It was really cute."

"Everyone was cheering along," Shane adds, creating an entire hype squad for the story.

"And then he shimmied over to me, held out his hand, and said, *May I have this dance?*"

Tyreek chuckles again. "I don't know if that's cringe or smooth."

"Definitely smooth." Shane picks up my hand and laces our fingers together. But when the other couple isn't looking, he digs his thumb into the center of my palm. It's a warning. "And look what I got out of it. I guess making an ass out of yourself in front of all of Boston is worth it."

Okay, that was kind of romantic. I notice Lynsey's expression shift from amused to…I'm not quite sure. She's very proficient at masking her emotions.

"So, what, you just dance now?" she says to Shane. I think it's supposed to be a joke, but I hear the edge to her voice.

"Guess so," he answers with a shrug. Then he shocks the hell out of me by adding, "Diana and I are doing that dance competition. NUABC."

Her eyes flash. "You're not serious."

I recover quickly from my own surprise. "Yup, I managed to wear him down," I confirm, snuggling closer to Shane. "Why? Are you competing too?"

"I've competed every year since I was sixteen." Her jaw is tight. "Since when are you interested in ballroom dancing, Lindy?"

Oh yes, she's pissed that Shane's partnering up with me. I bet he never wanted to do it with her. Not that he's actually my partner. This is a charade, and one that's clearly working.

"Diana twisted my arm." He offers a rueful grin. "I have a hard time saying no to her."

"Damn right you do." I press a kiss to his clean-shaven cheek.

The phone I set on the coffee table suddenly dings with an alert, and I disentangle from Shane to peek at it.

"All good?" he asks.

"Yeah, sorry. It's a notification that *Fling or Forever* voting has closed."

"Shit, was this the Sugar Shack release? Did you vote?"

"Obviously."

"Who did you pick to return to the hacienda?"

"Todd and Ky."

"Todd!" Shane growls. "The habitual cheater?"

"He's entertaining!"

On the other end of the couch, Tyreek stares at us in amusement. "Fling or what? Is this a reality show? Oh wait." He pokes Lynsey in the side of her thigh. "Babe, that's the one you watch, right?"

She nods absently at him, but she's laser-focused in my direction. "You've got him dancing *and* following reality TV? I'm impressed."

This time she doesn't bother trying to cloak it with humor. Her tone is clipped and holds a touch of resentment.

I'm pretty sure this girl hates me, but I don't know how much sympathy I can muster for her. She's sitting there with her boyfriend at her side. She has no right to be overtly hostile to her ex-boyfriend's fake girlfriend.

Honestly, this is fun. I'm absolutely nailing this role. And I've only just begun.

Shane's going to kill me.

CHAPTER FIFTEEN
SHANE

Have you always been this hot?

I'M GOING TO KILL DIANA.

I knew she was going to bust my balls and take great enjoyment from it, but I didn't expect our epic love story to involve me wooing her via dance. Now, while Lynsey uses the bathroom and Tyreek's in the kitchen making a call, Diana puts on some music and skips toward me on bare feet. Her heels are abandoned on the floor near the couch.

"What are you doing?" I ask warily.

"I feel like dancing." She pulls me toward the bay window next to the balcony door.

I let her manhandle me only because I'd like a second alone with her, and this gives me the opportunity to say, "I hate you."

"No, you don't. You love me. I'm your girlfriend and we're madly in love."

Beaming, she places one hand on my shoulder and slides the other into my palm. I instinctively clasp her waist and draw her closer, and damn, she's a lot shorter than I realized. Whenever I danced with Lynsey, I didn't have to bend my head this low to get to eye level. With Diana, I'm nearly a foot taller.

Fuck, she's a little spitfire in that tight dress. She looks delicious. Almost makes up for all the pain and suffering she's putting me through tonight. But I guess that's what I get for enlisting her help.

"Stop laying it on so thick," I warn in a low voice.

"Why? It's making her jealous."

That gives me pause. "You think?" I had a feeling, but Lynsey can be hard to read.

"Absolutely," Diana says. "When you said we were going to do the competition?" She points two fingers at her eyes. "Daggers. Like, I felt them stabbing into me. Spin me."

Grinning, I lift our joined hands so she can execute a little spin, then pull her toward me again.

Diana studies our feet, as if she's critiquing me. "Your footwork's not bad."

"We're literally just moving back and forth and side to side."

"Hey, a lot of men can't even do that."

Tyreek returns to the living area, smiling at us. To be honest, he's a decent guy. Soft-spoken, easy to talk to. I wanted to hate him, but I can't.

"Diana, here's that routine I was telling you about," he says. He'd been trying to track down a video of one of the cheerleading routines the BU squad performed last year.

"Oh, perfect. I'm dying to see it."

Diana lets go of me and darts to the couch. She plops down next to Tyreek as he plays the video for her.

Lynsey emerges from the hall a moment later, joining me by the balcony door. She follows my gaze to our respective partners. Well, her partner. Mine's a fraud.

I can't believe she has a boyfriend. And I can't believe she had the nerve to show up with him. It's a huge slap in the face. Makes me angry every time I think about it, but I can't let it show. Besides, I don't want Tyreek thinking I've got beef with him. It's all Lynsey.

"Some warning would've been nice," I murmur to her. This is our first moment alone since they arrived. She literally hasn't left his side.

"Yes. It would have," she agrees tightly.

I glance at her in surprise. "Seriously? You think *I* should have warned *you*?"

Our voices are hushed, but I don't think Diana or Tyreek even notice. They're engrossed with the video.

"You didn't tell me you were dating anyone."

"Right back at you, Lynz. Also, I'm not the one showing up at your house with Diana asking her to sleep over."

"I'm sorry. I didn't think it would be a big deal. We've been broken up for a year, Shane."

"How long have you been seeing him?"

"About a month. We met at a party in Boston. He's friends with Monique's cousin."

So she was with him when we spoke on the phone a couple weeks ago. Would've been nice if she'd filled me in then. I get it—she doesn't owe me anything. She doesn't have to update me about her love life. But it still feels shitty to be kept in the dark and then ambushed on my doorstep.

"You're not mad, are you?" She studies my expression.

"No, of course not." I take a step away. "I'm going to grab another beer. You want anything?"

"No, thanks."

I cross the room toward the kitchen and hope she doesn't notice the stiffness of my stride. I'm annoyed as fuck. I would never have blindsided her like this. Never would've dreamed of bringing my new girlfriend to Lynsey's apartment for an overnight. And I realize I'm going to have to give them my goddamn bed now. It's only the polite thing to do.

Awesome. Now I'll have to burn those sheets.

When Diana sees me in the kitchen, she pats Tyreek's arm

and tells him she'll be right back. A moment later she's beside me, hopping up to sit on the counter.

"Come here, Boyfriend," she teases.

Closing the fridge, I put on my boyfriend face and walk toward her. I can't help but notice that her dress has ridden up so high her thighs are pretty much bare. If she parts her legs even half an inch, I'll be able to see her panties.

If she's wearing any.

The thought summons a sizzle of heat that makes my dick twitch.

Diana grabs me by the belt loops and tugs me into the cradle of those tanned thighs. Then she laces her hands around my neck to pull my face close to hers.

"Are you okay?" she asks quietly. There's genuine concern in her voice.

"I'm fine."

"Your mask is starting to slip."

"I know," I admit.

I plant my hands on her knees and gaze down at her.

It suddenly registers how fucking hot she is. When I let her in earlier, I recognized she looked good, but now I'm *really* taking in the sight of her, and it's quite a sight. Her green eyes seem brighter. That red lipstick is killer. Her cleavage is top-notch. She's a weapon.

"Why are you staring at me?" Her cheeks are flushed, either from the whiskey or the dancing. She doesn't seem wasted, though.

"Have you always been this hot?" I muse.

Her mouth falls open. Then a laugh slides out. "Well, yes. I have."

"You look good, Dixon."

"I know."

I lock my gaze to hers. My mouth feels a bit dry.

She lifts a brow. "Are you waiting for me to return the compliment?"

"No. I know I look good. I always do."

Diana laughs again. Something about the soft, melodious sound has my body tightening. Before I can stop myself, I drag my thumb along her cheek. Damn, her skin is so smooth.

I glance over my shoulder. Lynsey and Tyreek are laughing at something on his phone.

If Lynsey's gaze were on me right now, I don't know if I would be licking my lips and murmuring, "I have a confession to make, Dixon."

I think she's also affected by this strange thread of tension moving between us. When we kissed during the dare game, she pretended it didn't get her hot, but her responses said otherwise. Her hitched breath. Her pulse racing when I touched her wrist. Pupils dilated.

I'm seeing all those same signs now.

"What is it?" she asks.

"I sort of want to kiss you."

"Are you drunk?" She sounds amused.

"Maybe just a little. Are you?"

"Maybe just a little." She visibly shivers when I cup her cheek, then inhales when I use my other hand to lightly caress her bare thigh. Her skin is burning to the touch.

"Do you want me to?" The question comes out hoarse from the sudden desire clamped around my throat.

Diana dons a thoughtful look.

Then she eases forward slightly and presses her lips against mine.

It's a soft kiss. An exploration. Like putting one foot into the hot tub to test the temperature. It starts as a warm rush bubbling around you. And then, when you realize how fucking good it feels, you submerge yourself. Let it consume you. That's what happens in a nanosecond. I'm submerged and consumed. She tastes like whiskey and temptation, and I never want this to end. This kiss is pure fire.

Our mouths pressed together, slicking over each other, her lips parting, her tongue coming out to touch mine. My heart is beating too fast. Diana makes a little sound. It's hard to hear over the music. But it vibrates against my lips.

"Hey, Shane, what's the Wi-Fi again? I got kicked off—oh, sorry." Tyreek chuckles softly.

Diana and I break apart. I swipe my hand over my mouth, while she hastily shoves a strand of hair that came loose of her top knot behind her ear.

"No, I'm sorry," I call back. I clear my throat. "Forgot we weren't alone."

I'm not even lying. I completely forgot Lynsey and her boyfriend were here. I was so absorbed in that kiss, a meteor could have hit Meadow Hill, and I would have obliviously and happily died with my tongue in Diana's mouth. The pool party kiss was hot. This one? Blistering inferno. My dick's never been this hard from one kiss.

Moistening my suddenly dry lips, I spare a glance at the couch. Lynsey's gaze finds mine. I can't decipher her expression.

But I can clearly read Diana's—a mixture of lust and shock.

I know exactly how she feels.

CHAPTER SIXTEEN
DIANA

Lack of control

THIS MAKES TWO.

Two times.

Two whole times that I've kissed Shane Lindley.

It's Saturday morning and I'm sprawled on a lounge chair, staring up at the clouds and obsessing over the fact that I kissed Shane last night. Again. And this time it wasn't because he goaded me into it and I was trying to win a party game.

I *wanted* to.

I clench my teeth and glare at one cloud formation in particular—the one that looks like two swans kissing. Stupid cloud swans. Rubbing it in my face.

I blame my make-out with Shane on the foul whiskey. I was very, very drunk.

You were not very, very drunk.

Oh my God. It's true. I was tipsy at best.

I hear the slap of flip-flops on concrete and look up to see Shane approach in a pair of red swim trunks and a white T-shirt. He sets a full coffee mug on the table beside me, then spreads an oversized striped towel over the chair next to mine.

There's only one other person out here this morning. Veronika sits on the other side of the rectangular pool, reading a romance novel with a shirtless guy on the cover. As much as I like to make fun of her for banging all the pool boys, I do admire her no-fucks-given attitude. She's in her midfifties and living her best single life after a drawn-out divorce. No husband, no kids. Living the dream over there.

Her head lifts the moment Shane arrives, appreciation filling her eyes. Great. I guess we'll be having this awkward chat in front of an audience.

"Hey." His voice has some gravel to it, and he looks tired.

"Hey."

As Shane lies down and stretches his legs out, I can't help but notice that his body just dominates that chair. It goes on forever. But I guess that's what happens when you're six-one with stupidly long legs and a broad, sculpted chest.

I twist my head toward him. "Where are your houseguests?"

"Gone, thank fuck. Lynsey's Briar tour started at nine."

"Are they coming back here later?"

"No." Once again, his tone is awash with relief. "She's going straight back to Connecticut after her interviews."

I study his chiseled profile, unable to curtail the memory of how it felt to run my fingers along that defined jaw. How soft the little hairs at his nape were beneath my fingertips before I curled my hand around his neck to kiss him deeper.

I quickly wrench my gaze away. Oh my God. Despite my mouth's traitorous behavior as of late, I'm *not* into him. He annoys me.

Oblivious to my inner turmoil, Shane starts scrolling on his phone. Completely ignoring me.

I huff out a breath. "Are we seriously not going to talk about it?"

He chuckles.

Across the deck, Veronika has sat up a little straighter and set her book down. She's openly watching us now. I hope she can't lip read.

"We made out, Dixon. No biggie." He sounds unbothered.

"It's never happening again," I say firmly.

"That's fine."

"What do you mean, that's fine?"

He puts down his phone and raises a brow. "Do you *want* it to happen again?"

"Of course not. I just want to make sure we're on the same page. I only kissed you because I got caught up in my girlfriend role."

"You don't have to explain it. I'm on the same page."

"So you were playing a part too?"

"No, I wanted to kiss you."

That shuts me up.

Shane laughs. "Dixon. It was a kiss. You're making a big deal out of it."

"I'm not making any deal out of it."

"Okay, good."

"Great."

"Excellent."

"Brilliant." He's chuckling again. "Thank you, by the way." He shifts his face back to the water. "I know you're not my biggest fan, but you still came over and helped me out. I appreciate it."

"You're welcome. And I have the perfect way for you to repay me."

He glances over suspiciously.

"Okay, picture this," I start with a beaming smile.

"No."

"*Picture* this. You and me. Gliding across the ballroom floor together in an elegant Viennese waltz."

"No."

"I'm not done!"

"Nope. You lost me at waltz."

Desperation rises inside me and brings a pout to my lips. "Please? Kenji bailed on me, and now I'm totally screwed. You showed some solid coordination last night. You have the raw talent, I'm sure of it. *And* you already told Lynsey you were entering the competition with me."

"Yes, I said it in the moment." He looks amused. "I wasn't planning on following through."

"What are you going to tell her, then?" I challenge.

"I don't know. I'll say it fell through. You found a new partner. Coach wouldn't let me do it during the hockey season." He shrugs. "There's lots of reasons why I might need to back out."

"Come on, Shane, please."

He directs another snicker my way. "You don't even like me, and you want us to be dance partners?"

I jut out my chin. "You don't have to like your dance partner."

"I'm not doing it."

"How about a blowjob?"

"I'm listening."

I grin at him. "Great. I'll find a good escort service and see if they'll give you one on the down low—"

"From *you*, Dixon," he interrupts with a smirk. "It's your mouth or no mouth."

"Perv. I will *never* blow you."

"I know. That's why I'm satisfied I'll never have to be your dance partner."

I let out a loud moan. "Every time I start to like you, you turn around and decide to ruin my life."

Shane curls over in laughter, which only heightens my irritation. Here I was, sincerely extending an olive branch to this man in the form of dance, and he's throwing it back in my face. Mocking me.

The chiming of my phone interrupts us. I stifle a groan after I check the screen. It's Percy. My ex has texted about ten times since I told him we couldn't be friends, and he's about one more text away from getting blocked.

> I know you're avoiding me. Can we please talk?

I ignore the message and grumble in irritation.

"Bad news?"

"No. Just my ex."

"Still bugging you?"

"Yes. He still thinks he has a chance of winning me back." I make an exasperated noise. "Seriously, what is wrong with you guys? Why can't you just go away after you get dumped? Why can't you get the message?"

"Ouch."

"Aw, I didn't mean you. I meant..." I suddenly remember what we were up to last night and why. "Oh, oops. I guess I do mean you. Sorry."

"I'm not trying to win her back," he insists.

"No? So you're telling me you didn't kiss me last night to make her jealous? To show her what she's missing?"

Shane's voice becomes gravelly again. "I can honestly say that in that moment, Lynsey was the last thing I was thinking about."

Our gazes lock for a second. A ripple of heat travels between us.

Oh no. Nope. This tingling between my legs is *not* good.

"You do want her back, though," I say, pushing the issue.

He doesn't answer for a long time, which is all the answer I need.

"I just had this whole future in mind, you know? For the two of us."

That catches me off-guard. "Future? I didn't realize fuckboys thought that far ahead."

"I'm not a fuckboy."

I lift a brow.

"I know it seems like it. I'm sure Gigi told you I went a little sex-crazed this year."

"You single-handedly tried to bang the entire cheer team."

"That's an exaggeration. But yeah, I did hook up a lot." He sighs. "But it's not what I want. I think I had to get all that out of my system to accept I'm a relationship guy."

I'm not sure I believe him, but I can't deny he seems sincere.

I have to get ready for work, so I leave Shane at the pool and head upstairs, where I stuff my work clothes in my backpack because I wouldn't be caught dead walking to work in my uniform. Della's Diner is literally the most outdated place in the world. It's very retro. The uniforms are super tacky, but the customers seem to love the blue-polyester getup with its white collar and matching apron. The managers do let us wear white sneakers instead of roller skates or some awful shit. And although I'm sure they'd love for us to style our hair in beehives, ponytails are tolerated.

My shift flies by. Saturday nights always do. It's so busy I can never check the time, so I'm always pleasantly surprised when the diner suddenly clears out without warning, and I realize it's thirty minutes till closing. It's my favorite time of the night.

I'm behind the pie counter cleaning up when the bell over the door rings, and a customer enters the fluorescent-lit room.

Percy.

My jaw tightens. I was stacking cups, and now I slam one down a little too hard. I don't mean to put so much force behind it, but thankfully the glass doesn't shatter.

"Are you okay?" asks Dev, the other remaining server. Everyone else has left for the night.

"I'm fine." I nod curtly toward our new arrival. "I'll take this one. I know him."

I march over as Percy is sliding into a booth.

"What are you doing here?" I ask angrily.

He holds up both hands in surrender. "Grabbing a cup of coffee."

"Percy."

"And hoping we can have a quick chat."

"I've said all I need to say."

"Well, I haven't said what I needed to say." His voice rises, drawing Dev's attention.

My colleague tips his chin in a silent question, and I respond with the slight shake of my head. I can handle it.

I give Percy a warning look. "This is where I work. Please."

"Fine. I'll leave—*if* you agree to talk to me after your shift." Fortitude hardens his eyes. "I'll meet you outside?"

I release an internal scream. Oh my God. I've had guys become obsessed with me in the past but never to this extent. I don't know what to do about it. Is this stalking? I don't think it qualifies as that yet, but this is the second time he's shown up unannounced.

It's making me uncomfortable, and I don't like this feeling. The uneasiness, the lack of control. I'm usually an expert at handling tough situations. I always have been. My dad says it's his favorite thing about me. Aside from fixing a shower, if there's a situation that needs fixing, you go to Diana Dixon. If you need someone to defend you, to tell someone else off, to throw down, you go to Diana Dixon.

I thought I drew a hard line with Percy last weekend, but evidently, I wasn't harsh enough. And that's the only reason I agree to meet him after my shift. It's time to lay down the law.

Percy waits on the sidewalk when I exit the diner thirty minutes later. His cheeks hold a slight flush, and when he greets me, I catch a whiff of alcohol on his breath.

"Have you been drinking?" I ask warily.

"I grabbed a beer at Malone's while I was waiting for you. But don't worry, I'm fine to drive. I'll give you a lift home. We can talk in the car."

"No. I want to walk."

A frown creases his brow. "I'm not drunk."

"I didn't think you were. I'd just rather walk." The last thing I want right now is to be trapped in a car with Percy.

"Okay, then. Let's walk."

My chest is so tight, I can feel my ribs trying to poke through the skin.

Ten more minutes of my life, I assure myself, as we head off down the sidewalk. I can suck it up for ten more minutes.

"I have something important to say," he starts, his tone ringing earnestly. "I take full responsibility for the breakdown of our relationship, Diana. I've had months to reflect on my actions, but it wasn't until our last fight, when you pointed out my insecurities, that I was finally able to examine the entire situation from your point of view. And it finally sunk in. How much I would hate it if you were accusing me of hooking up with other women—"

"Percy," I cut in. He's wasting his breath here.

"And you're right, the accusations were uncalled for. That's something I'm going to have to work on. And I *have* been working on it—"

"Percy," I interrupt again.

"All I'm asking you for is a chance. Let me prove to you that I'm still the witty, nerdy grad student you met at the Coffee Hut who couldn't tell the difference between a push and pull door."

I manage a weak laugh. "I know you're that guy."

"Then give me a chance to prove it."

We're not far from Meadow Hill now, and I count the steps longingly. Percy believes he stands a chance of convincing me, but I have no interest in getting back together with him. I want this entire ordeal to be over. I've never had such a needy, insecure boyfriend. And truthfully, I've gotten the ick.

"I'll be honest, Diana. You're the most beautiful woman I've ever been with, and that intimidates me. It's difficult when your girlfriend looks like you, you know?"

Two more minutes.

I try to quicken my stride, but I'm short and can't move that fast.

"So try to see it from *my* point of view? It's hard knowing that you get attention and that other men are leering at you. Because, come on, we know what they're thinking. They're all picturing you naked."

"Who cares what they're thinking?" I say in aggravation. "Just because they might be picturing me naked doesn't mean I'm going to sleep with them. You must have a really low opinion of me if you think I can't walk ten feet without spreading my legs open for someone. Like, this is ridiculous. It's insulting."

"That's not what I'm saying at all." He adjusts his pace to match my fast strides, groaning with frustration. There's a note of anger there too, which I don't like.

"Percy, I understand what you're saying." Actually, I don't at all, but whatever. Let's humor him. "But I'm not interested in getting back together."

"Even if I'm working on my issues?"

"Even then."

"So, what, we spend six months together and you just throw me away? Couples work through stuff together. They help each other with their issues."

"It's not my responsibility to help you with your insecurities!"

Now *I'm* angry. And once my temper has been triggered, there's no going back. It's probably my worst trait, but there's nothing I can do about it at this moment. He's literally exhausted the last iota of my patience.

"I'm going to be brutally honest with you right now. *I don't want to be with you.* I don't want to help you work through your issues." We're about fifteen yards from the main gate of Meadow Hill, but I'm too wound up to walk. I halt in the middle of the sidewalk and slap my hands on my hips. "We're not together anymore. We will never be together again."

"Is there someone else?" he demands.

Oh my God!

I want to scream. But it's obvious this man has zero respect for my boundaries and even more obvious he's never going to comprehend that I simply don't want to be with him. To Percy, if I don't want him, that *must* mean there's another guy involved.

And since that's clearly the only way his brain will register what I'm saying, I shout, "Yes!"

He rears back as if I've struck him. "What?"

"Yes, there is someone else. I'm seeing someone new."

He hisses out a breath. "Is it the hockey player?"

"Yep. Right again. We're done, okay? So please, just move on. The way *I've* moved on."

I start to walk, but he grabs my arm and tugs me backwards. I don't know if he means to be so rough, but it feels like my arm is jolted out of its socket.

"Let go of me."

"You fucking bitch," he snaps, and the mask completely shatters, revealing angry red eyes, flushed cheeks, and lips twisted in a snarl. His fingers curl around my forearm like a steel band. "You made me grovel and beg and this entire time you were doing exactly what I *knew* you were doing!"

"Let go of me," I repeat.

When I try to shrug his hand off, his grip tightens.

"*Let go of me.*" My free hand fumbles out to try to push him away.

"Fucking *bitch.*"

The next thing I know, his fist snaps forward.

And then he hits me.

CHAPTER SEVENTEEN
SHANE

If you want me, I'm yours

"HEY, LINDY."

This is the first time Lynsey has called me since we broke up. She's texted a few times, sure, to say "hope you're doing well" or whatever platitude, but she never made an effort to reach out and hear my voice. Until now.

"Hey," I say, hiding a smile. "How's it going?"

It's been a few days since Diana and I nailed our stellar performance of Boyfriend and Girlfriend: Madly in Love. Although maybe *madly in lust* is more accurate, considering I ended up making out with her in my kitchen. At the time, I thought Lynsey seemed bothered that I was with another woman, but after days of radio silence, I gave up on that notion.

And now look who's calling.

"Thanks again for letting us stay over last weekend."

"No problem. Tyreek seems like a solid guy."

"Yeah." Lynsey pauses. "Diana seemed cool too."

"She is."

"She's very…loud."

My smile springs free. "Nah. She just seems loud because you're quiet."

"I don't mean loud as in volume. She's just so outspoken. Seems like she has a big personality."

Is that an insult toward Diana? Lynsey's tone is completely benign, so I can't be sure.

"Anyway, I called to say I officially filed the transfer paperwork with my Liberty advisor. I'll be attending Briar in the fall."

"Wow, okay, big move. What about housing?"

"When I did my interview, the department head told me there're a few singles left in the senior dorm. Can't remember what the building was called, but she said it's where all the dance majors live."

"You'll be living on campus? Not with Tyreek?"

She laughs. "*Way* too soon for that. We've only been dating a month. Besides, I don't want to make the commute from Boston. I know it's only an hour or so, but it's still kind of a pain in the butt. Why wake up early to commute when I can wake up early to rehearse?"

I admire her work ethic. I always have.

"I'll have to figure out a way to rehearse with Sergei, though. Maybe find somewhere halfway between Liberty and Briar."

"Right. NUABC. How are you two going to manage that?"

"We passed the prelim, so we're already in the competition. I feel like weekend rehearsals should suffice. Or..." she trails off teasingly, "I could always steal you away."

I bite my lip to suppress a laugh. "Oh, is that so?"

Okay, she's definitely flirting right now.

"Maybe." She pauses for a second. "Honestly, though..." Her tone takes on a bitter note. "I'm a little annoyed that you're partnering with her when I asked you to do it every year and you said no every time."

Regret tugs on my insides. I shouldn't have lied about the competition. I think I got a little too into the role of Boyfriend. And, yes, I wanted to make Lynsey jealous. But I hadn't been trying to hurt her, and her next question, soft and pained, tells me I did.

"I don't get it. You're suddenly interested in dance?"

"No, it's not that. It's…" I decide to lay the blame on Dixon. She won't mind. "Diana's hard to say no to."

There's a long, tense beat.

"Yeah," Lynsey finally says. "It does seem like she has you wrapped around her little finger, the way she bosses you around."

"She doesn't boss me around."

"Shane, she *totally* bosses you around. During our entire relationship, I don't think I heard you argue with me about anything. Meanwhile, the entire night I was at your place, you two were bickering about something. That's not healthy."

"I guess." I wrinkle my forehead. "We're not actually arguing, though. It's all in good fun—"

"Anyway, I like that you're competing." She cuts me off as if I hadn't spoken. "It shows a lot of growth. Tells me that maybe now you're capable of being there for someone else. Putting them first."

Her comment triggers equal parts joy and annoyance. I like that she's seeing something good in me, but it bothers me how quick she is to dismiss the times I was there for her. Just because I didn't want to enter dance competitions with her doesn't mean I wasn't sitting in the front row at all her performances, cheering her on.

But maybe I could have done more. Tried harder. I'm probably more selfish than most people, but that's because of hockey. It makes you selfish. You're devoting all your time and energy to a sport and not a girlfriend. So she's right. Maybe I didn't always put her first. Maybe I didn't quite find that balance between hockey and girlfriends, but given the chance, I know I can navigate those two worlds better now. I've seen people around me do it. Like Ryder, who only cared about hockey his entire life and yet was somehow able to convince a woman to marry him. And from what I can tell, the marriage hasn't changed his performance on the ice, and the ice hasn't affected his marriage.

So why can't I do it?

"I guess I have matured a little," I say with a wry chuckle. "Or a lot, considering I'm willing to do the tango in front of an audience."

"Oh, is the tango one of your events? What categories are you entered in?"

"Actually, I'm not sure. We're still working on our video for the prelims." Look at me, spitting out the NUABC lingo.

"Well, let me know if you qualify."

"Why? You feeling threatened? Are you and Sergei gonna try to scope us out? Spy on us to steal our routines?"

"I'm not worried," she says haughtily.

"You should be because we're coming for you, girl."

"Oh, really?"

"Yup."

"Bring it." She laughs. "Anyway, I'll keep you posted on the transfer. Talk to you later, Lindy."

We hang up and my whole body is buzzing. I want to tell someone about this, but no one's going to give a rat's ass that my ex-girlfriend called me. Every single one of my boys will rag on me mercilessly.

But...my new "girlfriend" might be supportive. I brighten at the thought. I've heard Diana shuffling around next door all morning. I don't know what she's doing, but it sounds like she's been walking back and forth through her apartment for hours.

In high spirits, I pop over next door and knock loudly. "Hey, it's me. Let me in."

"Go away. I'm busy" is her muffled response.

I knock again. Louder.

"Quiet!" comes a shout from downstairs.

"Oh, lay off it, Niall!" I shout back. "Come on, Dixon, I have news."

After a brief silence, I hear her approach the door. "Fine, but don't be alarmed when you see my face."

"Why would I be alarmed—"

The door swings open, and I hiss in a shocked breath.

She's sporting quite the black eye. Not a full-on shiner, but she's bruised and swollen underneath her eye and above her cheekbone. The coloring is a reddish blue, rather than black and purple, which tells me the bruising is a couple days old.

I try to recall the last time I saw her. Not since Saturday morning, I realize. Shit, how have we not run into each other even once in four days? All I've been doing is golfing, working out, and swimming, and two out of those three activities have taken place in our shared apartment complex. Where the hell has Diana been?

"What happened?" I exclaim. "Are you okay?"

"Cheer camp," she says ruefully.

My jaw drops. "What are they doing over there? Making you guys compete in blood sports?"

"The other counselors and I were showing the girls how to form a pyramid, and I was on top. Took an elbow to the face when the thing collapsed."

"Damn. Have you been icing it?"

"I have. Fucking sucks, though. Anyway, what's up?"

I trail after her into her apartment. I notice she's cleared the coffee table away from the couch and rolled up that super-tacky burgundy rug; it's leaning against the wall by the fish tank. I glance at the big, empty space she's created.

"What are you doing in here? I've been hearing you move around all morning."

"I'm practicing some choreography I want to teach the kids tomorrow."

"Have you found a ballroom dance partner yet?"

"No," she says glumly.

"That's not true." I tip my head at her, grinning. "You have."

Diana narrows her eyes. Well, her other eye. The left one was already squinty thanks to the swelling.

"I just got off the phone with Lynsey. She told me I'm exhibiting

great maturity and growth by entering this dance competition. So…"
I shrug. "If you want me, I'm yours."

For the first time since I moved in next door, a huge, genuine smile—one that's directed at *me*—stretches across her face.

"Are you for real?"

"Yep. Let's dance, Dixon."

Diana once again shocks me—she steps forward and wraps her arms around my waist. Pressing the non-injured side of her face against my chest, she hugs me tightly. I'm so stunned, I stand there with my arms dangling at my sides.

"Thank you," she says softly. "I really needed this."

I don't know if she's talking about the dancing or the hug or something entirely different altogether, but the way her voice catches elicits a pang of concern.

I force myself to shrug it off because I know Diana and how prickly she gets when you poke too hard into her business.

So I merely return the hug and say, "We're going to crush this thing."

CHAPTER EIGHTEEN
DIANA

A fading nightmare

"ALL RIGHT, MAJESTIC EAGLES," I ANNOUNCE. "LET'S RUN THROUGH these jumps one last time and then we'll call it a day, okay?"

As Fatima and I count them in, the girls spring to action, giving it their all. Toe touches have been tough for some of them, particularly Chloe and Harper. They can get their legs up but not out, or vice versa.

"Why is my toe touch so low?" Chloe whines after she lands. Her forehead is shiny from exertion.

I walk over to her. "Because your legs aren't far apart enough. The farther apart you can get them, the higher your touches will be. This is why we keep harping to you about stretching. Gotta get that flexibility started young."

Fatima claps her hands. "Let's do the tuck jumps."

"Tuck jumps are so boring," Harper grumbles.

"They're great for the core," I tell the group, patting my abdomen. "Tumblers—" I glance at Tatiana and Kerry, our strongest gymnasts. "You guys in particular need to practice your tuck jumps. The more core strength you can build, the stronger tumblers you'll become."

We work on the final set of jumps, and everyone is smiling and sweaty when we dismiss them. The girls stream toward the locker room while Fatima tails after them.

"You coming?" she calls over her shoulder.

"It's my turn to put away the mats," I call back.

"Cool. If I'm gone before you're done, I'll see you tomorrow."

The moment the gym is empty, my smile collapses like a cheap tent.

Keeping that smile plastered on my face all week is one of the hardest things I've ever done.

I've been an emotional wreck since Percy hit me.

According to him, it was an accident. He claimed it was involuntary. That when I pushed him, his first instinct was to defend himself. Maybe that's true. Probably not. Either way, I don't want to make a big thing out of it. I don't. I can't.

I fucking *can't*.

Tears well up, and I blink rapidly to disperse them. I quickly stack up the mats, eager to get home.

I pray the other counselors have already left for the day as I trudge toward the locker room. Fortunately, it's empty, and since I usually change clothes at home, I grab my keys, sunglasses, and purse from my locker and hurry toward the door.

I falter midstep when my reflection in the wall of mirrors catches my attention. My gaze homes in on the ugly bruise around my left eye. An anguished sob gets caught in my throat, and I forcibly swallow it down. For a second, I can't breathe. Suddenly I'm back there. That night. Completely stunned, reeling from the pain of Percy's fist smashing into my face.

No one's ever hit me before.

It doesn't matter if it was an accident. It still fucking hurt. I told everyone at cheer camp that I accidentally caught Kenji's elbow to the face during dance rehearsal. I told Shane, and Gigi when I saw her the other day, that the same thing happened at camp during a pyramid collapse.

I don't know why I couldn't just tell them the truth.

You do know why.

Yeah. I do. It's for the same reason I didn't call my dad the second it happened, even though every instinct in my body was ordering me to.

Every instinct except for one—fear. The moment Percy's knuckles connected with my face, fight-or-flight kicked in, and the latter won in a landslide. I couldn't do anything but run. Run from Percy, run from the embarrassment, run from the urge to call my father for help. Because Dad would've made me go to the police, and that was the last thing I wanted to do in that moment.

I still don't. I *refuse* to make a big deal out of it. And the truth is, I did provoke him. I did try to shove him. So what's the point of reporting it to the cops when, in all likelihood, it won't go further than an uncomfortable interview?

I want to put this entire humiliating incident out of my mind. It's over and done with. I'm not worried about Percy coming near me again. Although he's been texting apologies all week, I've made it clear that I want nothing to do with him ever again. I've also kept every single one of his messages, screenshots of them saved in a folder on my phone.

My knees feel too wobbly to walk, so I sink onto the long wooden bench and scroll through those messages now.

The first one was sent less than five minutes after I stumbled into my condo that night and raced upstairs to ice my face.

PERCY:

Diana, I'm so sorry. That was a complete accident. I did NOT mean to hit you. It was an entirely instinctive response to you trying to push me.

ME:

I tried to push you because you grabbed my arm. You wouldn't let go when I asked you to let go—three times.

ME:

Don't EVER contact me again. FUCKING EVER.

PERCY:

It was an accident. Please believe me.

When I don't answer, his texts continue to stream in. They arrive daily, rife with excuses.

PERCY:

It was a reflex. Completely unintentional.

PERCY:

Are you okay?

PERCY:

I understand why you're angry, but I truly am sorry. You pushed me and my reaction was purely instinctual.

PERCY:

I didn't mean to hurt you.

PERCY:

I don't hit women.

PERCY:

You know that's not who I am.

The last message is from me to him. In no uncertain terms, I spell out what's what.

ME:

> You need to leave me alone. If you don't,
> I'm going to the police. I'm really fucking
> serious right now. I'm going to block you
> now, and I don't want you in my life anymore.
> Goodbye, Percy. Have a nice life. Fuck off.

I followed through on the threat and blocked him. I don't know whether he kept messaging after that. I can only assume he did. But on my end, it's completely closed off.

Along with the screenshots, I've also been monitoring my bruise. I took pictures of it the first night, and every day since. I don't know why. I don't plan on pressing charges. I believe him when he says he didn't mean to do it, yet I can't erase the memory of his eyes. For one terrifying moment, those brown irises had been downright feral. Although perhaps that only backs up his defense, that it was an animalistic instinct to defend himself because he thought—

What? That you were a threat? You're 5'1" and 110 pounds! What the hell were you going to do to him?

The incredulous voice in my head is correct, of course. But I still silence it. I don't want to dwell on this. I don't want to think about Percy anymore or remember that surreal, foreign sensation of fear clamped around my windpipe.

I force myself to rise from the bench and leave the locker room. I can't hide in here forever. I can't hide in my apartment, either, which is what I've been doing for days, and as I head down the sidewalk away from the high school, I vow not to let what Percy did turn me into something I'm not. A coward and a shut-in. A basket case.

When my phone rings in my hand, I flinch instinctively. Luckily, Percy hasn't found a way to contact me. But it is my dad calling, which is probably even worse. I'm expected to put on a brave face when I'm talking to Dad. Or maybe not *expected*; it's not something he's explicitly stated he requires of me. But falling apart in front of my father is not an option. I can't remember the last time I cried in his presence or showed even a sliver of vulnerability.

"Hey, kiddo," he says after I answer the call.

"Hey, good timing. I just got out of camp. I'm walking home."

"Perfect. I wanted to touch base. Make sure the shower temperature is still to your liking."

"Yep, it's great."

"How's life? Everything good?"

"Everything's great."

"You sure?" Concern fills his voice. "That didn't sound very convincing."

Shit. I paste on a brighter tone, but I'm not the best liar, so I opt for a half-truth.

"Mostly great," I amend. "Percy is still kind of bugging me."

"The ex?"

"Yes. He can't get the hint that I don't want to get back together."

Dad chuckles. "Well, I'd offer to beat him up for you, but I know you're perfectly capable of handling him on your own."

"You know it." I laugh weakly. "Don't worry. I already told him to fuck off."

"That's my girl." Dad changes the subject. "Oh, about the Labor Day potluck—Larissa's asking if you'll make your potato and bacon salad."

"Of course. I legit don't know how to cook anything else."

His laughter tickles my ear. "I still can't believe your mother paid all that money for you to take those cooking classes a couple summers ago."

"Major fail," I agree.

The worst part of that was, the only reason I capitulated was because Mom implied that we'd be taking the class together. Like a sucker, I allowed myself to think she truly wanted to bond with me. Turned out she never intended for us to do it together. She signed me up because my grandmother, her mother, made a disparaging comment the previous Christmas about what a shame it was that I'm such a terrible cook, and Mom can't look bad in front of her proper southern family. That's unacceptable.

"I can't wait to have you home," Dad says gruffly.

A lump of emotion clogs my throat. "Me too."

"All right, I gotta go, kiddo. Talk to you later. Love you."

"Love you too."

The tears threaten to spill over again. My dad has such faith in me. My whole life, he's raved about how resilient I am. How there's nobody else he'd rather have his back.

Going to the police about Percy would be so damn embarrassing. Dad knows *everyone* in law enforcement, so even if I wanted to hide that I was pressing charges, the news would eventually travel back to him. And then my mother would find out too, and knowing her, she'd say it was my fault for provoking Percy. Mom always scolds that I need to watch my temper.

At home, remembering my vow not to let Percy's actions send me into hiding, I change out of my camp clothes and into a swimsuit. Shane and I are supposed to go over details for the competition, so I text him to meet at the pool instead of my apartment, then force myself to go outside and walk the path toward the swimming pool.

My pulse quickens the closer I get. I've avoided all the neighbors this week because of my face, but I assure myself it's fine. If someone asks, I can feed them the same excuse I gave Shane and Gigi.

To my relief, the pool area is deserted when I arrive. I find a pair of loungers, get settled, and pull up the NUABC website on my phone. I need to reexamine my entire strategy. Kenji and I were going to perform the tango for our audition video, but with Shane's height, I think we might have a better shot qualifying with a Latin dance.

I still can't believe he agreed to be my partner. When Shane showed up the other day, I was still reeling over what happened with Percy, and suddenly someone was offering me a lifeline, a distraction.

Sure, that someone was Shane Lindley, but I'd been looking forward to competing for a whole year, and now the opportunity was back in my grasp.

"Jesus Christ, Dixon," Shane grumbles five minutes later. He's lying on the chair beside mine, also scrolling through the website. Cursing, he lifts his head in dismay. "This is intense. What is this? The American Nine? Dixon! This says we have to do *nine* dances! Four ballroom and five Latin."

"Relax. We're not entered in that event."

"How are we entered in anything if we haven't even qualified?"

"Because you send in the application before the prelims. Kenji and I signed up for American Smooth Duo and American Rhythm Solo."

He relaxes. "Oh, okay—" Then he pales. "Wait. What? That's two events."

"Yup."

"We're doing *two* dances?"

"Three, actually."

He stares at me in appalled accusation.

"It'll be okay. You've got this. The duo event is the tango and waltz. Solo is the cha cha."

Shane looks sick. "Dixon."

"What?"

"I will not, nor will I ever, perform a dance called the cha cha."

"Okay." I shrug. "You can call Lynsey and tell her we're dropping out."

"Fuck."

I grin. "We'll do the cha cha for the audition. I think you'll take to it better."

Shane glares at me.

"What's going on here?" a throaty voice inquires.

We look up at Veronika's approach. Our resident femme fatale is wearing a filmy, white cover-up over a very indecent leopard-print bikini, her unnaturally red hair loose around her shoulders.

She wags her finger mischievously. "You two have been spending a lot of time together. Is there romance in the air?"

"Oh my God, never. But we are entering a dance competition together."

"No, we're not," Shane denies immediately. His expression is a warning.

I see how it is. He's ashamed of our rhythmic connection.

"What?" I shrug at him. "They're going to see us practicing anyway. We'll be holding a lot of gym sessions."

"Oooh, sounds kinky," Veronika says.

I smother a laugh.

"Well, enjoy," she chirps before wandering toward her usual chair and umbrella. It's the one with a direct line of sight to the path, so she can see all the comings and goings of Meadow Hill.

"Anyway, back to this," Shane grumbles, holding up his phone. "I'm not doing more than one dance."

"We're doing three, and this isn't a negotiation." I tip my head. "What's the problem, Lindley? You don't think you can hack it?"

"Oh, you know I can."

"Exactly. Which is why we're doing three dances. I'm going for a swim now. You can sulk in private."

I dive into the deep end, enjoying the sensation of the cold water engulfing my body. For the first time in days, I feel confident again. Strong. It's like everything with Percy never happened. Just a fading nightmare I never have to revisit. Soon the bruise will fade entirely, and there'll be no remnants left of that horrible night.

A sense of calm washes over me as I swim laps. I zone out, focusing on propelling my body through the water, welcoming the burn in my muscles. When I stop to catch my breath in the shallow end, I notice a few more neighbors have arrived. I love summers in Meadow Hill. There's a real sense of community here.

I backstroke toward the deep end, where I heave myself out of the water so I can say hi to Priya, who sits at a table with Marnie and Dave.

"It's a college student," Dave is saying.

"Who's a college student?" I ask curiously, catching the tail end of their conversation. Water drips off my body as I approach the table. I glance over my shoulder. "Hey, Lindley, fetch me a towel?"

"Say please," he calls out.

"No," I call back.

Priya looks amused. "Wait, do we like him now?" She speaks a little too loudly.

"I knew it!" Shane, who's strolling toward us with my towel, glowers at me. "I *knew* you instigated a shunning program."

"I did not instigate a shunning program," I lie.

"Did she?" Shane asks Priya.

"Doctor-patient confidentiality," she answers smugly.

"Marnie?" he demands.

I glance at Marnie, winking. With a straight face, she says, "You're imagining it, honey. Nobody is shunning you."

"Stone-cold evil. All of you," he accuses, then shoves the towel at me. "You don't even deserve this towel."

Dave snickers under his breath.

Marnie redirects the group back to the topic at hand. "The renter of Sweet Birch 1A arrived today," she tells me.

Veronika saunters over in her white cover-up. "Are we talking about the Garrisons' rental?"

Marnie nods. "We just saw him in the parking lot unloading some boxes. He's going to be staying here the full six weeks. Handsome guy. Young."

Veronika perks up. "How young?" she inquires. Because she's Veronika and she's gross.

"I don't know, maybe mid to late twenties?" Marnie answers. "He said he's a grad student at Briar."

Guard shooting up, I tighten my grip on the towel. "Did you catch his name?"

Dave purses his lips. "Peter something?"

His wife lets out a laugh. "Honey. *Peter?* How can you forget his name? It was Percival."

Shock slams into me. Oh my fucking God.

No.

Absolutely not.

"Percival?" I burst out, anger whipping inside me. "Are you sure that was his name?"

"Unlike this doofus"—Marnie points at her husband—"it's not a name I'm likely to forget."

Priya eyes me in concern. "What's wrong?"

"That's my ex." I wrap the towel tighter around me, already backing away from their table. "I'm sorry, I have to go and figure out what the hell is going on."

Shane chases after me as I hurry toward our chairs to throw on my clothes. I gather my stuff and leave the pool area, Shane on my tail as we step onto the main path.

"That can't possibly be your ex moving into our building," he says in amusement. "Can it?"

"Sure sounds like it," I mutter, and I want to tell him it's not even remotely funny. It's the *furthest* thing from funny. But I can't say a word because I already lied to him about how I got this bruise. "Do you know any other Percivals who are grad students at Briar?"

"No, but I'm sure there has to be another one."

"Oh, fuck off, Shane. Come on."

"Hey, don't take it out on me."

Panic fills my throat and weakens my palms. "I'm sorry. I didn't mean to snap at you. I'm just…"

I stop walking and bury my face in my hands for a moment, trying to calm myself. If Percy is actually in Meadow Hill, I don't know what I'm going to do. What *can* I do?

Something else suddenly occurs to me, a reminder of what I said to Percy the night he hit me.

"Oh my God," I groan into my palms. I lift my head and stare at Shane helplessly. "The last time I saw Percy, I told him you were my boyfriend."

Shane's amusement returns in the form of a loud laugh. "What? Why would you do that?"

"Because apparently this is a thing we do now, okay? We tell our exes that we're boyfriend and girlfriend."

My hands are still shaking. I press them to my sides and hope Shane doesn't notice. What game is Percy playing? He punches me and then moves into my apartment complex? I want to cry, but I put on a steely face and pretend I'm angry about the latter and not the former.

"Lindley," I say in misery. "Before I go over to Sweet Birch to confront him, I need you to agree to be my boyfriend."

He shrugs. "Sure, let's go. I owe you one."

"Not just for today. I'm talking about the entire time he's here."

"Didn't Marnie say he's renting the unit for six weeks?" Shane demands.

I bite my lip. "You said so yourself—you owe me one."

"Dixon. I asked you to be my girlfriend for one night. You're asking me to give up my whole summer."

"Give up what? You already said you don't want to sleep around, so it's not like you'll be bringing random women home all summer. Right?"

"Right, but—"

"And all you were planning to do this summer was take it easy. Being my fake boyfriend doesn't change your plans at all. *And* it gives you more opportunities to make your ex jealous," I finish, grasping at as many straws as I can.

"So you're trying to make Percy jealous?"

"No, I want him to leave me alone!"

Shane's forehead creases at my outburst. "Dixon…" he starts warily. "What exactly is going on?"

I feel the desperation rising again, gripping my throat in its talons. I can't have Percy living here, but I also can't have Shane knowing Percy is the reason for the bruise on my face. It's so fucking mortifying.

I start walking again. Standing still is making me feel dizzy. Shane matches my stride, and I feel his gaze boring into the side of my face.

"I don't want him here." I hate how small my voice sounds. "I broke up with him and he can't accept it. Please, Lindley, it's only six weeks. Once he's gone, we can tell everyone we broke up."

"Wait, you want us to lie to people we know? Even Gigi and Ryder?"

"Just while Percy is here. I don't want it getting back to him that we might be faking it."

That's a lie. The reason I don't want to tell Gigi that Shane and I are faking it for Percy's expense is because her first question is going to be *why*.

Why am I playing games instead of telling Percy to fuck off? *Why* am I putting on a charade instead of marching headfirst into battle?

And those *whys* require me to tell the truth.

That he hit me.

That I'm scared of having him around me.

That I've never felt more ashamed in my life.

My brain is a tangled jumble of thoughts. Some of them might be irrational. I recognize that. But I can't do it. I can't tell my friends that my ex-boyfriend *hit* me. I tried, damn it. I saw Gigi this week. I opened my mouth, fully prepared to confess that Percy gave me this black eye, but the words refused to come out. Instead, I fed her the lie.

"Gigi's never gonna believe it," Shane says wryly.

"Sure she will. Besides, she's going to be distracted by the wedding and honeymoon." I implore him. "Please? I'd feel better... safer...if he thinks I have a boyfriend."

"Safer?" Shane echoes, wary again.

"I mean in the sense that he won't show up at my door with breakfast and make me uncomfortable," I say smoothly.

Speaking of uncomfortable, the devil himself suddenly appears on the path. Dressed in khakis and a white T-shirt, Percy's arms are full of two cardboard boxes that have the words TEXTBOOKS written on them in black marker.

I halt. Our eyes lock, and there's no mistaking the flash of guilt in his. This is the first time I've seen him since the night at Della's, and while being in his proximity again triggers a jolt of deep disgust, I also feel a twinge of fear. And that's what pisses me off the most.

I refuse to be afraid of this asshole.

I stalk forward, not mincing words. "I don't know what kind of game you're playing—"

"This isn't a game," he interrupts quietly. "You knew I was looking for housing, Diana."

"And you had to move *here*?"

My hands are trembling again, this time with rage. How *dare* he? How fucking dare he?

"It was either that or spend weeks at that fleabag motel on the outskirts of town. I can't afford to stay at the inn on Main Street for six weeks. This is the best option until my new townhouse becomes available in September."

It sounds on the up-and-up, but I don't buy it.

I notice his gaze is fixed on my face. On the fading bruise that *he* inflicted.

Shane is only a few feet away, so I know Percy won't dream of bringing up what happened the other night, but he does lower his voice and ask, "Are you okay?"

I ignore the question. "You know what? I don't care about your reasoning for why you're here. It doesn't change a damn thing between us. My last text to you made it clear where I stand."

Wincing, he has the decency to appear shamefaced again.

"Oh, and while we're here." I beckon Shane closer, then take his hand and, very blatantly, intertwine our fingers. "This is my boyfriend, Shane."

Shane doesn't go in for a handshake. He nods and says, "Nice to meet you, bro."

Percy tightens his lips for a second. "Nice to meet you too. If you'll excuse me…" He lifts the boxes slightly. "I have to finish unpacking."

As he walks past us, I turn to stare at his retreating back. His shoulders are stiffer than boards. As if *he's* the aggrieved party.

"You all right?" Shane asks gruffly. He's still holding my hand, almost like he knows I need the support, otherwise I'll keel over.

No, I'm not all right, I want to say.

The need to tell someone what happened is almost suffocating. I want to tell Shane. And Gigi. And my dad. Yet I can't summon the words. They're like a frightened animal cowering in the corner, and no matter how hard I try to coax them out, they refuse. They're stuck.

The confession burns in my throat, and then, for one panicky second, constricts it entirely. No air gets in, and suddenly I can't breathe. This has happened more than once this week.

"I'm fine," I manage to say. Miraculously, my voice sounds completely normal.

Shane seems oblivious to the turmoil roiling inside me as we walk to Red Birch, climbing the stairs to the second floor. "When do you want to start rehearsing?"

"For what?" I'm too distracted by my racing heart to focus on what he's asking.

"The competition?" he prompts, chuckling. "And when are we filming this audition?"

"Right. Sorry. We don't have to send the video until the end of August, but we should hit the ground running. How about rehearsal on Saturday? I'm only working breakfast and lunch shifts this weekend, so I'm free both evenings."

"Sounds good. Text me."

We part ways in the hall, and I practically dive into the solace of my apartment, where I can hyperventilate to my heart's content.

"Oh my God, Skip," I moan at my fish. "What the hell is happening?"

Breathing hard, I collapse onto the couch and fight the onslaught of sensation. The contents of my stomach threaten to come up. I really feel like I might throw up. I take a deep breath, then another, until the twisting, churning queasiness starts to dissipate. But my heart is still beating too fast for comfort. It can't be healthy for a heart to pound this hard.

Why does this keep happening?

You're having anxiety attacks.

No, damn it. I can't be.

I *never* feel anxiety. Even before a cheer competition, the nerves come in the form of giddy excitement. Fear isn't something I feel often, and when I do, it's entirely justified. Like that time Gigi and I were walking down a dark alley in Boston and heard a car backfire. I genuinely thought it was a gunshot, and the resulting jolt of adrenaline injected into my bloodstream had been intense.

Or when Dad's next door neighbor's dog got loose during the Labor Day potluck last summer. The huge Doberman went tearing toward a group of children, and for a second, my heart was in my throat because I truly thought he was going to maul them. Turned out the dog was great with kids. All he did was steal their ball and then make them chase him while the kids shrieked with laughter.

Both those incidents elicited fear, and it made sense. I *thought* there was danger. But I'm not in any danger right now. There's no reason for even a twinge of panic.

I sit on the couch, breathing in and out, willing my pulse to slow.

Eventually, the anxiety fades, but the unhappiness remains tight in my chest. I can't let this keep happening. I am not a weak person. I am not afraid of anything, especially not a pathetic, insecure man like Percy Forsythe.

Starting right now, I need to find a way to let this go.

GIGI:

Are we still on for tomorrow night? If so, I'm thinking dinner at the Indian place near Fenway. Then drinks at that martini bar we really liked?

ME:

Yeah, I'm still down!

ME:

Oooh yes, I love that restaurant. Def want to go back there

ME:

Shane and I are dating now

ME:

Which martini bar? The one near the Ritz?

GIGI:

Wait. What?

GIGI:

What do you mean you and Shane are dating??

GIGI:

Answer me!

GIGI:

● ● ●

CHAPTER NINETEEN
SHANE

Trial boyfriend

"I DON'T WANT TO GET MARRIED ANYMORE."

The glum statement comes from Ryder, who sits on the other end of the couch, stone faced.

I do my best not to laugh at him. "Hate to break it to you, bro, but you're already married."

It's Friday night, and I'm over at the townhouse that, until a few weeks ago, I shared with Ryder and Beckett. Now, Will's in my old room, and soon Ryder will be moving in with his new wife. Who he's already thinking of forsaking, it appears.

I know where he's coming from, though. From what he's told me, Gigi's family has gone overboard with this wedding. A wedding they're only having because Gigi's father, the legendary Garrett Graham, is apparently a secret softie and wants to walk his only daughter down the aisle. I don't begrudge him that—I can totally see my dad doing the same thing with Maryanne. Not that she's ever getting married. Maryanne's precious cargo. I've already decided that when she turns sixteen, I'm going to sit her down and talk to her about the benefits of becoming a nun. I think a convent would be a really good place for her.

"Maybe it's not too late to get a divorce," Ryder says, his tone so hopeful that I can't help but snort.

"You don't want a divorce. You're obsessed with that woman." I shrug. "Besides, the wedding won't be too bad. I, for one, am looking forward to getting absolutely wasted and seeing how many bridesmaids Beckett manages to hook up with."

"I mean, you're already banging the maid of honor, so that's at least one he can't score with."

Not quite, but now that Dixon told Gigi we were dating, it's understandable that Ryder thinks we've banged each other already. I suppose I could let him keep thinking it, but I also don't want to besmirch Diana's reputation.

"Actually, we haven't had sex yet," I say.

"Bullshit."

"It's true. We're taking it slow."

"Since when do you take things slow?" The question comes from Will, who pokes his head out of the kitchen. It's just him and Ryder here, while Beckett is in Australia.

He walks in chugging a bottle of water and dressed like he's going out. Dark jeans encase his long legs, and his blue button-down is the same light shade as his eyes.

"You off somewhere?" Ryder asks.

"Yeah, heading to the city," Will tells him. "Actually, I'm meeting your wife and your girlfriend"—he nods toward me—"for drinks."

Ryder narrows his eyes. "Gisele said it was girls' night."

"What can I tell ya? Diana invited me." He flashes me a smug look. "Your girlfriend likes me better than you."

"Probably," I agree. "I annoy the fuck out of her."

Ryder snickers. "How did this happen, anyway?"

"Nah, I saw it coming," Will says. "They made out at the pool party, and we all had to pretend it was for a dare."

I ignore Will's smirk and glance at Ryder. "I don't know. It sort of happened and now I've got a girlfriend."

He lifts his eyebrows. "Made it exclusive pretty fast."

"I can't exactly *not* be exclusive. She's Gigi's best friend and

I'm not looking to get murdered. But don't read too much into it. Girlfriend is just for lack of a better term."

"Dude, he's downplaying it," Will says to Ryder. "It's serious as fuck. He entered a dance competition with her."

My best friend's head swings toward me. I swallow a groan. I was hoping to keep that to myself for a while longer.

"What do you mean you entered a *dance competition*? What's happened to you since you moved out? Who are you?"

"You're asking who *I* am? You got married," I shoot back. "You changed first, man. Don't put this on me. You're the one who ruined our friendship."

He snickers and flips up his middle finger.

"How did you know about the dance thing?" I direct the question to Will. I'm deeply suspicious now.

"Diana announced it on Ride or Dance."

"What the fuck is Ride or Dance?" Then it hits me, the memory of her and Kenji filming that day at the pool. "Oh no. She didn't."

Will grins at me.

Leaning toward the coffee table, I grab my phone. A minute later, the screen shows the latest video from Diana's ridiculous dance account. My stomach drops when I realize she has over a hundred thousand followers. Kill me now.

The volume is on silent, so I turn it up and press play. Diana's high, bubbly voice blares out of my phone.

"Hello, dancers! I wanted to give you a quick update on NUABC. Kenji is out. No, don't get all dramatic. We didn't have a huge fight. He simply decided that superyachts are more important than me. Although, who can blame him? Superyachts probably are more important than me. But yes, he's going to be spending his summer on the Mediterranean, which means he won't be able to compete, so I've had to find a new partner. And I think, judging by all the comments on our last video, a lot of you will be happy with this partner reveal. You guessed it—I am indeed talking about Asshole Neighbor."

Ryder snorts mid-sip of his beer.

"Oh, and you'll love this too. Asshole Neighbor is now also Trial Boyfriend."

"Trial?" I growl.

Will starts laughing. My friends are dicks.

"I've decided to give him a shot to prove that he is worthy of my love. So yes, we are dancing, and we are dating. We are dance dating. It's going to be glorious. Our rehearsals start this weekend, so stay tuned for some Asshole Neighbor content and all the grief I anticipate him bringing me. All right, I'm off to bed. Good night, dancers."

"She is so lame." I groan.

"I think she's cute," Will says.

"Why don't you date her, then?"

"I'll make sure to tell her you said that when we're having drinks tonight. Anyway, yeah, I gotta go." He glances at Ryder. "Don't expect me back tonight. I'll probably crash at my cousin Rob's in Boston. I think he's joining us for drinks."

I shake my head. "How are you and 'Rob'—" I make quotations.

"Why are you using air quotes? Are you implying that Rob is not real?"

"—on a double date with Ryder's wife and my girlfriend, while he and I are here, *not* on a date with them?" I finish in disbelief.

"I don't know. Some guys have all the luck." Will gives an exaggerated shrug and saunters out of the living room.

After the front door closes, Ryder's dark blue eyes grow sober again. "Look, about you and Diana. Be careful, okay? Like you said, she's Gigi's best friend."

"Trust me, you don't have to worry."

Literally. Because it's fake.

"Honestly," I insist when I note his dubious expression. "I can't see this lasting too long."

"No?"

"She's not really my type. You know I prefer a more serious girl. Someone who's on the same page as me."

"And what page is that?"

"The long-term kind." I shrug. "Dixon is great, but she lives in the moment. She acts on these whims, throws herself into random new projects. She's the kind of person who's going to, like, take off to Budapest for a year. I don't think she's wanting to settle down anytime soon. We're just having fun."

"Fair enough." He rubs the side of his face, thoughtful. "But if you truly don't see anything long-term with her, don't let her get attached."

"Nah. She's the one insisting we keep it casual," I lie. "The girlfriend-boyfriend label is just easier to say than 'this is my friends with benefits,' you know?"

He relaxes. "Got it. So it's more of a friends-with benefits-sitch."

"Exactly."

"But you haven't had sex." He's skeptical again.

"Not yet. But I assume we'll be banging by like, tomorrow."

He snickers. "All right."

"What about you?" I say, eager to change the subject. "Married life treating you okay? You're not tired of Gisele yet?"

"Never." His face softens anytime Gigi is mentioned. And whenever that raw, unconcealed love floods his face, it almost feels like you're intruding. Like you've been given a window into an intensely personal thing that doesn't belong to you.

But the dude simply can't disguise his feelings for the woman, which is funny, because Luke Ryder is an expert at hiding his emotions. Since I've known him, I've never been a hundred percent sure where his head's at. But there's no uncertainty with Gigi. He adores her. Worships her. She's his entire life and he would die for her. It's telegraphed in his eyes the moment you say her name.

"But I'm really not excited about this wedding," he admits in a pained voice.

"I'm sorry. But I got you, man. Whatever you need."

He sighs. "Thanks, brother. I'm gonna need you to ply me with alcohol so I can forget about how many people will be there. Maybe rub my back while I puke."

I laugh. "You'll be fine."

"Oh, hey. I forgot to ask you—do you want to help out at the Hockey Kings camp? It's in a few weeks."

"Oh, right. That's in August. Which Harvard guy did they pick to coach with you?"

"Troy Talvo."

"He's good," I say begrudgingly.

"The boys are playing a game on the last day and we need some linesmen. You in?"

"Will Garrett and Connelly be there?"

"It's their camp."

"Then yes."

Chuckling, he rolls his eyes at me. "That's the only way you'll do it? Not out of the goodness of your heart?"

I grin at him. "I will ruthlessly pursue my own interests and I'll never apologize for it."

"Dude, Diana can do so much better than you."

"Ha. Like Gigi earned herself a prince."

"You're probably right about that. They're both way out of our leagues."

CHAPTER TWENTY
DIANA

Vertical sex

I COME HOME FROM WORK ON SATURDAY AFTERNOON ALL PUMPED UP to rehearse with Shane, only to discover he's still out golfing with Will. Ugh, such a spoiled brat. I know he likes to joke about being a rich boy, but this dude's seriously living the dream. What other twenty-one-year-old has the luxury of spending his entire summer golfing and honing his physique?

While I wait for him to get back, I catch up on *Fling or Forever*, enthralled by an epic catfight between Faith and Ky. Donovan is still running a long con on Leni, and either I'm paranoid or this new chick Marissa is trying to sink her claws into the Connor. Girl, keep walking.

Around seven, Shane texts to say he's ready, and we head downstairs. I've decided to hold our first rehearsal outside, since it's such a perfect evening. Warm but not too hot, and breezy enough to cool the sweat. Meadow Hill has a tennis court, but I think it'll be easier to practice on the grass, so Shane and I set up camp in a small clearing in front of the courts. I'm wearing little black booty shorts and a neon-orange sports bra, and I've come prepared with an external speaker, my laptop, and a tripod.

"How was your girls' night with Gisele and Will?" Shane asks dryly, while I adjust the height of the tripod.

"It was fun. I'm meeting Gigi again tomorrow after my breakfast shift for a dress fitting and then she's coming over for a swim."

"Excellent. Make sure you both wear your skimpiest bikinis."

"Only if you wear your Speedo."

"Deal." He dips his head, distracted for a moment by his phone. It looks like he's typing an entire essay.

"Stop texting your ex," I taunt. "We've got work to do."

He glances up, rolling his eyes. "It's my dad."

"You text your dad in multiple paragraphs?"

"Yeah. He's my best friend. We talk about shit. Got a problem with that?"

I want to call him a dork, but I can't deny it's sort of heartwarming. My dad and I are close too, but we don't engage in long, ongoing text conversations.

"Okay, let's start." I approach Shane, all business. "I assume you know the basic steps of the cha cha?"

He stares at me. "No. Why would you assume that?"

"You dated a dancer for four years."

"She's a ballerina. And just because *she* dances ballet doesn't mean *I* know ballet. It's not like I was going around doing pirouettes and jetés and—oh shit, I guess I do know some dance steps."

I swallow a laugh. Shane's funny sometimes, I'll give him that. And he happens to look really fucking good in his rehearsal clothes. I told him to wear something more form-fitting, so he's in a tight white T-shirt and black joggers. The pants are a thinner material than sweatpants, and although they're not skin tight either, they do pull tight against his groin when he walks, outlining his generous penis. I still think about how it felt pressed against me when I was in his lap. Why is this thing so big? And—oh my god, something occurs to me. What if it's even bigger? What if he only had a *semi* at the pool party? Like, he might have the largest penis of anyone on earth. It could be like twenty-five inches.

"Dixon."

I snap out of it.

"What the hell's the matter with you? Your face is redder than a tomato. Are you having an allergic reaction or something?"

Lovely. My face turned red thinking about Shane's twenty-five-inch penis.

I shake myself out of it. I don't know what I like less, blushing at the thought of Shane's equipment or this recent spate of anxiety attacks because my ex-boyfriend smacked me in the face.

I believe the word is punched?

I grit my teeth and turn away from Shane so he doesn't witness the dangerous mixture of rage and helplessness I know is flooding my eyes.

It's like there are two Dianas inside me. One of them is furious. She's saying, *What is the matter with you? Go to the cops. Punish him.* And the other one is cowering and crippled with shame, ordering me not to waste any more energy on this fucking catastrophe. The bruise has healed, and Percy is blocked from contacting me.

So really, everything is fine now.

It has to be fine.

"Let me finish setting up and then we can get started," I say, keeping my back to Shane as I set up my tripod.

"Do we really have to film this?"

He sounds so upset that I spin around, needing to verify his expression. Sure enough, his unhappiness appears genuine. I falter then, as I realize I never asked for his consent.

"Ah, fuck." Remorse flutters through me. "I guess we don't have to film this if you really don't want to."

"I'm not going to embarrass myself in front of your gazillion followers."

I crack a smile. "You know how many followers I have?"

"I creeped the account the other night." He scowls at me. "*Trial girlfriend.*"

I snicker, but my humor fades when I realize what this means.

"Look, I'm going to be honest. I make a bit of money by monetizing my posts." I shrug awkwardly. "It helps pay for groceries and stuff. I don't expect you to understand because I'm sure you don't pay for anything—"

He frowns.

"Sorry, I'm not trying to insult you. Truly. I'm only stating a fact. Like, I doubt that you and I have the same expenses."

"No, I get it," he says gruffly. "We don't."

"Right." I bite my lip. "All I'm saying is, these silly dance videos help me out in terms of money."

I do my best to ignore the prickly sensation caused by my confession. I hate admitting weakness or showing vulnerability, especially in front of someone like Shane, who comes from means. Not that I come from poverty. I inherited a major windfall in the form of this condo, and yes, I could sell it the way Thomas did with Aunt Jennifer's other investment property and take the cash. But I like having a home. Something that belongs to me. Cash is easy to blow, but an apartment is forever. It can be a lifelong investment.

"So yeah, I *can* work my way around it. Post some solo stuff when I'm rehearsing on my own. But the content with me and Kenji did stupidly well." I give him a hopeful look. "If it helps, I'll split any ad revenue with you. It's not a lot, but—"

"No," Shane interrupts. "I don't need that at all. Whatever, just film us. But I get approval of everything you post, so I don't look like too much of an ass. I don't trust your editing."

He shouldn't. I definitely would've given him the asshole edit. I hide a smile and set up the equipment.

"Okay." I stalk toward him. "Our basic rhythm is slow, quick quick, slow, quick quick."

"That's easy enough."

"Don't get cocky. The cha cha is all about timing. One misstep and you've ruined everything."

"But no pressure."

"Our starting position is facing each other, and the only step you need to know right now is the chasse step. Start with your weight on your left foot. Left foot, Lindley!"

"Sorry, I was looking at your foot."

I position his hands—his right one on my left shoulder blade, his left in my right hand. He's got big hands, probably on account of his two-foot dick. As we slowly run through the steps, heat rushes through me, and I know it's not from the warm breeze snaking over our bodies. I really need to stop hypothesizing about his penis.

Normally, I love the cha cha. It's fast and lively and makes me feel like a kid. But Shane's expression is anything but jovial.

"This is supposed to be a fun dance!" I chastise him. "You look like you're in a prison camp performing for your captors. Smile."

He bares his teeth.

I almost keel over laughing, which messes up our rhythm again.

"Sorry, let's start over. And stop staring at your feet. We need to maintain eye contact the entire time. It's how we communicate. Look at me, not your feet."

"But then how do I know if they're doing what they're supposed to be doing!" He sounds frazzled, his forehead creased with frustration.

"Ready?" I restart the music and count us in. "Slow step to the right, quick-quick to the left. Slow, quick quick, slow, quick quick." I yelp when Shane nearly crushes my toes in my sneakers. "Okay, stop. That wasn't it at all. We need to work on our timing." I sigh because that's going to be the hardest part, doing this in sync. "Your quick steps need to be quicker."

He groans. "This is the worst thing I've ever experienced in my life." He turns toward the camera. "Don't judge me."

"No, we got this," I assure him. "Trust me."

Although his footwork is better next time, his body remains stiffer than a brick wall.

"The cha cha is all about the hips. Every step, roll your hips. Like this." I show him.

"I'm not doing that."

"Yes, you are. Push your hip out when you do the chasse step. Then pop it back in on the cha cha step."

"No."

"Yes."

"No."

"Just a little more hip movement," I encourage. "You can do it."

He growls at me. "I'm a hockey player. My hips don't move that way."

"I guarantee they do."

I plant my hands on his waist, then bring them around to the top of his butt.

"Dixon," he says in amusement. "What are you doing?"

"It's all in the ass and glutes. I promise. Can I touch your butt?"

"Obviously."

I slide my hands down so I'm cupping his buttocks. Jesus. This is the tightest, most muscular ass I've *ever* felt. I've dated athletes before, but Shane's butt is something else.

"You have the ass of a marble statue," I marvel.

He smirks. "I know."

"All right, not to be crude"—I peek over my shoulder at the camera—"cover your children's ears, people. But dancing is basically vertical sex. You're too rigid, Lindley. You need to move your hips the way you would if we were…you know."

His eyes gleam. "Are you asking me to vertically fuck you?"

"Shane," I warn. I lightly smack his butt. "C'mon, let's repeat that step."

"While you squeeze my ass?"

"Yes, trust me. I'll be able to show you how to relax the hips."

"This sounds like the premise for a really bad porn scene."

"You wish."

After I count us in again, Shane thrusts his hips as if he's trying to bang his way through my body. It rips a wave of laughter out of me.

"No, you have to *roll* the hips." I squeeze the sides of his ass. "Here. Move from here."

We try again, and this time his movements are a bit looser and less pornographic.

"See? You feel the difference, right?"

An angry voice interrupts our moment of progress. "What's the meaning of this?"

I glance over my shoulder to see our neighbor Carla stalking toward us. "Oh, hey, Carla. We're rehearsing for a dance competition."

She crosses her arms over the front of her flower-patterned silk blouse. "Is one of the requirements fondling each other's rear ends?"

"No, but it's more enjoyable this way," Shane says, winking at her.

My hands drop from the rear end in question. "Sorry. Nope. I realize how this looks." I fight a laugh as I offer a fuming Carla a reassuring smile. "I promise we're not engaging in lewd behavior."

"You'd better not be," she replies primly. "With that said, I will be raising this at the HOA meeting."

"Wouldn't expect anything else, Carla." I give her a wave as she marches away in a huff.

"I don't understand the people in this apartment complex," Shane muses, watching Carla go.

"Sometimes I think it's some bizarre government experiment where they placed all these random people to see what would happen. Like, everyone has a unique role to play but nobody knows what the roles are."

"Why are you and I here?" He sounds intrigued.

I think it over. "You're here because..."

"I'm the wildcard." His eyes light up. "They're all like, what the fuck's he gonna do?"

"Sure." I pat his arm. "You're the wildcard."

We practice for another thirty minutes, and as much as I don't want to accept it, I think the cha cha is a lost cause, at least for the preliminary process. I have no doubt I could bring Shane's skills up to a decent level in time for the competition itself in October, but the audition video is due in a few weeks. There's no way he'll be good enough by then, and I'm worried we won't qualify if we go with the cha cha. I'll give it a few more sessions, but I suspect we'll have a better chance with the tango.

"What are you up to now?" Shane asks on our walk back to Red Birch.

"I need to finish watching last night's *FoF*. I'm dying to see who gets released from the Sugar Shack."

"I can tell you if you want. I watched it last night."

I swivel my head toward him. "I'm sorry, what?"

He shrugs. "Didn't have anything better to do. Anyway," he says, ignoring the giggles I'm convulsing with at his expense, "why don't I go pick up some dinner? We'll finish watching your episode, then watch the new one. And then, maybe, you know…"

I stop in the middle of the path and eye him in amusement. "No, I *don't* know."

Shane waggles his eyebrows. "We go to the bedroom and…"

"Are you asking me to have sex with you?"

"You don't have to look so repulsed."

I snicker at him. "We don't even like each other."

"We tolerate each other," he protests.

"Oh, what an endorsement to get me into bed! *I tolerate you, Diana. Please, let me make sweet love to you.*"

"That's not what I meant. All I'm saying is, we ought to consider a friends-with-benefits-type situation."

"I thought you said you don't want to do one-night stands anymore."

"This wouldn't be a one-night stand. It'll be a long-term thing. I mean, if we already have to pretend to be all over each other this summer for Percy's sake, we might as well put our hands on each other for real. What do you have to lose?"

"My patience. My dignity. My purity."

Shane releases an exasperated breath. "Must you keep pretending this isn't a thing?" He vaguely waves at his body.

"What are you pointing at?"

"My dick. You need to quit acting like it doesn't get you hot."

"Oh my God, you're so arrogant."

He just grins. "So...about this friends-with-benefits proposal?"

I slap my forehead in mock remembrance. "Oh, shit, I forgot to tell you. I actually screen all of my friends with benefits very, very carefully. There's a whole application process."

Shane plays along. "Oh, is there. May I have a copy of the application?"

"Unfortunately, I'm in the process of editing it to make it more in-depth, so I'm not open to applicants at this time. But maybe you can apply next year."

He nods solemnly. "Please let me know when a slot opens up again."

"You will be the first person I notify," I promise. "And by first, I mean dead last."

We're passing Sweet Birch when Percy suddenly exits the front door. The paranoid part of my brain wonders if he's been lying in wait. Hiding in the lobby waiting for his opportunity to pop outside. But my logical side says that's crazy. He couldn't have timed this so well.

His expression darkens when he spots us, but he recovers quickly and pastes on a weak smile.

Shane stops, but I reach for his hand to pull him forward. "Keep walking," I murmur.

"Diana," Percy calls at our backs. "Do you have a second?"

I ignore him and quicken my pace, practically dragging Shane along. The anxiety rises again, compressing my throat. It's a familiar sensation now, and I *hate* that it's familiar. Thanks to Percy, I feel helpless and trapped. I want to call my dad and beg him to come here, to heave Percy up by the collar and throw him into a different fucking state. But I can't ask my father to solve my problems. I have to solve them myself.

I inhale as many deep breaths as I can, but I only feel more light-headed by the time we enter our lobby.

I don't know what Shane sees on my face—I pray it's not fear—but whatever it is makes his jaw tense. "Do you want me to go have a word with him?"

"No. I'm hoping if I ignore him, he'll eventually go away."

That doesn't seem to satisfy Shane, but after a beat, he shrugs. "Fine. Let me know if you change your mind." We reach the top of the stairs. "What should we get for dinner?"

I realize my appetite is completely gone. The sight of Percy's face annihilated it.

"You know what, I changed my mind about dinner. I have a headache," I lie. "I think I'm going to take a shower and lie down for a bit."

"Are you sure—"

"Later, Lindley." I slide into my apartment before Shane can argue.

CHAPTER TWENTY-ONE
SHANE

We've gone viral

DIANA AND GIGI RETURN FROM THEIR DRESS FITTING AROUND TWO ON Sunday. It's still a scorcher of a day, and Ryder ends up joining us at the Meadow Hill pool, the four of us claiming a set of loungers and slathering ourselves in sunscreen.

While the girls sunbathe, I kick Ryder's ass in a race that draws loud cheers from the rowdy teenage boys in the pool with us. Dave and Marnie's kids are allowed to talk to me now that the neighbors don't hate me anymore. Veronika, of course, is sprawled in her usual lounge chair, blatantly checking out Ryder and me. It's a perfect pool day with good friends, sunshine, and beer.

The only problem is, Diana and I keep forgetting we're supposed to be dating. Around our best friends, we fall naturally back into our old roles. Those roles being Diana hates Shane, and Shane's only goal in life is to piss her off.

Heaving myself out of the pool, I watch as Diana points something out in the clouds for Gigi. "There. *There.* Do you see it?"

Gigi slides her sunglasses on to get a better view. "Nope."

I towel off and settle in the chair next to Diana's, while Ryder stretches out beside his wife.

"What are we looking at?" I ask curiously.

"That cloud up there is shaped like a magician. He's wearing a top hat and holding a rabbit in one hand and a huge butcher knife in the other."

"That's dark," I tell her.

"Hey, *I* didn't do this. That's what the clouds are saying today."

I roll my eyes at her. "You have issues."

"You didn't even try to see it," Diana accuses.

"Why would I? It's not there."

"*Try.*"

"Fine. Where?"

"See that break between the two clouds just left of the sun?"

I suck in a breath. "Holy shit. That rabbit's about to get his throat sliced."

Diana's entire face brightens. "Do you really see it?"

"*No.* No, Dixon. Of course not."

She grumbles in annoyance. "Why did you even pretend to play along?"

"Because it's fun getting you excited and then destroying your dreams."

"I dislike you immensely."

"Oh no. How will I ever sleep at night with that knowledge keeping me up?"

A dry voice interrupts us.

"Are you sure you two are together?" Gigi inquires, raising a brow.

Although she's joking, I don't miss the gleam of skepticism in her gray eyes.

And although I did tell Ryder we were dating, it feels wrong putting on this deliberate act in front of our best friends.

I glance at Diana in an unspoken *maybe we should fess up.* Her guilty look confirms she's also having trouble blatantly lying. Resignation enters her green eyes, and I suspect she's about to come clean—until her ex enters the pool area.

"Fucking hell," she mutters under her breath.

Gigi straightens up. "What?"

Diana nods toward the other side of the deck.

"Who's that?" Ryder asks.

"My ex-boyfriend," she answers grimly. "He decided to rent out the apartment three buildings down from me. Because he's a sociopath."

Ryder sits up. He's wearing shades, but the taut set of his jaw reveals his thoughts on the matter. "Is this asshole stalking you?"

Diana's gaze is glued to Percy. Although we're talking quietly, he must know we're talking about him.

On the other side of the swimming pool, he lays down a towel and takes his shirt off. For a physics student, he's not in bad shape. He's tall and lean but has some muscle to him. Not as bulky as me and Ryder, but I assume he doesn't spend as much time in the gym or playing competitive hockey.

He settles on the chaise and rests a paperback novel on his knee. I can't make out the title of the book, but I'd bet a hundred bucks he's pretending to read.

"He claims he had nowhere else to go," Diana tells Ryder. "His townhouse doesn't free up until September first, and he's teaching a class at Briar this summer, so he needs to stay local."

"And you don't believe him?" Ryder says.

"Nope. He can't get over this breakup. And he's…" She hesitates, visibly frustrated. "Whatever. He'll be gone soon."

"Does he know about you two?" Gigi asks, shifting a finger from me to Diana.

"Yep," Diana answers. "Which is another reason he's over there pretending to read and glaring at us."

I glance at Percy. I don't think I've seen him flip a page yet.

"Come on, Girlfriend," I say. "Let's cool off. I can see that temper of yours heating up."

"Fine." She lets me tug her off the chair. That slamming body of

hers is barely covered by a tiny red bikini. She adjusts the two trian-
gles as she walks toward the shallow end.

I know my next move could backfire on me and ignite her
temper even more, but I grab her arm and draw her toward me.

"Where do you think you're going?" I taunt.

A yelp escapes her lips when I scoop her into my arms and run
toward the pool. I jump, and then we're airborne for a second before
we hit the water with a loud splash. Diana is sputtering with laughter when her head pops out of the water.

"Oh, you asshole," she says, smacking me in the chest. But her
eyes are dancing.

See? I know how to cheer Dixon up.

We swim side by side for a while and eventually wind up in the
middle of the pool. I can stand in this section, but she can't, so she
wraps her legs and arms around me, clinging to my body like a koala
hanging onto a tree.

"Can you really not touch the ground here?" I ask.

"No! I'm short."

"Must be a terrible way to go through life."

I walk us backward until my shoulder blades bump the side of
the pool near our chairs. Diana twists around so her back is flush
against my chest. I wrap my arms around her, tilting my head to the
sky. I don't see any murderous magicians, but suddenly I'm looking
for shapes everywhere. Dixon rubs off on me in the strangest ways.

"What kind of thoughts do you think a cloud would have if it
was sentient?" I ask her.

"I can't even begin to answer that question."

I absently play with the end of her wet ponytail. "I think he'd
think, what the hell am I doing up here?"

There's a beat of silence, and then Diana bursts out laughing,
waves splashing everywhere as she shudders in my arms.

"Oh my God, why are you so weird?" she howls.

"Shut up."

I hear Gigi giggling from her chair. "Okay, I take it back."

"What?" Diana says, glancing over.

"You two are kind of perfect for each other."

I don't know if Percy heard that, but I notice his cloudy eyes flick in our direction before he lowers them back to his novel.

"Why won't he go away?" Diana mutters to me.

"Do you want me to go over there and say something? Because I'm happy to."

"No. He legally rented the Garrison place. What are we supposed to do about that?"

"You could file some sort of complaint with Brenda?"

"He hasn't done anything that warrants kicking him out of the building. Trust me, I've read the handbook."

Of course she has.

"He'll be gone soon," I assure her. "And until then, I will diligently serve as your boyfriend."

"Thank you." Genuine gratitude softens her face.

It's odd to see it. I didn't think Diana was capable of being rattled by an ex-boyfriend, but for someone who enjoys confrontation, she sure doesn't want one with this dude.

"Have you spoken to Lynsey lately?" she asks, still using my body as a chair.

"No." I keep my voice low because I don't want Ryder overhearing. He's been knocking me for the last year about not being over my ex.

"We should post some pics of us on social media. Make her jealous," Diana says devilishly. Before I can object, she holds onto the side of the pool and calls out to Gigi. "Hey, G, can you take a picture of us?"

"Sure." There's a rustling sound as Gigi climbs off her lounger. Then she chuckles. "Um. D? You have five thousand notifications. Literally."

"Sure."

"I'm serious."

Confused, Diana dries her hands with the towel Gigi hands her and checks her phone. A moment later, she starts to laugh again.

"Oh my God. Lindley. We've gone viral."

Dread twists my stomach. "No."

"Our last video has…wait for it…two and a half million views. And counting."

Oh, Jesus. Two and a half million people watched me do the cha cha and thrust my hips?

Kill me now.

"This is incredible." She's still laughing, shaking her head in amazement as she gives Gigi the phone back. "We'll celebrate this later."

"We will not," I tell her, but she's already looping her arms around my neck again and forcing me to pose for a photo.

"Let's see a kiss," Gigi says, holding up the phone.

I dutifully bend my head and bring my lips to Diana's. When we pull apart, Diana glances at Gigi. "Thanks, G."

"No problem. You know me, just your personal photographer, following you around."

"That's part of the best-friend duty!" Diana calls as Gigi returns to her chair.

We stay in the water, swimming toward the shallow end. But even though Diana can reach the ground here, she still wraps her legs around me again. I hold on to her ass, while the sun beats down on our heads.

I fixate on Diana's lips. I remember kissing those lips in my kitchen. How delicious they tasted. How good her tongue felt in my mouth. The way she used it, with that teasing little swirl—

"Why are you staring at me?"

"I was thinking about the swirl move you did with your tongue when we made out."

She lightly punches my shoulder. Droplets of water splash onto my arm.

"Hey, you asked." I teasingly drag my fingers over the swell of her ass. "Don't tell me you haven't been thinking about it."

"Not one iota of brain power has gone toward that kiss."

"Bullshit. I'm not the only one who was affected."

"Sorry to break it to you, but you were."

I give her ass cheeks a discreet squeeze. When her lips part, I take full advantage and press my mouth to hers, sliding my tongue through that seam. Despite her surprised noise, Diana kisses me back. I'm rock-hard within seconds, and I know she can feel it.

I pull my mouth away when I hear a loud slapping against the deck. We turn to see Percy's retreating back as he leaves the pool.

"Point made," I hear Gigi say from her chair.

Fuck. To be honest, I totally forgot about Diana's ex. There was no point being made. I simply wanted to kiss her and to prove I turn her on.

"See," I murmur. "It affects you as much as it affects me."

She reaches down between us, and my lips barely contain a groan when she lightly squeezes my erection.

"Really... Because the way I see it, if we're both so affected... why am I the only one who can get out of the pool?"

She laughs and swims off toward the ladder. And she's right. I can't get out without inviting Ryder's merciless taunting. All I can do is stay in the water with my erection and wait it out.

TRIAL BOYFRIEND LEARNS THE CHA CHA

495.8K   5.8K comments. 23K shares

@ginnyloo43
omg the sexual tension

@dancegurll
🔥🔥🔥

@stlouisballroomassociation
Incredible! So nice to see young people taking an
interest in this timeless art. More of this content!

@iheartballroomdancing
You two are amazing!

@meghan_johnson2
girl, your boyfriend is so fucking hot

@dancingdonna_nyc
#couplegoals

CHAPTER TWENTY-TWO

SHANE

My daughter will never date a hockey player

AUGUST

"Is it just me or are those the two best-looking men you've ever seen in your life? They're better looking than most male celebrities."

"They're beautiful," I agree.

"I don't know if men like being called beautiful."

"Not my problem. They are."

From the away bench at center ice, Will and I stand on skates, ogling Garrett Graham and Jake Connelly. Two NHL superstars. One Hall of Famer. Two beautiful men.

I've already texted my dad a few photos of them, which I discreetly snapped when nobody was looking. Or at least I hope nobody noticed, because that's some stalker shit right there. But I know Dad would get a huge kick out of seeing this.

"Okay—fuck, marry, kill," I say.

"Who are we killing?" Will furrows his brow. "There's only two of them."

"The wife of the one you want to marry."

Taking the request oddly seriously, he studies both men from head to toe as they engage in discussion on the other side of the rink. They're wearing black pants and navy-blue hoodies that are identical at first glance, until you peer closer and see Graham's sweatshirt has the Bruins logo, while Connelly's is the Oilers. Jake's forehead creases as he listens intently to Garrett.

Will finally answers. "Fuck Graham. Marry Connelly. Kill Connelly's wife before she kills me for stealing her husband."

"Good call." Brenna Connelly is terrifying. I've seen her cut down men twice her size on her TSBN sports show. She knows her hockey better than all the analysts at the network combined.

"Oh shit. Plot twist," Will mumbles under his breath. "Check out his body."

John Logan skates over to join the trio. He's refereeing today's game too. Another Stanley Cup winner. Another legend.

How is this my life?

"Dude, his physique is ridiculous," I rave.

"You guys realize we're here, right?"

Will and I twist toward the row of teenage boys on the bench behind us. They range from sixteen to eighteen years old, and every single one of them stares at us like we've lost the plot.

"You shouldn't objectify men like that," one kid says earnestly.

"Besides," the guy next to him adds, "if you're really gonna give out awards for the most beautiful, that one over there obviously wins."

He points at a fourth man who's gliding toward the small group of men. The newcomer is tall, blond, and looks like a male model. He's snapping on a black helmet as he joins the others.

"Dude," gripes the player at the end of the bench. "That's my dad."

I examine the teen, instantly noting the resemblance. His name is Beau, and although his hair is a shade darker than his father's, he has the same green eyes and chiseled features. He hasn't completely filled out yet, but he's already tall and built. I fear for the opponents he'll be facing in a couple years.

"Refs!" Graham blows his whistle to get our attention. He waves Will and me over.

Will eyes me nervously. "Don't let me say anything to embarrass myself."

"Same."

Garrett greets us with a smile and introduces us to John Logan, who needs no introduction, and Dean Di Laurentis, who as it turns out is the head coach of the Yale women's hockey team. Like Will and me, Logan and Dean are decked out in striped long-sleeves, black helmets, and whistles around their necks. But the two men also wear orange armbands, since they're refs and we're lowly linesmen.

Ryder and Troy Talvo round out the group. As assistant coaches, they had the difficult task of helping Garrett and Jake select today's two teams. Ryder said they chose the players based on their strengths and weaknesses, having worked with them all week.

Garrett is about to give us instructions when his gaze sharply veers toward the home bench. "Hey, G," he calls. "Hold up. I want to talk to you before you go!"

"Oh shit, I didn't realize they were leaving. Give me a sec too." Ryder pushes off on his blades, skating after his father-in-law.

Gigi waits for them at the bench, leaning over the side to give Ryder a quick kiss before turning to speak to her father. She's not alone—a girl with light-brown hair wanders away from Gigi toward the other bench to speak to some of the boys. She's wearing cutoff shorts and a black tank top that bears her midriff, and there isn't a single teenage boy on that bench who isn't checking her out.

As we wait for Garrett and Ryder, Will and I awkwardly stand with our fellow refs while I try not to leer at John Logan's shoulders. They're enormous. How is he still so fit at his age? I mean, okay, he's not ancient. Early forties maybe. But still. The man is in better shape than a lot of guys my age.

"You're late," Dean hollers at yet another newcomer.

A man with auburn hair skates over, his blades hissing as he comes to a stop. He rolls his eyes at Dean. "Calm yourself. I'm not even reffing. Just here for the entertainment." Noticing Will and me, he smiles. "Hey. I'm Tucker."

"Shane," I say, reaching to shake his hand. "This is Will."

"Did you guys all play together in college?" Troy Talvo asks, gesturing between the three men. "I heard Garrett say something like that."

"Briar hockey, baby," Dean confirms, flashing a perfect white smile. "We were unstoppable."

Logan nods, blue eyes gleaming. "Back-to-back Frozen Four wins. Damn. That was something, huh?"

"That's our plan for this season," I tell the men. "We killed it last year, so now we—"

I startle when Logan suddenly growls. "Nope. No fucking way, Dean. This is not fucking happening. Go get your boy."

I follow his gaze and see Beau Di Laurentis hugging the girl in the crop top. They're clearly happy to see each other.

"Chill. It's just a hug," Dean replies, unbothered.

"His hand grazed her lower back."

"His hand didn't graze shit."

Logan's tone remains deadly. "It's not happening. I'm not letting a Di Laurentis corrupt her."

"He's only sixteen, and he's not doing anything."

Trying not to laugh, I interrupt their heated exchange. "I take it that's your daughter and that's his son?" I ask Logan.

"No, that's my daughter, and *that* is his future fuckboy."

"I mean, the kid's old enough to already be one," I hedge, while Will snickers softly.

Logan glares at me. So does Dean.

"Sorry." I hold up my hands. "It's true. Sixteen is old, bro. I mean, when did *you* lose your virginity?"

"I didn't," Dean says primly. "I've never had the joy of laying with a woman."

Will, Tucker, and I start laughing, but Logan's expression lacks all traces of humor.

"I was fourteen." He's visibly upset. "Oh, for fuck's sake. Why did we ever have a child? We *knew* there was a fifty percent chance it would be a daughter."

Dean grins at Logan's dramatics. "Relax. Look—Blake's hugging AJ now. Go bother Connelly."

"My daughter will never date a hockey player," Logan says ominously. "I know what they're like."

"What about you?" I ask Tucker. "Any daughters in danger of being corrupted?"

He drags a hand over his reddish beard, snorting loudly. "My girls would eat these boys alive."

"Heartbreakers, the both of them," Dean agrees.

Garrett and Ryder rejoin the group, and we go over the game plan.

"All right, so you're aware of what to call and what not to call?" Graham asks the refs.

"Only call penalties against my kid. And let him punch people in the teeth if he wants," Dean says with a straight face.

We all snicker.

"Yeah, we're going to do the opposite of that," Connelly says with a sigh.

"How aggressive are we allowed to let it get?" I ask them.

"As aggressive as you want as long as it's within the rules. A few of these boys are headed right for the NHL next month. We're not going easy on them."

Sometimes I wish I went that route too, but I don't think I was prepared at eighteen to play professional hockey. Too young and dumb. I wanted to get college under my belt first, before I went to Chicago and unleashed myself on the world.

Garrett claps his hands. "We're treating this as a real game. Three full periods. High pressure."

Jake nods. "Let's do it."

"Get ready to be slaughtered," Garrett tells Connelly with a big smile. "Son-in-law and I got this."

"Nah. Harvard men get it done."

"He calls you Son-in-law?" I grin at Ryder as the men skate off.

He sighs. "Yeah. Either that or Mr. Ryder."

"At least he likes you now," Will says helpfully.

"I mean, 'likes' is pushing it. Tolerates me is more accurate. But he knows I'd die for his daughter, so that's all that really matters."

The game gets underway. Part of Ryder's and Talvo's job was to organize the lines as if they were putting together their own team. Team Graham's first line features Beau Di Laurentis. Team Connelly lucked out with Jake's son AJ and Gray Davenport on the same line.

I don't follow high school hockey too closely, but even I know about this trio. They're the three best players in the country, and I heard they've all already committed to playing for Briar in a couple of years. With that kind star power on the lineup, it's going to take a lot of flukes and upsets to wrench that Frozen Four trophy out of Jensen's hands. There's a reason he's the winningest coach in college hockey and probably the highest earner. He not only recruits the greatest players, but then after they leave, he gets their kids too. Lucky bastard.

It's so much fun to watch these boys play. They remind me of myself when I was a teen. The sheer determination. The grit. The balls to make risky plays before your collegiate coaches discipline that recklessness out of you.

Right off the bat, it's obvious that Beau possesses the overall skill. Puck protection, stickhandling, shooting. His instincts are incredible, and I'm floored by his ability to keep a cool head under pressure. AJ has the speed, though, like his old man. And while Gray's dad played forward in his days, Gray is a deadly defenseman. He doesn't let Di Laurentis anywhere near the net on any of his shifts.

I'm starting to think Graham's team is going to take the drumming of a lifetime, but I've underestimated Ryder and his father-in-law. Connelly and Talvo's strategy was to pack the first line with all the superstars. Graham and Ryder, on the other hand, assigned a superstar to each line, so there's always one great player on the ice at all times.

When Connelly's first line leaves the ice, Graham's second-line superstar scores a goal the moment Davenport is off the ice.

Will and I are on opposite sides, keeping a vigilant eye on the state of play. At one point, I blow an offside whistle on Connelly's kid. Connelly almost lunges out of the bench toward me, coach and hockey dad rolled into one. I've seen many of them, red-faced and screaming, on the sidelines during my own high school games.

"He was over the line, asshole!" Connelly growls at me.

I skate over politely. "One more outburst from you, and I'm throwing you out of this game, Coach."

Oh my God. I can't believe I got to say that to Jake Connelly. This is the greatest day of my life.

He harrumphs but is befittingly shamefaced.

"You can't go calling people assholes," I hear Talvo reprimanding Connelly afterward, and I smother a laugh. "We're Harvard. We're better than that."

"Sorry, lost my head."

The game remains at that level of intensity all the way until the last second of the third period. Team Graham's spread-the-love strategy pays off—they win 3–2, courtesy of a game-winning goal by Beau, who demonstrates why he has the reputation for delivering in clutch situations. Beau's dad skates over and throws an arm around his shoulders, saying, "Atta boy."

I skate to the bench and check my phone, but my dad hasn't responded to any of this afternoon's texts, not even the photo of Graham and Logan laughing so hard they're almost falling over. It makes me furrow my brow because Dad never takes more than an hour or so to text back. I shrug it off, though. Maybe he and Mom are just busy with Maryanne.

Ryder breaks away from the other coaches and skates up to me and Will. "Garrett and the others are taking us all out for drinks," he says. "You two in?"

Will and I gawk at him.

"What?"

"What the fuck kind of question is that?" I say. "Of course we're in."

"Idiot," Will mumbles.

I glance at Will. "You've gotten a lot meaner since you started bro'ing out with Beck. I love it."

He smiles. "Thank you."

CHAPTER TWENTY-THREE
DIANA

Do you want me to take it out?

AT ELEVEN THIRTY, SHANE BARRELS THROUGH MY OPEN DOOR BEFORE I can even invite him in. Which I wasn't planning to do because it's late Thursday night and I'm in the middle of an *FoF* marathon. I'm two episodes behind.

"I'm drunk," he announces.

I gape at him as he brazenly breezes into my living room. He's wearing cargo shorts and a tank top, and for some reason, he's holding a brown paper bag in his hands.

"You realize you don't live here, right?"

"I *should* live here," he says nonsensically.

His brown eyes drift toward the TV screen, which is paused on Donovan's sleazy British face.

"Sweet. Let's do this. We need to catch up before Saturday."

I press my lips together to stop a laugh. "Why's that?"

"Because Saturday is a Sugar Shack release. *Super* important." He cocks an arrogant brow at my expression. "That's right, I know the lingo now. And you know what? I'm not ashamed to say I like this show. It's entertaining. The women are hot. And some of the dudes are hilarious. Like the Connor. There isn't a single episode where he doesn't have me in hysterics."

It's a struggle not to fall on the floor laughing. Shane's drunk, all right. No way would he admit any of this sober.

"And *look!* I even picked up refreshments. *And* I had to walk into the liquor store with *John Logan* and ask the clerk for assistance because I couldn't find this on the shelf. I looked like a total loser. John Logan laughed at me, Dixon. Because of *you.*"

With a flourish, he removes a bottle of the Pink Stuff from the paper bag.

Surprise flickers in my eyes. "You stopped to buy my favorite drink?"

"Only the best for my fake girlfriend."

A smile creeps onto my face despite my resistance. Damn it. I hate to admit it, but this jackass is growing on me.

"Fine," I relent, taking the pink bottle from him. "I'll get us some glasses."

As I walk to the kitchen, Shane ambles toward the fish tank. "What's up, Skip?" he greets the goldfish. "Hey, Dixon," he calls over his shoulder. "Are we sure he's in good health? He looks fat."

"Oh, he's in terrible health. He's on diet food."

"There's diet fish food?"

"Yeah, I have to special order it from some weird lady in Florida. She makes it herself. But it doesn't matter what I do to try to help this asshole. He doesn't lose weight."

"Aww, leave him alone. He's just a husky boy who loves his pirate's chest."

I grin when I see Shane peering into the tank, his face pressed up right against the glass.

"He's got, like, dead eyes."

"I know. It's very unnerving." I carry two wineglasses filled to the brim with pink liquid and set them both on the coffee table. "How was your hockey thing?"

"Legends, Dixon. I spent the whole day and night with *legends.*" He sighs happily. "It was fucking spectacular."

"I'm glad you had a good time." I reach for the remote. "All right. There's a selection ceremony at the end of this episode. Any predictions about who Marissa is going to choose?"

"One hundred percent Steven."

"Hate to break it to you, but she's totally making a play for Connor."

"No way. Zoey's too beloved. You can't be the person to send Zoey home and expect to win a single vote in the finale. Even Marissa's not that dumb. I'm sticking with Steven."

I sip my drink and focus on the screen. About ten minutes in, Ky and new boy Juan get to spend the night in the Sugar Suite.

And I'm not going to lie.

It gets hot.

I gulp down some more alcohol as the couple starts making out on a white bed adorned with rose petals. There's no actual nudity, but we catch tantalizing glimpses of Ky tossing her lacy red bra onto the floor. Juan sliding her thong down her tanned legs. Juan's boxers getting flung across the suite.

A second later, the couple is under the duvet, and it looks like he's operating a jackhammer in there.

"That's ferociously fast," I remark. "And they went from kissing to super penetration in five seconds. Where's the foreplay?"

"What's super penetration?"

"*That.* The entire bed is shaking. How is this fun for her? There's no way this girl's having an orgasm."

"I don't know. Maybe she asked for it. Maybe she was like, *Don't go down on me, Juan. I need to be pounded, preferably at a speed of sixty miles an hour, in order to come.*"

I burst out laughing, nearly spitting my drink all over the couch.

"What about you?" Shane asks curiously.

"What about me?"

"What gets you off?"

"Nope." I set down my glass. "We are not talking about this."

"Why not?"

"Because we're in a fake relationship. We're not friends who talk about their kinks."

"I think we should reevaluate your fake-girlfriend duties."

"My only duties are to make you appear somewhat palatable to your ex-girlfriend."

"Oh, fuck off." He polishes off the rest of his drink and leans forward to refill his glass.

"You're hitting the pink stuff pretty hard," I say, lifting a brow.

"I'm already drunk. What's a bit more drunker?"

"Was that English?"

Shane's not paying attention to me anymore. "Holy shit, did this chick *really* just tell the Connor that she can make him happier than Zoey? Swear to God, if she picks him, I'm gonna—shut up, Dixon! Shut up. Jeff's about to pick."

"I'm not talking. You're the one who's talking!"

I can honestly say that Drunk Shane might be my favorite Shane.

We cheer when Jeff picks Leni, breaking her bond with Donovan. Then it's the moment of truth. Marissa, the brunette who's shaken up the hacienda, stands and smooths out the bottom of her white minidress. The camera pans from Steven's face to Connor's. They're the two guys she's been talking to the most and the two guys in the most solid relationships.

"If Steven's picked, you and I become friends with benefits," Shane pipes up. "If it's the Connor, I go home and jerk off."

I snort. "Either way you go home and jerk off, sweetie."

"I have no loyalties here," Marissa tells the group. "I came in here knowing I was going to ruffle some feathers. Tonight, I have to stay true to my heart and choose the person I think I have the strongest connection with. So, the boy I want to walk the path to forever with is…" The music grows dramatic. "…Connor."

Shane growls in outrage as Zoey's heartbroken face fills the screen.

"I told you," I say with a sigh.

The host of the show addresses the group in her crisp British accent.

"Zoey and Donovan, your bonds have been broken. You will join the other singles in the Sugar Shack. I'm sorry, but it was just a fling. The rest of you are still on the road to forever."

Shane is agape, so upset about Zoey's banishment that I can't help but reach over to squeeze his arm. Of course, he chooses that moment to move his arm, and my hand ends up in his lap instead.

Grinning, he peers down at his crotch. "If you wanted to undo my pants, you could have just asked."

I snatch my hand back. "I'm not undoing your pants."

"Would it kill you to admit that you're attracted to me?"

It might. Because I'm not attracted to men like Shane. The annoying kind. The cocky kind. I've dated athletes before, but I'm drawn to a specific personality type. Someone with a more level head. Someone more mature than me, if I'm being honest. Someone to keep me in line when my temper strikes. Shane only activates it. We'd be way too fiery together.

On one hand, that means the sex has the potential to be off-the-charts hot.

On the other hand, I'm not opening that door. Not because I'm against casual sex. Sometimes I prefer it depending on the man. But going there with Shane feels like a bad idea. He's best friends with my best friend's husband *and* he lives next door. If a sexual relationship explodes in our face—which seems quite likely judging by our clashing personalities—it'll only make things awkward, and then I'll have two people in Meadow Hill I need to avoid. It's in my best interest to resist this temptation.

"Don't you think it's time you were honest with yourself?" Shane's question drips with seduction.

I try to scoot away, but he stops me by taking my hand. His fingertips brush against mine.

"You've already kissed me thrice," he continues.

A laugh pops out. "Thrice, huh?"

"Mmm-hmm." Those dark eyes linger on me, looking me up and down. Is he picturing me naked? I have a feeling he is. "First time on a dare, second time for the benefit of your ex, third time for the benefit of mine."

"Doesn't matter what the motivation was. All that matters is the end result."

"What was the end result?" I find myself asking.

"It got you wet."

A bolt of heat spears into me.

I walked right into that one.

I swallow. "No, it didn't."

"Dixon, don't lie to me. You're better than that. I can tell from your expression that I'm right." He lets out a ragged groan. "Why do you have to be so stubborn? You want this as much as I do."

That catches me off-guard. "You want it?"

"Are you kidding? Of course I do."

My cheeks grow warm in response. "Well, that doesn't matter because it's not happening."

Frustration thickens his voice. "So there's nothing I can say or do to convince you to go into that bedroom with me? Nothing at all?"

"Nothing," I answer, pretending my mouth isn't dryer than cotton. "You're wasting your time."

"What if I kissed you?"

"You'd have to ask me first, and I don't consent."

"What if I take off my pants?"

"Well, then you'll be sitting there with no pants on."

"You're infuriating."

"Because I won't have sex with you?"

"No, because you can't admit you want to."

"It's a new sensation for you, isn't it? Rejection."

"I can handle rejection. I can't handle lies."

"You lied pretty easily to Lynsey about our fake relationship."

"You have an answer for everything."

I let out a breath. "It's not a good idea. To be honest, half the time I think you're messing with me anyway. I don't trust you. You're all over the place, Lindley. One day you're a fuckboy, the next day you want a relationship, the day after that you want to be friends with benefits. I can't trust what you say."

He's incredulous. "You really don't trust that I'm attracted to you? *Look* at this." He smooths his hand over his cargo shorts, stretching the fabric taut so I can see the erection pressing against it. "I've got a semi, and that's just from you arguing with me."

I almost choke on my tongue. That's a semi? God, I was right. His generous penis is way more than generous. What's bigger than generous? Considerable? Substantial?

"You like what you see," he says knowingly.

Realizing I've been staring at his crotch, I wrestle my gaze away.

"Admit it. You want your hand to be the hand that's doing this." He cups his substantial package and smirks at me.

My throat goes arid. I cough when he starts dragging his palm up and down the length of him. "Oh my God," I croak.

"Oh my God, what? Would you like me to stop?"

I'm glued to my seat, watching him intently. And I'm not even drunk. There's no excuse for this behavior.

"Tell me to stop." Desire etches into his features as his hand continues its lazy strokes.

I open my mouth. I want to try to form the word *stop*. But no sound comes out.

"You know what I think? I think you want to know what it's like," Shane drawls.

I gulp again. "What what's like?"

"Being with someone when you're not the one calling the shots in the bedroom."

I don't expect that answer. "What makes you think I call the shots in the bedroom?"

"Your personality." He chuckles. Still stroking himself. And yeah, the bulge is even bigger now. He catches where my gaze has gone and arches a brow. "Do you want me to take it out?"

I manage to choke out the word "No."

He drags his tongue over his top lip. "Okay. We'll save that for later. Anyway, back to your bossiness in the bedroom."

"I'm not bossy in the bedroom."

He's right, though. I *do* call the shots. I like to dictate encounters, control the pace. Percy was good at letting me do that. Initially I expected him to be more dominant because of his age, but he was fairly submissive in bed. If anything, he tried to make it more emotional. Softer. Whenever I wanted it to be dirtier, he'd make me feel embarrassed for even asking.

Shane isn't going to be submissive.

And maybe that's why I'm fighting it so hard. Because he's not wrong—my entire body is on fire. I *am* wet, and my clit is throbbing. I want his mouth on me. I want his dick in me.

I cough again, squirming on the couch.

"Say the word," he says mockingly. "Say the word and I'll give it to you."

Somehow, I manage to regain my faculties. "No."

After a long, strained silence, he curses in frustration. "Fine. Then if you'll excuse me, I'm going to go next door and take care of this."

"Fine," I echo weakly.

And I stay rooted in my seat and let him go.

CHAPTER TWENTY-FOUR

SHANE

Anything is a tango thing if you make it so

"Don't forget—the tango isn't a dance," Diana explains, resting both hands on her slim hips. It's raining outside, so we're rehearsing in the Meadow Hill gym. Which normally wouldn't be a problem, but the same way I now attract an audience in this damn gym, so does Diana apparently.

We've got three dudes here pretending to work out, which means three pairs of eyes glued to Diana's ass as she saunters off to grab a bottle of water. She and I have set up camp on the mats where I usually do my deadlifts. We're in perfect view of Ralph, who's using the treadmill at the end of the row, walking impossibly slow. Liam Garrison is playing the role of "man who bench presses." And rounding out the trio is Dave from Weeping Willow, who's spent less time rowing on his machine and more time watching Diana stretch.

I don't blame them. Her ass looks incredible in those skintight shorts. And although her sports bra offers some padding, it doesn't stop her breasts from jiggling whenever she moves. Everything about her is worthy of ogling. Her bare stomach. Tanned skin. Hair in a high ponytail.

She's utterly edible. And I want to take a big bite.

"Lindley, pay attention."

I snap out of it. "The tango isn't a dance. Got it." I pause. "Wait. So what is it, then?"

"It's a promise."

"A promise of what?"

"The best sex of your life."

Damned if that doesn't make my groin clench.

"You're dancing, but really, you want to be in bed. But you can't, so you have to let out all that sexual frustration on the dance floor."

She's preaching to the choir. Sexual frustration has become the story of my life. Because of Diana Dixon, of all people. We've been rehearsing the tango every night this week, and it's getting more and more difficult to have her body so close to mine and *not* take her clothes off.

I picked up the tango steps a lot faster than I did with the cha cha, so rehearsals are kicking into next gear. It isn't long before we're in position, marching up and down the gym mats in a routine I'm quickly becoming proficient at.

"And one, two, three, four, five-six, seven, eight. One, two, three, four, five-six, seven, eight. Perfect. Nice, we *got* this. Make sure you're a bit quicker on the fifth count."

Tango is a walking dance. In theory it sounds simple, but it's more difficult than it looks. You need to bend your knees a lot. It's very bendy.

"Oh my God, Shane, you're doing amazing!"

"You're such a cheerleader," I grumble, but I'm not really complaining.

Confession: doing this with Diana is fun. She's an endless well of gusto. A bundle of energy. She doesn't stop, and I sort of love it when the cheerleader in her comes out. This woman just pumps you up. If I suffered from low self-esteem, I'd hire her to follow me around and boost me up all day, telling me how remarkable I am.

And another confession: I like to dance.

Sure, I still can't get my hips to move exactly the way Diana wants them to, but I've always had rhythm, and I feel this dumb tango music in my blood as I lead Diana forward, then slide my hand over her upper back and dip her.

I wish we could do some cool lifts, but when I raise the idea again now, Dixon says it's not really "a tango thing."

"I think anything is a 'tango' thing if you make it so," I retort. I twist around to the ever-present camera. "Back me up here, guys."

"Do not back him up," Diana says, angrily pointing at the tripod.

We're not filming live, but it's unsettling to think that this video will be seen by hundreds of thousands of people. Since our first viral video, Ride or Dance's follower count soared from a measly 100K to over 450K. We've had three more posts with a million-plus views, and Diana's been gushing about the ad revenue.

"We need to stick to the routine. It scored perfect tens from the judges on *Dance Me to the Moon*," Diana says, naming the reality show she's been stealing choreography from.

"Yeah, but we don't want to copy it completely. Let's think outside the box. One lift," I beg. "Please?"

She caves. "Fine. Let's try it. We'll do those same two slow beats for a count of four, and on the quick five-six, you can lift me."

"I like where your head is at." I nod in approval.

Diana raises her arms to tighten the elastic of her ponytail, which draws my focus to her breasts in that neon-pink sports bra. She wears a lot of neon. It suits her. And those perky tits suit her too. She's like a sexy little pocket rocket.

I don't mind that she's still pretending she's not attracted to me. I need someone who will make me work for it a little. I'm a man who loves a chase. But I hate that the ball's entirely in her court. I made it clear the other night that I was down for...anything. Literally anything. But Diana's too stubborn for her own good. I have no idea what it will take to win her over. She just needs to, I don't know, swallow her pride. And then swallow my dick.

I choke on a laugh.

"What are you all giggly about?"

"Nothing."

Diana narrows her eyes. "Are you having impure thoughts?"

"Of course. Me and everyone else in this gym."

She glances toward the trio of men, and they all quickly swing their gazes away. Liam fiddles with the weight. Dave starts randomly punching buttons to change the setting on his rower. And that shameful Ralph, father of three daughters not much younger than Diana, pretends to be on his phone.

"All right. Let's do a practice lift," Diana says. "I want to gauge the height we should aim for." She moves to stand in front of the wall of mirrors. "Come behind me."

Yes, please.

I step up behind her.

"Hands on my waist."

God, why are we wearing clothes for this?

I swallow through my dry mouth and obey her, planting both palms on her hips.

"No, like this." She covers my hands with hers and drags them an inch lower. "You need to lift me from here. It's a more stable base. Okay, on the count of three, lift straight up. Not too high."

I do what she says, holding her suspended in the air, and we examine ourselves in the mirror. Her arms are extended, legs together, toes pointed downward.

"Good form," I say.

She laughs. "Stop talking shit."

"Actually, *excellent* form. And check out this landing technique," I rave after I set her down.

"Let's do it again, weirdo. I want to see something."

I grip her hips and heave her up.

"Don't put me down yet." She looks thoughtful as she studies our reflection.

I admire her flat stomach and the perfect lines of her body. The way my fingers curve perfectly around her waist. My cock twitches behind my joggers.

"Is it just me, or are you picturing us naked too?" I ask the mirror.

Diana groans. "Oh my God. Put me down." She slides down my body, and I don't know if she does it on purpose, but her ass presses against my dick in a torturous glide. "This is important. We're filming in a week."

"I think we could film it now and we'll do okay."

"'Okay' is not going to cut it." She gasps. "Are you trying to sabotage us? Are you a saboteur?"

"I'm not a saboteur, you fucking psycho. All I'm saying is, I think we're decent enough to show the judges we're not going to embarrass their stupid organization. Isn't that the whole point of this audition? Because a bunch of ballroom snobs got pissy that all these shitty amateurs were entering their precious competition?"

"Yes, but that doesn't mean I'm half-assing the audition. We don't take chances with dance."

"Dance is all about risk-taking." I turn toward the camera. "Back me up, guys."

"Do not back him up," she orders. "Dance is about discipline. And passion. Passionate discipline."

I stare at her. "Why are you like this?"

She ignores that. "Let's run through the entire routine one more time and then call it a night."

For the last time this rehearsal, we run through our tango routine to the music pouring out of Diana's external speaker. By the time we get to the final dip, we're both breathing hard. We finish to a smattering of applause. I look at our audience consisting of three men who just want to bone Diana and give them a little bow.

"Thank you, kind gentlemen." I walk to the bench where I threw down my towel and wipe down my face. Diana does the same. Her neck is arched as she dabs her towel over the sheen of sweat on her cleavage.

I notice Ralph's eyes glaze over.

"Dude," I reprimand, "you have three daughters. Show a little respect. Or discretion."

He sheepishly hurries out of the gym.

"Dinner and *FoF* tonight?" I ask Diana when we're back in Red Birch. It's sort of our routine now.

"Can't. I'm grabbing dinner with Will."

A frown touches my lips. "You're going out with my teammate?"

"Yes."

"And I'm not invited?"

"No, it's a him-and-me thing."

I don't know why, but that makes my shoulders tense. "But I'm your boyfriend. Is he trying to take you on a date?"

"Of course not. We're friends."

"But I'm your boyfriend," I repeat.

"My fake boyfriend," she corrects.

"*He* doesn't know that." I scowl. "Why is Will asking you on dates?"

She stops outside the door of 2A. "He asked me, as a friend, to have dinner with him tonight. It's not a date, and I am the most loyal fake girlfriend you will ever have. I fake love you, Shane. I want to fake marry you and have your fake babies. Okay?"

I glare at her. "Uncalled for. I can't believe you brought our fake children into this."

"Why are *you* like this?" She huffs out a breath. "I'll see you at rehearsal tomorrow."

She leaves me in the hall staring at her closed door.

I unlock my own door and stomp into my apartment, not quite sure why I'm so riled up. Am I annoyed that Larsen might be making a move on a woman he believes is my girlfriend? Or am

I bothered that Diana is choosing to hang out with him tonight instead of me?

Motherfucker.

I think it's the latter.

I think this unpleasant sensation slogging through my veins is jealousy.

What if she decides she actually likes Larsen and wants to date him for real? My brain has finally reconciled with the fact that I might be a tiny bit interested in starting something up with her. Fine, not a tiny bit. Ever since I accurately guessed her kinks, I haven't been able to stop thinking about fucking her.

I saw it in her eyes, how badly she wants to relinquish control, and that intrigues me to no end. I've never met a woman who might want to explore that kind of stuff with me. Lynsey sure didn't. But Diana wants a guy who will take charge. Someone who can fulfill her darkest, dirtiest fantasies.

Why the hell should Will Larsen get to explore that with her?

Nope.

If anyone is getting that honor, it's going to be me.

CHAPTER TWENTY-FIVE
DIANA

You win

> Turns out the restaurant has a dress code now. Wear something semi-fancy.

WILL THROWS ME THAT CURVEBALL TWENTY MINUTES BEFORE HE'S supposed to pick me up. Men! How does he expect me to make myself look "semi-fancy" in the span of *twenty minutes*?

Sighing, I ditch my jeans and halter top on the bed and approach my closet to find something more suitable for a nice dinner. I flip through hangers until I find a shimmering red dress. I slide the smooth fabric off the rack and wriggle into it, then put my hair up in a neat bun and apply some red lipstick that perfectly matches the dress.

There. Semi-fancy.

Will picks me up, looking hot in a white button-down shirt and black trousers. His brown hair is shorter than the last time I saw him, giving him a more boyish vibe.

"Jesus." He whistles as I slide into the passenger side. "I really hope Lindley didn't see you leave the house looking like that. Otherwise, he'll think I'm taking you out on a date and kick my ass."

"He already thinks it's a date," I answer, grinning. "I got interrogated hardcore earlier."

We chat on the way to the restaurant, a very familiar corner location on Main Street. "Wasn't this a breakfast place last week?" I ask in confusion.

"Last month," he corrects, snickering. "Last week they were the sushi place."

I hope *this* venture sticks because we're greeted by a very appealing ambiance when we walk inside. It's a Mediterranean restaurant now, offering small, secluded tables hidden between tropical palm fronds you might find in Greece and framed photographs of Santorini and the Greek islands lining the white stucco walls. There's even a live band. Well, a guitarist and a guy softly playing the bongos. But it's still cool. I like it here now.

Will doesn't get a chance to pull out my chair—an overeager waiter appears out of nowhere to do it for him. He then seats Will too and snaps open our napkins with an elaborate flourish, handing them to us to put in our laps. We're both trying not to laugh as he ends his extravagant show by offering us a pair of red leatherbound menus.

Once he's gone, we take a moment to study the menus.

"Welp." Will lifts his head and flashes an innocent smile. "It's all Greek to me."

I laugh so loud it comes out as a snort. "Oh my God, that was so lame."

But I mean, he's not wrong. The entire menu is written in Greek. I can make no sense of the foreign characters on the page. There isn't even an English option underneath.

I purse my lips. "I think I know why this owner keeps rebranding."

"Yeah, I think so too."

We're forced to ask the waiter to translate every single item, which takes forever. Finally, we order our meals and settle back in our chairs, while soft guitar music wafts all around us. Will spends some time complaining about his father, who's been putting up a

fight about Will wanting to spend a year in Europe after graduation. I learn that Mr. Larsen is a congressman who splits his time
between DC and Connecticut with Will's stepmom. We bond over
stepmoms for a bit, as it turns out we both like ours. His parents
aren't divorced, though; his mom died when he was four, and he was
raised by a troop of nannies until his dad remarried.

Eventually, I steer the subject toward Beckett because the curiosity is eating at me.

"How's it going with Beck? He's coming back soon, right?"

"Next week."

I don't miss the way Will's features strain. "Uh-oh. The situation
is still bothering you?"

"A little. Maybe it would be different if I'd been with someone
since he left. But I haven't met anyone I vibe with."

"So your last encounter is still that awkward one where you kept
picturing Beck."

"Yup." He sounds glum.

"Okay. Well. Where are we on the arousal scale now? When you
think about hooking up with Beckett and a woman, is it less of a
turnoff? Or more?"

He sighs.

"More, huh?"

"It's all I fucking think about," he mumbles.

"Honestly, I think you're stressing way too hard about this.
Everyone has their kinks."

"Yeah?" he challenges. "What's yours?"

"None of your business."

Will grins.

"So what are you going to do when Beckett gets home?"

"I don't know."

"Have you talked to him since he left?"

The question startles him. "Sure. We text every day. He's my best
friend."

"Then don't you think you should be talking to *him* about all this? Tell him what's been bothering you?"

"Maybe."

He sounds noncommittal. Typical guy. Yes, let's keep everything bottled up instead. That's always a splendid idea.

The rest of dinner passes over decent food and some excellent conversation. I really like Will. He started off as Gigi's friend, but he and I have grown closer now that we're both in Hastings for the summer. And maybe it makes me an asshole because he's so stressed about it, but I'm all over this Will and Beckett situation. I don't know if I could ever have a threesome myself, but I can't deny the fantasy is appealing. It doesn't hurt that Will and Beck are two ludicrously attractive hockey players. I can see how any girl would be tempted to be crushed between those two hard bodies.

The waiter is clearing away our empty plates when I get a text from Shane. I expect some grumbly complaint about me being out with Will. Instead, I find a link to a document. Okay. That's weird.

I have to pee, so I decide to open the message in the bathroom. One, because it's rude to check it in front of Will, and two, because I'm afraid to check it in front of Will.

And I'm far too curious to wait until I get home.

After I do my business and wash my hands, I find a follow-up text from Shane. All it says is: you win.

I click the link and almost die laughing on the tiled floor.

It's an application.

A literal application for the position of my friend with benefits.

Hilarious headings assault my eyes. Name. Penis size. Skills—oh my God. He listed all his favorite sex positions in order of what he considers himself most skilled at, to least skilled. Reverse cowgirl is on the bottom.

My laughter bounces off the acoustics in the bathroom. If I hadn't just peed, I might actually pee myself. And yet despite the sheer absurdity of what I'm reading, I can't fight the rush of arousal that floods my bloodstream.

Under turn-ons, he wrote:

Calling the shots.
Not against being watched.

My breath catches, heat tickling the tips of my breasts. Under final thoughts, he was more articulate:

As your fake boyfriend and real friend with benefits, I take the duty of pleasuring you very seriously. I guarantee at least one orgasm per session, whether by tongue, finger, or cock.

My entire body clenches. The idea of his mouth or fingers or tongue anywhere on me makes my heart speed up.

I will worship your body, respect it, and fuck you like you've never been fucked before. Thank you for your consideration.

I stare at the screen until it times out and turns black. Jesus. I inhale a long, unsteady breath, just as another message pops up.

SHANE:

So? Do I have the job?

CHAPTER TWENTY-SIX
DIANA

Initiative

"THAT'S WHAT YOU WORE OUT WITH HIM?" SHANE GROWLS WHEN HE opens his front door.

I stay rooted in the doorway. "Yes."

"And you still insist it wasn't a date?"

"It wasn't. We just went to a nice restaurant."

Shane can't take his eyes off me. "Please tell me that's the dress you're wearing for our audition video."

"No, that one is sheer so you can see the leotard underneath."

"Fuck," he groans. Then he notices I haven't moved an inch. "Are you coming in?"

I don't budge from the threshold. "Not until we discuss the Dixon rules."

"You and your rules. Can we at least discuss them inside, so Niall doesn't voice his opinion?"

Good point. I follow Shane into the living room, where I maintain some distance between us. He's showered and changed since our rehearsal, because he smells like soap and is wearing a gray Eastwood College T-shirt and black sweatpants that ride low on his trim hips. One defined oblique is revealed, and my fingers tingle with the urge to touch it.

"Did you like my application?" His eyes are twinkling.

"It's very well written," I answer begrudgingly.

"I knew you'd enjoy it." Winking, he takes a step toward me. "So let's talk about the rules."

I take a step back. "Only one rule. Respect."

Shane is startled. "What do you mean?"

"I mean, we respect each other in all parts of this. Yes, it's just sex. No, there won't be feelings involved. But even a friends-with-benefits situation requires a level of respect. I'm not your sex toy."

He reels. "Christ. Of course not."

"And I don't want you sleeping with other people."

"I won't." Assurance rings in his tone. "I already told you I'm not interested in sleeping around anymore, and I'd never put you at any risk."

"Okay, good. Oh. And condoms," I finish.

"Obvs."

"With that said, I'm on the pill, so if we both get tested, I'm cool going without." I heave a sigh. "Because I kind of hate condoms."

He groans again. "Are you seriously standing there telling me how badly you want to go bareback? Are you trying to make me ejaculate?"

"*If* there are two clean bills of health," I reiterate.

He tips his head. "What was your favorite thing in the application? What made me stand out as a candidate?"

I hide a smile. "I'm not answering that."

"Nah, I think you should. You know what I like. It's only fair I know what you like. Did anything stand out?"

I hesitate. "I *might* have liked the part about you calling the shots."

His lips curve. "Yeah. I had a feeling. Why is that?"

It's a very easy question to answer. Because in every aspect of my life, I'm always in full control. I became cheer captain in sophomore year, which is unheard of. I call the shots at practices and I run my squad like a well-oiled machine. To my dad and brother, I'm an unstoppable force of nature. I go after what I want. I throw myself 100% into every project I undertake.

This isn't to say I'm inflexible. I like control, but I'm not a control freak—I can easily give up the reins if needed. I'm a perfectionist, but I don't break down if something isn't perfect.

And when it comes to sex, there's nothing I'd like more than to be ordered around.

Respectfully, of course.

"Because I'm more often in control than out of it. And the guys I've dated never took much initiative in the bedroom," I confess to Shane.

"That's what you want to see? Initiative?"

I nod slowly.

"Okay then. Go to the bedroom," he says in a low voice. "Wait for me there."

"Wait for you," I echo uneasily, swallowing hard.

He stands there, taunting me with that tall, broad body. I can see the thick ridge of his dick straining beneath his pants. They're black, so it's hard to tell if he's fully hard. Thanks to his application, I now know precisely how big it is, and my thighs clench at the thought of him inside me.

"Bedroom," he repeats, tone sharpening.

I take a breath. Then I go to his bedroom without a word.

I examine my surroundings, eyeing the neatly made bed, soft gray area rug, and shiny mahogany dresser. I can't believe I'm doing this. Why am I in Shane Lindley's bedroom? What's wrong with me?

And where the hell is he?

I hear him moving around the kitchen. I hear running water. Is he pouring himself a glass of water? Indignation rises inside me, quickening my pulse. I worry he's playing me for a fool, but at the same time, the anticipation he's building is excruciating. There's an actual pain between my legs. A knot of agony. Everything feels hot and tight, my entire body clenching with need as I wait for him to return.

Finally, Shane fills the doorway. He watches me for a moment, eyes growing heavy lidded. Then he pulls his T-shirt off by the collar, every muscle of his chest rippling as he tosses the shirt on an upholstered chair in the corner.

"Take your hair down," he says brusquely.

I gulp again. I did not expect my night to end like this. Or that I would be following Shane Lindley's orders and not fighting back. Not arguing or quarrelling with him, or telling him to do it for me.

Without a word, I pull on the elastic that's keeping my bun secured. I slide it onto my wrist and shake my hair out. Brush it out with my fingers, so it's streaming down my shoulders.

Heat flares in Shane's eyes. He strides past me to sit on the foot of the bed, muscular thighs splayed open. "Come here."

I stand in front of him. One large hand reaches out and touches my knee, then moves higher, slipping beneath the hem of my dress, pulling the material up with it until he reveals the waistband of my thong. He dips a finger underneath the strap, tugs on it teasingly, but doesn't take it off.

He peers up at me. With the ceiling light fixture shining down on his face, I suddenly realize that his eyes aren't just brown. They're a dark hazel, deep-green flecks in his irises, like a lush rainforest at night.

I stand there silently. Waiting.

He laughs. A low, husky sound. Approval flickers in those gorgeous eyes.

"I really like this obedient Diana Dixon," he drawls.

"Don't push your luck," I warn, though my voice sounds shaky. "Or the bad bitch will be back."

"The bad bitch hasn't gone anywhere. She's right here. Dying to get fucked."

I bite my lip as a jolt of need courses through me. If you told me last year that I'd be standing in Shane's bedroom, waiting for him to issue another command, I would have laughed in your face.

"Take your panties off." His hand slips out from under my skirt. "But keep the dress on."

Heart pounding, I slide my thong down my legs and then kick it away. The scrap of lace lies abandoned on the floor near my bare feet.

"God, you're so fucking obedient." He licks his bottom lip. "Straddle me."

I'm breathing hard as I climb on top of him. Shane plants his hands on my waist and slowly glides them upward, stopping to gently squeeze my breasts before coming to a stop at the spaghetti straps of my dress. He nudges them off my shoulders, and I shiver. His fingertips are rough, calluses rasping over my skin, as he yanks the bodice of my dress down.

He groans when he sees I'm not wearing a bra. I often don't, as my B cup doesn't always necessitate it.

"These are cute," he mumbles.

"Are you calling my boobs cute?"

His lips quirk in a smile. "What's wrong with that?"

"They're not supposed to be cute," I object. "They're supposed to be sexy. Luscious."

"Oh, trust me, they're sexy. And luscious. And perky. And fuckin' cute."

He traces the swell of each breast with his thumbs. The delicious scrape against my sensitive skin is almost too much. When his thumb drags over one nipple, I make a sound of desperation and my hips rock forward.

"Interesting," he says.

"What?"

"You're sensitive." He squeezes my nipple between his thumb and forefinger, gives it a gentle roll, and I feel a gush of moisture between my legs. Pooling there.

"*Very* sensitive," he corrects, grinning. "Ever had an orgasm from someone sucking on your nipples?"

"No, but I've gotten pretty close," I admit.

He brings his mouth to one breast and takes my nipple in his mouth, flicking his tongue over it. I swallow a moan and shift aimlessly in his lap.

"Horny little thing," Shane mocks.

He chuckles against my flesh, vibrations pulsating through my body. Then he drags his mouth to my other nipple and sucks gently, while his palms cup my breasts, squeezing.

When I'm moving too much, rocking too hard, he plants a hand on my hip to steady me. "Fuck, you're dying for it."

I have trouble finding my voice. "I need…"

"Tell me what you need," he mutters, lashing his tongue over my nipple.

"I need you to touch me."

"Where?"

"Between my legs. Please. Touch me."

My God, I'm actually begging for it. What's happening to me?

"No." Shane pats my ass. "Get up."

I slide off his lap. My knees are shaking. Pulse racing. I can feel my heartbeat in my temples. In my throat. Throbbing in my clit.

He smiles knowingly, fully aware of what's happening to my body. "Take my pants off."

My fingers tremble as I reach for his waistband. This is the hottest sexual encounter I've ever had, and I'm not even naked. *He's* not even naked—yet. He is a second later, when I pull his pants down.

I'm robbed of breath at the sight of his dick. It's as substantial as I expected it to be. And it elicits a peculiar, agitated sensation that travels through my body and throbs between my legs. I want him in me. I *need* him in me. Though to be honest, I don't know if he's even going to fit.

Shane gives his erection a slow, deliberate stroke. Then he locks our gazes and says, "Get on your knees, Diana."

CHAPTER TWENTY-SEVEN
SHANE

Ask me nicely

DIANA IS THE STUFF OF FANTASIES. MY LITERAL FANTASIES. SHE'S LETTING me order her around without a single complaint, and we both know she loves it. A flush of desire reddens her cheeks. She's still in that sexy red dress, but it's pulled down to reveal her delectable tits. I don't order her to take the dress off, though. I like that she's still half-covered. That I still haven't seen her pussy. For some reason that makes this even hotter.

She sinks to her knees. I'm so turned on, I know there's no way I'll be able to fuck her for more than three seconds if I don't take the edge off first.

"Wrap your hand around me."

She moans and does what I say. The feel of her warm fist closed around my cock is next level.

"Put your tongue on it," I mutter. "Get it nice and wet and ready for your mouth."

Another moan.

My pulse races as she begins licking the head of my cock, circling it with her tongue. Her hand moves tentatively along my shaft.

"Tighter."

She squeezes me, and I groan. Meanwhile, that obedient tongue continues to lick, making my shaft glisten.

"Your mouth, Dixon. I need it now."

I know I'm big, but fuck, the sight of her lips stretched around my dick is hot enough to make my head spin.

"Make me come." My voice is low. Hoarse from lust and thick with promise. "If you do a good job, you'll get a reward."

She releases me with a soft pop. Interest flickers in her eyes, mingling with the heat of desire there. "What's the reward?"

"I'll let you decide." I smile at her. "My tongue or my fingers."

Her breath hitches. She strokes her hand over me again. "Not this?"

"No. You're not ready for it. We're going to have to work our way up to it."

"I don't know, I'm pretty wet already."

I groan again. "Stop distracting me. Give me what I want."

She grips my dick and goes back to sucking it. Christ, she can barely get me in her mouth. Maybe halfway. So she has to use her hand too.

It takes effort not to thrust full force into her mouth. I let her take the lead, trust her to get me where I need to go. Truth is, it's not going to take much for me to blow this load. She looks so fucking incredible on her knees in front of me.

Platinum hair tousled from being tied and released.

Eager mouth sucking me up.

The little noises she's making.

Jesus.

My balls are drawn up so tight, it's like they've disappeared into my body. Every muscle is clenched right along with them. I finish faster than I ever have before. There's no controlling myself. She makes me hotter than anyone has in a long time.

"I'm coming," I warn her. I'll let her decide how she wants it.

Diana releases my cock and jerks me through the release. I groan and come on her tits. She doesn't seem to mind. She's biting her lip. Her other hand is between her legs.

"I didn't say you could touch yourself," I growl, even as I'm still releasing the last few drops of the most mind-blowing climax. It was fast and forceful, like a sudden downpour, and I'm nowhere near sated. I'm still so hard and so ready for another round.

But I made her a promise.

Diana rises to her feet, her dress around her waist. I pull the fabric down her legs and then throw it away.

"On the bed," I tell her.

She scrambles for the mattress. I have a feeling this is the only time I'll ever see Diana Dixon submissive, and I'm going to enjoy every last second of it.

Still breathing hard, I stroke my dick. There's still a drop of come on the tip, and I rub my thumb over it as I rake my gaze over Diana's naked body.

"Tongue or fingers?" My voice is raspy.

"Tongue," she says.

"Good choice."

I kneel at the foot of the bed and run both hands over her smooth legs. She shivers when I stroke her calves and shins before gripping her ankles to pull her body forward so her thighs are inches from my face.

"Ask me to lick it."

Her breath catches. I peer up to find her watching me, pupils dilated, lids heavy.

"Ask me," I repeat.

Her chest rises on a deep inhalation.

"Lick it," she whispers.

Smiling, I spread her thighs and bring my mouth between her legs. When my tongue comes out for a taste, it short circuits my brain. She's goddamn delicious. I just want to lap her up, but I can't. I need to tease her a little. I've been with enough women to know that foreplay is necessary, not optional. They need to be ready for me.

I lick her pussy while she rocks against me. We don't speak. The only sounds in the bedroom are her needy moans and my greedy ones, because her pussy is like a drug, and I need more. I slip one finger inside her, and when she clamps around me, I realize this is going to take a while. I add a second finger, and she moans so loudly, I can't stop a chuckle.

"Damn, Dixon. You want it bad."

"I know. What's wrong with me?" She sounds agonized.

I lift my head. My lips are covered with her arousal. "Nothing's wrong with you. This pussy is the rightest thing I've ever felt."

It's not difficult to guess what Diana likes. And if she's faking it, she's doing a damn good job. Breathless noises. Soft gasps. The whispered "fuck"s she chokes out when I push my fingers in and out.

I add another finger. "Tell me if it's too much." We're at three now.

She rises on her elbows and peers down at me. Her eyes are completely hazy. She bites her lip as she watches what I'm doing to her. As I slide that third finger in and push it into an impossibly tight space.

"You take it so good, baby. I can't wait to be inside you."

She moans.

"You're going to come for me now, okay? When you give me this orgasm, I'll give you my cock."

She sucks in another breath. "I'll try."

"That's my girl."

I gently thrust my fingers inside her and bring my tongue back to toy with her clit. I know she's getting close, but she keeps squirming and moaning in agitation, not getting where she needs to go.

Remembering the near violent jerk of her body when I sucked her nipples, I reach a hand up to give one of those puckered buds a tight pinch. And Diana goes off like a rocket. She comes with a gasp, and I find myself grinning against her pussy as she takes every ounce of pleasure I have to offer, grinding herself on my face.

By the time I withdraw my fingers and lift my head, she's panting hard. Her pussy is swollen and glistening.

"There you go," I murmur in approval. "You did such a good job."

My cock is like an iron spike. I leave her on the bed, blissed out. Her eyes track me as I retrieve a condom and roll it on. She watches as I rummage in the top drawer.

"What are you looking for?"

"We might need some lube."

"Trust me, we don't." She laughs weakly. "Just get over here already."

It's the only order she's issued since this wildly erotic interaction began, so I let her have this one. Besides, she's not wrong. I tease one finger through her slit and discover she's dripping wet.

"That orgasm wasn't enough?" I grin at her. "You almost crushed my face."

"Nowhere near enough. I'm dying to know what it's like to come around *that*." Her gaze is glued to my erection.

I climb onto the bed and cover her body with mine, my lips coming down to kiss her. But I don't get inside her yet. I'm trapped between her, throbbing, my dick seeking an outlet, hips moving to find it. Our tongues tangle as I drive the kiss deeper. She's a phenomenal kisser. And those noises. I can't get enough of those noises. I'm not a fan of over-the-top porn-star moans and shrieks. Diana doesn't do any of that. She's vocal, but it comes from the most primal place.

I grab a pillow. "Lift your ass," I say, and slide it under her. I know from experience it's the best way for her to take me in this position.

I grip my dick and tease it into her pussy. Even an inch has us both sweating. I push another inch in. She looks like she wants to crawl out of her skin.

"Fucking hell, Lindley. Give me more."

"Ask me nicely."

Heat flares in her eyes. It's the first time she's challenged me. "I want it now."

"This isn't your show. It's mine. If you want to come, you have to ask me very nicely to put it inside you. Ask me for another inch and say please."

Her throat dips in a swallow. "Give me another inch, please."

My lips curve in a smile. Having Dixon submit to me is the hottest thing that's ever happened in my bedroom.

I give her another inch, and she lets out a happy breath.

"Another one," she begs.

"Yeah? You want more of this?"

"Please."

Very slowly, I push in. "Halfway, baby."

"Half!" She groans. "Oh my God. I already feel so full. How are you not all the way in? Give me more."

I give her more.

"More. Please, Shane."

Every breathy plea does my head in. I push forward, not with my entire length but deep enough that I feel her around me like a tight glove. Enough that it rolls her eyes to the top of her head and has her clinging to me. She starts rocking.

"Slowly," I warn. "Get used to it."

"I'm used to it," she says stubbornly.

"Dixon—"

"Fuck me. Please. Please, Shane, please."

Diana Dixon is begging me to fuck her. I never would've imagined this last year, when she was mocking me about my fuckboy ways, vowing she would never have me. Well, she has me now. She has all of me. Well, almost all of me.

I'm not going to lord this over her, though. This isn't some sort of humiliation fetish. This is about making her feel good. Taking control so she doesn't have to. Showing her that her pleasure matters to me as much as mine.

I go slow despite her pleas. Because the buildup is everything. Deep, measured thrusts. Her fingers dig into my ass, and her teeth bite into my shoulder.

"You're a feral little thing," I grunt.

She responds by biting me harder. The sting of pain triggers another bolt of pleasure. I speed up. Yeah, the train has left the station. I can't control the pace anymore. No one's in control but my hips and her pussy swallowing me up.

But I still have some willpower left in me. "Are you going to get there again?" I grind out. I'm wound up tight. So hard for her.

"I think so. Keep hitting that spot."

I angle my hips. "This one?"

"Mmm-hmm. Yes. Right there. Don't stop."

I pound into her. My body is on fire. Heart thundering. I'm officially in the danger zone. That point where a woman tells me *not* to stop what I'm doing because she's about to come, which means *I'm* about to come, which means soon I'm going to stop exactly what I'm doing because I'm too far gone.

I hold off as best as I can, trying to think about anything but the fact that her pussy is about to spasm around me. I kiss her, biting back a curse when she nips at my lower lip. *Fuck.* My willpower shatters, and I hope to God she comes too because I'm done. Pleasure explodes inside of me. I shudder, tempo abandoned, as the orgasm is ripped from me.

I'm a destroyed and demolished mess, panting hard. I collapse on top of her and feel our hearts beating in unison. A fast, throbbing rhythm.

I growl in her ear, "Please tell me you came."

Her breathless laughter vibrates against my chest. "Yes."

"Thank God." I roll us over and pull her warm, pliant body on top of me. "That was the best fake sex I've ever had," I tell her, and she laughs even harder.

FWB APPLICATION

NAME	Shane Michael Lindley
HEIGHT	6' 1½"
DICK	9"
JOB TITLE	Friends with Benefits for Diana Dixon
WHY I WANT THIS JOB	I would like to have sex with you

EXPERIENCE

Lost virginity at age 16 and have been diligently using my penis ever since

STRENGTHS	Tongue, fingers, cock. Stellar dirty talk
WEAKNESSES	I provide too many orgasms. I create soreness due to large penis size
TURN-ONS	Calling the shots. Not against being watched
TURN-OFFS	Sharing

FAVORITE SEXUAL POSITIONS + SKILL LEVEL AT SAID POSITION:
(1 = decent, 5 = excellent)

Missionary (5)	Spooning (4)
Doggy-style (5)	Lazy Dog (4)
Cowgirl (4)	Reverse Cowgirl (1)

FINAL THOUGHTS

As your fake boyfriend and real friend with benefits, I take the duty of pleasuring you very seriously. I guarantee at least one orgasm per session, whether by tongue, finger, or cock. I will worship your body, respect it, and fuck you like you've never been fucked before. Thank you for your consideration.

CHAPTER TWENTY-EIGHT
DIANA

September sausage fest

I slept with Shane Lindley, and I don't regret it.

Because sex with Shane is sort of incredible.

Fine, no sort of about it.

Hands down, it was the best sex of my life. And now that this orgasm ball is in motion, I can't stop it from rolling all over me. We've slept together every night for the past three days, although I've drawn the line at staying over because I'm not about to cuddle in bed with Shane Lindley like an actual couple. I'm strictly using him for…well, for so much, I've lost count.

I'm using him as a dance partner.

As my bodyguard for Percy.

As a dick provider.

Oh, and he's a better reality show watcher than Gigi. He actually catches all the episodes. Gigi claims she doesn't have time to watch an episode every single night because what kind of show requires that kind of commitment from their viewers, and to that I say *a true fan* makes the commitment. And Shane is proving himself to be a true fan. He's strangely protective of Zoey. And not even because he wants to bang her! I asked, and he adamantly insisted she's not his type.

On Sunday morning, I wake up to a familiar text. The same one I've received three days in a row now.

SHANE:

Morning sex?

I lazily type a response.

ME:

I can't. HOA meeting.

SHANE:

Oh shit. Forgot about that. Get dressed.
Meet you in the hall.

He's coming to another meeting?

I suppose I don't blame him. There's literally no greater entertainment. I look forward to these meetings the way I imagine the bloodthirsty citizens of Rome poured into the Colosseum on alternate Sundays.

On our way to the Sycamore, I muse to Shane, "If my aunt hadn't died, I'd never know the joys of Meadow Hill HOA meetings."

"One, that's macabre as fuck. And two, after the meeting—you, me, naked?"

"No, I have to go to work. But we will definitely be naked when I get back." A groan slips out. "Oh my God, why am I like this? You and your stupid dicksand."

"Dicksand?"

"Yeah, like quicksand. But your dick is the trap, and I've been sucked into it."

"Wouldn't your pussy be the quicksand 'cause it's the one sucking my dick into it?"

We stare at each other for a moment.

"Why are we like this?" he sighs.

"I don't know, but—wait, no, don't say *we. You. You* are the weird one."

Although the way that we get one another's eccentricities is a tad unsettling. The last person I want to form a kindred weirdness connection with is Shane Lindley.

"Your ex isn't going to be here, is he?" Shane asks as we enter the building.

My stomach drops at the mention of Percy.

It seems like I only manage to keep my anxiety at bay so long as I don't allow myself to remember Percy exists. But then I see him on the path or someone brings him up, and the panic returns. In an instant, I feel that phantom pain in my eye, that suffocating tightness in my throat, and I remember I'm not the Diana I was a month ago.

I'm the Diana who lets a man hit her.

"Dixon?" Shane is oblivious to my inner turmoil.

"Oh, sorry. No, Percy's not an owner. Renters aren't allowed to attend these meetings."

The conference room is full when we enter, but Priya saved my usual seat in the front row. I'm about to tell Shane he's relegated to the back when, on Priya's other side, Veronika pats the empty chair next to *her* and says, "Shane, I saved you seat."

I reach down and give his butt a discreet slap. "Go get your cougar, tiger."

"I hate you," he mumbles.

We take our seats, and Brenda gets the meeting going with an agenda item I couldn't care less about.

September Sausage Fest.

You'd think Shane would be as bored as I am, but to my total astonishment, my fake boyfriend and real lover becomes more animated than a teen girl gushing about her favorite pop star. He starts rambling about his favorite butcher in Boston and how if we *really* want to experience sausage, we need to talk to Gustav, who recently started selling a sweet Italian sausage flavored with fennel and garlic, which is *almost* as good as Gustav's pork kielbasa, with its savory, slightly smoked taste.

"You know what," Shane says, cutting himself off midsentence. "I think I should get added to the neighbors' group chat. I'll send all the details there."

At the head table, Brenda eyes him with suspicion. "I thought you found group chats too stressful."

"I've grown a lot since my last meeting. I feel confident I can handle the pressure of the group chat now." He winks at Veronika, who giggles.

"I'll add you." Niall speaks up, albeit grudgingly. "But only because I like a good kielbasa."

Shane grins at him. "Don't we all, my man."

Niall doesn't smile back.

Since it's impossible to get through an entire meeting without high drama, the shit hits the fan after Brenda opens the floor for concerns and complaints.

At the end of the front row, Carla shoots to her feet.

"I have a complaint. Enough is enough," she tells the board. "She needs to be banned from the pool completely!"

Nobody has to ask who "she" is.

Veronika is quick to defend herself. "What? I deserve to swim as much as anyone else."

"Do you know how she stares at my son Carl? He can't go swimming anymore, he's too anxious."

"Maybe he isn't anxious because of me but because his mother Carla is such a narcissist, she named her own child Carl." Veronika folds her arms.

Shane tries to stop a laugh but fails, so it comes out as a wheezy snort.

Carla's jaw drops. "What's that supposed to mean?"

"Come on, it's weird. We all think it's weird, right?" Veronika asks the room.

"I hate to agree with Veronika," Niall mutters, "but I have always thought that."

"Ugh!" Carla groans. "I swear, if she doesn't have limitations set on her, I'm leaving the building. I will move somewhere else. We can't live with this tramp ruining our community day in and day out."

"Carla," Brenda says, "we have no way to expel Veronika from the pool. She already paid her fine, and she hasn't broken any new pool regulations to warrant suspension."

"Okay, fine," Carla huffs. "I want to propose a new rule. Diana, can you put it in the minutes?"

"Yeah, of course." I hastily flip to the next page of my minutes notebook.

"Motion to add a formal rule disallowing whores from being at the pool."

"You know what?" Veronika screeches and lunges for Carla.

Carla screams in horror, jumping out of her chair and seeking safety behind the board members' table. But Veronika keeps lunging, and now Brenda has her hands out between the two of them. Niall gets up to hold Veronika back, but she's like a feral animal.

"That's it!" I've never heard Brenda lose control, but she's yelling at the whole room now. "The meeting is canceled today! I don't know why we can't get through one damn HOA meeting without a dire incident! Everyone, go home! Veronika, get off the freaking table!"

Shane and I shuffle outside. I have to hold on to his arm for support because I'm laughing too hard.

"I can't believe that just happened!" Tears leak out the corners of my eyes.

"I never want to move out of this complex," he says between deep, shuddering laughs.

Once we calm down, we step outside into the sunshine. The

other neighbors are also scattering, pouring out of the Sycamore and disappearing down the path.

"I think you should blow off work," Shane says. There's no mistaking the heat in his eyes.

"No. That's not how jobs work."

"Fine. Do you want a ride?" he offers.

"Thank you, but I think I'll walk. It's such a nice day."

"All right, catch you later."

He leans in and I lean back.

"What was that?" I demand.

Shane blinks. "Oh my God. I was gonna kiss you goodbye."

"Yeah, no. We're not doing that."

I'm giggling to myself as I leave for my shift at Della's. On my lunch break, I check my phone to discover some activity in the neighbors' chat. Niall, the traitor, followed through and added Shane, who's already sent a few messages. Aw, look at him participating!

I work my magic.

ME:

> Guys, Shane dropped his phone in the pool and it's completely dead. And somehow he also lost all his messages and contacts and we don't know if he'll ever get them back.

YOU HAVE REMOVED SHANE LINDLEY FROM THE GROUP NEIGHBORS.

I instantly get a message from Shane.

SHANE:

> Why won't you let me have this!!

ME:

> Because you want it too bad.

CHAPTER TWENTY-NINE
SHANE

Omigosh

"THANKS FOR DOING THIS," DAD SAYS AS MARYANNE BOUNDS INTO MY condo. She has a purple rolling suitcase in tow. Not a carry-on but a full-size one an adult would take on a European vacation for a month. It's covered with stickers brandishing ridiculous science slogans, like: UP AND ATOM!

And: SCIENCE IS MY SUPERPOWER.

And my favorite: STEMINIST IN TRAINING.

"Of course," I tell my father. "You know I love my quality time with the squirt."

Maryanne tugs on my hand. "Shane, which one is my room?"

"There's only one room, remember? And it's yours."

"Really?"

"Yep, all yours for the next two nights." I gesture to the sectional, where I've already stacked sheets and a blanket. "I'll be on the sofa."

She bounces into the room, dragging her suitcase behind her. "I'm going to unpack!" she screams.

I turn back to Dad. "How much did she pack? She's only here for the weekend."

"Yeah, your mom tried to calm her down, but she's excited to be spending the weekend with her big brother. It makes her feel very grownup."

It's my parents' wedding anniversary. They're throwing a huge party for it next weekend, but they wanted a solo celebration too, so Dad's taking Mom away for the weekend. Maryanne usually stays with our aunt Ashley when they go away, but it's summer and I've literally got nothing else going on, so I offered to babysit.

Dad leans against the kitchen counter, and when he reaches up to run a hand through his scruffy blond hair, I notice his arms appear even slimmer than the last time I saw him. He's giving me a run for my money with how hard he's working out this summer. We chat about the Hockey Kings camp, and I tell him how surreal it was being on the ice with bona fide legends.

"That'll be you next year, kid."

"I can't wait." Excitement surges in my blood. "I'll make sure you have tickets to every away game just in case you decide to fly out to one."

The look on his face is bittersweet. "I'm holding you to that. Hey, Princess, come here. Give your dad a hug."

Maryanne barrels out and wraps her arms around his waist.

"Don't give Shane too much trouble."

"I won't. And don't worry, I'll make sure he stays out of trouble too."

God, I love this kid.

After he leaves, I turn to Maryanne. "All right, what do you want to do? I thought we'd go to Della's for dinner. They have a gazillion pie options and old-fashioned milkshake glasses."

Her eyes light up. "Okay!"

"But that won't be for a couple more hours. Unless you're hungry right now."

"No, I'm not hungry. I want to make a volcano."

"What?"

"A volcano." She sports a huge smile. "Don't worry! I brought all the instructions and all the supplies."

A minute later, I understand exactly why her suitcase is so massive. At some point when Mom wasn't looking, Maryanne packed a literal arsenal. I'm talking newspaper, baking soda, vinegar, tubes of acrylic paint, dishwashing detergent, and every other ingredient and tool required for her secret project.

"Oh my God. How are you my sister?" I sigh.

"You mean because I'm way more awesome than you? I know. I wonder that too sometimes, but I don't question why God decided to give you to me."

I burst out laughing. This kid, man.

"So *why* are we making a volcano?"

"Because Daddy and I watched a really cool show last week about a *huge* volcano eruption." Her eyes go wider than saucers. "Have you ever heard of a place called Pompeii?"

I try not to laugh again. "I might be familiar with it. Why?"

"It was totally destroyed by a volcano. The eruption lasted *eighteen hours*! And it covered everything in ash. Ash people everywhere!"

"The more I get to know you, the more I think you really are a psychopath."

"They died, Shane. I can't change the past. Anyway, I really want to make a volcano. We did one in school last year and I've been dying to make another one ever since, and then we watched the Pompeii show and I asked Mom and Dad *again*, but they were too busy arguing—"

"Wait, why were they arguing?"

"I don't know. But then Mom *finally* came to my room and said we didn't have the time or the supplies." Maryanne flashes a big, toothy grin. "Well, guess who has the time and the supplies!"

Spoiler alert: it's us.

In no time at all, I'm sticking strips of papier-mâché onto a volcano we construct using crumpled newspaper and a cake tray. In the disaster zone that was formerly my kitchen, Maryanne molds our mini-Vesuvius so the top is narrower than the base, while I work hard to create the most epic reconstruction of the city of Pompeii at the bottom of the volcano. Maryanne is more artistic than me, but I think my papier-mâché trees are quite impressive. Despite what *some* people might say, they do not look like blobs.

When my phone buzzes on the other counter, my hands are too sticky, so I turn to my sister. "Can you check who that is?"

She goes to peek. "It's a text message from Dixon. Something about Zoey."

My sister quickly recites Diana's message before I can stop her, but luckily it's not R-rated.

"'Don't forget to watch foff tonight. Fingers crossed Zoey gets voted back in.'" Maryanne wrinkles her nose. "What's foff? Who's Zoey? Who's Dixon?"

"My neighbor Diana. She's just talking about this silly dating show we watch."

"You watch it?" Maryanne starts to giggle.

"Hey, don't knock it till you try it."

"Okay, I'll tell her to come over and watch it here."

"No—"

Maryanne is already typing. I have no idea what, but it's too late to stop her. She sends the text and darts back to our workstation.

My suspicions are triggered when a couple minutes later, there's a tentative knock on the door. Followed by Diana's cautious voice.

"Lindley, are you okay?"

"Yeah, I'm fine," I holler toward the door. "Why?"

There's a long pause, then, "Should I call Lucas?"

The hell is she talking about? Who's Lucas? Does she mean Ryder?

"Do you mean Ryder?" I say in confusion.

"Shane. As your girlfriend, I need to tell you, I'm very concerned."

Maryanne gasps. "Your *girlfriend*?"

"Who's in there?" Diana shouts. "Shane!"

I glower at my sister. "Go let her in, would ya?"

A moment later, Diana appears in the kitchen. Hair in a ponytail, she's wearing a white tank top and pink shorts.

Why does she always have to wear the tiniest shorts? It drives me fucking crazy. Every time she bends over in those short-shorts, it exposes nearly her whole ass. And I'm obsessed with that ass. I've had my hands and mouth all over it on a nightly basis, and I'm nowhere near sick of it.

Sex with Diana only gets better. The memory of each encounter is like a cold sip of water after a hard workout—it's so satisfying, you gotta let out a little noise. And she's been my cool cup of water for more than a week now.

I'm loving this FWB situation we've got going on. And it's not just because she's a slamming hottie, though she damn well is. But I've slept with my share of sexy women, and that by itself is not enough to keep me interested. Nah, it's that she's so sassy. I love a woman who will talk back and put me in my place. Dixon does that in spades. I never know what crazy shit is going to come out of her mouth, and I sort of love it.

"What was the Lucas thing?" I ask in confusion.

"Oh, I was trying to use a code," she explains. "If you played along like his name was Lucas, then I would know that you were in trouble. Being held hostage or something."

"Why would you think I was in trouble?"

She's already ignoring me, her gaze shifting about two feet lower. "Hi, I'm Diana. And you are?"

"I'm Maryanne. It's lovely to meet you." My sister sticks out her hand.

"The manners on this kid. I like it." Diana responds with a vigorous handshake, then eyes our project in amusement. "What are you guys doing?"

"We're recreating the Pompeii eruption."

Diana's mouth opens for a second, then closes, then opens again. "Look, I'm all for science. But isn't that a bit insensitive? A lot of people died."

"We're going to say a prayer in their honor before we erupt," Maryanne says earnestly.

I sigh. This kid is so awesome, you can't even call her out for being politically incorrect.

"Sure," Diana says, clearly fighting a smile. "I guess that makes sense."

"Why did you think I was in trouble?" I repeat, not letting it go. I walk over to the sink to wash off the gluey substance.

"Because of your text message."

I dry my hands before grabbing my phone. I laugh when I see what Maryanne wrote.

ME:

> Omigosh. Come over and we'll watch it here. Omigosh. So excited about Zoey!

Diana's response is equally entertaining.

DIXON:

> I don't appreciate the sarcasm.

"I do not say things like 'oh my gosh,' neither as three words nor one," I growl at Maryanne.

"But it saves time." My sister studies Diana like she's one of Maryanne's microscope slides. "Are you really my brother's girlfriend? He said you were his neighbor."

"I'm both." Diana turns to me for confirmation, as if to verify whether to tell the truth.

I nod slightly because my sister looks so excited at the notion, I figure we might as well let her have it. I can say we broke up after the summer ends.

"You're just as pretty as his last girlfriend," she announces. "Maybe *more*."

Diana's lips twitch. "I'm flattered. I've met his last girlfriend, and she is stunning."

"You're stunning too," Maryanne says firmly.

"Well, thank you. I think you have both of us beat, though."

Maryanne beams at the compliment and offers an even bigger one in return. "Do you want to help us with Pompeii?"

"Sure. Put me to work."

I'm not surprised in the slightest that Diana and my sister become fast friends. Our volcano ends up being a smashing success, with Maryanne's lava mixture inflicting maximum damage as it bubbles out the top and pours over the sides. The red food coloring adds an extra layer of morbid to the entire project.

Later, after Maryanne discovers that Diana is a cheerleader and teaches girls her age at spirit camp, she begs Diana to teach her some moves. Next thing I know, we're outside practicing cartwheels, which quickly evolves into Diana coercing me to show Maryanne the tango routine we filmed for our NUABC audition. We're still waiting for the results, but I have a good feeling about it.

Diana joins us for dinner, and Maryanne is tuckered out by the time we get home, claiming she wants to go to bed early. Or so I think. Apparently, she's awake enough to text our mother a play-by-play of our entire day. I know this because, ten minutes after Maryanne retires into the bedroom, I receive a message from my mother.

MOM:

> I'm sorry, my only son has a new girlfriend and I have to find out from his ten-year-old sister? And you've entered a dance competition? This is a betrayal to the mother-son code, and we will discuss it at length when you are home next weekend for the anniversary party.

Then there's a follow-up.

MOM:

> Actually, bring your girlfriend to the party.
> We'd love to meet her.

CHAPTER THIRTY
DIANA

Interesting development

"YOU DIDN'T HAVE TO DO THIS," SHANE SAYS AS WE PULL OFF THE INTER-state. It's the tenth time during our three-hour drive that he's informed me I didn't have to tag along. One might think he's the one second-guessing our weekend jaunt.

Me, I'm happy as a clam in the passenger side of his Mercedes. I *love* this car. I wish I could steal it from him. The seats are stupidly comfortable, and every time I'm in here, it smells incredible. You'd think having a hockey bag perpetually in the trunk would give it that smelly boy fragrance, but it still boasts that expensive leather scent. It's intoxicating. I vow to be well-off enough one day to afford a Mercedes.

"We both know I couldn't say no to your sister," I tell Shane.

Last weekend, Maryanne overheard Shane laughing about how his mom wanted me to come to their anniversary party, and the next thing I knew, I had this cute kid tugging on my hand and pleading, "Please come!"

Seriously, those big, dark eyes? Can't say no to them. Besides, I love a good party.

"Hey, is Lynsey going to be there?"

"At my parents' anniversary party? Uh, no." His tone is dry.

"Did your parents like her when you were together?"

"I think so." He keeps his gaze straight ahead as he flicks the turn signal. "They said they did."

The response lacks conviction. Interesting. The nosy part of me rears its head. Hopefully I can poke Shane's parents this weekend and get the real story. Because if they weren't enthusiastically welcoming the girl he dated for *four* years, then there's definitely a story to be told.

Shane gives me a sideways look. "Are you really not bothered about attending a family event with me?"

"No. Why would I be?"

"You're not nervous?"

"I don't get nervous."

He seems impressed. "Ever?"

"Nope."

Well, except for those pesky anxiety attacks that I'm apparently unable to keep at bay anymore. I thought if I just didn't think about Percy, they would go away. But lately I've been waking up to random bursts of panic. This morning, for example, I opened my eyes and the first thought that breached my mind was the memory of Percy's fist flying toward my face. They started coming at night too if I'm working the late shift at Della's. I finally had to inform my manager I needed fewer evening shifts, blaming the schedule change on my dance rehearsals.

The only saving grace about this entire fucked-up situation is that Percy has kept his distance at Meadow Hill. I assume it's because of Shane, and I'm beyond grateful to have Shane at the apartment complex...

...words I never thought I'd say in my entire life.

But if Shane weren't around, I can't imagine how excruciating it would be running into Percy on the path or at the pool. I'd be locked in my apartment, probably suffering from even more anxiety attacks than I am right now.

"When we're there, let's try to tone down all the fighting, okay?" Shane's voice draws me back to the present. "The fighting?" I echo.

"You know." He grins. "The way you're constantly bitching at me about something."

"I don't bitch at you."

"Sure you do."

"I simply point out truths that you don't enjoy hearing. It's not my fault your ego can't handle it."

"My ego is doing fine, thank you very—*this*," he interrupts himself, waving a hand between us. "This is what I mean. The bickering. My parents aren't like that. They're super chill and madly in love. They don't fight or make fun of each other."

"I don't know if that's boring or sweet."

"Nah, trust me, they're fun to be around. They're not boring. All I'm saying is, let's tone it down."

"You mean me." I fight a bristle of annoyance. "You want me to tone *me* down."

"Come on, you know that's not what I mean."

No, I *don't* know that. But whatever. It's a good thing we're not actually together because that's not something I'd ever want to hear from a boyfriend. That I ought to tone any part of my personality down. It means he doesn't love me for who I am. It means—

And *why* am I dissecting how Shane feels about me? All I care about is how good *he* makes *me* feel—in bed. And oh my God, does he know what he's doing in that department.

In fact, the only thing that "bothers" me about spending the weekend in Heartsong, Vermont, with Shane's family is that it likely means we won't be having sex.

A winding country road unfurls ahead of us as Shane drives past a blue sign that welcomes us to Heartsong. Not long after, I find myself in a literal storybook. A quaint, little town nestled between rolling hills and framed by a canopy of oak trees. The air carries the scent of grass and wildflowers into my open window.

Up ahead, I spot another sign: a vintage wooden one proudly declaring the town's name again.

"Oh my God, this is the most Vermont thing I've ever seen."

He sighs. "I know."

We cruise down Main Street, which is lined by storefronts frozen in time—a general store, a pharmacy, a cidery, a tavern. Each building is adorned with colorful awnings and ornate metalwork. When the town square comes into view, I honest to God gasp. The square features a clock tower *and* a fountain.

We pass a small park where children are shrieking with laughter and an ice cream shop that has a line down the block of hopeful patrons.

"God, it's like a quaint town ate a quaint small town and then threw up over a third quaint town to create a—"

"I get the point," he cuts in, snorting.

"Like, I'm talking nauseatingly cute. This is where you grew up?"

"Yep. I was born in Burlington, which is where my parents met. But they moved out here after they had me. How about you?"

"Not far from here, actually," I reveal. "I grew up in a small town too. Oak Ridges. It's in northern Massachusetts, right by the Vermont border."

"Oh wow, that is close. I drive past it all the time."

"My dad and stepmom live there. My mom's from Savannah, but she went to MIT and then got a job as a professor in Boston. Met my dad there."

"He's a cop, right?"

"SWAT."

"That's hardcore."

"I know. If you ever meet him, ask him to tell you some of his stories. He's been involved in two hostage crises, one where they had to shoot the hostage taker."

Shane whistles under his breath. "Shit. Did he pull the trigger?"

"No, one of his snipers did, but he gave the order. Dad says sometimes that's even harder to swallow. The knowledge that you ordered someone's death but then had someone else do the dirty work."

"Yeah, I can't even imagine."

He turns right on a residential street lined with more of those ancient trees. Sunlight filters through the leaves, casting a dappled pattern on the road. This town is stunning.

"This is us," Shane says, pulling into the wide driveway in front of a beautiful Victorian home with a wraparound porch and three-car garage. "Ready, Girlfriend?"

"Born ready, Boyfriend."

Inside, we're welcomed by Shane's parents and a Maryanne tornado who throws her arms around my waist in an ecstatic hug.

"You came!" she exclaims. "I'm so happy!"

I'm obsessed with Shane's parents from the moment I meet them. His dad, Ryan, is all jokes and smiles, and his mom is more welcoming than I expected. Usually, I'm a hit with my boyfriends' dads, while the moms grill me at every chance they get. But April Lindley, while asking the occasional prying question about my relationship with her son, treats me like a long-lost daughter from the get-go.

I feel a bit bad lying about our relationship, but the more we talk, the more I realize I'm not doing much lying. I laugh about how he annoyed me all year. How a part of me still can't believe I let him convince me to be his girlfriend. And none of that is a lie—swap the word *girlfriend* for *friend with benefits*, and that's exactly what happened.

God help me, but we're friends now. We have a TV show we watch together almost every night. We're dance partners, for Pete's sake. A fact that Shane's mom finds downright hilarious when we discuss it during dinner.

"I don't even want to know how you got that boy to agree to this," April says, giggling into her water glass.

"You must be something special," his dad agrees, grinning at me.

The Lindleys make an unlikely couple. April is elegant. Extremely put-together. She's wearing khakis and a silk blouse for a dinner in her own house. Ryan, meanwhile, gives off scruffy vibes with his sweatpants and dirty-blond hair to his chin. He looks like he should be surfing the waves, not running a successful, multimillion-dollar business.

And then Maryanne, well, she's Maryanne. She shows me her room, her science trophies, her favorite books. My head is spinning by the time she takes me to the guest room, where I'll be staying. I'm sort of relieved by the Lindley house rule: no sleeping in the same room. If I were sharing a bed with Shane, there's no way his considerable penis wouldn't make an appearance, and there's no chance in hell of me being quiet while he uses it on me. Better to resist temptation.

I deposit my weekend bag on the bed and fish out a pair of loose plaid pants and a T-shirt. Maryanne informed us that we were watching a movie after dinner, and I want to throw on some comfy clothes. Shane's making the popcorn as we speak. I also pull out my little black dress and hang it in the closet. It's what I'm wearing for the anniversary party tomorrow.

"Hey." Shane appears in the doorway. "My mom says if you need extra pillows or blankets, they're in the linen closet next to the guest bath."

"Thanks. Close the door? I want to change."

He steps in and shuts the door behind him. As I pull off my tight top and replace it with the baggy tee, Shane tips his head, his eyes gleaming with seduction.

"Do you want me to sneak in here after everyone's asleep?"

I was *just* thinking how we shouldn't have sex. Which means the answer to that question should be no.

Yet when I open my mouth, the wrong one-syllable word slips out. "Yes."

The Lindley anniversary party is being held in a large private room at a restaurant that doubles as a banquet hall. When we walk in, we're greeted by the animated hum of conversation and the inviting aroma of Italian food. The large room, with its soft lighting, earthy tones, and rustic wooden furniture, offers a warm ambiance that brings a smile to my lips. At the far end of the room is a small band playing acoustic bluegrass music.

I think I'm in love with Heartsong, Vermont.

There are about sixty people in attendance, but Shane only has time to make a few introductions before we're ushered to our table for dinner. All the tables are adorned with simple centerpieces, and we've been seated with his parents, sister, his mother's twin Ashley, and Shane's maternal grandparents.

Like I told Shane yesterday, I don't get nervous for these events. Tonight is no exception, although that could have something to do with how friendly and welcoming everybody is.

While the restaurant staff moves gracefully among the tables, Shane's family regales us with stories that have me in hysterics. Turns out Shane's parents were high school sweethearts. His grandmother tells me about the first time April brought Shane's dad home to meet her parents, how a seventeen-year-old Ryan was so desperate to make a good impression on his girlfriend's parents that he didn't want to admit his stomach couldn't handle spicy food. So when April's mom served him a five-alarm chili for dinner, he ate every last bite—and wound up a red-faced, snot-nosed, puking mess in their upstairs bathroom.

Shane's grandfather pipes up, telling me that's when he knew "the white boy was a keeper." According to April's father, you know a man truly loves a woman when he's willing to humiliate himself in front of her family.

I don't know if I'm imagining it, but I swear I glimpse sadness on Mr. Lindley's face while his in-laws tell the story. He reaches for

April's hand, and this time I know I'm not imagining the way she squeezes his hand, almost as if in warning. Yet when their eyes lock during her sister's toast, there's no disguising the love they feel for each other.

"You're lucky," I whisper to Shane as the staff begins clearing our plates. "I love my stepmom, but sometimes the little kid in me still wishes my parents had stayed together."

"Honestly, I couldn't even imagine what I would do if my folks got divorced. My whole life, they've set the bar, you know? Showed me what love is actually supposed to look like." In an uncharacteristic moment of vulnerability, Shane's voice cracks.

My heart softens at that. It's nice to see the deep love for his parents reflected in Shane's eyes. I get the feeling he has a lot more depth to him than he's willing to show. That he's more than the cocky, obnoxious hockey player who wants to get in my pants.

So of course, he has to ruin the moment by staring at my boobs.

"Stop looking at my cleavage," I scold.

"I can't help it. Like, how is there that much of it? Your tits aren't that big."

"You're not supposed to comment on a woman's breast size. It's uncouth."

"I didn't say I don't like them." He drags his tongue over his lips. "I don't discriminate. All shapes and sizes are welcome in Lindley Land."

"Ew. Shane."

He just snickers. He's incorrigible.

With dinner over, the dancing starts. The room transforms from a chill acoustic affair to a lively party, the band now playing a mixture of blues, country, and soul.

The dance floor, always a sight to behold, beckons to me. I think that's the reason I never feel out of place at parties. Even ones like this, where I hardly know a soul. As long as there's music in the air and something solid beneath my feet, I will always belong.

I'm about to pull Shane on his feet to dance when his father surprises me by asking me first.

"How about it, Diana?" Ryan offers his hand and a smile.

"Absolutely."

We join the growing group of people on the dance floor. Shane's dad curls one palm around my waist and grips my hand with the other, and we start moving to the up-tempo beat. The loud music, combined with sounds of chatter and clinking glasses, makes it difficult to hear each other, so he brings his face closer to my ear.

"You're an interesting development," he teases. "Different."

"What do you mean?"

He shrugs and spins me around, displaying some pretty decent footwork.

"Hey, you're a good dancer," I inform him, pleasantly surprised. "Better than Shane." Grinning, I cock my head. "Do you want to do the competition with me instead?"

"I certainly do not," he says cheerfully.

I laugh. "Fair enough. It's not for everyone."

"I still can't believe you dragged my son into it."

"Yeah, he's being a very good sport," I say grudgingly. Curiosity continues to tug at me. "What do you mean I'm different?"

Just saying that word—*different*—brings a slight clench of insecurity to my chest. Because I know he's right. I *am* different. I've always felt it and not only because I'm weird and have a temper.

I'm different from my family in Savannah, who view me as this outspoken, confrontational girl corrupted by the north, who doesn't know when to sit quietly and look pretty.

I'm different from my little brother, who's so freakishly smart and determined to save the world.

And I'm definitely different from my mom, who doesn't think I'm intelligent enough to be in the same room as her.

I suppose that's why I love the way my dad sees me—as unstoppable, invincible. I know there's only one opinion that *should* matter, and that's my own. But to me, the person whose lens I want to view myself through is my father's. Because his vision of me is the best one.

"You make him laugh a lot," Shane's dad says, his rough voice jolting me from my depressing thoughts.

I crack a smile. "I think I just annoy him a lot."

"That too."

"Thanks," I say with mock hurt.

Ryan smiles. "But he needs that. My boy needs the challenge." His gaze drifts across the room. "All Lindley men do."

He's gazing at Shane's mom, who's chatting with her twin and a few other women I wasn't introduced to. An uneasy feeling pricks at me when I notice the longing in his eyes. The hint of sorrow. I'm sure of it now, and I find myself praying that Shane's parents aren't having issues. They seem like such a great couple.

Ryan spins me around again. "I also notice how much more relaxed he is. Around you, I mean."

Compared to Lynsey? I want to ask.

I resist the urge. I already have the answer anyway, because I saw it for myself, how Shane acted when Lynsey was around. That night, he'd been more serious. Guarded, watching his words. I don't know if that was to impress Lynsey or to avoid angering her, but I certainly noticed a difference. I find it validating that his parents also observed his change of behavior with his ex. Or at least I suspect they did.

"I like you two together," Ryan says. "I think—"

"May I cut in?"

Shane, of course.

His dad relinquishes me without complaint, clapping his son on the shoulder before walking off. Shane takes his place, placing one arm around my waist to pull me close.

"Should we perform our tango for the guests?" I tease.

"I'd rather die."

I press my face against his chest to smother a laugh. "And you say *I'm* the dramatic one."

When I raise my head, he's once again fixated on my cleavage. Warmth spreads through me, and not just because his eyes are telegraphing how badly he wants me naked. Dancing with Shane is pretty great. He's so tall and I'm so short, so it really shouldn't work, but somehow it does. We fit together.

"What was my dad saying to you?" he asks curiously.

"Oh, you know. That I'm wonderful and he loves seeing us together and I'm the best girlfriend you've ever had."

"Yes. I'm sure he said all that. In those exact words."

"Well, he did say he liked us together. That part is true."

"You know who else would like us together?" Shane winks at me.

"Your penis."

"Exactly."

To: diana@rideordance.com
From: admin@nuabc.com

Dear Ms. Dixon,

We are pleased to inform you that your entry for this year's National Upper Amateur Ballroom Competition has been approved. You are entered in the following categories:

American Smooth Duo

American Rhythm Solo

Please see the attached welcome package for important information.

Best,
Susan Hiram
Director of Operations

CHAPTER THIRTY-ONE
DIANA

Dicksand

A WEEK AFTER MY VISIT WITH SHANE'S FAMILY, I HAVE MY FINAL DRESS fitting in Boston for Gigi's wedding. Once we're done, I go out for dinner with Gigi and her cousin Blake, another bridesmaid. Blake will be attending Briar next month, entering the freshman class, and I'm excited to have her around. Few people on this planet rival Blake Logan's sarcasm.

Since I'm drowning in ad money thanks to Ride or Dance, I decide to splurge and take an Uber back to Hastings instead of riding the bus. I text Shane as I'm letting myself into the Sycamore. We made plans tonight to celebrate the most important news anyone has ever received in the history of all of human civilization.

NUABC, bitches! Here we come.

ME:

Almost home.

SHANE:

Are you wearing a dress?

It's an odd inquiry and yet not odd at all coming from Shane.

Yes. Why?

SHANE:

Keep the dress on. Take the panties off.
Leave your door unlocked.

Those three concise sentences send a thrill shooting through me. God. I didn't realize how much I was into this. It's common knowledge that I wear the pants in my relationships.

But I adore not wearing the pants in the bedroom.

Or the panties, apparently.

Like he asked, I leave my door unlocked. Shane walks in not long after I do. He's shirtless and barefoot, a pair of worn jeans hanging low on his hips. He's so disgustingly attractive that I can't tear my gaze off him.

"Did you follow my instructions?" he asks, tipping his chin.

"Yes."

"Let me see."

Lips curving, I teasingly lift the bottom of my dress to reveal I'm not wearing anything underneath.

"Good girl," he praises.

He walks over to me, one hand curling around my waist, the other around the back of my neck as he bends down to kiss me. Our tongues meet, and as always, it sends an electric shock to my core. He cups my ass and lifts me up, and my legs wrap around him instinctively as we make out.

Slowly, he moves forward until my back is flush against the wall next to the balcony door. His hips are moving, the zipper and button of his jeans grinding over the thin material of my dress, creating delicious pressure against my pussy.

"I want to fuck you right here against this wall," he mutters in my ear.

"Do it," I beg.

I'm gasping for air. I don't even need foreplay. I'm dripping wet, and when he slides one hand off my ass and brings it between my legs, he groans loudly. He feels how ready I am.

"I forgot, I have something for you," he says suddenly.

To my dismay, he lowers me to the ground, my legs finding footing again. He reaches into his back pocket for his phone.

"Is now the time?" I demand.

"Trust me, it is."

He pulls up a photo and hands me the phone. My heart does an eager somersault. It's a doctor's report, dated two days ago. A clean bill of health.

"Look at you, chlamydia free," I tease. We've both met my requirements now. I sent him my results last week. I got tested at the health clinic when I went to renew my birth control.

"But," he says, reaching into his other pocket, "I brought a condom just in case."

He holds up the little plastic square. I take it from his hand, twist it between my fingers a couple times. Shane watches me. Then I flick it away. It plinks against a framed photograph next to the TV and falls to the floor.

Shane's eyes are smoldering. "You sure?"

"Yes."

And then we're kissing again. Now his hands are frantic, palming my breasts over my dress, slipping between my thighs again, one long finger sliding inside me.

I clench around him, crying out in pleasure before registering that the balcony door is open.

"Hold on, let's close this," I say, wrenching my mouth away from his. "Then you can fuck me against the wall to your heart's content."

"Or," he counters. His wicked gaze flicks toward the doorway. "Get on the balcony."

"What? No. We can't."

"Nah. I think we need to be out there."

My feet move of their own volition until I'm standing outside. My balcony overlooks the pool, but it's night, and nobody is out there. The Meadow Hill grounds are quiet. Other than the soft lights on the path and bluish glow from the pool, the courtyard is bathed in shadows.

"Stay here," Shane says in a low voice.

My heart rate accelerates as he steps back into my apartment. One by one, I see all the lights turning off. When he returns, he's already undoing his jeans.

"Shane," I warn. "Anyone can see us."

"Maybe before. Those lights were like a beacon. Now if anyone looks up here, it's too dark to make out what we're doing."

I swallow the anticipation lining my throat. "And what are we doing?"

Rather than answer, he lifts my dress up from behind.

"Hands on the railing."

My body is pulsating with pure need as I step forward and curl both hands over the edge of the balcony. We're only one story above, but it feels like a dizzying height from here. Or maybe I'm dizzy with desire.

Shane eases up behind me. I twist my head. His jeans are still on but undone. With one hand, he takes his dick out.

"Eyes forward," he whispers.

Swallowing again, I turn my head and gaze out at the pool. From the front, I'm fully covered. From the back, my ass is exposed to Shane's ministrations. I feel the tip of his cock gliding up and down between my ass cheeks.

He brings his mouth close to my ear. "If you make a noise, I'll stop."

Oh my God.

We're out in the open. The warm, late-summer breeze floats over us, tickling my scorching cheeks. Shane drags his dick down my ass, toward the place that's aching for him. I bite my lip hard to stop from crying out when the tip pushes inside me. He's the one who makes noise, much to my delight. A strangled groan.

"Quiet or we'll have to stop," I mock.

That earns me the sting of his teeth as he bends down to bite my shoulder. "You have no idea how amazing this feels. You're drenching my cock."

He's right, I am. This is the first time we've gone bareback, and I'm so wet. Everything about this encounter is turning me on. The night air. The fact that we're out in the open. To a passerby, it would appear like we're simply standing on the balcony with Shane behind me. Admiring the stars, perhaps.

Only I know that half his dick is lodged inside me.

He inches back, withdrawing until only the very tip hovers at my opening. Then, with an equally indolent stroke, he pushes forward, inch by inch. He does that once, twice, a dozen times. It's excruciating. The pace is sheer torment. There's nothing I want more than to buck my ass against him and fuck him hard and rough, but when I try to push back, he digs his fingers into my left ass cheek in a rebuke.

"Don't move. Just stand there and take it."

That should piss me off, but it doesn't. I *want* to take it. I want to stand here and let him fuck me. Fast, slow, any way he wants.

His lips are at my ear again. "Trust that I can take you there."

I bite the inside of my cheek. It's difficult to yield to him because I know my body better than he does. I know what I need.

But I'm wrong. Shane also knows what I need. He proves that by pushing me forward slightly, positioning me so I'm directly in front of one of the vertical railing slats.

"Bend your knees a little." His hands are still on my ass. His dick still inside me.

As I do what he says, he nudges me forward and my clit touches the slat.

I moan.

"Diana," he warns.

"Sorry." I gulp wildly.

Oh my God. Now, every time he thrusts, there's gentle pressure on my clit from the railing. This has gone from torment to pure torture. My heart is beating way too fast. I can't even hear my thoughts anymore. Not that it matters. There's only one thought left in my head anyway, and it's *more, more, more.*

He gives it to me, pulling back, then filling me nearly to the hilt, rotating his hips each time. I hear his breathing quicken. He's not even touching me with his hands. He's got both on the railing on either side of my body, his fingers next to my clenched fists.

My clit is throbbing. The next time it gets pushed into the railing, I start to feel that impatient burn of need. This is the naughtiest sex I've ever had. I want to move faster, but he asked me to trust him to get me there, so I do. And it isn't long before he's fucking me in long, deep strokes. I feel the orgasm trying to breach the surface. If he goes a little faster, just a little bit faster—

"Hi there."

I freeze. Shane goes completely still.

Down below, Dave and Marnie stroll down the path holding their tennis rackets.

Now? *Now* is the time they're choosing to go play tennis?

Fine, the courts are lit until midnight, and they are a tennis family, so I guess it's not terribly out of character. But still.

"Nice night, huh?" Shane's voice holds a rasp of gravel.

"Gorgeous," Dave confirms.

"What are you two up to?" Marnie chirps.

I'm getting fucked as we speak, I almost blurt out.

I can't decide if this is the most embarrassing thing that's ever happened to me or the hottest. My breathing quickens. Shane's dick is buried inside me. And this couple is standing below us, chatting as if I'm not about to have an orgasm in front of them.

"Diana and I were arguing about whether or not that's Orion's belt or a random cluster of stars." He points above our heads. "I think it's a random cluster. She's certain it's Orion."

Dave and Marnie crane their necks toward the dark sky.

I assumed that was a ruse on Shane's part to give him an opportunity to pull out, but he doesn't. He stays lodged inside me. His hand imperceptibly grazes my hip. I shiver. I rock back against him ever so softly and hear a muffled curse.

"Nope. Sorry, Diana, it's not Orion's belt," Dave confirms. "You lose."

No, I think I win. Because holy shit, this feels *so good*.

"Anyway, maybe we can play doubles some time," Marnie says with a bright smile. She holds up her tennis racket.

"Yeah, for sure," Shane says easily.

"Wonderful. Anyway, enjoy the rest of your night," she says, and then they meander off, moving too slow for my comfort.

Once they're gone, Shane folds his arms around my chest and walks us backward into the apartment. This time, he shuts the balcony door.

"You're evil," I accuse. "Do you think they knew?"

"Oh, they had no idea. They're the most clueless couple I've ever met in my life. Plus, I don't think they remember what sex is. I heard Dave telling Ralph in the gym the other day that they're in a dead bedroom."

"Aw, that's sad."

He looks like he's trying not to laugh. "Can we stop talking about Dave and Marnie's lack of a sex life and focus on the fact that I'm inside you right now?"

"Oh, right. I forgot." I give him an innocent smile.

That gets me a smack on the ass. He pushes me toward the couch and bends me over so I'm draped across the arm.

"Sorry, baby. This is going to be fast."

"That's okay," I say, and grip one of the sofa cushions as he starts fucking me again.

It's a punishing rhythm, hips snapping, filling me with long, deep strokes that bring black dots to my vision. My pelvis grinds against the couch. I couldn't stop the orgasm even if I tried. It's almost overwhelming, waves of release crashing into me until I'm a puddle of orgasmic mush. I hear him groan as he spills inside me. We're both gasping for air.

We stay in that position, catching our breath. God. It only gets better with this man. It's not fair. He's not supposed to be this good at sex.

Finally, he pulls out with the utmost gentleness.

"Stay right there," he says gruffly. "I'll go grab something to clean you up."

It's a reminder that we didn't use a condom, and I realize that's why my brain short-circuited. Sex without a condom hits different for me. It's just too mind-blowing.

After we've cleaned up, Shane asks if I want to get under a blanket and watch a movie, but I shake my head.

"No," I say. "We might fall asleep."

"So?"

"So we're not doing the whole spending-the-night thing," I remind him. I gesture around my living room. "This is my space." I point to the wall that separates our apartments. "That's your space." I point to our genitals. "And this is our space."

Shane snickers. "Got it. Friends with benefits. Sleeping over— not a benefit."

"Exactly."

"All right. Then I'll leave you to your own devices, Dixon. Same time again tomorrow?"

I sigh. I want to say no, but we both know I won't mean it.

I'm too deep in his dicksand.

CHAPTER THIRTY-TWO

DIANA

Bigger is better

"MY MAKEUP IS DONE. DEAD. BURY IT AND DELIVER THE EULOGY." I sigh at my reflection in the mirror.

I suppose my face didn't stand a chance, considering it just witnessed the most emotional wedding ceremony of all time. And the rampant emotions didn't even come from the bride and groom! Sure, Gigi had tears in her eyes when she recited her vows, and I swear I heard Ryder's voice crack several times, but the real emotional floodgates were opened by Gigi's parents, who both cried the entire time. Garrett Graham battling tears when he handed his daughter over to Ryder was probably the sweetest thing I've ever seen.

"Trust me, all of our makeup is ruined," Mya Bell says wryly. My gorgeous, statuesque co–maid of honor joins me at the full-length mirror, dragging a delicate finger over her smudged mascara.

"Seriously, I need a touch-up if we're going to take photos at the reception." This comes from the most beautiful woman in the world: Alexandra Tucker.

With her glossy dark hair, big brown eyes, and flawless, symmetrical features, she's a perfect ten. It's crazy that I'm just standing here, you know, next to a *supermodel*. Whenever I see these influencer models online, I assume every part of their appearance has been filtered to high heaven. With Alex, I was confident she couldn't be *that* different in person since I've seen her walk runways and that's hard to filter, but I swear she's even better in the flesh. Standing here beside her, I can't find a single flaw.

And when they say lightning doesn't strike twice, well, joke's on them. It does. Because Alex's older sister, Jamie, is drop-dead gorgeous too. Jamie inherited their dad's red hair, and her features are a bit softer than Alex's, but I honestly wouldn't want to be in the position to choose who's more beautiful. It's impossible.

Jamie stands across the room chatting with her mom, Sabrina. They're both lawyers. That Tucker gene pool is something else. Beauty *and* brains.

Molly Fitzgerald nearly knocks the two women over. She's bouncing with excitement after nailing her very first flower-girl assignment. Molly's mother, Summer, finally catches her and says, "I like the energy. But maybe we can bring it down to a five?"

"Yes, because *you're* perfectly capable of controlling your energy levels," Brenna Jensen drawls at the impeccably dressed blond. Neither woman was in the wedding party, but as close friends of the family, they're able to take advantage of the bridal suite.

There are *a lot* of beautiful women in this room. It makes me a little self-conscious. I guess Mya shares the sentiment because she pulls me aside and whispers, "Am I the only one intimidated here?"

"Nope."

She's still eyeing Alex Tucker. "Okay, good. Because this is kind of surreal."

It is. And it only gets more surreal when we arrive at the reception, which is being held outdoors on the manicured country club grounds. The entire area is adorned with delicate fairy lights that twinkle like stars in the early evening sky. Even the weather is apparently enamored with the Grahams because it bestowed them with the perfect evening. A clear, warm night without a drop of moisture in the air.

The head table sits under a wooden pergola decorated with white flowers and trailing green vines. The rest of the tables, covered in ivory silk linens and floral centerpieces in hues of sage and white, surround a gleaming dance floor.

I walk in on Beckett's arm. He's back from Australia, looking tanned, handsome, and completely fuckable in his black suit. We take our seats at the bridal party table, all our gazes focusing on the head table where Gigi and Ryder sit like royalty with her parents. Since Ryder is parentless, Hannah sits on one side of him while Garrett sits next to Gigi.

I'm gratified that I don't have to give a speech; Mya takes on the onus of charming the five hundred guests in attendance. I'm not usually scared of public speaking, but this is way too intimidating. Hockey royalty. Supermodels. Media personalities that Garrett has worked with and befriended over the years. Let's be honest—this wedding is for the parents. But Gigi loves hers enough to give them this gift after eloping, and Ryder loves her enough to give her whatever she wants.

I sit beside Shane, whose appreciative eyes rake over me. "You look so good," he mutters in my ear.

"So do you."

Seriously, he fills out that suit like nobody's business. I've been watching him work out all summer, and it shows. He's broader than he was last year. His pecs are more defined. Biceps are huge. Ass feels more muscular when I'm digging my fingers into it while he fucks me—

"Stop thinking dirty thoughts." His clean-shaven cheek caresses my chin as he speaks at my ear again. He knows me too well.

The post-dinner speeches go on and on and on and on. Every single one of Gigi's six godparents insists on coming up to the dais to say something. Ryder's half brother and best man, Owen McKay, delivers a touching speech that has everybody crying. There's no fixing this makeup. This is my life now.

Over dinner, I chat with Mya, talk to Blake Logan about her freshman schedule at Briar, and bicker with Shane.

"I can't believe this is a thing." Mya flicks her french-tipped fingers between us.

"I know, right?" Shane drawls. "She's really punching up."

"Oh, fuck off. You're the one who's punching. I'm so out of your league, it's not even funny."

"Truth," Beckett says, raising his champagne glass.

The neighboring tables are even more boisterous than our own. The entire Briar hockey program is here, men's *and* women's teams. Champagne flows freely, the clinking of crystal glasses and loud bursts of laughter echoing all around us.

There was a string quartet playing gentle classical music during dinner, but now a live band takes the stage. Gigi and Ryder stand up, and I can see the resignation in Ryder's blue eyes as the six-foot-five, ten-inch-dick groom is forced to be the center of attention again.

A gazebo draped in billowing fabrics serves as the backdrop for the newlyweds' first dance. It's spectacular. Gigi's aunt knocked this wedding out of the park and into outer space.

As they dance under the moonlit sky, surrounded by the soft glow of fairy lights, Gigi and Ryder only have eyes for each other.

And just when I think I can't cry any harder, their dance ends and Hannah Graham steps onto the stage. She's utterly stunning in a slate-gray gown that hugs her body, the material shimmering with every step. She exudes pure grace, and the hush that falls over the room brings goose bumps to my flesh.

As the first notes of the piano fill the air, Hannah starts to sing. To this day, I'll never understand why she chose to focus on songwriting instead of performing. Her voice is so beautiful. Rich and emotive, each note piercing right into your soul. I barely pay attention to the lyrics, although Blake whispers to me that it's an old lullaby Hannah used to sing to the twins when they were little. Gigi is bawling, and even her brother, Wyatt, has tears in his eyes.

This wedding is next level.

Hannah's final notes linger in the air. There's a moment of dead silence before the guests erupt in applause.

And then the party starts.

The dance floor has the same strands of fairy lights suspended above it, creating a starlit canopy. I laugh in delight when Shane pulls me to my feet before I can even ask him to dance.

"I've converted you!" I accuse.

He links our fingers and tugs me toward the floor. "I have a confession to make," he says ruefully. "I've always liked dancing."

"Seriously? And you still put up such a big fight?"

"I said *dancing*, not this ballroom torture you're putting me through. I'm just saying, I enjoy dancing in general. Chugging champagne, busting loose at a wedding. It's fucking great."

He's right. There's nothing I love more than a good wedding. And an intoxicating beat. And the feel of Shane's big hands running over my body. There's nothing sexual about his touch, though. It feels nice.

"I can't wait to have one of these," he confesses.

I blink. "A wedding?"

"Yup."

"Yeah, okay. Sure."

"I'm serious." His eyes are bright and earnest.

"You want a wedding," I say skeptically.

"A big one," Shane confirms. "Bigger is better." He winks. "That's what I've heard anyway."

I give him a little shove, but he just pulls me closer again. I don't mind the slow dance. Yeah, I don't mind having his muscular body against mine one iota.

"And when do you plan on having this wedding?" I ask him.

That gets me a shrug. "Honestly, the sooner the better. I always wanted to get married young. Wouldn't mind being a young dad, either."

My eyebrows shoot up. "Really."

"Sure. As long as it doesn't interfere with hockey, why not."

I grin at him. "You're naive if you think that won't interfere with hockey. These things you say you want—a wife, kids. They need to come first, you get that, right? How do you expect to juggle that with your NHL career?"

He frowns. "Lots of NHL players have wives and families and still play the game."

"Would they walk out of a game if their wife needed them?" I challenge.

"That's a loaded question. Depends on what she needed."

"She's giving birth."

Shane shrugs. "Russell Doolie missed the birth of his first child because of a playoffs game. His wife was cool with it—she's the one who told him to finish out the series."

"Fair enough. Then I guess you need to make sure you marry someone who's okay with making those sacrifices. Not many women would be."

He gives me a curious look. "Would you?"

"I don't know," I answer truthfully. Then I shrug. "But it doesn't really matter because I don't plan on having kids till my early thirties. Do you know how much work those things are?"

Shane snickers. We're interrupted a moment later by Beckett, who grabs Shane and whisks him away to do celebratory shots with the entire men's hockey team.

I'm suddenly reminded of the wedding I went to with Percy last year. As much as I loathe even having his name inside my brain, because it triggers my anxiety, the memory lingers. A friend from high school got married, and I brought Percy as my plus-one. He barely said a word to anyone the whole time and kept a deadly grip on my hand or a possessive arm around my shoulders whenever anyone with a penis tried to talk to me. I broke up with him not long after that. I was starting to notice that behavior happening far too often for my liking.

Unlike Percy, Shane doesn't care who I talk to or dance with. For the next hour, everyone goes wild on the dance floor. The hockey boys are just the right amount of tipsy, though I imagine they'll be properly drunk once more of the older folks start heading out and it's only us young'uns closing down the country club.

But now it's nearing midnight, and the crowd still hasn't dissipated. If anything, the older guests are as drunk as the young ones. I've lost count of how much champagne I've drunk, and a part of me wonders if I'm mishearing it when I stumble onto Shane and Garrett near the bar discussing *Fling or Forever*. But it's no secret that Gigi's dad is a fan of the show.

"He's so snakey," Garrett is saying.

"Yeah, but he didn't deserve to be mugged off."

I make an exasperated noise as I glare at the two men. "Just because Donovan is a Brit doesn't mean you are! Stop using British slang. It's embarrassing."

Shane is defiant. "So you're okay with Donovan cracking on with Ky?"

"Oh my God, I'm not defending Donovan! Leni is a national treasure. I'm just saying, stop being weird!"

Shane flicks an eyebrow up at Garrett. "And she considers herself a superfan."

"I'm leaving now." I roll my eyes and wander off to find someone normal to talk to. I scan the guests mingling on the well-manicured lawn and spot Ryder standing at the edge of the dance floor.

I join him, following his gaze to see Gigi dancing with friends. She is absolutely radiant. Glowing. Her reception dress is a floor-length satin number that clings to her body like a second skin. Her hair is loose, dark waves streaming down her shoulders.

I give Ryder a pat on the arm. "Do I need to give you the whole speech, or does it go without saying?"

He glances over wryly. "What, hurt her and I'll kill you?"

"Okay, so you know it already."

"Trust me, I've gotten it from every single uncle, aunt, cousin. Her dad, obviously—"

"Obviously."

"And even Hannah gave the speech, although hers was accompanied by a hug so I don't know if I should take it seriously."

"Oh, you should. She'll cut a bitch."

Ryder chuckles.

Before my next foray onto the dance floor, I chug some water, use the bathroom, and then return to the throng of bodies. While Shane dances with Mya, I dance with Beckett, then Will, then Gigi's twin brother, who flashes his lady-killer smile at me.

"Hey, beautiful," he says easily, wrapping his arm around my waist. His dark-green eyes narrow in appreciation as they roam my gown-clad body.

Wyatt has sex eyes. He always manages to look seductive, even when he's not flirting.

"Hey, hottie," I respond as I rest both palms on his broad shoulders.

It's a shame that Gigi has a strict hands-off rule when it comes to her brother. When I met her freshman year, she made that stance clear. Her exact words were, "Unless you can see yourself marrying him, you will *not* be going to bed with him."

I could've tested that rule over the years, but despite the obvious chemistry between us, Wyatt and I never went there. Because while I might have fun with him for a night, I absolutely cannot see myself marrying him. He's too laid-back. Not only would I eat him alive but I suspect his go-with-the-flow attitude would eventually drive me up the wall.

Wyatt and I get to dance for all of one minute before Shane cuts in.

"Are you going to pee on me now to mark your territory?" I mock as I loop my arms around his neck.

Shane cups my ass to bring me flush against his body. We're

not dancing so much as standing there with our bodies pressed together.

"So you and Wyatt Graham," he starts.

"What about us?" I play dumb.

"Did you ever sleep with him?"

I raise a brow at him. "What would you do if I said yes?"

Shane grinds his lower body against mine, his chin dropping onto my shoulder so he can whisper in my ear. "I'd take you home and drill you so hard that you won't remember a time when my dick wasn't in you."

Jesus.

I swallow the sudden rush of moisture that fills my mouth.

"So did you?" He searches my face.

"No," I admit. Then, just to rile him up, I add, "But maybe I should. Maybe I'll go home with him tonight."

A growl sounds in my ear.

"What?" I say innocently.

Shane skims his hand up my bare arm, lightly grazing the side of my breast, and cups my cheek with his palm. His fingertips tease the side of my jaw.

"No man is allowed to touch you but me, Dixon." His voice is low. Thick with desire. "And if one tries, I'll rip his fucking hands off."

A hot shiver rolls through me. It's strange, because earlier I was thinking how unattractive Percy's possessiveness was, how the behavior led to our breakup. And yet Shane's growly threat doesn't make me bat an eye. Lindley doesn't scare me.

But the way I'm starting to feel about him does.

To: Brenda@meadowhillhoa.com
Re: Inappropriate Noises

Brenda,

I would like to lodge a formal complaint against my upstairs neighbors, Red Birch residents 2A and 2B. I am citing the noise ordinances outlined in Section 3 Paragraph 2 of the Meadow Hill Homeowners' Handbook.

In the last two weeks, I have heard noises in the form of vocal expression (moaning, whimpering) inappropriate language (expletives such as "fuck" and "goddamn"), and structural disturbances (loud thumping against walls, excessive bedspring squeaking).

As per S3 P2, the recourse for such conduct should result in a fine, as I'm sure you are aware. Please address in the next HOA meeting. I am available most evenings and weekends if you would like to discuss further.

Sincerely,
Niall Gentry
Red Birch, 1B

CHAPTER THIRTY-THREE

SHANE

Shane is the sausage king

SEPTEMBER

"This is what I've always dreamed of."

"What?" Diana says suspiciously from the driver's seat. I have benevolently allowed her to drive to Oak Ridges, but that's only because I need to read through a bunch of the emails Coach Jensen sent regarding the upcoming season. Practice starts next week.

"Meeting my fake girlfriend's real family," I explain with a grin.

Ironically, she didn't even ask me to come to this end-of-summer potluck at her dad's place. I invited *myself*. But what else was I going to do once I heard it's not just any old potluck—it's a bring-your-own-meat event. And yes, there are a million jokes I could be making about the kind of meat I can bring Diana, but who has time to make jokes when they can be thinking about all the sausage they picked up from Gustav's.

"I mean, I already spent the weekend with yours," she says. "At this point, we should be announcing our engagement."

"I'm not announcing our fake engagement to your SWAT leader father. He'll kick my ass when I leave you at the altar."

Diana snorts. "We both know I'm the one who's not showing up for our wedding."

"Hey, is your mom going to be there today?"

She starts to laugh. "Absolutely not. Even if she and my dad were on great terms—and they're on cordial terms at best—she's not a fan of my stepmother. Larissa is too common for her."

"What the hell does that mean?"

"Well, my mom is a pretentious academia snob, and Larissa is a hairdresser, so put two and two together."

"I don't know, if I had to pick, I'd rather get a haircut than a lecture about philosophy or whatever. More practical."

"You should tell that to my mom if you ever meet her. Which hopefully you won't because she'd probably hate you."

I tense slightly. "Why? Because I'm half Black?"

"No, because you play hockey, and she thinks jocks are dumb. My mom isn't a racist. She's a snob."

Now I chuckle. "I guess I'll take it."

Diana's tone grows troubled. "It must be really hard going into certain situations wondering if someone is going to be racist or not."

"It's not fun," I admit. "And it's weird, because part of me is so fucking lucky for growing up with the privilege I've had, and the parents I have. But it's like sometimes none of that matters when I'm walking in the electronics section of a store and I get security guards following me."

"Fucking assholes." Diana growls on my behalf, which is cute.

"Yup. It sucks. But I try to remind myself that I'm more privileged than most, and hold on to that, I guess." I look over curiously. "Is your mom really going to think I'm dumb?"

"Probably. She doesn't take athletes seriously. I dated a football player in high school, and every time he came over, she complained she was losing brain cells just being around him. Meanwhile, he's one of the smartest people I've ever met. He's majoring in mathematics at Notre Dame."

"She sounds kind of insufferable."

"She can be."

Diana hits a pothole, making the Mercedes bounce.

"Hey," I growl. "Be careful."

"Sorry—"

"We've got a cooler full of sausage in the back."

"Oh. You're worried about the sausage. I thought you were concerned about the tires." She shakes her head at me. "I can't believe you spent that much money on meat."

"You said your father was a meat fan."

"You're *such* a suck-up."

"I mean, he's your dad *and* he's a cop. I'm not an idiot. I don't really want to get on his bad side. And trust me, once you taste these veal bratwursts, you'll understand why they cost so much."

She shrugs and slows down when she notices another pothole. "Eh. You know I don't care about food."

Yeah, I've noticed. Diana eats whatever's available. "I don't get you. Food is awesome."

"Food is fuel. I don't care what it tastes like. And I can eat anything because my gag reflex is nonexistent."

"Damn right it is." I wink at her.

She rolls her eyes.

Truth is, though, she takes my cock so good. Fuck. I shiver just thinking about it.

"Don't get horny," she warns. "We're not stopping for car sex."

"Or we could stop for car sex."

"We are not stopping." She's laughing again.

"We should've driven up last night instead of early this morning," I grumble. "Then we'd be having morning sex right now."

"I had to work," she reminds me.

"You could've called in sick."

"Shane. Not everybody is a lady of leisure like you."

I snicker.

"Seriously." She gives me a sidelong look. "You have to stop doing that."

"Doing what?"

"Telling everyone to blow off work. You do it all the time. With me, with your friends. Some people can't do that."

"I'm joking. I know they're not actually going to do it."

"Yeah, but it's your cavalier attitude toward this stuff. Like, yes. We're all aware that *you* can blow off work. It's a bit insulting sometimes, the way you act like having a job is beneath you."

Well, damn. I've been put in my place.

And suddenly my mind is running through every conversation I've ever had with everyone I've ever known.

Do I really do that?

"I guess I have been making fun of Will lately," I say pensively, discomfort roiling inside me. "About how he's cheaping out on his backpacking trip. But he's rich too! Why would he travel on a shoestring budget when his dad's a congressman?"

"Maybe he wants to pay his own way." She lifts a brow at me. "Unlike some people."

I glare at her. But we both know she's not wrong, and now I feel like a total asshole.

"Stop making me self-reflect," I grumble.

She just laughs.

Oak Ridges is eerily similar to my own hometown. I didn't expect to have so much in common with Diana Dixon, but it turns out we do. We both grew up in small towns. We both have younger siblings. And we're so sexually compatible, it's not even funny.

Diana parks the car in the driveway of a modest house with white siding and a tidy lawn. We're greeted at the front door by Diana's father, who is not at all what I expected. The square jaw and blond buzz cut make sense, but I was picturing a big, hulking guy wearing camouflage gear and at least seven feet tall. Tom Dixon is shorter than I am, maybe around five nine. But what he lacks in height, he makes up for in build. He's got beefy shoulders, a barrel chest, and biceps the size of my thighs.

"This is the new boyfriend?" he says after Diana introduces us.

"Yeah."

"Welcome." He eyes the cooler in my hands. "What you brought today, son, is really going to determine whether I like you or not."

I snicker. "Trust me, you're going to love this."

"Shane is the sausage king," Diana sighs.

"I've got a guy in Boston," I reveal to Mr. Dixon. "Nobody knows about him. He operates a tiny little butcher shop in Back Bay between a laundromat and—"

"A Korean karaoke place," he finishes.

My mouth falls open. "You know Gustav?"

"Kid, I've been going to Gustav since before you were born. I know Gustav Senior!"

"No shit!"

He all but snatches the cooler from me. "Ah, I gotta see what Gustav gave you."

We race into the kitchen like a pair of schoolboys. Tom opens the cooler, his entire face scrunched in concentration as he examines the selection of sausages I brought.

"Well?" I say, holding my breath.

He lifts his head. "We're best friends now. Diana, please excuse us."

She rolls her eyes. "I'm gonna go find Thomas. You weirdos entertain yourselves."

Once she's gone, Diana's dad gives me a once-over. After an unnervingly long silence, he asks, "Do you treat my daughter with respect?"

The question startles me. "Of course," I say sincerely.

He nods. "You seem all right."

And that, other than the barbecue variety, is the only grilling I encounter for the rest of the day.

We exit through the sliding doors and emerge into a sprawling backyard where the tantalizing aroma of sizzling meat hangs in the air. An enormous, weathered barbecue stands on the stone patio at the base of the wooden deck, sending billowing plumes of smoke into the clear, blue sky.

"Wow, this is sort of a big deal," I remark.

Colorful picnic tables are scattered across the lawn, covered with checkered tablecloths. Children play on the grass, their laughter mingling with the sounds of dozens of conversations going on at once and the occasional clink of utensils against plates.

The grill is being manned by two men who turn out to be the snipers on Mr. Dixon's SWAT team, only instead of rifles, they're armed with long spatulas and basting brushes. I peek at the barbecue. Flames are dancing beneath a gridiron laden with various cuts of meat. Racks of ribs, marinated chicken skewers, and thick, juicy burgers sizzle and crackle as they cook to perfection. The tantalizing scent of barbecue sauce and seasonings wafts through the air, making my mouth water in anticipation.

"I'm in heaven," I tell Diana when she joins us. "You've literally redeemed yourself in my eyes."

That gets me a punch on the arm.

We dodge a group of kids darting around the yard in a game of tag and approach a row of tables that offers an impressive array of side dishes, from creamy mashed potatoes to bowls of fresh salads.

Diana introduces me to her stepmother, Larissa, a dark-haired woman with playful eyes. She's standing with a young man with blond hair parted to the right and a smooth baby face. It's Diana's younger brother, Thomas, who flew back from South America to attend this shindig and is flying back early tomorrow morning.

I gape at him. "Isn't that a lot of travel for a few hours of barbecue?"

He grins ruefully. "I would literally be disowned if I didn't make it home for the potluck. Like you've got to be dead or dying."

"It's true," Larissa confirms.

Despite his boyish appearance, Thomas is super mature and more sarcastic than I expect. He's on the premed path but took a gap year to volunteer with an aid organization.

As we chat, I sling my arm around Diana's bare shoulder, absently stroking her warm flesh. Despite the fact that there is an unsettling number of cops here, I'm having a good time. The food is amazing, and we gorge ourselves all afternoon, to the point where I force myself to stop eating before I get a stomachache. We play a game of cornhole with two men from the Boston PD. One of them pulls me aside afterward to talk hockey, and the next thing I know, he's calling his friends over.

"Hey, Johnny! This kid's playing in the NHL next season."

"What!"

Several men wander toward us, all of them massive hockey fans. Their favorite cop bar in Boston doubles as a Bruins bar, and they proceed to give me some shit for going to Chicago.

"Hey, it's not like I had a choice in who drafted me," I protest.

"I'll allow it," one says, slugging back the rest of his lager.

I discover one of them almost went pro. And he would have been at UConn around the same time as my dad.

"Do you know Ryan Lindley?" I ask him.

"Sure do. Why?"

"That's my dad."

"No shit! You're his kid?"

I brace myself for the next question—*then why aren't you pasty white like him*? Dad and I have gotten that question a couple times when we've run into old acquaintances of his, who weren't aware he was in an interracial marriage. Although my parents have been greeted with almost unilateral tolerance in Heartsong, I know not everyone is so open-minded.

But this man seems unfazed by my skin tone. "How's Ry doing?" he asks me.

"He's great. Owns a bunch of properties in Vermont and runs a property management company."

"Good for him. That was a real shame what happened in that game."

"You saw it?"

"Yeah, of course. I was a couple of years behind him, but we were teammates. The whole team and I were over the fucking moon to see him go pro. It was a real sobering thing, you know? Watching him go down like that. I'm glad he picked himself up and made something of himself."

"That's what hockey players do."

He slaps me on the shoulder. "That's what we do, kid."

I head back to the grill to check if Diana's dad needs help. The sun is dipping lower, casting long shadows across the lawn. People are starting to leave, coming up to hug Tom and Larissa. They shake Tom's hand and tell him he outdid himself this year.

I search the yard for Diana, wondering where she's disappeared to, and finally spot her chatting with a bulky young man in shorts and a Boston PD tank top.

Thomas joins us at the grill. "So my sister roped you into her dance stuff, huh?"

"Yup," I say glumly.

The kid smirks. "She sent me your audition video. That was a pretty good tango, dude."

"I'm sorry, what?" Tom asks in amusement.

Thomas fills his dad in. "Shane's partnering with Di for her ballroom competition. Kenji ditched her."

Larissa gives me a nod of approval. "Good for you. Takes some real confidence."

"I am nothing if not confident." My tone is absent-minded as my gaze once again drifts toward Diana and Mr. Boston PD.

A small firestorm brews in my chest. I don't know why seeing her laughing with this guy makes me burn, but it does.

Thomas notices my distraction. "They're just talking," he says with another smirk.

I glower at him. "I don't care."

"Right. That's why you keep looking over there. Watching them almost as vigilantly as Dad."

My head swings toward Tom Senior. "You don't like that guy either, huh?"

"Ha," Thomas says gleefully. "I knew you didn't like him."

"He's my sergeant's boy. Just passed the academy. A damned beat cop and already thinks he deserves a spot on SWAT. That kind of arrogance bothers me." Tom shrugs. "But Di can handle herself. She's tough as nails."

"She is," I agree.

Thomas grins. "Did she ever tell you about the time she beat up a kid twice her size on the playground because he tried to make her eat ants?"

Diana's dad lets out a howl of laughter. "Aw man, I forgot about that. She was eleven, I think. Maybe twelve. The school called me at work, and I had to leave a weapons training seminar to pick her up because her mom was out of town. Got to the school and found her sitting in the principal's office, not a mark on her. Meanwhile, this boy has a bloody nose and there's all these ants caked into the blood because she shoved his face in the dirt after she hit him. Said only one of them would be eating bugs that day and it sure wasn't gonna be her."

Diana arrives in time for the end of story, sighing when she sees my face. "It's not as psychotic as it sounds."

"My God. I knew you were feral," I accuse.

"Stop scaring him with stories about me beating people up, Dad." She seems embarrassed, but something else flickers through her expression too. Anxiety, maybe? "We don't want to give him the wrong idea. I'm actually a huge wimp."

Tom Senior slings his arm around his daughter's shoulders and plants a kiss on her temple. "Nothing wimpy about you." He glances at me with a smile. "This is the toughest girl you'll ever meet."

Diana smiles too, but I notice it doesn't quite reach her eyes.

CHAPTER THIRTY-FOUR
SHANE

Senior year, boys

HOCKEY'S BACK, BABY.

This is the day I've been looking forward to all summer. It's what I've trained hard for, and my strength and conditioning have definitely paid off. I've gained weight, added a lot of muscle. Hell, I'm probably more agile too, thanks to those dancing lessons. But I'll never admit it to Dixon.

It feels great returning to the Graham Center, Briar's state-of-the-art hockey facilities. The women's team uses this rink too, but they don't officially start practice for another week.

I walk in the building, breathing in the familiar scent of the lobby as I tilt my head and let my gaze roam over the pennants and jerseys hanging from the rafters. The display case against the back wall contains our latest Frozen Four trophy and all the previous ones Coach Jensen and the coaches before him secured for Briar. Jensen's won more championships than any other coach in the history of this university. It's cool to see and an impressive legacy to leave behind if he ever retires.

I stride down the hall, feeling like I'm on top of the world.

I slide into the locker room and find a few of my teammates also showed up early, including Ryder. It's weird not driving with him to practice anymore, now that we don't live together. It's even weirder that last week I was dancing at his stupidly extravagant wedding.

"Hello, Mr. Graham," I say in a formal tone.

He rolls his eyes as he pulls his shirt off, revealing a bulky chest with abs that rival mine. I'm not the only one who stayed in shape this summer.

More guys stream in. Case Colson, Gigi's ex and our co-captain. Nazzy and his wingman, Patrick. Austin and Tristan, who are now sophomores. Beckett strolls in looking tanned and well fucked. Soon he and Will are laughing about something in front of Will's stall. All the juniors are seniors now, and it's a bummer not seeing our old seniors in the room, like Micah, Rand, our goalie Joe.

"I am so fucking ready for this season," I tell my friends. "Senior year, boys. All we gotta do is bring that trophy home again, then we're off to the pros."

"Well, you are," Beckett says as he undoes his jeans.

I glance over. "Have you decided what you're going to do after graduation?"

"No idea, mate."

Beckett's an environmental science major, but he's never actually talked about what kind of job he'll get when he leaves school. I know Will wants to travel. Ryder will be in Dallas. I'll be in Chicago. Colson in Tampa. Next year is going to be interesting.

I strip out of my street clothes and shove them into my stall. Our black-and-silver practice uniforms are freshly laundered. Skates newly sharpened. I can't wait to get out there.

The air inside the rink is brisk, carrying the scent of freshly resurfaced ice. The fluorescent lights glint off the polished surface as we gather around Coach Jensen at center ice. He's a tall, imposing man with buzzed hair, shrewd eyes, and an aversion to words. He greets us with a curt, "Welcome back." That's it.

During the warm-up skate, I notice some of the guys are looking out of sorts. And it becomes more evident when Jensen gets us doing some skating drills. I don't blame the freshmen for being a little slow on the jump—this is their first season at Briar and their nerves are buzzing. The sophomores and juniors, however, know better. They know precisely what to expect.

Clearly seeing what I am, Coach blows his whistle and skates toward us from the boards. He singles out the kid standing next to Austin Pope. Phillip Donaldson, who wasn't a starter last year.

"What the hell are you doing?" Jensen demands. "Did you do a single push-up during the offseason?"

Donaldson mumbles something.

"What was that?"

"I said sorry, Coach."

"And you?" Jensen points a scary finger at Nazem. "Looking a little out of breath there, Talis."

Standing next to Nazzy, Patrick can't stop a snort. "Yeah, that's what happens when you spend your whole summer partying on Milford Lake."

"I spent the summer with *you* and your stupid family," Nazzy growls at him. "You were just as wasted as I was."

Jensen snarls at them both. "Yeah, and it shows. Donaldson, Kansas Kid, Nazem. Laps for the rest of practice."

I lift a brow. Whoa. If Jensen doesn't deem them good enough for today's drills, that means they're *really* out of shape.

"All right," Coach snaps. "We're going to do a blitz breakout drill. I need to see who else decided to be lazy this summer."

Ryder and I exchange a look. Blitzes are high-intensity and not usually the kind of drills you do on Day One. They're supposed to teach players how to work together under extreme pressure and require precise passing, quick transitions, and rapid decisions.

Jensen brusquely sets up the drill while we all listen intently, our breath visible in the crisp air.

"Speed is key," he finishes, that sharp gaze moving over the dozens of bodies on the ice. As if he's trying to assess which one of us might be a little pudgy under our practice jersey. "I want that puck in the offensive zone before the defense knows what hit 'em. Let's go."

The anticipation is palpable as we spread out across the ice. I nod at Colson and Pope, my linemates for this drill. The familiar adrenaline rush that always precedes a challenging exercise is injected directly into my blood. When the puck drops, the rink comes alive with the scrape of skates against ice.

I burst forward in powerful strides, propelling myself toward the puck. Case snatches it first. His stickhandling skills are on full display. As the defenders advance on us to thwart the breakaway, Colson snaps the puck to Pope, who passes it to me.

We absolutely crush this drill. Our lightning-fast passes keep the defenders at bay, the puck zipping between us in a blur of black on the white canvas of the ice. I'm on fire as I weave through the defenders with a combination of finesse and brute force, leaving them scrambling to catch up to me.

As we cross the blue line, Colson executes a perfectly timed crisscross, disorienting Beckett and the other d-men, while our new starting goalie, Todd Nelson, braces for the impending assault. I unleash a slapshot that evades Nelson's grasp and smashes into the back of the net with a satisfying thud.

The guys on the bench erupt in cheers and hollers.

"Holy shit, Lindley," Jordan Trager crows as he skates out to take my place. "What was that!"

I grin at him, riding the exhilaration of my total domination. I've never felt more on top of my game, and it doesn't go unnoticed.

After practice, Jensen whistles to call me over. "Lindley! The fuck did you put in your cereal this summer?"

I shrug modestly. "Nothing. Just stuck to a high-intensity exercise regimen. I added swimming to my workouts too. It makes a real difference."

He raises a dark brow. "Is that all?"

A groove digs into my forehead. "What, you think I'm shooting HGH or some shit? I'm not an idiot."

"Didn't think you were, but shit, you're looking sharp. And if *I* notice how sharp you're looking, the officials are going to notice too. So keep your nose clean this year. We might have a lot of random drug tests coming our way thanks to you."

Damn. I look so good, he's worried people might suspect I'm using performance enhancers? I think that's simultaneously a compliment and an insult.

In the locker room, some of the guys are organizing drinks at Malone's. Nazzy is one of them, showing he didn't learn shit from Jensen's lecture during practice.

"You in?" he asks me.

"Can't. I've got a thing tonight."

Will grins from his locker. "Why don't you tell them about your thing?"

"Why don't you kindly fuck off?"

"Wait, what's going on?" Patrick stumbles over in excitement. He and Nazzy like nothing better than to find new ammo to rag people about. They're the two most competitive guys on the team and the two biggest jokers. Competitive with each other, jokers with everyone else.

"Lindley entered a dance competition," Will tells the room.

I glare at him. "Traitor."

"What? They were going to find out anyway."

"You're in a dance competition?" Patrick doubles over laughing.

Nazzy, though, appears oddly impressed. "No shit."

"Yeah, I'm doing it with—" I stop abruptly.

"Go ahead, finish that sentence," Ryder says dryly.

"My girlfriend," I mutter.

Nazzy gawks at me like I'm a rare zoo animal "You have a girlfriend now? What the hell. We don't see you for one summer and you go from Raging Fuckboy to Mr. Salsa-dancing Monogamy?"

"First of all, we're not entered in a salsa category," I say coldly. Patrick howls.

"We're doing the tango and the waltz."

He howls louder.

"Think you might be missing one," Ryder drawls. Asshole's being unusually talkative today. "Isn't there a third dance?"

"You know, I preferred you when you didn't say a word. Go back to being the brooding asshole who doesn't speak, please and thank you."

"What's the third dance?" Beckett's chuckling as he laces up his shoes. Locks of blond hair fall onto his forehead.

"The cha cha," I grind out. Then I flip up both middle fingers. "And go fuck yourselves. All of you."

Their laughter tickles my back as I stomp out of the locker room. Along with it being our first practice, it's also the first day of classes. I've got Media Ethics starting in thirty minutes on the west end of campus, so I have to hike over to the cluster of buildings that houses most of the social science lecture halls.

Five minutes into my speed walk, I bump into Lynsey.

I experience a burst of genuine shock. Even though she confirmed she'd be attending Briar, I honestly didn't think I'd ever see her on campus. She hasn't contacted me at all, either, since the day she called at the end of July.

We both halt in our tracks.

Her dark eyes crinkle at the sight of me, lips curving. "Hi."

"Hi." That familiar smile softens something in my chest.

Neither of us seems to know if we should embrace, so we stand there for a moment before she finally steps forward to give me an awkward hug.

"How've you been?" she asks after we break apart.

"I'm good. How about you? How are you settling in? All moved into the dorm?"

Lynsey nods. "I have a single in Halston House near the

performance center. Tyreek helped me move my stuff in this weekend."

I nod back. "How's he doing?"

"He's great. Excited for the basketball season." She pauses. "How's Diana?"

"Also great."

"So you're still together." Her expression is hard to decipher.

"Yep," I confirm.

There's another beat of awkwardness. A couple months ago, I was desperate to hear her voice. Now I'm unsure of what to say to her. I can't flirt—she has a boyfriend. And even if I wanted to flirt, it feels disrespectful toward Diana to do that. She and I might not be together, but we still have sex almost every night.

Lynsey finally puts an end to the discomfort. "Should we get together now that we're on the same campus? Maybe have coffee sometime next week?" she suggests.

Despite myself, my heart flips, and it pisses me off that she still has this effect on me. I don't want her to.

"Sure," I say, nodding slowly. "Sounds good."

CHAPTER THIRTY-FIVE
DIANA

SOS

"It's all about the quick steps. Pretend we're dancing in a fairy tale. Like we're at Cinderella's ball."

"Why on earth would that help me with the steps? We're not cartoons. We're doing this for real."

Shane tries to mimic my steps, cursing when he messes up for the third time. It's Thursday, and we both had early classes that let out by four, so we're squeezing in a waltz rehearsal.

"Why can't you lead?" he grumbles.

"Because the man leads."

"Aren't we trying to smash the patriarchy?"

"Yep, but the competitive ballroom dance world hasn't gotten that memo yet. Ergo, the man leads."

We start over, dancing across the Meadow Hill gym as the tempo gets faster.

"What the hell!" Shane yelps. "Why is this speeding up?"

"It's the Viennese waltz."

"So?"

"So it's a dance of elegance and speed."

The music reaches its crescendo and we finish in an unimpressive skid.

"Yeah," I muse. "It needs more work."

"You think?"

A disgruntled Shane stomps off to go use the bathroom out in the hall. We've already chugged two bottles of water each during this rehearsal. We're in a difficult spot now. We've pretty much nailed our tango routine. We're okay at the cha cha.

But the waltz is killing us.

"Hey, check this out," I say when Shane returns.

I'm lying on the mat, one leg crossed over my knee and my phone resting on it. Shane flops down beside me, one big arm reaching out to accept the phone.

I can't take my gaze off his biceps, the way they always ripple whenever he moves his arms. He's so ripped and it's fucking sexy. Makes it hard to concentrate.

I snap out of my ogling and press play on the video.

"Watch," I say grimly.

A female voice chirps out of the phone speaker.

"We're Martinique and Viktor, and this is what we have to say to Ride or Dance!"

Shane hisses. "That's us. We're Ride or Dance!"

"Well aware," I reply, trying not to laugh.

The video cuts to a couple dancing the tango. With her flawless brown skin and almond-shaped eyes, Martinique is ethnically ambiguous and drop-dead gorgeous. And *tall*. She has those endless legs I've always coveted, which means she and her partner, the fair-haired Viktor, line up perfectly for the tango. The natural way they move together only serves to highlight my biggest fear—the height discrepancy between me and Shane. Our tango is good, but it could be so much better.

"The tango is our Everest," I mumble.

"What do you mean?"

"Kenji's small. That's one of the reasons we liked the tango. But it's our biggest impediment, Shane—your height."

"Maybe it's *your* height that's the impediment."

"No, my height is perfect. It lets you do all the cool lifts. You're too tall to tango."

"There's no such thing as too tall to tango," he says smugly.

I sigh.

On the screen, Martinique executes a graceful spin, her hand extending in a flourish. Viktor takes it, and they both turn to address the camera.

"We're coming for you, Ride or Dance," Viktor says with a smirk.

Shane gasps. "These dickheads are trolling us!"

"See? I told you." I pull up their profile and squawk in outrage. "They have a hundred thousand followers."

"Whatever. We're at four eighty-two K."

"You know the exact number?" I tease.

"I'm ballparking. But it was four eighty-two the last time I checked. It's probably eight million now."

I adore Shane's flair for hyperbole. It matches my own.

At the potluck, my brother teased me about catching feelings for Shane, and it's been haunting me ever since. At first, I kept assuring myself it was bullshit. Of course I don't have feelings for him. We're just dancing. And having incredible sex. And enjoying each other's company. Why would anyone think there's feelings involved? Geez.

But...

Yeah. It's getting harder to pretend I'm not into Shane. He's hilarious. Great in bed. So easy to talk to. Sweet when he wants to be.

Lately I've been wondering if maybe I want more than just a friends-with-benefits arrangement. Maybe I want—

"Holy shit," Shane says, jolting me from my thoughts. "And they're recruiting trolls in the comments."

"What do you mean?"

"They're telling their followers to go to *our* page and comment that Viktor and Martinique are better than us." Shane spits out an expletive. "Who do these assholes think they are? And check out this dude. I could bench press him. I don't care if he's like six four. He's a twig."

"Calm yourself, big boy."

"Okay, little one."

I grin at him. "Those are not becoming nicknames."

"I don't know. I like big boy. A lot." He leers at me.

I hop to my feet. "All right, practice is over. I need to rethink the choreography for this waltz before we go any further. Might have to go take a dance class or two."

"Isn't that what this is? Dance classes?"

"I mean with professionals."

Shane eyes me.

"What?"

"It's an amateur competition, Dixon. Do you really need to put that much effort into it?"

"Have you met me? I can't half-ass anything, even if I wanted to. I'm either one hundred percent in or I don't do it."

He nods. "Yeah, I get it. I feel the same about hockey."

"So, yeah, let me think up some easier choreography."

"Is that what you want to get into eventually? Choreography?"

I shrug. "I haven't had enough formal training to choreograph real dancers, but I'd enjoy being a cheer coach and doing choreography for competitions. I think I'd be really good at it."

"I think so too." He trails after me toward the door. "I'm gonna grab a shower before I come over for the finale. If that's still the plan for tonight."

"Obviously." The winners of *Fling or Forever* are being announced tonight.

Upstairs, I take a quick shower to rinse off the dance sweat, then put on comfy clothes, feeling lighter than I have in months. I know a large part of that has to do with Percy no longer being at Meadow Hill. The Garrisons are back from Atlanta and back in Sweet Birch, and Percy is all the way across town at his new townhouse.

It's a huge weight off my chest, being able to walk down the path without worrying about bumping into him. Without worrying about seeing him at the pool. I can already feel my anxiety lessening. Now, when I picture his face, my throat only closes up a little, not completely. My hands tremble but don't shake.

I'm hoping the more time that passes—and the more physical distance between me and Percy—the less anxiety I'll feel. Until maybe one day I won't feel it at all.

Shane and I reconvene an hour later in my apartment. I pour myself a glass of the Pink Stuff, since tonight is basically my last chance to drink without worrying about hangovers. Saturday is the first football game of the year, and the squad needs to be in elite shape for the season opener. But I know Shane has hockey practice tomorrow morning, so I raise a brow when he gets himself a beer.

"Should you be drinking when you have practice?"

"Just one. You'll have to get drunk enough for the both of us."

The episode starts with Zoey and the Connor on their final date aboard a luxury yacht. After Zoey was voted back into the hacienda from the Sugar Shack, Connor was like a new man. Realizing how close he'd come to losing her, he went above and beyond to prove to her that she was the only woman for him. His transformation has been amazing. We've watched him go from a douchebag radio host who rated women's breasts on a scale of "lickable" to "motor-boatable," to a sweet, thoughtful, grown man in love.

Or so I thought.

Halfway through the finale, Jasmine tells Zoey that the Connor told Ben that he might not be ready for a serious commitment.

"What!" I shout at the screen. "What are you *saying* right now? Stop trying to sabotage them!"

Shane is agape. "Do you think Connor actually said that? I don't remember them showing a scene like that."

"Jas is totally stirring up trouble," I say firmly. "There's no way."

But then Ben backs Jasmine up, confirming to Zoey that Connor did indeed say it.

"Oh my God," I moan.

"What the fuck was he thinking?" Shane growls.

Zoey starts to cry. For the next fifteen minutes, we're glued to the screen. The Connor does some damage control, scrambling to reassure Zoey that he and Ben had the commitment conversation nearly a month ago. But Ben and Jas insist it was "just the other night."

"They're lying," Shane says. "They're totally trying to knock Zoey and Connor out of the Forever Couple running."

"Fuckin' saboteurs."

We're still ranting about Jas and Ben when Will sends me an SOS. That's literally what the message says. "SOS" and nothing more.

Grinning, I unlock my phone.

"Who is it?" Shane asks.

"Will," I say as I type a response.

ME:

What's up?

WILL:

Beck just invited someone home tonight.

ME:

And you want to join them.

WILL:

So fucking much.

ME:

So do it.

WILL:

> I can't. I need to be strong. Can I crash at your place?

ME:

> You can't keep coming over here to avoid threesomes.

WILL:

> She's the hottest girl I've ever seen, Diana.

ME:

> I thought *I* was the hottest girl you've ever seen.

WILL:

> Right, of course. My apologies.

Shane peers over my shoulder. "Are you sexting with my teammate?"

"No."

"I saw your last message! You're asking him to say you're hot."

"It was a joke."

"No. No way." He points a warning finger at me. "You're not going to make me into a cuck, Dixon."

I snort. "I'm not making you into a cuck."

"I mean it. You can't expect me to be your fake boyfriend and then flirt with my friends. It makes me look like a fool."

"Fine. Good point," I relent. "You know what? I'm sorry. I won't flirt with Will when he's here."

"What do you mean when he's here?"

"He's coming over to crash."

"Again?" Shane narrows his eyes. "Why does he have to? He's

got a three-bedroom townhouse. Even if he's plastered at the bar and needs to walk home, he can just walk home. To his *own home*."

"It's a whole thing," I say vaguely.

"Elaborate, please." Shane sounds exasperated.

I don't want to betray Will's confidence, but…maybe this is something Shane can help him with. Because the fact is, Will can't keep running from his problems and hiding from Beckett in Meadow Hill every time the guy brings a woman home.

Shane's usually pretty good at reserving judgment. Maybe he can talk some sense into Will where I'm failing.

"Okay, so…" I hesitate. "I'm going to tell you something, but you can't breathe a word of it to anyone."

Turns out I'm the worst secret-keeper ever. But I trust that Shane's not going to say anything. He hasn't blabbed about our fake relationship after all, and it's been months.

"Will doesn't want to be at home when Beckett has a girl over," I tell him.

He frowns. "Why the hell not?"

"So you know how the two of them like to…?" I let the question hang.

"Screw the same women at the same time?" Shane finishes dryly.

"See?" I accuse. "That's why his head is so messed up. He's afraid of the judgment. Society is so judgey."

"Hey, I'm not judging. Everyone has their kinks." Shane grins. "Like how you enjoy it when I boss you around and how I enjoy bossing you around."

"But you're not into threesomes?"

"No, I wouldn't share you with someone." He meets my curious gaze. "I'd let him watch, though."

Heat tingles between my legs. "Look but don't touch?"

"Exactly." Shane moves closer, resting his hand on my leg. A thoughtful gleam enters his eyes as he lightly strokes my thigh. "Would you let someone watch me fuck you?"

I swallow. "Maybe. Depends on who, I guess." I gulp again. "But we digress. We're talking about Will. The threeways are starting to make him feel like there's something wrong with him. He's trying to take a break from it."

"So he's coming over tonight in order to keep his dick in his pants?"

"Pretty much, yeah." I sigh. "I don't know if he'll raise the subject with you, but if he ever does, maybe you can talk some sense into him. Tell him it's really not a big deal if he has a threesome kink."

"I'll see what I can do." He glances back at the screen. "Oh shit. British host is back. This is it."

Shane and I watch the rest of the finale. I breathe in relief when Zoey and the Connor patch things up, then crow in triumph after it's revealed that Ben and Jasmine were lying about when the commitment comment was made.

"I love you," Connor's telling Zoey now. "With all my heart. A month ago, I wasn't ready to commit to you. To anyone, really. But I'm ready now, Zo. I want you to be my girlfriend. Not just in the hacienda but in the real world."

"I want that too," Zoey says shyly.

The British host then asks the final two couples to stand in the gazebo, where the public voting is revealed. Shane and I are cheering when Zoey and the Connor win the final vote to be crowned the Forever Couple. Well, I'm cheering. But Shane looks pleased, and I'm certain he's doing flips and roundoffs in his head.

Around ten o'clock, Richard from the Sycamore buzzes to let me know Will has arrived, and a few minutes later I'm letting him into my apartment. He greets me with a hug, then walks over to say hi to Shane.

"What are we watching?" Will glances at the TV.

"Nothing," Shane lies.

I notice he changed the channel from TRN to TSBN when I went to answer the door. Football preseason highlights now flash on the screen. Oooh. Someone doesn't want Will to see us watching the *FoF* reunion show.

"I'm actually heading home now," Shane says. "I wanted to go to bed early tonight."

Will wrinkles his brow. "You're not crashing here?"

"Why would he crash here when he has his own bed?" I answer for Shane. "I don't need him clinging to me all night and suffocating me with his love."

"You fuckin' love my love," Shane grumbles. He gives Will a firm look. "She loves my love."

Will snorts.

"Do you need a ride to practice tomorrow morning?" Shane asks his teammate.

"Yeah, that'd be great."

"Cool. Alarm's set for seven thirty. I'll knock on the door at eight. If you're not ready, I'm gone."

"I'll be up," Will promises.

"Let me walk you out," I say, linking my arm through Shane's.

At the door, he gives me a deep, elaborate kiss with more tongue than necessary.

"You don't have to lay it on so thick. He already believes we're dating," I mumble against his lips, although I'm not really complaining. Shane's kisses melt my brain.

"I can't believe we don't get to fuck tonight," he mumbles back.

If it were up to Shane's libido, we would be having sex at least twice a day. Again, no complaints from me. I've never had sex this good in my life.

I lock up after he leaves and return to tackle my nightly skincare routine. This time I don't rope Will into it, but he stands in the bathroom doorway, watching me in the mirror.

"You and Lindley are still going strong, huh?"

"Who would have thought, right?"

"I mean, no one." Will snorts. "You gave him so much shit last year."

"Yeah, 'cause he's obnoxious. That hasn't changed."

"Exactly. That hasn't changed. So what's different now?"

"His dick," I confess. "I've fallen into his dicksand."

Will nods solemnly. "I'm sorry."

Once my face is nicely moisturized, I set Will up on the couch with clean sheets, two pillows, and a thick blanket. Despite what some people might think, I do respect Shane enough to not share a bed with his teammate. Fake relationship or not, we're still exclusive friends with benefits, and I wouldn't be thrilled if *he* was sleeping with another woman in his bed, even if they were platonic. But that's because I'm a possessive bitch. Even over my temporary man.

"Thanks again," Will says gruffly. "I'm sorry I keep imposing on you."

"It's not an imposition, I promise." I give him a kiss on the cheek and then go to my bedroom, climbing under the covers.

I can't fall asleep, though. Because…goddamn it, I want to have sex. I've grown so accustomed to a Shane orgasm before bed, and now my body is humming beneath my duvet.

Around eleven thirty, I still can't sleep, and now I'm thirsty, so I leave my room and go to the kitchen. As I tiptoe past the couch, I peek at Will, who's passed out on his back, snoring softly. He's completely out.

I pour myself a glass of water, and as I lean against the counter to drink, my gaze once again travels toward Will. Maybe there's no harm in a quickie. I can just hop next door, get off, and come back. Will won't even notice. He's dead to the world.

Back in my bedroom, I pull out my phone and text Shane.

ME:

Changed my mind. Quickie?

SHANE:

> Thank God. I couldn't sleep. I was about to jerk off.

SHANE:

> I'll come over.

ME:

> But Will's here.

SHANE:

> Yeah, and my bedroom wall is right behind your living room where he's sleeping.

We don't have to use your bed, I start to type, but he's already followed up with, On my way.

CHAPTER THIRTY-SIX
DIANA

You're really going to do this, huh?

I TIPTOE THROUGH THE MAIN ROOM TO LET SHANE IN. THE MOMENT I open the door, I press my fingers to my lips to indicate he needs to be quiet. I didn't turn on any lights, so we're bathed in shadows as we quietly walk past the kitchen. I try to let the bluish light from Skip's fish tank guide my way, but it's still hard to see, and I curse when my knee slams into the small island. A jolt of pain travels up my leg.

"You okay?" he asks.

"No," I whimper, bending over to press my hand against my kneecap. "Mother*fucker*."

"Don't worry. Let's go to your room and I'll kiss it and make it better." There's a pause. "Or..."

I lift my head to see his eyes gleaming in the darkness.

"What?"

"Maybe I'll kiss you now."

I glance toward the couch at a sleeping Will. When I turn my head back, Shane's lips are right there. He kisses me, his tongue sliding through my parted lips to touch my own. He circles it, exploring my mouth as his hand moves downward, fingers dipping beneath the waistband of my shorts.

"Shane." A hushed warning.

He breaks the kiss. I feel him searching my face. "Say the word and we'll take this to the bedroom."

That's exactly what we should do—take this to the bedroom. But the excitement tingling in my clit tells me to stay put. The idea of getting caught is more thrilling than I thought it would be.

"Tell me what you want," he urges softly. "Stay here or go to your room?"

It's hard to speak through the lump of arousal in my throat. I finally find my voice, managing to get out one throaty syllable.

"Stay."

His lips curve. He gently pushes me backward until my butt hits the edge of the counter. Then his hand is back inside my pajama shorts, teasing me over the fabric of my underwear. His knuckles reach the top of my mound just as I hear a husky noise from the couch.

I freeze. But Will is only shifting positions, rolling onto his side.

Shane and I wait several agonizing beats. My heart has never pounded harder.

Finally, he resumes his ministrations, rubbing me in slow, lazy caresses. As if he has all the time in the world to play with my pussy. As if his teammate isn't lying ten feet away and might wake up at any second.

I hiss in a breath when Shane slips his hand inside my panties. My legs spread as his fingers seek and find my drenched pussy.

He drags one finger through my slit, and my legs seem to lose all strength. I sag forward. Shane steadies me, chuckling quietly.

"Up," he says, and the next thing I know, he's lifting me onto the counter.

I fall back onto my elbows and peer down at him. Licking his lips, he sinks to his knees in front of me, pulling my shorts and panties down my legs. Alarm flutters through me, as I didn't expect to be naked from the waist down. I thought our clothes would stay on, that we'd tease each other through the barriers.

But I can't deny it excites me to be lying here on the counter on full display.

"Will is right there," I whisper in an unconvincing objection. "What if he's awake?"

"Then he can watch you come."

My breath hitches.

Shane studies my face and quirks his lips in another smile. "You like that idea."

I swallow another lump of pure, relentless lust. "It was all the threesome talk about him and Beckett. Got in my head."

"Dirty girl." Shane continues to watch me. "Is that what you want? To wake him up and ask him to join us?"

I don't miss the way he brings his hand to his groin to do some rearranging behind his sweatpants.

"Is that what *you* want?" I counter.

"I told you I don't like to share."

"You're not sharing. You're bragging."

"What am I bragging about?"

I spread my legs. "How good this pussy is."

My wanton action rips a groan from his throat.

We instantly look at the couch. Will still lies on his side, face turned in our direction but eyes shut. His chest rises and falls in even intervals.

"Jesus, Dixon," Shane grinds out. "Stop talking like that. I'm leaking precome."

I feel a clench between my legs. "Let me taste."

My plea makes him groan again, but this time it's muffled by his teeth digging into his bottom lip. Without a word, he stands and positions his body in front of my face. Keeping his back to the couch, he eases the front of his sweatpants down and releases his cock. It springs up, thick and eager. Sure enough, moisture beads at the tip.

His breathing is ragged as he fists his erection and slowly brings it to my waiting mouth. I lick the tip, and it twitches for me while my tongue explores him.

Shane releases a quiet, strangled noise. I wrap my lips around him and let him push a few inches into my mouth. I can never take him too deep because of his massive size. Even with half his length, I can feel him at the back of my throat.

His fingers thread through my hair, guiding my head along his shaft. I feel myself getting impossibly wetter. It's hard not to be turned on by the sound of his unsteady exhalations and the taste of him on my tongue.

"That's enough," he warns when I tighten the suction of my lips.

I almost weep when he takes his dick away. But he atones for that sin by returning to the cradle of my thighs and dropping to his knees. My hips buck into his hungry, sucking mouth, taking every ounce of pleasure he has to offer.

I'm sprawled on the kitchen counter, half-naked, a feast for Shane's tongue and Will's eyes should he open them. But I don't care about the latter. The heart-pounding sensations Shane is creating in my body are all I can focus on.

I can feel the orgasm trying to surface. Black dots flash through my vision, my surroundings threatening to fade, but I blink and force myself to stay in the present. I don't want to miss a second of this. When Shane's tongue flicks over my clit, every nerve ending in my body comes alive. Firing on all cylinders.

I gasp, so close to detonating. So close—

He wrenches his mouth away, and I almost wail in disappointment.

"Please don't stop," I whisper pleadingly.

But he's already on his feet. He grips his dick, his features taut, hungry. "Sorry, baby, I fucking can't take it anymore. I need you."

Despite the persistent throbbing in my clit, an orgasm that's now eluding me, I can't fault him. I've never seen him look this desperate. His lips are pulled tight over his teeth, eyes on fire as he steps between my legs.

"Put me inside you."

I reach between us to grip him. I'm so drenched that he glides inside effortlessly. I suck in air as he grinds into me, my hips reflexively pushing against him. I've never been filled like this by any other man. The friction of him inside me tickles nerves I didn't know existed.

"So you're really going to do this, huh?"

I jolt at the sound of Will's resigned voice.

Oh God.

My cheeks are scorching as I twist my head in Will's direction. His face is almost entirely illuminated by the glow of the fish tank. I swallow when I see the unmistakeable glint of arousal.

"Sorry, did we wake you?" Shane drawls.

"Obviously," Will says dryly.

Shane flicks his gaze toward the couch. "I'd send Dixon over there to tuck you in and sing you a lullaby, but we're a little busy right now."

"Yeah, I can see that."

Shane pauses thoughtfully. "Do you like what you see?"

"What the hell do you think?"

"You like watching me fuck my girl?"

Will doesn't answer. Then he lets out a breath. "Don't you two want to move this to the bedroom or something?"

Neither of us moves. Shane is still inside me. It's crazy. I should tell him to stop, cover myself up, run into the bedroom. But I remain motionless. My pulse throbs between my legs. I know Shane can feel it rippling around him.

"We're good where we are," he mutters, his hungry gaze locked on my face. "But you're welcome to go hide in the bedroom if this offends your delicate eyes."

I see Will shift beneath the blanket as he holds eye contact with me. There's a question in his expression.

"Remember we talked about kinks?" I say wryly. "This is his. He likes to be watched."

Will's tongue comes out to lick at the corner of his mouth.

"What about you, Di? Do you want me to stay and watch you get fucked?"

A shiver skitters up my spine. His voice is low. Seductive.

I nod slowly.

Will nods back. "Say it out loud." It's a command, not a suggestion. "I need to hear your consent."

I clear the lust from my throat. "Yes. Stay."

Smiling, Shane withdraws and then pushes his cock inside me with a fast, deep stroke, drawing an involuntary moan from my lips.

Will makes a strangled noise. "Jesus, Lindley."

"You have no idea how wet she is," Shane tells him, his breathing quickening as he slides out again, then plunges back in. "My dick is soaked."

Will doesn't answer. He's wholly focused on me. I should feel exposed, but I don't. I'm on fire, every nerve ending crackling with anticipation.

Shane pulls out again, dragging his tip up and down my slit as he continues talking to Will. "I bet you wish you could be over here right now, don't you, Larsen?"

That thick cock fills me again. I moan.

When Will still doesn't respond, Shane spares him another glance. "I know what you're thinking. You want your dick in my girl's mouth while I fuck her."

"Yes" is the hoarse reply.

Oh my God.

"Well, too bad. I don't share," Shane mocks. "But you can keep watching."

He strokes my clit and I feel a shudder of pleasure. I tear my gaze off Will and focus on Shane. On the chiseled features stretched taut with his desire. On the enormous dick stuffed inside me.

He leans forward, sweatpants down to expose his bare ass. Big hands travel up my stomach to cup my breasts over my sleep shirt, rubbing my nipples between his fingers. It sparks an electric current through my body. My breasts are stupidly sensitive.

"Feel good?" he asks, toying with my nipples as he fucks me nice and slow.

"Mmm-hmm."

Shane curls his muscular body over my quivering one and bends his head to kiss me with reckless abandon. I whimper against his greedy tongue, clinging to his shoulders, scraping my nails down his back. All the while, his hips keep moving.

He licks his lips as he straightens up, one hand flat on my belly as he lightly rubs his fingertips over my clit.

"You like that he's watching you take my dick."

I nod wordlessly.

"You take it so good, baby." His fingers tease me, pressing down on that sensitive nub. "Look at you, Dixon. Stretched all around my cock. You're so tight."

My hips start to move too. He's not even fully in, damn it. He's too big. But my body is greedy. I make a low, desperate noise, trying to buck myself against him.

Shane chuckles.

"Will," he says without looking over.

"Yeah?"

"Get yourself off watching us."

There's a muffled groan.

I see movement from the corner of my eye. Pulse racing, I turn my head in time to see Will sliding his hand under the blanket. This is the raunchiest, kinkiest, most arousing thing I've ever experienced. I should feel gross and objectified, but I don't.

Will rolls onto his back. He pushes his boxers down. I catch a shadowy glimpse of his fist moving over his shaft. His face is turned in my direction. He's biting his lip.

"If you come before Diana, I'll let you decide where I shoot my load."

Will groans.

I do too.

Oh my God.

Shane braces his hands on the counter and fucks me so deep I'm seeing stars again. My body contracts around his cock, pinpricks of pleasure traveling over my skin.

"Better hurry, though," Shane warns. "She's close. She's squeezing me so tight, it's only a matter of seconds."

How am I *not* supposed to be close when Shane is hitting the most incredible spot and Will is working his cock in long, steady strokes, pleasuring himself to the sight of us?

Shane slides his hands beneath my ass, lifting it a little so he can plunge deeper. He goes faster and faster, and I can't stop the onslaught of sensation. The orgasm is rising. I feel the familiar tingle building up.

I gulp for air. "You're gonna make me come."

"Do it. Show Larsen how much you like taking this dick."

Squeezing my ass with one hand, Shane uses his other one to rub my clit again, all the while maintaining that torturous pace, those deep strokes.

A wave of ecstasy rolls through me. I don't try to hold it back; I couldn't if I wanted to. My fingers splay out on the counter, shivers consuming my entire body as I experience one of the best releases of my life.

Shane doesn't stop drilling into me after my orgasm passes. He still has to reach his own. But he's close—I know by the primal grunts that leave his mouth.

"Sorry, Will, you weren't fast enough," Shane mutters, then groans when my inner muscles clamp around him, still contracting from orgasm.

Will is groaning too, stroking himself while his gaze remains glued to me and Shane. To the place where we're joined. To Shane's thumb still grazing my clit.

"I'm coming," Will mumbles, and an answering bolt of desire shoots through me.

I don't know where to look. At Will, who's jerking himself to release all over his abs? At Shane, who's now shuddering as he spills himself inside me?

It takes forever for my heartbeat to regulate. I feel the muscles in Shane's stomach relax as he gently withdraws from my body. He's breathing hard. Eyes still devouring me.

"Doing okay there, Will?" he calls blithely.

"Fuck. Yeah."

Chuckling, Shane tugs his sweatpants up and then cleans me with a soft paper towel, his touch tender. Without a word, he picks my shorts and underwear off the floor and puts them on me. My legs are wobbling as he helps me off the counter. My bare feet hit the floor.

Shane dips his head to plant a kiss on my lips. "I'm off," he says, winking at me. "Night, Dixon."

A strangled laugh sputters out. "Night, Lindley."

He takes a few steps toward the entryway, then glances over his shoulder. "Night, Larsen."

CHAPTER THIRTY-SEVEN

DIANA

Fixer-upper

A WEEK INTO THE NEW SEMESTER, I RUN INTO SHANE'S EX-GIRLFRIEND on the tree-lined quad. I know Shane saw her already, but this is my first Lynsey encounter in the Briar wild.

As usual, her smile holds a trace of coldness. I don't know if aloof is simply her default state or if it's because I'm dating her ex.

Lynsey closes the distance between us, sauntering toward me in a pair of dark-blue skinny jeans and a black tank top with lace trim. Her hair is arranged in a tight bun. I swear, this woman is elegance personified. In comparison, I feel almost juvenile in my black-and-silver Briar cheerleading uniform.

"Diana, hey."

"Hi." I paste on a friendly smile. "How was your first week?"

"Overwhelming," she admits. "This campus is a lot bigger than Liberty. I keep having to check my map." She shows me her phone screen, which is open to a map of Briar.

"Where do you need to be?" This time my smile isn't forced. I get it. I remember being a freshman here. I was late to every class for a solid week.

"The Greenley building. It's supposed to be somewhere around here."

"Come on, I'll walk with you. I'm going in that direction."

"Thanks. Do you have class?" she asks.

"Cheer practice. The sports facilities and gyms are on the way to Greenley."

We fall into stride together, dodging a group of guys in Briar football jerseys. They're fans, not players, and they all whistle at me as I pass in my pleated cheer skirt. I ignore them and keep walking.

"How's it going with Shane?" Lynsey tips her head toward me. "He said you're still seeing each other."

"We are, yeah. And it's going pretty great."

More than great, in fact. Our friends-with-benefits arrangement has proven to be fruitful and resulted in some of the raunchiest sex I've ever had in my life. Like with Will watching us while Shane fucked me on the kitchen counter? Never thought that's something I'd be doing.

"How's Tyreek?" I ask her.

"He's good." Her tone is noncommittal.

I raise an eyebrow. "I sense some hesitation. Everything okay on that front?"

"I don't know." She shrugs. "BU is only an hour away, but it seems like anytime I ask him to come here, he convinces me to come up to Boston instead. It's not super long distance, but he'll have to come during the week because I've still got rehearsals."

"I can't believe you're entered in the American Nine," I say, unable to stop a note of grudging respect. "You must be phenomenal."

"I can't believe you managed to get Shane to enter *one* event, let alone three." Her tone becomes rueful. "It's nice to see him maturing. Growing into the man I always knew he could be."

I bristle on his behalf. "What was he like before?"

"Selfish," she says bluntly. "He had a one-track mind, and that track was hockey."

"I mean, it still is." I shrug. "But maybe now he's better able to incorporate other items into his schedule."

"Yeah, well, he didn't do that with me." Annoyance clouds her expression. "No offense to you, but it's frustrating, you know? It's like you have this fixer-upper house that you're pouring all your time and energy into, and then when it's beautifully renovated, you don't even get to live in it."

It's difficult to keep my jaw closed. Is she seriously comparing Shane to a run-down house that she, what? Slapped a coat of paint on and made better? Bitch.

He was fine the way he was, I want to retort.

But at the same time, I have no idea what he was like in high school. Maybe he was a total bonehead and a terrible boyfriend.

"Someone else is reaping the benefits," she says, waving a hand toward me as she continues with her insensitive analogy. "And it makes you want to dip into your savings and buy that house back."

I don't know if she's joking, but I laugh regardless because it's so ridiculous. Does she truly think she can just snap her fingers and get him back?

"I don't think it's going to be that easy." I gesture at myself. "You know, on account of his girlfriend."

"It was a joke."

"No," I say evenly. "I don't think it was."

Any lingering humor fades. "It was a joke," she repeats.

"Really."

We stare at each other for a minute. Her unwavering gaze doesn't bother me. I jerk a finger toward the ivy-colored building twenty yards away.

"That's you right there."

"Thank you." Lynsey takes a step forward, then stops to look over her shoulder. "I don't want Shane back, Diana." She pauses meaningfully, a smirk forming on her pouty mouth. "If I did, though, it wouldn't be that hard to get him."

With that, she saunters off.

I'm utterly fuming as I walk into the gym a few minutes later.

What the *hell* was that? This chick actually thinks she can steal my man?

He's not your man.

Okay, but *she* doesn't know that.

And she has a boyfriend of her own! What kind of selfish-ass bitch goes around threatening to steal someone's boyfriend when she's got one at home?

He's not your real boyfriend.

Well, maybe he fucking should be, I silently snap at the voice in my head.

My volatile response to Lynsey's threat gives me pause. Is that what I really want? For Shane to be my boyfriend? My mind is suddenly a jumbled mess.

The only thing I'm certain about is that I cannot fucking stand Shane's ex.

I stomp into the locker room and yank open my locker, so I can shove my backpack into it. Then I take a long, calming breath.

I can't go into practice this riled up. You need a cool head when you're performing stunts and tumbling routines where one misstep can mean a broken bone or a concussion. Not only that, but I have an added dose of pressure when it comes to this squad. Not only am I the captain, but I'm also one of three flyers and the top girl. That means I'm at the top of the pyramid, which is fucking terrifying. The pressure is liable to choke you alive if you let it.

As captain, I always show up early for practice so I can check in beforehand with our coach, Nayesha. So I'm startled when I hear footsteps nearing the locker room door. A lot of them. Which is even weirder. One girl might show up thirty minutes early, but not the three that enter a moment later.

Suddenly I find myself on the receiving end of three grave expressions.

"Sit down, Captain," Audrey says.

It's sort of a random trio. Crystal and Audrey are friendly but not close, and Madison doesn't really interact with either of them. The only thing they have in common is…

Shane.

Goddamn it, Lindley.

Is his fan club going to beat me up in the locker room for getting with him? I told Crystal during our first cheer practice this week that I was seeing Shane. It was a full-disclosure, I-need-to-be-transparent chat that I really didn't want to have but forced myself to because I knew eventually it would get around.

"Sit down," Crystal urges, and that's when I realize they don't actually look mad.

They're concerned.

"I'm going to keep standing, if you don't mind."

They all cross their arms in identical poses. Crystal speaks up in a firm tone.

"This is an intervention, Diana."

ARCHENEMIES

- [ ] *Madame Cotillard*
- [ ] *Shane Lindley*
- [ ] *Constantine Zayn*
- [ ] *Viktor and Martinique*
- [ ] *Lynsey Whitcomb*
- [ ] _____

CHAPTER THIRTY-EIGHT

SHANE

Wait, are you flirting?

OUR FIRST GAME ISN'T UNTIL NEXT WEEKEND, SO I'M ABLE TO ATTEND the football team's season opener in our home stadium with Ryder, Gigi, and a few other teammates. Freshman Blake Logan also tags along. On our way to pick her up from the dorms, Gigi tells me she promised Blake's dad that she'd watch out for Blake.

Blake's dad being John fuckin' Logan. It's surreal to me, the idea of having John Logan, one of the best defensemen of the last couple decades, as your father.

I wonder what my life would have been like if my dad's NHL journey had ended differently. Hell, I might not even be here. Maybe he would've been so absorbed in the professional hockey lifestyle that he decided to hold off on having children for a few years. Or never had them at all.

In the stands near the fifty-yard line, I sit between Patrick Armstrong and Blake, who boasts those fresh-faced girl-next-door looks with a light smattering of freckles and her brown hair arranged in a side braid. But that body is *dangerous*, hugged by tight jeans and a halter top that bares her midriff. I can understand why John Logan enlisted some bodyguards. Dudes are going to be all over this chick.

On the field, the football team is looking incredible. It's only their first game, but I'm impressed by how well they gel. Our quarterback connects with every pass, and our superstar wide receiver is on fire tonight. He's a junior now, but his sophomore season was equally explosive. I wasn't able to catch as many games as I would've liked, but I remember the entire campus buzzing about Isaac Grant last year.

During halftime, Diana leads her squad in a lively, stunt-heavy routine, knocking it out of the park, of course. I can't take my eyes off her. That short cheerleading uniform reveals a lot of leg and a lot of stomach as she's tossed through the air by the men on the team. I can't wait to fuck her tonight.

After the game, Diana meets us in the parking lot, bouncing on her white tennis shoes. She's still in her uniform, hair in a high ponytail, eyes shining.

"You killed it," Gigi tells her.

"Thanks, babe." She hugs the girls. "Ready for your first frat party, Blakey?"

"Yeah, excited about the party, Blakey?" I mock.

Blake rolls her eyes at me. "One, don't ever call me Blakey. Only Di is allowed. And two, I'm being dragged to this thing against my wishes. I've been promised the full college experience and apparently that involves drunk frat guys."

"She needs to be initiated into campus life," Diana says firmly. "It's not college without drunk frat boys."

Diana, Blake, Patrick, and Austin Pope pile into my Mercedes. I'm not planning on drinking tonight, so I'm the DD, chauffeuring us to Greek Row.

"Did you see the way Madison was glaring at me in the parking lot?" I grumble to Diana. I can still feel the cheerleader's dour gaze boring into me.

She reaches over from the passenger side, resting her hand on my thigh. "Can't charm them all, babe."

"I still can't believe the cheerleaders held an intervention for you. About *me*."

Patrick chortles from the back seat. "For real?"

Diana twists around to grin at him. "It was amazing. I wish I'd filmed it."

"What, do they all hate you or something?" Blake asks curiously.

"They sure didn't hate me when they were moaning my name," I taunt.

Diana smacks my arm. "Uncouth!"

"Got it," Blake says in amusement. "So you broke all their hearts."

"Their hearts shouldn't have been involved in the first place," I argue. "Seriously. This is why I think casual sex is some sick joke. A hoax society decided to play on us. Seems like it only upsets people."

"Honestly, I deserved the intervention," Diana sighs. "It was payback for all the times I told them how awful you were. To them this must seem like I've lost my mind."

The frat house comes into view, and I park twenty yards away on the street. I'd like some distance between my Mercedes and inebriated assholes, thank you very much.

Music reverberates so loudly that I can feel the beat standing on the sidewalk outside of Kappa Nu. People are filtering in and out, some of them already stumbling even though it's only eight o'clock. Neon lights flash out of the front door, and the deafening music combined with the inadequate lighting is a headache waiting to happen. I sort of wish I were drinking.

Diana links her arm through Blake's. "Now, seeing as this is your first official college party, don't let the boys in there give you the wrong idea of men," she warns. "These are not men—they are overgrown children. They think fart jokes are funny, and their flirting consists of holding your legs during a keg stand and saying 'nice tits.'"

"It's true," Patrick confirms to Blake. "By the way, nice tits."

She grins at him.

We enter the frat house, Diana walking ahead of me, hips swinging and ass swaying in that tiny skirt.

I capture her waist and tug her backward. "Want to go upstairs and sit on my face?" I whisper in her ear.

She shivers. "Stop tempting me."

As the others venture deeper into the party, we remain in the hall, my body pressed against her back. I slip both hands under her skirt and cup her ass. Diana squirms.

I rest my chin on her shoulder. "You know, considering all the cheerleaders I've been with—"

"All five thousand of them?"

"All million of them. I've never actually fucked anyone while they're wearing a cheer uniform."

Her answer is a taunt. "Who says I'm going to let you fuck me?"

"Is your hand under her skirt?" Beckett drawls, coming up to us with Will in tow.

"No," I lie.

"I can see it."

"You're hallucinating."

Diana laughs. I give her ass cheek a little swat before sliding my hands out. Will glances at me. He doesn't say anything, but I'm sure he's thinking about what happened in Diana's apartment that night. I think about it often.

It wasn't awkward, either, when he and I drove to practice the next morning. I expected it to be, but we chatted in the car as if nothing had happened. I guess Will's used to playing it cool after a night of kinky sex. God knows he has experience with it these days.

"Dixon!" someone shouts when we enter the crowded living room.

For a second I'm startled because I'm the one who calls her that. Isaac Grant, star wide receiver, saunters toward us holding a red cup full of beer and sporting a victorious grin. He has every right to gloat. He finished that game with ten catches for a hundred and eighty-two yards, two touchdowns. He's a weapon.

Isaac throws an arm around Diana and smacks a kiss on her cheek.

I try to ignore the sizzle of jealousy that heats my blood. The cheer team attends every football game, so the players and cheerleaders spend a lot of time together, I get that. Diana's bound to be close with some players.

But Grant triggers my possessive side. He's a good-looking dude. Tanned skin, chiseled jaw, at least six four, and ripped. His only flaw? He's a ginger. Although admittedly, his hair is more auburn with blond highlights as opposed to creepy orange.

I greet Isaac with a nod. "Hey, bro. Good game."

"Thanks." He doesn't miss the way I reach for Diana's hand. "Dixon, this your boyfriend?"

"Yup."

He continues to size me up. "Basketball?"

"Hockey."

"Nice. You hockey bros are tough as nails."

"Damn right."

Grant's interested gaze shifts toward Blake. "Who's your friend?" he asks Diana.

"This is Blake. Blake, Isaac."

Almost instantly, he lays on the charm. "What did you think of the game, gorgeous?"

Blake looks amused. "Why do you assume I went to your game?"

"You didn't?"

"No, I did." She flicks up an eyebrow. "That second TD catch was impressive."

"I aim to please." Grant proceeds to crank it up to another level, going on about the game while throwing in several double entendres to hint that his physical prowess extends beyond the field.

He's midsentence when Blake cuts him off.

"Wait, are you flirting?"

Isaac looks startled.

I snort into my drink.

"Oh, you were. Got it. I thought we were all just listening to you tell us how great you were, but then you made that comment about your strong hands and nimble fingers, and I was like, oh shit. He's flirting." She glances at Diana. "I'm sorry. That was rude. Is he a close friend of yours?"

I keel over in laughter because this man can get any girl he wants and a freshman just demolished his ego in five seconds.

Isaac narrows his eyes. "What did you say your name was again?"

Diana can't control her own laughter. "Oh, now he's pretending he doesn't know your name," she tells Blake. Giggling, she strokes a soothing hand over Grant's broad shoulder. "It's okay, sweetie. Just abort. Go somewhere else and lick your wounds."

Eyes narrowed, he saunters off to save face. And yet, for the next hour, I keep catching him staring at Blake. Diana notices too.

"I think you've intrigued our superstar," she says. "Tread carefully, though, because his reputation is warranted. I think he's slept with every cheerleader on the team, even the ones with boyfriends."

"Including you?" I growl.

"No." Then she sighs. "We just made out."

Blake snickers into her beer. I know I shouldn't encourage underage drinking, but so far, she's only had one, and I'm keeping a close eye.

"You don't have to worry," Blake assures us. "I'm allergic to arrogant men."

Like Diana warned her, the frat boys become more and more juvenile the drunker they get, but the party doesn't get as rowdy as I expect. Aside from one Kappa Nu pledge streaking naked down the street and another one jumping off the roof into the backyard pool, it's fairly tame for a Greek Row kegger.

I dance with Diana and Blake. Chat with Ryder and the guys. I ask Will to join me at the driving range tomorrow morning, and when he says he can't, Diana tugs on my arm.

"I'll come with you if you want," she offers.

"Really?"

"Sure. You were at that club almost every day this summer. I want to see what all the fuss is about."

Later, we're watching a competitive game of beer pong in the dining room when Isaac Grant braves Blake's sharp tongue again and joins us. His biceps flex beneath a black T-shirt with the Briar football logo.

"What do you want for breakfast tomorrow?" he asks Blake.

A frown creases her forehead. "Breakfast?"

He winks. "You're spending the night at my place—it's only fair I buy you breakfast."

"Smooth," I tell him.

Blake remains unimpressed. "Sorry. I've got plans." She tips her head at Diana. "I think I've had enough of this party. Are you ready to go?"

CHAPTER THIRTY-NINE

SHANE

Open book

THE FOLLOWING MORNING, I PARK THE CAR IN THE MEMBERS' LOT AT the country club and turn to my two companions. Blake crashed at Diana's condo last night, so she's tagging along again. The three of us grabbed breakfast—sans Isaac Grant, poor bastard—before heading to the driving range.

"Have you ever been golfing?" I ask Blake.

"Yes." She purses her lips. "I hate it."

That doesn't bode well. And I know for a fact Diana hasn't. She's not even dressed for golf. She's wearing a crop T-shirt and yoga pants that stop above her calves. A blond braid hangs down her back and a pair of big black sunglasses sit on her cute nose.

Blake is taking advantage of the warm September weather in a thin white tank top and tiny denim shorts. They're not indecent by any means, at least not enough to invite the ire of the country club puritans, but she'll definitely be drawing some eyes.

Since I only own a set of men's clubs, we stop at the rental hut first to grab some clubs for the girls.

"I can get it," Diana offers.

"Nah, it's on me. I have a membership."

After the kid in the hut charges the rental to my account, I shoulder both bags as we walk the flower-lined path toward the driving range. The scent of freshly cut grass hangs in the air. We find a far spot away from most of the other golfers.

Diana stares at me expectantly.

"What?" I say as I slide my driver out of the bag. I remove the cover and smooth my hand over the sleek surface.

"You said you were gonna teach me how to golf," she reminds me.

"We literally just got here."

"Yeah, and I thought we'd get right down to business." She pouts. "I expected you to do something really hot."

"Yeah," Blake agrees. "I thought you'd lean in real close and put your arms around me very seductively and then whisper, *It's all in the grip.*"

I throw my head back and laugh. "Okay—one, I'm using that line from now on. And two, I'm pretty sure your father would rip my tongue out if I ever said that to you and amputate my hands if I ever touched you. Therefore, I will only instruct you from a discreet distance."

Blake flicks up an eyebrow. "Coward."

"Coward," Diana echoes tauntingly.

"Really, Dixon? You want me to put my hands on another woman and whisper seductively to her?"

"In the spirit of golf, I would accept it."

I snort. "All right, pull out that driver. Let's work on your swing."

Diana reaches into the women's bag.

"I've been told the key to a perfect swing is all in the grip." I wink at her. "And I know for a fact you've got a phenomenal grip."

Blake sighs. "I know you're talking about handjobs, and I don't like it."

I shrug. "I'm not sorry."

"He never is," Diana tells her.

I stand next to Diana and show her how to properly hold the

driver. When she mimics the grip I demonstrate, I reach down to adjust her fingers.

"There. Perfect. Now widen your stance. You want your feet shoulder-width apart. Relax your shoulders too."

I turn to Blake to offer the same advice—in time to see her drive the ball a hundred and forty yards.

My jaw drops. "What the hell, Logan?"

"Oh, I'm not bad at golf," she says with a smirk. "I just said I hate it."

"Don't ever deceive me again."

Laughing, she places another ball on her tee. Seeing as how she doesn't need my help, I leave her to it.

I set Diana's ball for her and then step back. "It's all about timing and coordination," I advise. "Keep your eye on the ball. You got this."

She doesn't got it.

At least not right away. Diana shanks her first swing, sending tufts of grass flying all over my shoes. But the failure only fuels her. Suddenly she gets that adorable furrow in her brow, the one that tells me she's about to overcome a challenge or die trying.

She nails her second swing, driving the ball about sixty yards.

"Did you see that?" Diana spins around. "That was beautiful."

"It *was* beautiful," I say, fighting a smile. "Now let's work on your distance."

She throws her arms up in a victory pose, and I notice a few guys in their mid to late twenties blatantly checking her out. Yeah, my fake girlfriend's hot.

If I'm being honest, though…this isn't feeling very fake anymore. Sure, we're friends with benefits, but those benefits are starting to extend beyond the sexual variety. We're constantly texting. Calling each other. Dancing together. Hell, I brought her along for my last afternoon of me-time before the hockey season is officially underway. And not only she is *not* complaining about spending her morning at the driving range but she's making a sincere effort to learn.

The only other woman I've taken golfing is Lynsey. Yes, my ex used to do me the honor of coming with me once, maybe twice a year if I was lucky. And one of those times was for my birthday because I begged her to play eighteen holes with me.

I remember that birthday vividly. Lynsey sat in the golf cart most of the time checking her phone, totally missing when I nailed a hole-in-one on the course. She'd mustered up some enthusiasm at my proud roar, but I could tell she didn't give a shit.

Now, I stand here envisioning myself hitting a hole-in-one with Diana on the green beside me. Christ. Dixon would probably perform an entire cheer routine to celebrate my achievement. The certainty of that elicits a rush of pleasure.

Oh man. My chest is tight with emotion now. I'm such a fuckin' sap.

As I switch to a nine iron so I can work on my shorter game, I grin at the sight of Diana hyping Blake up. "You got this, Blakey. I think you can add an extra five yards to your next drive."

"God, you're such a cheerleader," Blake says dryly.

"I can't help it." Diana bounces on her heels. "I just want people to do well." When she wanders back to me, genuine excitement dances in her green eyes. "This is so much fun. Thanks for bringing us."

"I'm glad you're here," I say thickly.

Whatever she sees on my face has a smile tugging on her lips. "Is that so?"

"It is so. And I'm glad you're actually having fun."

"I'm having a blast. I think next time we should play a whole game."

I swallow the sudden obstruction in my throat. "Yeah, we should. It's, uh, really cool having you here."

It's hard to articulate how I feel right now. It's almost a bit ridiculous, feeling this level of joy and tenderness over something as silly as a woman showing enthusiasm for one of my hobbies.

Diana frowns, and I know she's reading my mind. "Did Lynsey hate golf or something? What, did her family die in a tragic golfing accident and she can never play the game again?"

"No, her family is alive and well." I shrug. "She came golfing on my birthday if I asked her to, but that's about it. She didn't show much interest in the things I was into."

"And I bet you attended all her dance competitions and sat in the front row holding a huge sign that said *dance baby dance*."

"I mean, no, there were no signs involved." I snicker. "But yes, of course I went to her performances."

"Don't take this the wrong way, but…" Her tone is careful. "This relationship sounds like it was very one-sided."

I glance over at Blake, who's checking her phone several feet away. Then I lower my voice. "What does that mean?"

"It means it sounds like you did all the heavy lifting. Or rather, all the heavy bending."

"That's not true."

Diana goes quiet for a moment. When she speaks, it's with a chord of hurt. "Remember on the way to your parents' house, how you told me to tone myself down? When we were talking in the car?"

Her indictment evokes a spark of guilt. Shit. I don't even remember saying that. But I apologize nonetheless.

"I'm sorry. That was a crappy thing to say."

"Yes, it was. And Percy did the same thing sometimes, telling me I needed to change something about myself." Diana cringes at the sound of his name, as if it's painful leaving her mouth. "But that's not my point. What I'm trying to say is—from what I've seen and heard, you're the one toning yourself down."

"What do you mean?" I ask warily.

"Pardon the super-cheesy expression, but it's like Lynsey dims some of your light."

A frown twists my lips.

"It seems like you were trying really hard to impress her or something."

"Okay, that sounds pathetic."

"It's not. It's only natural to want to make the person you're with happy. You do want to impress them. But it sounds like you made all the compromises. It had to be your *birthday* for her to do an activity you enjoyed. What did she do to support *you*? Did she come to your hockey games?"

I shift in discomfort. "She was busy with rehearsals."

Diana doesn't comment on that, but her expression says, *I rest my case.*

She falls silent again, then lets out a breath. "I just get the sense that this relationship might not have been as magical as you remember. Because from an outsider's perspective, it doesn't seem like the healthiest." She shrugs. "And I suspect I'm not the only one who thinks that."

My frown deepens. "What do you mean?"

"Just some things your dad said. He told me that you laugh a lot when you're around me. That you act differently. He didn't specifically mention Lynsey, but it was implied that maybe you weren't yourself when you were with her."

I object to that. "Lynsey and I had great times together."

"I'm not saying you didn't. But I do wonder if you were ever truly yourself with her. Did you fully open up? Show her every part of you?"

"Oh my God, Diana," Blake interrupts. "Come see this."

"Sorry. I'll be right back." Diana squeezes my arm and walks over to peer at the phone Blake is holding out to her.

Her words leave me with a bad taste in my mouth and a jumble of thoughts in my brain.

Was I ever truly open with Lynsey?

The thing is…yes. I was open. I was vulnerable with her, sharing intimate parts of my psyche. I confessed to certain kinks—she didn't want to indulge me. I invited her to everything—she didn't want to come. And then, when she did come, she made it clear she wasn't having a great time.

Fuck. It bothers me that my dad thinks I acted differently around Lynsey. Like I was some chump who let a girl walk all over him.

But I never viewed our relationship like that. Yes, it had its issues, and maybe in hindsight, I did make the bulk of the compromises, but—

"Shane, come look at this."

I push the troubling thoughts aside and join the girls. Blake shows me a picture from Gigi and Ryder's wedding of a dark-haired man trying to do the splits on the dance floor.

"This is my dad's old teammate from Briar. Mike Hollis." Blake can't stop giggling. "This is right before he tore his pants and then his wife started yelling at him and made him go home."

I laugh. Oh yeah. I remember that dude. He and his wife were tearing up the dance floor all night. Blake scrolls through the rest of the pictures in the sequence, which show a petite woman with brown skin and dark hair reprimanding the man with the ripped trousers.

"These are hilarious," I say, before realizing something. "You know what, I haven't actually seen any pictures from the wedding, other the ones I took."

"Oh, I have a whole folder on my phone," Diana tells me.

"You do? Where's your phone?"

"It's on top of our golf bag."

"Nice. I'll grab it." I'm about to go when Blake suddenly gasps. "Oh my fucking God."

"What is it?" Diana asks.

"Isaac just messaged me."

Now Diana gasps. "Isaac Grant?"

I raise an eyebrow in amusement. "Mr. Superstar Wide Receiver? Check you out, Logan. Attracting the big guns."

"How did he get your number?" Diana looks like she's trying not to laugh.

With deep resignation, Blake reads out loud. "'Hey, it's Isaac. Don't ask how I got your number. It took me forever and I had to go through some pretty dark channels.'"

I snort.

"Then he sent a follow-up. This one says, 'Let's not beat around the bush. I want to see you again.'"

"Wow." I'm legit impressed. "Good for him."

Blake glares at me. "No, not good for him. This is basically stalking!"

"Nah. He's just shooting his shot. You should say yes."

"I can't believe I'm seconding this," Diana pipes up, "since he's such a massive manwhore, but I agree. I think he has a secret soft side."

"Yeah? If you two love him so much, you date him." Blake rolls her eyes. "Cocky football players aren't my type." She pauses. "Although I guess I'd prefer that to a cocky hockey player."

"What's wrong with hockey players?" I demand.

"My mom and I are football fans."

I stare at her, slack-jawed. "This is blasphemy. Your father's John Logan."

"Uh-huh, he is. I cheered at all his games growing up, and I guarantee I know more about hockey than most of your teammates. But if I have to choose a game to attend, I'd way rather be sitting behind the Patriots' bench than center ice at TD Garden."

"You are disowned." I shake my head at her.

Diana and Blake proceed to ignore me as the former tries to convince the latter not to respond with "Pass."

I no longer care about the conversation now that I know Blake is a traitor, so I go to find Diana's phone. I want to send myself those wedding photos.

"Is it in your albums?" I call over my shoulder.

"Yeah. In a folder called G's Wedding."

"Cool."

I grab the phone and unlock it; I already know the passcode because I've used her phone before. That's another difference between her and Lynsey. My ex would never give me the password to her phone. I don't think she was cheating or anything, though. That's just Lynsey's personality. She's a private person. Reserved. Diana, meanwhile, is an open book.

I head back to the girls, scrolling through Diana's photo albums. And that's when I realize she's not an open book at all.

CHAPTER FORTY

SHANE

That's not who I am

IT'S A STRUGGLE TO KEEP MY COMPOSURE AS DIANA AND I DRIVE BLAKE back to campus. Without a word, I pull into the parking lot behind Burton House, Blake's dorm, and kill the engine.

"Thanks for the ride," she says, reaching for the door handle. "This was fun."

"Don't ignore Isaac," Diana scolds as Blake hops out of the backseat. "Give him a chance."

"I don't think so."

Diana rolls down the window, shouting after her. "Give him a chance!"

"Nah" is the response floating in the wind.

Diana turns to me and grins.

I'm incapable of sharing in her humor. I cannot unsee what I saw in her phone. It's burned like a cattle brand into my brain.

Her smile slowly fades. "What's wrong?"

I take a breath. I can't find the words. I honestly don't know how to start because I'm so fucking livid.

"Shane, hey."

She reaches for my hand.

I shrug it off.

"Seriously, what's wrong?" Deep concern lines her voice. "You're freaking me out."

"Dixon." I drag another burst of oxygen into my aching lungs. "I am trying really hard right now not to explode and do something I'm going to regret."

"Regret?" Alarm widens her eyes. "What are you talking about?"

"I need you to be honest with me. I'm going to ask you a question and all I want from you is honesty. It's a yes or no. And I mean it. Don't lie."

She visibly gulps. "What is it?"

"Did your ex-boyfriend hit you?"

The car goes deadly silent. Diana's face pales, her expression stricken. I already know the answer before she even responds.

"Why are you asking me that?"

"Don't," I snap. "I asked for a yes or no. Did Percy hit you?"

After a long, tension-ridden silence, she says, "Yes."

Rage slams into me.

I grip the steering wheel with both hands, squeezing it until my knuckles turn white. I can't even think about putting the car in drive right now. Can't risk leaving this parking lot. Because if I do, I'll be tracking down Percy whatever the fuck his last name is and mowing him down with this car until he's a bloody pulp beneath my tires. And I don't give a shit if that makes me a psychopath. The knowledge that he laid his hands on Diana has dissolved my vision into a red haze. At this moment, I'm capable of murder.

"How did you…" She trails off.

"The folder on your phone," I bite out. "You should have moved it to one of your hidden folders."

"I didn't expect anyone to ever go through my phone," she says tightly.

"I didn't purposely go through it. I accidentally clicked it. And then what? I'm supposed to pretend I didn't see a picture of your *beaten face*?"

"It…it was just a black eye."

"Just a—!" I stop, taking a calming breath. I squeeze the steering wheel again before slowly lowering my hands. "Let me see it again."

"Why?"

"Because I only skimmed the messages. And I think it'll be easier to read rather than have you tell me, because I'm goddamn volatile right now and—"

"No, I get it," she cuts in. Hands shaking, she passes me her phone.

My heart batters against my ribs as I read through everything. Diana kept it all. From what I can gather, it happened after work. Percy showed up after her shift. Walked her home.

And fucking *hit* her.

He put his filthy, pathetic hands on her and—

I hiss out another breath. *Calm down.*

In his messages, Percy keeps insisting it was a reflex. Instinctual. But I saw the photo of her face. I saw her black eye in person. That was not instinctual. That was a sick asshole who hurt a defenseless woman.

Diana documented every text where he admits that he assaulted her. But he continues to blame *her* for it, saying she shoved him.

"Did you touch him?" I ask gruffly.

Her entire face collapses. "I didn't do anything. He grabbed my arm and I tried to push him off."

"Show me," I order. Not because I don't believe her, but because I require a visual of this in my head. So I have something to tell the cops after I murder this man. "Is this how he did it?"

I reach across the center console and grab her by the forearm. Gentle but firm.

"He grabbed you like this?"

She nods meekly.

"And what did you do?"

With her free hand, Diana shoves my shoulder.

"And then he punched you in the face." The rage bubbles up again. "*That* was his response to you pushing his shoulder?"

"Yes."

There's another beat.

"*Why the fuck didn't you go to the cops?*"

She flinches.

I immediately collect my temper.

"I'm sorry. No, Dixon, I'm sorry. This isn't on you. This is on him. I…" I hear my pulse thudding in my ears. "I don't understand why you wouldn't report this. Why did you lie and say you got hurt at cheer camp?" She told me she took an elbow to the face, for chrissake.

"Because it's embarrassing!"

Her voice cracks. So does a piece of my heart. I've never seen Diana look so destroyed. She sits in the passenger seat, completely stripped away of the confidence I've come to adore, tears streaming down her cheeks.

"That's not who I am, okay?"

"What does that mean?"

"It means I can take care of myself." Her voice trembles wildly. "You heard the stories my dad told you. I'm the one who kicks people's asses. I'm *not* the woman who gets hit by a man, all right? I didn't report it because I *can't* be that woman."

"Baby." I unbuckle my seat belt, then lean over to unbuckle hers. "Come here."

"No." She tries to twist away from me.

"Come here," I repeat, reaching for her.

This time she doesn't resist. She climbs into my lap and buries her face in my neck. We sit there in the dorm parking lot, and I hold her tight while barely restrained rage boils in my blood.

Diana straightens up, her tear-streaked face breaking my heart.

"I'm the strong one," she mumbles. "I'm the unstoppable one, and some fucking asshole punched me on the sidewalk. I can't go to the police."

"Yes, you can. And you should," I say firmly.

She bites her lower lip, which is still quivering.

"You have to, Dixon. You can't let him get away with this, and I think deep down you want to report it."

Moisture clings to her eyelashes again.

"You do. That's why you saved this folder on your phone. You documented what he did and kept it because you knew you might need to use it. Actually, no, not *might*—you knew you *should* use it."

Diana starts to cry again, shuddering in my arms. "I can't go to the police. My dad is going to find out—"

"You're right. He'll find out. And once he knows what happened, he'll probably be as murderous as I am. But he loves you. And he'll know, just like I do, that you didn't do anything wrong."

Her teeth gnaw at her lip. "I provoked him."

"You didn't provoke him. You broke up with him and told him to leave you alone. He followed you to work and then assaulted you. That's all you need to say to the cops. Trust me, no one is going to victim-blame or think you did anything to cause what happened."

"His lawyer will if we go to court. Oh my God." Panic lights her eyes. "I'm not going to court, Shane. I'm not fucking testifying."

"I doubt it'll even reach that point," I assure her. "I guarantee you he'll plea out." I gesture to the phone I dropped in the cup holder. "You've got pictures. You've got texts. His own words admitting it. This is a slam dunk."

"Sure, you say that now, and then suddenly the next year, or however long it'll take, will be spent dealing with this." She makes a desperate noise in the back of her throat. "I don't want him in my life anymore."

"I don't want him in your life either." I gently touch her chin, forcing her to meet my gaze. "But let me ask you this—do you want him to find a new girlfriend? Because what if his new girlfriend makes him mad and then he hits *her* and gives *her* a black eye?"

Something flashes in Diana's eyes. I think it's anger.

"Yes," I urge. "Good. Be angry, baby." She *needs* to be angry. "You didn't do anything wrong. You didn't invite this. You didn't deserve this. And you need to report this. If you do, I promise I'll go with you. I'll drive you to the police station in Hastings right now, and I won't leave your side." I stroke her cheek. "And if you want, I'll be there when you talk to your dad. But this isn't something you can sweep under the rug and—"

I stop suddenly.

"What is it?" she says.

"This is why you wanted me to pretend to be your boyfriend when he showed up at Meadow Hill," I realize, cursing softly. "You were scared of him."

I inhale through my nose and try to ground myself because once again, if Percy were in front of me, I'd be ripping his throat out with my bare hands.

"You should have told me," I say gruffly.

She avoids my gaze. "I was ashamed."

"You have nothing to be ashamed of."

"I'm the girl whose boyfriend hit her. It's pathetic."

"Diana, stop. I know this is coming from a place of emotion, but once you're able to take a step back and look at it rationally, you're going to realize that that's not who you are. There is nothing pathetic about you and never will be."

"Do you promise?"

"I promise. And I promise to support whatever you decide to do, even if I disagree with it. With that said…" I grasp her chin to force eye contact. "Can I take you to the police station?"

Her mouth starts quivering again.

Then she nods.

CHAPTER FORTY-ONE
DIANA

You're human

POLICE STATIONS SUCK. AND NOT ONLY BECAUSE THEY SMELL LIKE stale coffee and the fluorescent lights give you migraines. They make you feel like you're in trouble, even when you did nothing wrong. It's an irrational response, I get that, but I can't fight the feeling that everyone is judging me as I spend my Sunday at the station in Hastings.

I'm forced to go over my statement several times. The detective in charge prints all the photos and the text messages from my phone, then advises me they'll need to contact my phone provider and verify things on their end too. Time stamps and such. She says they'll do the same with Percy's phone, once they get a warrant for it, and that they plan on bringing him into the station this evening.

I plan to be long gone before that happens. The idea of facing him makes me want to throw up. Yes, I faced him all summer. But this is different. It's like we had this closet full of skeletons and both agreed to lock the door. And then, without his permission, I unlocked that door and shone a light onto what he did.

Percy's not going to be happy, and I think Detective Wendt recognizes that because she also advises me to get a restraining order against him. Which means I need to repeat the story *all over again* to another officer and make another statement. By the time that happens, my dad finally arrives.

I don't know how Shane got his number, but when Dad joins us at the station, he says Shane's the one who called him. True to his word, Shane hasn't left my side all day.

The cops said I could get a lawyer, but I didn't want to wait around for hours on end for my dad's attorney to show up. Besides, my statement is one hundred percent the truth. If Percy's lawyer wants to twist my words later, let him. I'll hire a lawyer once we get to the next step. According to Detective Wendt, this is all very preliminary anyway. She's really nice, and there was nothing but sympathy on her face when I explained why I waited months to report the assault. She said she understood.

Flanked by two uniformed officers, Wendt approaches as we're leaving the station. She says they're going to arrest Percy now and bring him in for questioning.

But it's not until Dad, Shane, and I are outside on the front steps that my father drops a bomb on us.

Turns out, Percy already has another assault charge on his record.

Shane curses. "Are you kidding me? Why didn't Detective Wendt tell us that when Diana was giving her statement?"

"They're not allowed to disclose it at this point in the investigation," Dad says in a flat tone. "But I got my chief to run Percival's name through our system at the precinct while I was driving down here. It showed up in the search."

"Who did he assault?" I ask weakly.

"His previous girlfriend. Chief Stanton didn't have access to the entire report, so we only know the basics."

It suddenly gets hard to breathe. "I can't believe he's done this before."

My father hangs his head. "This is on me. I should have done a background search when you started dating him."

"Dad, come on." I can't help but laugh despite the gravity of the situation. "Of course you're not going to run a background check on my boyfriend."

"That's what any good cop would do."

"Dad, stop."

"What exactly do we know about the other incident?" Shane presses.

Dad quickly fills us in, but he's right—there's not much to go on. Apparently, my ex-boyfriend assaulted a woman he dated when he was doing his undergrad in New York. And while Percy's lawyer pushed to get the charges dropped on account of it being his first offense, the case went forward because the victim's mother was some big shot who fought for it. Percy only got probation, though.

It doesn't surprise me that he decided not to share this juicy tidbit with me. Why would he? *Oh, by the way. I smacked my last girlfriend around too.*

But this demonstrates a history of violence, and as awful as it is to think another woman might've suffered, it does make me feel slightly better about my own situation. Makes me wonder if maybe what happened to me was inevitable.

Although I drove to the station with Shane, my father insists on driving me home. While he goes to get the car, I stand on the curb with Shane, furrowing my brow at him.

"How did you get my dad's number?"

He hesitates.

"Shane."

"I asked Gigi for it," he finally reveals.

Anxiety rushes through me. "You told her what Percy did?"

"Not at first. All I said was that you were at the police station and needed to call your dad. I told her you were okay, but she kept insisting on driving down from Boston unless I gave her some answers. So eventually I had to tell her the truth."

I reach into my purse for my phone. It was off during the interview, and now I turn it on to a flood of texts from Gigi.

GIGI:

Are you okay?

GIGI:

I really hope you're okay.

GIGI:

I'll have my phone on me at all times, literally glued to my hand, waiting for you to text back. Love you.

"Are you pissed?" Shane asks nervously.

"No, it's fine. I would've had to tell her anyway now that I've pressed charges."

My dad's pickup truck stops in front of us.

"See you at home?" Shane says. "I can come over."

"Maybe later?"

He nods. "Shoot me a text if you want me."

After a beat of hesitation, I step forward and give him a hug.

He hugs me back, and there's something almost desperate in the way he clings to me.

"Thanks for bringing me here," I say quietly.

Shane tucks my hair behind my ear, his voice thickening. "I hope you don't feel like I pushed you into it."

"No, you were right. Deep down I always knew it was the right thing to do. It needed to be done."

There's a reason I kept all that evidence. I think I knew I'd eventually be here, at this police station. My only regret is not doing it sooner. I hope to God that Percy's lawyer doesn't try to paint me as some scorned girlfriend who tried to score payback after the fact.

"And one more thing," Shane says, tugging on my hand before I can leave. "You *are* unstoppable. Don't let what this one asshole did convince you that you're anything other than unstoppable. You're Diana Dixon, for chrissake."

I crack a smile. "Damn right I am."

And yet in the truck, I don't feel very strong. My dad doesn't say much on the drive to Meadow Hill other than to ask how I'm doing at least four times. The fifth time he asks, we're walking down the path toward Red Birch, and I stop to sigh in exasperation.

"Dad, it's not like this happened last night. It happened months ago."

His jaw tightens. "Right. And I still don't understand why you wouldn't report it."

"I already explained why." I start walking again.

He chases after me. "Diana, you know what I do for a living. I protect people. If you told me, I could have protected you."

"It was already over and done with. The bruise healed."

"It *wasn't* done. This fucker moved into your apartment building!"

"I know, but I had Shane."

"And thank God that you had Shane!" Dad's face turns red, but I know he's not angry with me. He's upset. "What if Percy cornered you in the apartment? Did you *see* the layout we just walked through? That goddamn Sycamore building and now this winding path like we're in the goddamn Caribbean? What was your aunt thinking buying a unit here? What kind of security nightmare is this?"

"There are cameras everywhere," I remind him. "And you can't step foot on the property without going through the Sycamore building first."

"He was *in* the building, Diana. Do you not get that?"

Desperation clogs my throat. "No, I get it. I'm sorry. You're right."

"No. Don't apologize. I'm not blaming you for anything," he says as we enter Red Birch and climb to the second floor. "I'm just worried. You're my daughter. I don't want anything like this happening to you again."

"It won't."

"You're right. It won't. And now we're going to make sure it doesn't happen to anybody else."

"I'm sorry I waited so long to tell the police."

"I don't understand why you didn't tell *me*."

It's hard to speak past the lump in my throat. "Because you think I'm so tough."

Dad watches as I unlock my front door, an incredulous look on his face.

"You *are* tough, kiddo. Even after what this fucker did to you, you're still the toughest person I know." He trails inside after me, reaching for my hand to stop me from keeping my back to him. "Admitting that you're weak sometimes doesn't mean you're not strong. It means you're human."

"I didn't want you to think differently of me."

"I would never think differently of you. You didn't do anything wrong. You didn't invite this. Despite what you tried to put in your report, you didn't provoke this asshole. You were defending yourself, and his response was dangerously disproportionate. He left *marks* on you." Dad spits out a low, growled curse.

I sigh. "Are we going to need to get a restraining order against *you* to keep you away from him?"

"Probably," he says, deadly serious. "It's requiring all my willpower not to go and gather up the squad. Drive over to his house and disappear him."

"Disappearing people isn't even a SWAT tactic. Stop being so extra."

"It is when someone messes with your daughter." He chuckles. "And if you think I'm being extra, wait until your stepmother hears what this psycho did. She'll claw him up like a mama bear."

I groan suddenly. "Oh no. I'll have to tell Mom about this too, won't I?" Panic sparks in my gut. "Can you do it for me?"

Reluctance digs into his forehead. "Di. I think you need to be the one—"

"Please?" I beg. "I can't have this conversation with her. Not right now. I can't handle it. Can you just fill her in and tell her I'll talk to her about it when I'm ready?"

"If you really want me to do that, I will." He lets out a breath. "But I need you to understand something. You can handle anything that life throws your way. You will always be the strongest person I know. Hell, way stronger than I am."

"That's not true."

"I mean, I divorced your mother. *You* still have to keep dealing with her."

I manage a laugh. "She's not so bad."

"She isn't," he agrees. "But I do know you put on a front when you're with her because she brings out your insecurities. And then you put on this front with me, and with your brother, that nothing bothers you. But things *are* gonna bother you, and bad things are going to happen. They happen all the time, unfortunately. And it kills me that I can't stop them from happening to you. You're my entire life, you and Tommy."

A vise of emotion squeezes my heart.

"But here's the thing. Even though you're strong and capable of taking care of yourself—and I truly believe in that—you also need to be strong enough to know when to ask for help." His expression sharpens. "And when something like this happens? You fucking ask for help, Diana."

I bite my lip so hard, I feel a sting. "Okay."

We settle on the couch, and Dad runs me through what will likely happen with Percy. Basically, my role in this is over for the time being. Now it's a matter for the detectives to investigate and then the courts to handle if the DA pursues the case.

After Dad leaves, I take a shower and reflect on this day from hell. It started off so promising too. Golfing with Shane and Blake, having a great time. And somehow it ended with me having to sit in a sterile interrogation room and share my humiliation with total strangers.

I rub my face, letting the shower spray beat into my forehead. Fuck. I need to start reframing the way I think about this, I know that, but it's difficult not to view this as embarrassing.

I just need to keep reminding myself that what happened doesn't make me weak or pathetic. I would never dream of looking at victims of domestic abuse and thinking, *gee, they're so pathetic.* I would champion them until the death. So why can't I do the same for myself?

Although this isn't a new thought to me, for some reason it really takes root this time. No one deserves to be hit. No woman, no man, no child. An intimate partner should not be doing that to you, ex-boyfriend or not. It's not right.

What Percy did was *not right.*

I get out of the shower and towel off, then go to feed Skip. He death glares at me, and I death glare back. After his fat belly is full of diet food, I call Gigi and we spend the next hour talking about everything that happened. She's upset I didn't tell her about Percy and even more upset when I blubber on about how ashamed and mortified I felt. But she assures me, like my dad and Shane, that I didn't do a damn thing to provoke this.

When we hang up, I find a text from my dad.

DAD:

> I filled your mother in. Told her you would reach out when you're ready to talk. She said okay.

Hurt stabs into me at the glaring absence of my mom's name on my notifications list. She knows what happened with Percy and didn't even contact me? Yes, I said I'd reach out when I was ready, but she could've at least checked in. A one-line text would have sufficed. *Listen, I know you don't want to talk, but I'm here for you and I'm waiting.*

But that's not Mom's style. She's so unemotional. This entire situation probably makes her extremely uncomfortable.

I also find a message from Shane, asking if I'm doing okay. I type back a two-word answer.

> Come over.

He's in my apartment literally a minute later. Also showered and changed, clad in a T-shirt and sweatpants, his feet bare.

Those dark hazel eyes search my face. "Rough day, huh?"

"Understatement much?"

"Yeah, I know." He pulls me onto the couch and wraps his arm around me. "Should we watch something?"

"Sure."

As Shane scrolls through the rows of titles on my movie channel, he looks over glumly. "I can't believe I'm saying this, but I miss *Fling or Forever*."

"Me too," I moan.

"Do we really have to wait until May?"

"May? What kind of hope planet do you come from? The new season starts next July."

"*July?* We don't even get it in June?"

"It's tragic. The fan base has been petitioning for two seasons. Some reality shows have a summer and winter season, but so far, TRN hasn't caved. I don't know if they have the budget."

"What budget? It's not like they do anything extravagant."

"The hacienda is pretty extravagant. And that yacht where Zoey fucked the Connor for the first time must have cost a pretty penny to rent."

"I guess." He absently runs his fingers over my shoulder, scanning the film options. "Ugh. There's nothing good here."

I take the remote from him and turn off the TV. "Let's go to bed."

"It's only nine. You're tired?"

"I didn't mean we would be sleeping."

His lips curve. "Oh. Got it."

"I just need…" I give him an earnest look. "I need some TLC. Can this be a me-night?"

"Baby, it's always a you-night. Even when I'm calling the shots, it's always about you. You're the only one I care about in there."

Oh hell. When he says things like that, it's impossible to deny my feelings.

Shane surprises me by lifting me up. Laughing, I wrap my legs around his waist and hold on to his neck. He carries me as if I weigh nothing at all and lays me on the bed so freaking gently.

"I'm not going to break," I tease him. "I mean, I got punched in the face and survived."

"Too soon," he mutters. "Still makes me murderous."

"Sorry."

"You might have had months to deal with it, but I only found out this morning. It's still fresh for me."

"I get it. I won't make jokes about it. I promise."

"Thank you."

His big, muscular body hovers over me, supported by his elbows. He starts kissing my neck and a shiver runs through me.

"Shane?"

"Hmmm?" His lips explore the sensitive tendons of my throat.

"Thank you for being there today."

His breath is warm against my flesh. "You're my girlfriend. Where else would I be?"

He didn't say the word *fake*. Usually when we're alone, we refer to ourselves as fake boyfriend and girlfriend.

Rather than point that out, I close my eyes and lose myself in his ministrations. His lips trailing over my collarbone. His hands pushing my shirt up and then his mouth coming down on my stomach to kiss it. He kisses my abdomen and my rib cage. The valley between my breasts as he slides my shirt off my neck. When

I'm lying there in nothing but a pair of cotton bikini panties, he runs his hand over my bare legs, propped up on one elbow as he admires my body.

"You're gorgeous."

"Thank you."

Shane's eyebrows fly up. "Wow. You said thank you."

"What do I usually say?"

"*I know.*" He snorts.

I shudder out a laugh. "You know I'm joking when I do that."

"Yeah. And you know I'm dead serious when I tell you you're gorgeous. Because you are."

His hand skims upward again, flattening against my stomach as it climbs higher and higher until curling around my breast. He squeezes softly, fingers toying with my nipple. Then he lowers his head and slowly starts kissing my breasts.

Shane unleashes a flurry of sensations in my body. He leaves no inch of skin unkissed. It's sweet and slow and exactly what I need. I'm gasping by the time his mouth finally travels between my legs. He plants a kiss over my underwear, smiling as he lifts his head, then slides his fingers underneath the waistband and pulls them off my ass, down my legs, and throws them away. He spreads me open and licks a sweet swirl against my clit before dragging his tongue through my slit.

"I love doing this," he says hoarsely. "I love how responsive you are. The noises you make."

I bite my lip as I watch him. He's being so gentle. I know he probably thinks I'm an emotional wreck tonight, but I'm not. I would be fine if he wanted to be rough. But I don't mind sweet Shane. I don't mind these soft kisses. I don't mind the tenderness of his fingertips as they dance along my hip on their way up to my breasts. With his mouth locked on my clit, he uses his other hand to ease one finger inside me. It's the most exquisite torture.

"Don't stop," I plead as my hips begin to move.

"Never," he promises.

When I feel the telltale tingling, pleasure rippling and build-ing in my core, I start to squirm in agitation. My thighs tremble. Opening and closing of their own volition. Shane chuckles. He knows I'm close. And he knows what's happening to me right now. That desperation I feel when I need it so bad but for some reason my body won't give it to me.

He also knows exactly what I need to get there. He pinches my nipple and that's it. Game over. The orgasm floods my body. Not an explosion but delicious waves of pleasure that languidly spread through me. I feel warm and cozy as Shane climbs his way up my body to kiss me. I taste myself on his lips when our tongues meet.

He cups my face, and I hook my leg over his hip. I'm completely naked, squished up against his fully clothed body.

I sigh happily. "That was nice."

I wait for him to take off his pants, but he stays fully clothed, lazily kissing my neck again.

"You're not gonna fuck me?" I complain.

"Not yet." His breath tickles my chin. "I'm just enjoying this."

We lie there kissing for what feels like ages, until eventually he gets naked and eases his thick cock inside me. The feeling of him sliding in bare is utterly exquisite. I don't come again, but he does, groaning into my hair as he shudders with release. Afterward, I leave to clean up and pee, then crawl back into bed next to him. Shane throws the covers over us, and I peek up at him, smiling.

"Are you staying over?"

"Mmm-hmm. Is that cool?"

"Yes."

In the three months we've been doing this, we've never spent the night together. It's been our way to keep it strictly friends with benefits. Or rather, friends with most benefits except for sleeping over, because that feels a little too intimate.

My head rests on his chest, and it feels so good to have him holding me. For a second, I almost ask him what we are. I'm no longer fighting my feelings for this man. I want a real relationship with him, yet I'm still not sure if he wants to be serious with me. But I don't want to spoil the moment. We can get into that another time.

Right now, my only focus is melting into his arms. I don't want him to leave tonight. And clearly, he doesn't either because he snuggles even closer and doesn't let go of me the entire night.

CHAPTER FORTY-TWO

SHANE

A weekend thing that weird people do

OCTOBER

IT DIDN'T EVEN OCCUR TO ME THAT I MIGHT HAVE TO MISS THE DANCE competition.

That's right.

NUABC is scheduled in the middle of my hockey season.

Luckily—and I'm talking damn lucky here because Dixon would've straight-up murdered me—I *think* I can make it. The competition is in Boston and wraps up late afternoon, and the team happens to be facing Boston College that evening, so the timing lines up. Only problem is, I won't be able to ride the team bus, and I'll also have to go play a highly physical game of hockey immediately after an entire afternoon of ballroom dancing. I don't know if Coach Jensen is going to be cool with that.

But we're about to find out.

I rap my fingers against his open office door. "Hey, Coach. I need to talk to you about something."

His eyes darken with suspicion.

"Why are you looking at me like that?"

"Because anytime one of you dumbasses comes to talk to me

about something, it's something that fucking annoys me." He waves me in. "What's this about?"

I stand in front of his desk, awkwardly sliding my hands in my pockets. "Um."

"Spit it out, Lindley."

"So there's this dance competition," I start.

"Fuck's sake." He puts down his pen. "See? What did I tell you?"

"Okay, I know that sounds…"

"Stupid?" he supplies.

I choose to ignore his close-minded criticism toward my dance ambitions. "My girlfriend and I have been rehearsing all summer for this, but it only occurred to me yesterday, when we were finalizing some details, that I never asked when it was."

He stares at me. "You never asked when it was," he echoes.

"I knew it was October, but I never asked for the actual date." I hang my head in shame.

Coach Jensen sighs.

"I don't know why, but for some reason I just assumed it would be on a weeknight."

"Why would a dance competition be held on a weeknight? Seems like a weekend thing that weird people do."

"Hey, I'm doing it and I'm not weird."

He stares at me again.

"Anyway." I gulp. "It's this Saturday. And like I said, we've been training hard for this. We sent our audition tape at the end of August. We're ready to go."

"Lindley. You're a hockey player. I don't care what kind of dancing you want to do in your spare time. But you play for the Briar University men's ice hockey team"—he enunciates slowly, as if he's trying to teach the ABCs to a toddler—"and therefore, you will be at the game."

"Oh, no," I reassure him. "I think I can be at the game."

"You think?"

"No, I *know* I can be at the game." God, I fucking hope I can be at the game. "I just won't be on the bus. Our first event is at noon, and then the American Smooth Duo is at four, so I doubt I'll make it back to campus by six to board the bus. But!" I flash him a beaming smile. "I'll already be in Boston, so all I have to do is—"

"Dance your way to the rink?" he finishes politely.

I glare at him. "You know, you could be more supportive. It's bad enough that everyone else makes fun of me. But guys on this team view you as a father figure. You should be supporting their dancing careers, not spitting on them."

"As much as I love the sarcasm—" A muscle ticks in his jaw. "You don't fuck around with my hockey schedule. And what happens if you get injured while you're off doing the mambo?"

"We're not dancing the mambo. We're doing the tango, the waltz, and—you know what? Forget it. Doesn't matter. But I promise you, we've nailed down our routines. We're good. No risk of injury."

He cocks a brow. "*Why* are you doing this?"

That's a very good question.

Originally, I agreed to partner up with Diana to make Lynsey jealous, but I can't remember the last time I thought about my ex. I've been absorbed with hockey and Diana and school. These days, when Diana and I schedule a dance rehearsal, the only thing I'm thinking about is how much fun we're going to have.

"I'm doing this because I enjoy it." I chew on my lower lip. "And because I know how much she loves it."

Coach leans back in his chair, studying me with those shrewd eyes. "Look," he finally says. "I might come off as a hard-ass sometimes."

"Sometimes?"

He ignores that. "But there's nothing I respect more than a man who values his woman."

"Aww. Coach. You're adorable."

"Shut the fuck up." He jabs his finger in the air. "Anyway, that's what I've learned after two decades of marriage. Value your woman. Respect her. Show interest in her interests. And hopefully she does the same for you."

"She does."

He nods, pursing his lips for a moment. "We need to be at the rink at six thirty. Warm-up skate is at seven. Can you be there?"

"Absolutely. The winners are being announced at five thirty. And I checked the directions from the hotel to the arena. I can make it to the rink by six thirty with time to spare."

"Time to spare, huh?"

"Yes." I get a wary feeling. "What is it?"

He tips his head, pensive. "Just remembering a conversation I had the other day with my little granddaughter. Morgan. She asked me if I take my guys on field trips."

"No," I say with dread.

"And I said, why would I take them on field trips? They're grown men, and they're hockey players. They don't need to go to the fucking zoo. Well, I didn't say *fuck*. But I was thinking it," he grumbles. His expression takes on a gleam that I really, really don't like. "But talking to you, Lindley, has opened my eyes. Made me reconsider my entire stance on field trips."

"No," I repeat, the dread twisting into horror.

In a rare occurrence, much like a total solar eclipse, Coach Jensen smiles at me.

CHAPTER FORTY-THREE
SHANE

Confi-Dance

"This is intense."

I glance around the ballroom of the Silverwood Hotel and wonder if it's too late to run for my life. The cavernous room is bathed in the crystal glow of chandeliers, casting shadows over the rows and rows of white chairs arranged in a square with a raised stage in the middle. Gilded mirrors and ornate crown moldings adorn the walls, and the dance floor we'll be tangoing and cha-chaing on today is a gleaming, polished wood.

Some pairs are brave enough to warm up in front of their competitors. The faint strains of classical music float through the ballroom as a middle-aged couple glides across the floor in a waltz. Their feet barely touch the ground. Jesus. They're incredible. But their count is all wrong.

Or maybe…

"Dixon." I frown, poking her in the ribs. "We've made a mistake."

"What do you mean?"

"Our waltz is too fast!" I accuse. "We're going to make fools of ourselves. Did you not look up the proper count for—"

"Relax," she interrupts with a laugh. She pats my arm. "They're doing a standard waltz. We're doing the Viennese. Ours is supposed to be faster."

I relax. Then tense again when I try to take a breath and not enough air gets in. I tug on my too-tight bow tie. Why am I wearing this? Why the hell am I here?

The panic and second-guessing wreak havoc until I notice Diana's face, flushed with excitement, and that's when I remember why I'm here. Because she worked hard for this. And because I made a commitment.

"Don't worry. We've got this." Diana turns away from the floor and lifts her hands to my shoulders, giving them a firm massage, like she's hyping me to get into the boxing ring. "And if we fail spectacularly, who cares? I didn't sign up for this thinking we'd win. This was the most fun I've ever had."

"Me too," I admit. And I'm not lying.

A familiar white-blond head catches my eye. "Babe," I say under my breath. "Don't look now, but the enemies have arrived."

"Who—" She stops. Eyes narrowing. "Confi-Dance."

"Pricks."

Viktor and Martinique from Confi-Dance, their uncleverly-named social media channel, saunter toward us with unearned confi-dance. Martinique does look amazing, though, if not a bit over-the-top. Her ensemble is made up of a form-fitting leotard adorned with sequins and rhinestones, which seems like overkill, but it clings to her body and emphasizes her ample boobs. Her skirt is see-through and has more sequins on it in strategic places. I guess the bling is supposed to be eye-catching. Diana did say our outfits need to "dazzle."

Personally, I prefer Diana's outfit. Hers is all drama and flair, while Martinique just went for shiny.

Diana's red leotard, a stretchy fabric with only a hint of adorn-ments, features lacy sleeves with a delicate pattern that goes through her middle fingers to secure them to her wrists. It has a plunging neckline and an open back, and unlike Martinique, she won't have to worry about her tits bouncing around. Dixon's are small and perky and contained. She's wearing a flowy skirt with a high slit, and when we practiced our spins earlier, that material billowed all around her, the slit showcasing her footwork. Apparently, it's supposed to accentuate her movements. All I know is I can see a lot of thigh, and my dick is happy.

"Don't you look cute," Martinique chirps to Diana. She raises a thick, dark eyebrow at me. "Those pants are a bit tight, no?"

They are. Diana dressed me tonight and I complained endlessly. But it's imperative to show a united front in the face of our enemies.

"Me?" I counter, flicking my gaze toward Viktor. "I can see the outline of your balls, bro. You sure wearing white was a good idea?"

Viktor tightens his lips. "Don't try to get in my head. It won't work."

"Really? Because you seem mighty rattled."

"I don't rattle."

"If you say so."

"I don't rattle."

I grin at him. "Sure, bro."

"Bullying everyone around you as usual, huh, Ride or Dance?" Martinique says darkly.

"As usual?" Diana echoes, looking amused. "We've literally never spoken to another NUABC competitor in our entire lives."

"Exactly." Martinique's voice is snide. "Snobs aren't welcome here, Ride or Dance."

"Can you please stop calling us by our social media channel?" I ask politely. "It's very dehumanizing."

They both scowl at me.

"Okay, then. See you later, Confi-Dance." I glance at my girl. "Can we remove ourselves from this creepy showdown?"

"God yes."

We leave them in the ballroom shooting daggers into our backs.

"I think they might actually be off their rockers," I tell Diana.

"Certifiable." She's still shaking her head about it. "Come on, let's go backstage. I want to check my makeup."

The hotel is permitting contestants to use the adjacent banquet hall as a backstage area. The huge space is packed with dancers in various states of undress. There are a lot of sequins and man-bulges in this room.

Diana's shoes click on the tiled floor on the way to the area where we left our stuff. They look like low-heeled sandals to me, but Diana assured me they're real dance shoes.

She approaches one of the mirrors in the vanity area and drags a french-tipped fingernail beneath her eye to smooth out the line of her eye makeup.

Damn, she looks so hot right now. I wish she'd kept her hair down, but she said it would be too distracting. Instead, it's in a tight ponytail secured at the nape of her neck. A red flower is clipped over her left ear. Throw in the bold-red lips and smoky eyeshadow, and I want to bend her over the vanity table and drill her right here in front of everyone.

Once she's satisfied with her makeup, she turns to face me.

"Repeat after me," she says firmly. "We are going to captivate the audience."

"I'm not repeating that. And I'm not captivating my asshole teammates."

Diana can't control her laughter. "I still can't believe Coach Jensen is bringing the whole team to watch us. Why would he do that?"

"Because he's the devil." I harrumph. "I told you to contact the NUABC people and make sure they didn't give him tickets."

"They wouldn't have gone along with it. The afternoon audience is always too small. They want to fill those seats."

"My teammates are going to be heckling us the entire time. I hope you know that."

She pales. "They'd better not. That could affect our scores!"

It's chaos back here. I continue scoping out our competitors, but it's hard to know who is entered in which category. I do know that the Solo and Duo categories are up first, though, while the pairs competing in the five- or nine-dance events don't go on until late afternoon and evening. That includes Lynsey and her partner, Sergei, so I'm startled when I spot her in the crowd.

Lynsey walks toward us when she catches my eye. She's in sweats, but her makeup is perfect and her hair is pulled back in the bun I've seen her wear a thousand times during ballet performances. Meticulously styled with sparkly hair pins above her temples because that's Lynsey. Meticulous.

Seeing the two women together, Diana is all glamour while Lynsey is pure elegance. They couldn't be more different.

"Just wanted to come over and say good luck," my ex-girlfriend says. She acknowledges Diana with a nod, but those dark eyes are focused only on me.

"Thanks," I answer. "Right back at you."

The awkward interaction is cut short when a NUABC official announces that the Duo and Solo competitors need to take their seats in the contestant section. Diana and I return to the ballroom and find ourselves seated next to Confi-Dance, who glare at us. These people need to have sex more often.

In the middle of one section of chairs is the judges' table. There are six of them, each one stoic-faced with a clipboard in front of them. Classical music reverberates in the room as couple after couple begin to take the stage. Some pairs are pretty good, while others dance in a clunkier manner, like professional athletes lumbering around on celebrity dance shows.

"I think we're better than most of these pairs," Diana whispers to me. "This year's talent isn't as good as last year's. That bodes well."

"Babe," I whisper back. "We're not going to win or place. You know that, right?"

My prediction is punctuated when Viktor and Martinique execute a flawless foxtrot that has all the judges nodding to each other. Dickheads. And since all twenty pairs in our category have to perform their first dance before anyone goes twice, Diana and I are forced to follow Confi-Dance, which I hate. I don't want the last memory in the judges' heads to be that stupid perfect foxtrot.

Our first dance is the tango because Diana wants to come out strong right out of the gate. I haven't quite been able to master that damned Viennese waltz.

I'm riddled with nerves as we rise from our seats. I've never been nervous before a hockey game, even a championship one, yet I'm sweating from anxiety right now.

Loud yells and hollers blast through the ballroom as we step out onto the floor.

"Yeah, Lindley!"

"GO GET YOURS, LINDLEY!"

Diana gives me a pained look. "Why can't *my* friends be here?" she mumbles. Her cheerleaders are at an away game with the football team, which Diana had to get special permission from her coach to miss. And Gigi and the women's hockey team are playing in Providence.

"At least we've got a fan section," I mumble back, but knowing my teammates are out there only exacerbates my anxious state.

My pulse is racing. Nerves twisting in my gut. What the fuck am I doing here? I'm the most confident man you'll ever meet. Secure in my masculinity. But these pants are too damn tight, and so is this shirt, and the bow tie is just plain ridiculous—

"You okay?"

The sight of Diana's face pulls me off the panic ledge. She's flushed with excitement, and I have to tell myself not to puke. I can't let her down.

"All good," I croak out.

A voice comes over the PA system. "Next pair, please get in position."

God. Kill me.

Diana and I walk to the opposite ends of the polished floor. I swallow hard, rubbing my palms against the front of my obscenely tight pants. Whispers and the rustling of clothing echo around us as everyone waits for us to begin.

"I CAN SEE YOUR BULGE, LINDLEY!"

Jordan Trager's voice breaks the silence, and I wish murder were legal in Massachusetts because I'd kill him if I could.

As we wait for our music cue, the air is charged with anticipation. Finally, the melody fills the ballroom.

Pray for me.

Diana and I lock eyes. She's a vision in red and black, silk and lace. Her lips quirk in a smile. I grin back.

Then we both glide forward, marching toward each other in what Diana likes to call "our journey across the floor."

I extend my hand.

Diana slips hers into it.

Her other hand rests on my shoulder, and suddenly we're surrounded by the most melodramatic music, courtesy of my melodramatic woman. I command the dance floor with a confidence I only half feel. I don't have time to wonder if I look stupid. To care that I'm making an ass of myself in front of my hockey team. I'm going to nail this fucking routine if it kills me. Diana follows my lead, surrendering to me the same way she submits in the bedroom. She's the better dancer, but I'm the lead.

Her steps are precise. Mine are less so but not embarrassingly bad. We communicate with our eyes, knowing exactly what needs to be done. We've practiced this routine so many times, I know it by heart, but tonight it's more seductive than I intend.

My hand finds the small of her back. I caress it and her breath hitches.

Our chests meet, then retreat.

I hear cries of approval in the audience and loud cheering from my teammates, but I drown it out. Only concentrating on Diana, my footwork, and the motherfucking tango. Legs intertwined, I march us with growing confidence, following the seductive steps she choreographed for us. The sultry rhythm gets in my blood. It's intoxicating. It makes me want to fuck.

My fingers graze her back again, stroking seductively. Christ, this sexual tension is something else. An electric charge that's about to set fire to this ballroom. I don't even care that Coach Jensen is probably having a panic attack.

Diana's heels click on the floor, my feet working hard to match her step for step. Every dip and twist get us closer to the end, and I realize the audience is quiet now. Just watching us. Diana is drama personified, so our tango features a lot of dramatic pauses, and I hear a woman gasp over the music at one point.

Everyone is collectively holding their breath when I lift Diana. She slides down my body and I immediately hook her leg and we march again. Her body is like liquid in my arms, enthusiasm and sensuality radiating in her movements. She's so hot.

Our bodies arch, legs intertwine as the song reaches its climax. If we were naked, I'd be coming inside her right about now.

We execute a final dip to the cheers of the audience. The bottom of Diana's ponytail brushes the floor as I hold her in a low dip. She's suspended there like a sexy angel. With our eyes locked, the final pose is intimate and sexy as fuck. We hold it as the music dies.

My heart is racing. I'm panting, feeling like I just played a full period of hockey without a rest.

There's a brief silence before applause erupts in the ballroom.

Yeah. We killed it.

Diana beams at me. She's breathless too.

"We did it!" She throws her arms around me.

I lift her off her feet, glancing over to see the judges scribbling wildly on their clipboards.

"Fuck," I say as we hurry off the floor. "I wish this score wasn't combined with the waltz. I think based on the tango alone, we could've placed."

"Oh, look who's getting invested now," she teases.

I grin. "Dixon. We slayed that tango. You know that, right?"

Proof of that is in the sulking faces of Viktor and Martinique when we pass their seats. Aw, someone's looking confi-sad.

"Nice job," Martinique spits out, as if the words taste bad.

"Thank you," Diana says magnanimously.

We bypass the seating section because Diana needs to make a quick wardrobe change. The backstage area is still bustling. A few monitors against the wall show live footage of the routines being performed in the ballroom, and I notice Lynsey standing near one with her partner Sergei. When her gaze finds mine and she gives me a smile and a thumbs-up, I can't decipher her expression.

"You were incredible," Diana tells me, awe rippling in her voice. "No joke, Lindley. That was phenomenal."

I can't deny my ego gets a nice boost hearing that.

Diana opens her garment bag and pulls out another skirt. She slips out of her red, filmy one, replacing it with a pleated number that falls to her ankles. It's a shimmery white, and the black leotard combined with the white skirt seem to transform her.

I was wrong. Diana is glamour *and* elegance. She's both.

"The waltz is more flowy," she explains, noticing me watching her. "All those sweeping movements. The pleats will emphasize that."

"Of course," I play along. "And it'll show off those indecent ankles. Get all the dicks hard."

"Exactly."

We have the Viennese waltz and the cha cha left, but now that I've gotten one dance out of the way, my nerves are fading.

"I'm sorry in advance if we don't win or place," I say gruffly.

"Honestly, I don't care. I'm just so happy we did this." Her gaze softens, her tone now lacking that usual Diana sass. "Thank you."

"For what?" I say thickly.

She stands on the tips of her high heels and brushes a kiss over my lips. "For everything. Talking sense into me about Percy. Humoring me with this silly stuff." She waves a hand around the backstage area. "I was wrong about you, Lindley. Turns out you're actually a good guy."

CHAPTER FORTY-FOUR

SHANE

History

I ENTER THE LOCKER ROOM TO THE SOUND OF DEAFENING CHEERS. Nazzy and Patrick hop up on the bench and wave their towels around in the air. Trager has rolled up his jersey and is slapping asses with it. You'd think they just won the Stanley Cup finals, instead of watched me dance around in very tight clothing.

My teammates are all cheering and shouting and telling me how fucking amazing I did. I feel bad that I had to leave Diana there for the winners' announcements. All the afternoon events are being announced now, the evening winners revealed later tonight at the after-party. I don't know if an after-party full of amateur ballroom dancers would be the greatest thing ever or the cringiest. Either way, I won't find out because I've got a hockey game to play.

"Dude, that was shockingly good." Our co-captain, Case Colson, claps his hand over my shoulder. "And shockingly hot."

"Yeah. My dick twitched," Trager confirms.

I snort.

"I'm not even joking," he insists. "Like *damn*. You and Dixon were generating some serious heat."

We totally were.

"Thanks for coming," I tell them, throwing my backpack in

the locker. I'm still in my dance costume. I didn't bother changing into my street clothes at the hotel since I was only going to have to change again when I got to the rink. I unbutton my shirt and wrench the bow tie off.

"When do you find out who the winners are?" Will asks curiously, sliding his chest protector on.

"Diana is going to text me. Should be any minute now."

I set my phone on the shelf inside the locker and start to get dressed. I've got all my gear on except for my skates when I hear the alert.

A moment later, I release a loud whoop that captures the room's attention.

Beckett lifts a brow. "Well?"

"Fifth place, motherfuckers!"

The room erupts again.

Trager, who couldn't even stand the sight of me last semester, hauls me off my feet in a hug. Then he pulls back and wrinkles his nose. "Wait, is fifth place good? That sounds kind of bad."

"Nah, man, it's sick. Diana didn't think we'd even make top ten."

Speaking of Diana, another text pops up. My eyes nearly bug out of their sockets when I read it.

DIXON:

> The 5th place prize is TEN GRAND!

Je-sus. What kind of hardcore amateur dance competition is this? I saw on the website that the first-place pair wins fifty grand, and I remember seeing the top five were also in the money, but I assumed that meant like six hundred bucks. Who the hell is funding this shit? Is the mafia involved?

DIXON:

> That's FIVE THOUSAND DOLLARS each!

I smile at the phone. Yeah, obviously I plan to give her the entire amount. I'm sure she'll fight me on that, but I'll fight harder. I'll let her buy me a nice dinner or something, though.

> How did Confi-Dance do?

> Don't be mad.

> 3rd place.

Assholes.

I can't deny that Viktor and Martinique were damn good, though. And while our tango was explosive, our waltz was par, and the cha cha was basically a disaster. I'm still stunned that Diana and I cracked the top five. It's a satisfying culmination to an entire summer's worth of rehearsals. Fifth place is a solid achievement, and I'm proud of us. I'm proud of Diana, who throws herself wholeheart-edly into her projects. She told me last night that her next goal is to learn Spanish, and there's zero doubt in my mind that she'll be fluent by the end of the year. She's that kind of person. Pure dedication.

I can't believe I ever thought she was just a flighty cheerleader. I was so wrong about this woman.

Coach marches in to go over some last-minute strategy, his sharp gaze seeking out Beckett. "Dunne, I'm putting you on Lindley's line tonight."

Nice. I love it when Beck's on the ice with me. He's such a fuckin' goon. I always know I'm going to get the puck because Beckett will have all the opposing forwards tangled up against the boards. He's probably the best defenseman on the team.

He and I fist-bump, grinning at each other. We haven't played on the same line since Eastwood College. When we transferred to Briar, he was put on the first line with Ryder, Case, Will, and David Demaine. But now that Demaine and a bunch of other seniors graduated, Coach and his staff keep rearranging the lines, trying to find a configuration that works. Tonight, I'm playing with Austin Pope, last year's freshman superstar who's now a sophomore sensation, and a couple other sophomores who are still a little wet behind the ears. Beck will be a welcome addition.

"Hey, Coach," Nazem calls out. "Lindley placed fifth in the dance thing."

Jensen fixes me with a withering look. "If you're not first, you're last."

"Dude. Fifth place is awesome for my first dance competition. Come on, tell me I did a good job. You can do it, Coach—just one good job."

He glowers at me. But as he's turning away, I hear him mutter, "Good job" under his breath.

I laugh in delight. I always knew he was a big softie at heart.

He shocks me even further when he stops me at the locker room door, smacking my shoulder with a meaty hand. He waits for everyone else to stream out before saying, "It's nice to see you give the same kind of dedication to all your pursuits, Lindley. I gotta say, though, your cha cha is sloppy as fuck."

My jaw falls open. "What do you know about the cha cha?"

"My wife and I took dance lessons before our wedding," he reveals. "Had to learn five Latin dances."

"American or International?"

"International. It was the worst year of my life," he growls.

I can't stop a laugh.

"But it resulted in me marrying my woman and dancing a mean cha cha, so…" He shrugs. "You're better than that, Lindley. Practice harder."

He stomps off, and I stare after him. Chad Jensen is full of surprises, and, honestly, the gift that keeps on giving. I can't wait to tell the boys about—

Halfway down the hall, Coach turns to smirk at me. "If you try to tell anyone about this, I'll deny it. You will look like a fool."

Goddamn it.

How does he *know*?

———————

The game is fast-paced from the first puck drop. I'm still riding the high from the competition, and it only seems fitting that I score the winning goal. This is Shane's night. This is Shane's fuckin' house.

"*Yes*," Ryder growls, smacking my helmet as I heave myself over the wall. His line is done for the night, so he's on the bench enjoying the action without any of the pressure.

There are only forty seconds left in the third. Sure, Boston College can score two goals in that time—miracles do happen. But it's unlikely. Coach knows it and orders our third line to treat the rest of the game like a penalty kill, while the rest of us sit on the bench hollering for them to hold the line.

When the buzzer sounds, signaling the end of the third, everyone on the Briar bench surges to their feet, savoring the taste of victory. We were on fire tonight. Invincible. The atmosphere in the locker room afterward is sheer triumph.

"Gigi and Mya are outside with Diana," Ryder tells me, shouldering his hockey bag. "Mya came up for Gigi's game against Providence. We're all heading back to Hastings and meeting up at Malone's."

Perfect. I didn't even know my girl was here, but a quick glance at my phone confirms that Diana took an Uber here after the winners' announcement. She says she's waiting in the lobby.

When I step into the hallway, however, it's not Diana I find waiting for me.

It's Lynsey.

"Hey." I'm startled to see her, especially standing there in jeans and a black sweater rather than the dance costume she was wearing at the hotel. "Why aren't you at the NUABC after-party?"

"Decided to skip it."

"But aren't they announcing the winners of the American Nine?"

"Sergei will text me if we placed."

She shrugs, which is very atypical for Lynsey. She's usually very direct. And in all the years I've known her, she's never blown off an important event. Or at least, an event that's important to *her*.

I'm utterly baffled.

"Where's Tyreek?" I ask. "Was he in the crowd rooting for you?"

"No. Actually, we broke up."

"You did?"

She nods. "Last month."

"Oh." That's odd. She and I have bumped into each other a couple of times on campus since then, and she hasn't said a word about it.

"And I didn't go to the after-party because I wanted to watch your game instead. I caught the last period."

I hide my shock. "You came to watch me play?" And then I can't help myself. "Never really showed much interest before..."

"I know. That was crappy of me." She looks uncomfortable. "Can we go somewhere and talk?"

I hesitate.

"There's a little pub not far from here. Let's grab a quick drink." She falters. "Oh. Unless you have to be on the team bus."

"Not tonight. I drove myself because of the competition."

"Okay. Great." Her relief is unmistakable. "Then you can have a drink."

"I've got plans. I'm meeting everyone back in Hastings to celebrate our win."

"I won't take too much of your time, Lindy. You can still meet everyone there. You'll just be, what? Fifteen minutes late? Twenty?"

Her gaze is so earnest, and for a moment, she appears uncertain. I'm suddenly reminded of our first kiss. For all her bravado—even as a teenager, she acted like she was so sure of herself—when I went to kiss her that first time, cupping her cheek with my hand, she'd worn this same look. Uncertainty and hope. Eagerness mixed with fear.

"I've been doing a lot of self-reflecting since Ty and I broke up, and I need to get a few things off my chest. Please." When I hesitate again, she releases a frustrated breath. "I don't want to play the history card, but come on, Shane. I've known you since the eighth grade. You can spare twenty minutes for me."

She's right, I can.

Before I can answer, I catch sight of a familiar platinum ponytail at the end of the hall. When I see Diana break through the crowd, I glance at Lynsey and say, "I'll meet you out front. I'll come around with the car."

"Sounds good," she answers gratefully.

As Lynsey passes Diana, she greets her with a nod. I don't miss the suspicion darkening Diana's eyes as she approaches me. I hold out my arms, and even as she flies into them to hug me, I feel the rising tension.

"Fifth fuckin' place!" I exclaim. "I told you that tango was killer."

She brightens at that. "I can't believe how much money we won! This is really going to help me."

"I know. It's wild. What did fourth place get?"

"Twelve grand."

I nod decisively. "I know what we're aiming for next year."

Diana grins and takes my hand. Then, as if she's remembering what she just saw, the smile abruptly fades. "Why was Lynsey here?"

"She wants to talk." I pause for a second. "Gigi's here, right? Ryder said she's got her car?"

"Yeah," Diana answers uneasily. "Why?"

"Do you mind driving back to Hastings with her and Mya?

I'm going to grab a quick drink with Lynsey, but I'll meet you at Malone's right after. I'll be thirty minutes behind you, I promise."

Diana stares at me.

"What?" I run my hand over my close-cropped hair, lightly scraping my palm.

"You're grabbing a drink with Lynsey." Her tone is flat.

"I told you, she wants to talk."

"Yeah, I bet she does."

"It's not like that," I assure her.

The tension between us continues to rise. I can see Diana's mind spinning, her jaw working as she grits her teeth. She wants to say something. No, she wants to say *a lot* of things, and I've witnessed her temper enough times to know it's taking all her restraint not to explode on me.

She exhales slowly. "I don't want you to go with her."

My eyebrows fly up. "What?"

Torment creases her face. "I wasn't planning on saying this right now, in this hallway, but…this isn't pretend for me anymore, Shane."

"I know that." My voice is a little gruff.

"I have feelings for you. Real feelings. And I can't believe I'm saying this to Shane Lindley when last year you were the last person I wanted to speak to. But this is it. This is the truth. And I get it, okay? I know this whole thing started because you wanted to make her jealous, and I'm sure you were secretly hoping she would break up with Tyreek and take you back—"

"She and Tyreek did break up."

Diana shakes her head derisively. "See? That's why you can't go! She's trying to get back together with you."

Unhappiness washes over me. "Maybe. Or maybe not. Either way, I have no intention of getting back with her. Whatever it is she wants to talk about, she was pretty upset and I owe it to our history to hear her out."

"You don't owe her anything. She dumped you."

I reach for Diana, but she steps back, her cheeks reddening with anger.

"I don't want you to go. Please. I'm asking you not to."

"It's a conversation. Nothing more."

Silence falls between us. Voices from the lobby drift into the hall, animated chatter and muffled laughter, but Diana and I are at an impasse, neither of us making a sound.

Finally, she speaks. Her voice is colder than the Atlantic.

"All right, Shane. I see how this is."

Frustration clamps around my throat. "What do you mean?"

She laughs bitterly. "I literally just stood here and told you I have feelings for you, and you said nothing in return. So I see it, plain as day. I see where we're at. I see what this is to me, and I see what this is to you. And you know what? Just go with Lynsey. Hope you have fun."

Diana spins on her heel and marches off without a backward look.

CHAPTER FORTY-FIVE
DIANA

It's not a relationship

"You're not driving with Shane?" Gigi says when I practically drag her out of the arena and tell her I'm ready to go.

Mya's hurrying after us, dressed like she should be at an art gallery instead of a hockey game. She's sporting leather stiletto boots, tight black pants, and a gray cashmere sweater beneath her peacoat. The scarf is designer, of course. Mya Bell is stunning. She wants to be a surgeon, and I have no doubt her patients are really going to enjoy the view. This gorgeous creature, cutting them open.

"D?" Gigi pushes.

"Shane has somewhere else he needs to be," I say tersely.

She gives me a blank look. "Okay...?"

It's a question. I don't answer it.

We reach Gigi's SUV, and I slide into the backseat without fighting for shotgun like I normally would with Mya.

Gigi starts the engine and pulls away. I stare at the back of her head and try not to cry. It barely registers that there's not much chatter between her and Mya, so when Gigi stops at a red light a few minutes later and both women twist around to study me, I blink in confusion.

"What's wrong?" I ask them.

"Yes, what's wrong! What is wrong with *you*?" Gigi demands.

"Seriously," Mya agrees.

I shrug at them. "Nothing."

"You haven't said a single word in five minutes," Gigi says, incredulous. "You literally just came in fifth place in your favorite dance competition! It's all you've been obsessing about for like a year. I know you and Kenji only started rehearsing this summer, but you've been working on this choreography basically since last year's competition."

"So?"

"So you should be on cloud nine."

"You should be babbling about how you're going to rule the world," Mya says in that mocking voice of hers. She always likes to bust my ass, but that's okay because I bust hers right back.

"But instead, you're sitting there staring at nothing. You're not even on your phone. What happened?"

Shane doesn't want me.

The confession is desperate to surface, but I clamp it down, pressing my lips together. No. I will not give Lindley the satisfaction of crying about him to my friends. Then it makes it real.

It is real.

Not to him, it wasn't.

To my utter horror, tears sting my eyelids. I start blinking rapidly in a desperate attempt to contain them.

"What's wrong with your face?" Mya demands, and I realize she's watching me in the side mirror.

Gulping the lump in my throat, I swipe my coat sleeve against my suddenly burning eyes.

"Hey, Diana, seriously. What's going on?" Gigi looks concerned. "Did you get in a fight with Shane?"

"Not really." My voice shakes a little. "I mean, he went to meet up with his ex-girlfriend after I asked him not to."

"Whoa." Mya whistles softly.

"And she just broke up with her boyfriend and clearly wants him back. But you know…" Sarcasm drips from my voice. "He 'owes it to their history' to hear her out."

Mya's jaw drops.

Gigi curses. "Are you kidding me? What do you mean, hear her out? She's *obviously* trying to win him back."

"Yeah, that's what I said." I clench my teeth to stop my lips from quivering. "But whatever. It doesn't matter. He can do whatever the hell he wants."

"He's your boyfriend."

"Actually, he's not." A tired laugh slips out. "He never was."

The confession hangs in the car. A loud honk makes us all jump. The man in the car behind us is pissed that Gigi isn't going through the intersection. She holds her hand up in an apologetic wave and moves forward, heading in the direction of the interstate. It's about an hour drive back to Hastings, and after this bomb I dropped, I know it's not going to be a comfortable one.

"It started with him wanting to save face when Lynsey showed up at his apartment with her new boyfriend. So I went over there and, you know, pretended that we were dating. And then he returned the favor after Percy started harassing me."

"Gigi told me about that," Mya says, sounding upset. "How on earth did Percival turn into a stalker?"

"I know, right?" I bury my face in my hands and groan into my palms.

When I raise my head, I feel anxious and sad and pissed all in one. I was on such a high earlier. Especially after the tango. Sure, the cha cha was passable, and the Viennese waltz could have been better, but oh my God, *that tango.*

I've never experienced anything like it. The thrill that shot through me when Shane was commanding the floor with his presence, basically fucking me in front of the entire audience without removing a stitch of clothing. After that, everything else seemed anticlimactic. That tango lives in my blood. I'm not surprised we came in fifth.

What I am surprised about is that he chose Lynsey over me. Maybe I'm naive, but I truly believed he was done with her.

I say this out loud now, sighing unhappily.

"I saw the difference in him from the summer until now. We even ran into her once on campus and he didn't seem like he was pining anymore. He was giving me signals that he was into me."

Gigi bites her lip. "I think he *is* into you."

"Then why the hell did he go off with his ex-girlfriend?" Mya counters.

"You're not helping," chides Gigi.

"No, I *am* helping because we're not going to delude her into thinking that the guy is into her. This all started because he used her to make his ex jealous." Mya twists in her seat. "He told you he still had feelings for her, right?"

"In not so many words, yes."

"So feelings just don't go away."

"Yes, they do," Gigi insists. "Feelings *do* go away, and then you meet someone new and new feelings develop, and the old ones don't matter anymore."

"Clearly these old ones do because *he went with his ex*."

The two women continue to argue on my behalf. They're the devil and angel on each shoulder, except they're sitting in the passenger side and the driver's seat. And I don't know which one of them to believe.

Finally, I interrupt with a loud groan. "I'm with Mya here, G. It was a fake relationship, and it meant nothing to him."

"He entered a dance competition with you. He wouldn't have done that if you don't mean something to him."

"Yeah, as a friend. But his goal from the beginning was to get his ex back. And I begged him not to go with her tonight and he chose her. So that's proof of his intentions."

"I agree," Mya says.

My heart splinters. I can't believe he left. I can't believe he picked her. We've been together for months. We see each other every single day. It's like how the couples in the *Fling or Forever* hacienda maintain that time moves differently in there. One day in the hacienda is like three months of dating. Having Shane next door, being in contact with him every day, has accelerated this relationship.

It's not a relationship.

Right. I guess it isn't.

"Let's just drop it," I mutter. "He made his choice. Do you mind dropping me off at home first? I don't feel like going out."

"No problem," Gigi says quietly.

I barely say another word for the rest of the car ride. Eventually Gigi puts on music, and she and Mya talk quietly. They try to include me here and there, but I nod or mumble a yes or a no until they give up.

And right when I think this night can't get any worse, when Gigi turns onto the street toward my apartment complex, I see something that makes my blood run cold.

I've had my gaze glued out the window to avoid making conversation, which means I'm laser-focused on my surroundings and don't miss the familiar vehicle parked near the driveway of Meadow Hill. A dark-gray hatchback with an NYU sticker on the back bumper. As we drive past it, I catch a blur from the driver's seat.

"Stop the car," I blurt out.

"Why?" Gigi asks in concern. "What's wrong?"

"That was Percy back there. In the gray car."

When she keeps driving, I smack the back of her seat. "Gigi, stop the car."

"No. You have a restraining order against him."

"Exactly, and he's not allowed to be here."

The TRO distance requirement is one hundred yards, and he's parked *ten feet* from the entrance of my apartment complex. What is he thinking?

"Stop the car, damn it. I want to go over there and find out what he's up to."

"No," Gigi repeats, her tone brooking no argument. "The only thing you're doing right now is calling the police."

CHAPTER FORTY-SIX
SHANE

I was an accessory

"Thanks for doing this," Lynsey says.

We're in a small corner pub tucked away on a quaint cobblestone street. The interior is a blend of exposed brick walls, dark wooden beams, and a collection of tables, booths, and worn leather armchairs nestled in corners of the room. We find an empty pair of armchairs and sit across from each other.

It's not as crowded as I would expect for a Saturday night. Only the murmur of conversation and occasional burst of laughter fills the air, offering a more intimate environment. It makes this feel like a date. But it's not a date. And I'm distracted because I know Diana is pissed at me. It's going to take a lot of groveling to make this up to her.

"So what's up?" I ask Lynsey.

"I miss you."

My mouth snaps shut.

What?

Lynsey gives a self-deprecating smile. "Sorry, I didn't mean to hit you with that right out of the gate, but that's the gist of it. I miss you."

I'm not sure what to say, but I'm given a reprieve because the waitress arrives. I order a pint of IPA. Lynsey gets a tea. She's not much of a drinker.

Once the server's gone, I rub my cheek, then the side of my neck, before my jittery arm drops to my lap. "I don't know what to do with that," I admit.

"You could say you miss me too."

"I have said that," I remind her. Resentment floats through me. "I told you I missed you almost every time we talked. And you haven't said it back until now."

"I know."

"Which is sort of convenient, isn't it?" That pang of bitterness grows into a tight knot in my throat. "Up until a few weeks ago, you had a new boyfriend."

"It wasn't serious with Tyreek."

"It doesn't matter if it was serious. You were with somebody else. And I'm pretty sure if you hadn't been dating him, you wouldn't have even considered transferring to Briar."

Disbelief fills her eyes. "You think I transferred schools because of a *guy*? You know me better than that, Lindy. My future is far too important for me to act on whims."

Something about her indignant response rubs me the wrong way. It's one word. One word is the problem. *Her* future. Our entire relationship was about her future, her ballet schedule, her friends. Our lives revolved around what she wanted to do and where she wanted to go.

The realization smacks me in the face like a rogue hockey puck.

"I was an accessory," I say.

"What are you talking about?"

"In our relationship. I was an accessory. I did everything for you, and it's really fucking pathetic when I think about it. Every dance event that I could make it to, I was there. Front row center. And in four years, I can count on one hand the number of hockey games you attended."

"That's not true," she protests.

"Three," I tell her flatly. "Four if you count tonight. But I don't count tonight because I'm still not sure what tonight is. I have a very good idea, though."

"What do you mean?"

"You don't like seeing someone else playing with your toys."

A frown twists her lips.

"Yeah, that's exactly what this is." I shrug. "You're jealous that I'm with Diana."

"Oh, come on. I'm in no way threatened by some airhead cheerleader—"

"*Don't* disparage her. I won't have it."

She instantly backpedals. "That came out wrong. All I mean is, you're ambitious too. You also have a plan for your future. A solid one."

"So?"

"So how does this girl fit into it? That night at your apartment, every time I asked her a serious question—what she wants to do after graduation, what her goals are—she would shrug and say *I don't know* or *we'll see*. I know you, Shane. You can't be with someone who wings it through life."

"I can be with whoever I want. And just so you know, she's not without ambition. Anything that woman puts her mind to, she succeeds at."

It's the truth. Whether it's a dance competition, training for nationals, taking the minutes in the HOA meeting… Diana lives her life to the fullest, no matter what she's doing, no matter how mundane the activity. She's smart and driven, and she gives a shit about the people in her life. Her family, her friends. Although her Saturdays are write-offs because of football games, she's managed to attend all my Friday games. That's right—Diana Dixon has already come to more of my hockey games than Lynsey did the entire time we were together. She went *golfing* with me simply because she knows I enjoy it.

"Our relationship was all about you," I tell Lynsey. "I compromised on everything. Made sure all your needs were met. And you couldn't even be bothered to feign interest in my sport." I shake my head. "It wasn't all bad—"

"Really?" she interrupts bitterly. "Because you're making it sound like we had the worst relationship in the world. Why did you stay with me for four years, then, if I was so awful?"

"You weren't awful. That's not what I'm saying. We had a good relationship. Sometimes it was even great. But I'm starting to realize you broke up with me for a reason."

"Maybe I made a mistake."

"You didn't," I say simply. "We weren't right for each other. I thought we were, at least in the sense that we were both ambitious and knew what we wanted from our future. The thing is, though, you didn't want *me* in your future. That's why you broke up with me. And I'm happy now with somebody else."

The waitress returns with our drinks. But I'm already done here.

"Sorry, Lynz. I'll always value what we had, and I'm happy to remain friends, if and when you're ready for that. But..." I fish my wallet out of my pocket and pull out a twenty. "This should cover everything. Sorry. I can't stay. My girlfriend's waiting for me."

I leave my ex in the pub and hurry outside. Standing on the sidewalk, I call Diana, but her phone immediately goes to voicemail. Yeah, she's pissed.

Fuck.

I try Gigi next. Voicemail. Oh for two.

On the third call, I manage to get a response from Ryder.

"Hey, is my girlfriend with your wife? If so, can you put her on the phone?"

"They're not here."

A frown touches my lips. "What do you mean? Why not?"

"Diana didn't want to go to Malone's, so Gigi took her home. But me and the guys are here."

"Shit, is she that mad?"

"Who, Diana? I don't know. Gisele didn't say anything."

"All right, cool. Thanks."

I head back to the arena and jog toward my Mercedes. I make the hour drive to Hastings, tapping my fingers on the steering wheel the entire time. I'm antsy and desperate to get out of the car. I want to see Diana and explain why I had to go see Lynsey. That I have no intention of getting back together with her. I know I'm going to take some shit, probably get yelled at for an extended period, but I'm hoping she'll be able to see how sincere I am.

I get off the highway, bypassing downtown Hastings by taking the residential streets until I reach the cul-de-sac where Meadow Hill is located. I have to pass the main driveway on my way to the residence parking, and my spine stiffens when I notice the vehicle that's leaving at the same time I enter.

It's a police cruiser.

CHAPTER FORTY-SEVEN

SHANE

My real girlfriend

I BARREL THROUGH THE SYCAMORE LOBBY INTO THE BACK COURTYARD and race down the path toward our building. I gave Richard at the desk about three seconds to answer when I asked, "What's up with the police car?"

All he managed to get out was "There was an incident with Diana and—" before I was sprinting to Red Birch.

I take the stairs two at a time. Even over my thundering footsteps and thudding pulse, I hear Niall's muffled voice. "Walk quiet!"

I ignore him. At Diana's door, I push on the handle, but it's locked, so I start banging against the door.

"Dixon, let me in. Are you okay?"

Footsteps approach the door. Then it swings open, and I see Gigi.

"What happened?" I say instantly. "Where is she?"

"In the shower."

Gigi's grim face tells me whatever happened tonight wasn't good. I storm inside, peering past her shoulders to find Mya Bell, Gigi's former roommate, on Diana's couch. I give a terse nod of greeting. She flicks up her hand in a quick wave.

"Was it that fucking asshole?" I demand. "Percy?"

Gigi nods. "Yeah. He was basically, like, casing the apartment when we got here."

"What do you mean, casing?"

"I don't know, that's the best way I can explain it. He wasn't *on* the property, but a few yards away from the Meadow Hill sign." Anger colors her cheeks. "Diana spotted his car. She wanted to get out and confront him."

"I hope you didn't fucking let her."

"Of course not. We went right in and called the cops. They got here within three minutes, which was impressive. But I guess there's no crime in Hastings. They were probably just sitting around waiting for something to happen. The cops questioned Diana, then went to find Percy, who denied breaking the restraining order. He asserted he was beyond the minimum distance."

"He's supposed to stay a hundred yards away from her. If he was parked near the entrance of the driveway, that's not a hundred yards."

"He claimed where he was parked in relation to Red Birch itself and *this* apartment is exactly one hundred and eight yards. Supposedly he measured it using satellite imagery."

"Slimy prick."

"Yeah, Diana was pissed. So now it's a matter of semantics, and the restraining order is being revised to include this apartment as well as the main building. It was a whole shitshow, and Diana just had enough. Which is why I think you should leave."

I gape at her. "Like hell I'm leaving. I'm going to be right here when she gets out of the shower."

"Shane," Mya says tentatively.

I glance over. "What?"

"You don't have to put on the act anymore," Gigi explains. "We know this isn't a real relationship." She gestures from me toward the bathroom beyond the hall.

"She told us everything," Mya confirms.

"And I get it," Gigi says quietly. "That was really nice of you to pretend to be her boyfriend while Percy was living here. And you did good, convincing her to report what happened to her. But…"

"But what?" I snap.

"But you led her on."

My chest squeezes. "Is that what she thinks?"

"What else is she supposed to think?" Gigi's gray eyes flash at me. "She told you she had feelings for you, and you ditched her to go see your ex-girlfriend."

"Yeah, for closure," I mutter.

"What closure do you need? Didn't she dump your ass a year ago?" Mya remarks from the couch.

I scowl at her. "Can we stop with the commentary?" I scrape both hands over my scalp. "Yes, I screwed up, and I know she's pissed off. But there's nothing between me and Lynsey. I made it very clear to her tonight that I don't want to get back together."

"Regardless, I don't know if tonight is the night to be dealing with…whatever this is. This fake relationship—"

"It isn't fake," I burst out. "It's real as fuck. Do you not get that? I love her."

Gigi blinks. "Oh. Seriously?"

I scrub a hand over my face, uncomfortable under Gigi's and Mya's surprised scrutiny. My feelings for Diana have been percolating for months now, but this is the first time I've been able to give them a label. *Love.* I fucking love this girl.

I didn't expect the realization to strike in front of an audience, and I wish her friends would just leave already and let me go see my girl.

"Seriously," I mutter to Gigi. "So do me a favor and let me take it from here. Please."

"I'm not leaving."

"You said she's okay, right? She's pissed but not shaken up. He didn't touch her. So, please, just go. I really appreciate that you drove her home and stayed with her while the cops were here, but I'm asking you, very nicely, to go now so I can be alone with the woman I love."

After a long beat, Gigi nods. "Fine. But I'm calling her in an hour, and if she sounds even the least bit upset, I'm driving back and kicking you out myself."

"Fair. And I mean it—thank you for being here for her. You're a good friend. Both of you."

After they leave, I lock the door and return to the living room. I groan my frustration into my palms while trying to ignore the little spark of fear that asks, What if Gigi and Mya hadn't been with her? What if he somehow found a way to—

No, I can't even think about that.

But I should have been there, damn it.

"So you love me."

I look up and find Diana standing in the hall doorway. She's wrapped in that pink towel she was wearing the first time I saw her in this building. Her cheeks are red from the shower. She walks toward me on bare feet.

"You heard that, huh?" I say ruefully.

"Yep." Her green eyes sweep over me. "Did you mean it?"

"Do I ever say anything I don't mean?"

She shrugs. "I don't know. It sure looked like you meant it when you chose your ex over me."

"I didn't choose her over you. I know it seems like that, but I needed to go with her tonight. I had a suspicion I needed to confirm."

"What suspicion?"

"That my relationship with Lynsey was not as good as I thought it was."

My words bring a twinkle of humor to her eyes. She bites her lip.

"Are you trying not to laugh?" I demand.

"Sort of. I mean, it was so obvious. From everything you've said about her, it sounds like the relationship was the Lynsey Show and you were just a supporting cast member."

"I see that now. And I wanted to talk to her tonight so I could tell her all that. And to make sure she knows I don't want to get back together."

"But she tried to, didn't she? Just like I said she would."

"I had a feeling she would too," I admit.

Diana glares at me. "And yet you acted like the idea was *so* preposterous when I raised it."

"Look, when she said she broke up with Tyreek, it occurred to me she might try to rekindle things, but that's not why I wanted to see her."

"Really. You didn't want your little ego boost from knowing your ex is dying to get you back?"

"No. I didn't. I needed to have that final moment with her. We were together for four years. I wanted her to know that we weren't right for each other and that I've fallen in love with my girlfriend. My *real* girlfriend."

Diana is biting her lip again. But the smile cannot be contained. It bursts through, lighting her entire face. "I don't think you're lying to me."

"I'm not," I say softly. "I don't want anybody else, Dixon. I want you."

"Why?"

I furrow my brow.

"I'm serious. Why do you want me?" She's chewing on her bottom lip, and I can practically see the insecurities rolling off her. "I'm drama, remember? I needed to tone myself down before meeting your family—"

My chest clenches. "Fuck. I'm so sorry I ever gave you the idea that I wanted you to change yourself."

She clutches the top of her towel to keep it in place. "I won't," she says, unwavering. "Change myself, that is. I'm melodramatic and weird and I argue a lot, and that's my personality. If that scares someone—"

"Doesn't scare me," I interject. "I don't want you to change. I want you for you. Drama and all." I grin at her. "So will you please be my real girlfriend?"

Diana plants one hand on her hip. "I'll have to think about it."

"Gonna make me sweat, huh?" I chuckle.

"For a little while. But I'm not mad at you anymore."

"Good."

"And…" She lifts a brow. "I might be falling for you too."

"Fall*ing*?" I feign outrage. "But I've already fallen."

"I'm not telling you I love you on the night that you chose to go with your ex-girlfriend."

"Fine. I will await it with bated breath." I approach her towel-clad frame and touch her cheek. "Are you okay? Gigi told me what happened with Percy."

"I'm fine." She shakes her head in disbelief. "I just can't believe his arrogance. This sulking asshole sitting there in his car. He told the cops he was out for a drive and just *happened* to find himself at Meadow Hill, so he pulled over because he wanted to reminisce about our relationship. According to him, there was no malicious intent. It wasn't meant to be a threat."

"Bullshit."

"I know. But the cops aren't going to do anything because whoever wrote up the restraining order wasn't clear in their language, so he's off on a technicality. He didn't break it. But either way, I'm calling Detective Wendt in the morning."

"Don't worry, I'm not letting this creep anywhere near you. If he shows up here again, he's gonna have a word with Shane Junior and Shane the Third." I raise my right fist and then the left.

"We need better names for your fists," Diana says frankly.

"I know. In my defense, I've never called them anything before, so I was sort of winging it."

"We'll brainstorm."

"Maybe bring it up at the next HOA meeting," I suggest.

"Good idea." She's smiling.

I open my arms. The moment she steps into them, her towel falls to the floor.

I snicker and peer down. "Oh. The seduction has started?"

She snorts. "I'm not seducing you. But...now that I'm naked...I *guess* you can atone for tonight's sins and give me an orgasm."

Chuckling, I pick up her naked body, walk to the kitchen counter, and set her ass down on it. "I shall begin my atonement."

CHAPTER FORTY-EIGHT

SHANE

R Lindley

NOVEMBER

Diana and I spend Thanksgiving with each other's families. My family has dinner on Thursday, while the Dixons do theirs on Friday, and since our towns are within spitting distance of each other, we're able to do both. I like having a girlfriend again. Honestly, now that I'm all in, I realize there was never any point in fighting it last year. This is my natural state. I'm a girlfriend guy. That's just who I am.

On Thursday morning, we drive to Heartsong, where my little sister greets Diana like a long-lost friend, throwing her arms around her. She drags Diana upstairs to show her something, while I wander into the kitchen to help Mom.

"Where's Dad?" I ask her.

"He's in the den."

"Cool. Let me go say hi and then I'll help you with dinner."

"Sounds good, honey. Thank you."

I notice some strain around her eyes before she turns toward the stove. I step forward to touch her arm.

"Is everything okay?"

"It's fine. Cooking stresses me out, you know that. Go see your dad."

The den is Dad's domain, part man cave, part office. Filing cabinets take up an entire wall. Against a second wall is an array of computer monitors sitting on an L-shaped mahogany desk, with framed photographs and hockey memorabilia hanging above the desk. The third wall boasts a gas fireplace with two overstuffed armchairs and a coffee table in front of it.

I find Dad kneeling on the hardwood floor, rummaging through a big cardboard box.

"Hey. What are you doing?" I ask curiously.

"Hey, kid." He gets up to give me a quick hug. "Happy Thanksgiving."

I slap him on the back. "Happy Thanksgiving, old man."

"Who are you calling old? I'm still a spring chicken."

"Young people don't use phrases like *spring chicken*."

"Ouch." He clasps his heart as if I hurt him.

I gesture to the two boxes on the ground. "What's all this?"

"Oh, I have something for you. Remember I told you last month I was finally clearing out those boxes in the attic? I dragged a couple in here because I found some cool stuff I want to give you and Maryanne. No point letting it all sit in a dusty attic."

He walks to the desk and picks up a folded square of fabric. He unfolds it and holds the red-and-black garment up by the collar. It's a Chicago jersey, an old-school one from before they switched to their new uniforms. Grinning, he turns it over. The name LINDLEY is stitched onto the back.

"Holy shit," I exclaim. "Is that your Blackhawks jersey from when you played there?"

"You mean when I played five minutes of one game?" he says dryly.

"Still pretty fucking cool." I take the jersey from him, running my fingers over the seams on the logo. "This is actually what you were wearing for your first NHL game?"

"Yep. What I was wearing the night my career ended."

He doesn't sound too beat up about it, but I flinch at his blunt words.

He notices and shrugs. "I mourned that life a long time ago. Created something even better. Something to leave you and your sister that's more tangible than hockey money."

I grin. "I mean, we could have invested the hockey money."

"Hey, you can invest the real estate money too."

"Just kidding." I gesture to the jersey. "Are you really giving me this?"

"Yes, but I'm going to get it framed first."

"Will you sign it?"

"Absolutely."

Eyes shining, Dad grabs a metallic silver marker from his desk drawer and scribbles his name on a black section of the jersey.

R Lindley.

He looks so proud that tears sting my eyelids. Because, fuck, I can't even imagine having your dream stolen from you like that. In an instant. One second and it was done.

"Where's Diana?" he asks.

"She's upstairs with Maryanne."

Dad puts his arm around me and ruffles my head. I don't have a lot of hair, so he's basically just rubbing his palm over my buzzed scalp. "I'm happy you're home. Happy you're with Diana too. She's a good one."

"I think so too."

"Glad you came to your senses."

I raise a brow. "What's that supposed to mean?"

"Your mom and I were getting worried there that you might get back with Lynsey."

"Wow." I can't stop a laugh. "You really didn't like her, huh?"

"It wasn't about liking her. It was about liking her for *you*. She wasn't good for you. Too serious. Overly ambitious."

"Mom is serious and ambitious," I point out.

"Yep, and she suits me to a T. Because I'm a laid-back bum who needs a woman like her to motivate me." Dad leans against his deck, arms loosely crossed. "But you're not me. You're loud and brash and stubborn as hell. You need someone like Diana to put you in your place. Lynsey never did that because…" He shrugs. "Because, well, I suspect she was too self-absorbed to notice what you were up to."

I won't lie—it stings to hear that. And his words dispel any notion that they'd liked her. Clearly, they were just skilled at keeping their mouths shut.

"I wish you told me all this when we were dating," I admit. "Four years, dude. You might've saved me some time."

Dad chuckles. "You wouldn't have listened. Stubborn, remember?" He pushes away from the desk. "C'mon, let's go join the others."

Thanksgiving is a blast. We don't have any out-of-towners this year, but we're hosting Mom's parents, my aunt Ashley, a bunch of cousins from my dad's side, and more cousins from my mom's. We watch football, gorge ourselves at dinner, and play after-dinner charades.

It's the perfect day, except for one moment of tension between my parents. Dad wants to go for a walk after our guests leave, but my sister is so hopped up on sugar that Mom suggests we watch a movie instead. Dad pushes the issue, and eventually Mom caves, grumbling in annoyance as they bundle up and head out, leaving Diana and me alone in the house.

I waste no time grabbing her hand. "Upstairs! Now! Quickie!"

Diana can't stop laughing as we hurry upstairs. I know we have at least thirty minutes, but I bypass my bedroom just in case and pull her into the hall bath.

"Oooh, shower sex?" Her green eyes dance devilishly as I turn on the water.

I crank the temperature to hot and pull off my sweater, tossing it on the tiled floor. "I figure the spray will drown out any noises you make."

"Me? You're the noisiest man I've ever been with. You and your man moans."

"You love it when I moan in your ear," I say arrogantly, undoing my pants.

A moment later, my boxers hit the bath mat and I step into the shower. With the curtain still wide-open, I duck my head under the spray and let it course down my naked body.

"You coming?"

Diana makes quick work of her clothes and joins me. I see her ass bounce a bit as she steps in, and I don't hold back the urge to grab a fistful of it. As she pushes her ass into my naked torso, my cock begins to rise against those firm cheeks. I could slide into her right now and fuck her brains out. That's what my instincts are begging me to do. But I resist, because if I do that, the whole encounter will be over in two minutes. I want to make this last.

I start kissing her neck, and as I predicted, the spray masks her resulting moan.

"We should use this shower trick at home for Niall," I tell her while my lips continue to travel along her throat.

"He'll still hear us," she mumbles. "He has the ears of a cheetah."

I stop kissing. "Do cheetahs have really good hearing?"

"I don't know. I assume it's better than human hearing. Will you quit thinking about Niall and make yourself useful?"

I laugh against her hair, bringing my arms around so I can cup her breasts. Her skin is supple beneath my fingers. I turn her toward me because I don't want to merely feel her tits. I want to see them. I want to see the desire burning in her eyes.

"What are you waiting for?" Diana whispers.

Christ, I could stare at her all night, but if she wants me to take her, I'm happy to oblige. I reach between her legs, assessing how wet she is. Fucking drenched. I know she's going to take my cock without issue.

But the shower space is limiting, so I pick her up and lift her out of the tub. She curls her legs around me as I walk us to the counter, where I set her down gently.

The water in the shower is still running, but I don't care. The bathroom grows steamy around us. I can barely see our bodies in the fogged mirror.

I pull her to the very edge of the vanity while gripping my cock in one hand.

"Beg," I rasp.

A soft noise of desperation leaves her mouth. "Give it to me. Please."

Smiling, I push forward, giving her half my length. She groans, her hands stretching to the sides for something to grasp. She knocks over the toothbrush holder and soap bottle. They tumble into the sink basin.

"I wish I had more time to tease you," I say regretfully, my fingers caressing her hips. "But I don't, so I guess I'll just have to make you come."

Diana chokes midlaugh when I thrust deep. Over and over, until she's moaning with abandon. Every time I drive into her, her breasts jump up and jiggle, and I'm inspired with each pump to make them move again. So I move harder, faster.

I put one hand on the bathroom mirror to get a better grip, but it slides off because of the moisture. My handprint allows me to see our reflection, and now I'm not only looking at her but watching myself pump inside her. Fuck, we look so good.

"Harder," she whimpers.

Her breaths grow unsteady, mingling with the steam filling the small space. I listen to her increasingly throatier moans, slamming into her harder every time she begs.

I don't take my eyes off her, loving the way she gasps with each deep thrust.

"Give me that orgasm, baby. I want it."

I know what she needs, though. I bring one thumb to her clit, rubbing gently, and the other to her nipple, pinching not as gently, and Diana goes off. I'm too far gone myself, the incoming release tightening my balls and surging through me. Rope after rope of it shoots into her as she pulsates on my cock. Her legs tighten around me, pulling me in deeper.

It takes a moment to catch my breath. "Why are we so good together?" I croak.

"Dicksand," she mumbles.

"Pussysand," I correct.

But it doesn't matter which one of us is right. Our sex life is incomparable. It's otherworldly.

For the first time in a long time, I'm completely at peace with every single aspect of my life. Family. Girlfriend. Sex. Career path. I feel like I'm killing it in every department.

Including hockey, as we win yet another game on Saturday afternoon. The team doesn't get the whole weekend off for Thanksgiving. Our schedule chugs along as normal. So I'm on the ice the day after Diana and I see her family in Oak Ridges, unleashing slapshots on the UConn goalie and getting slammed into the boards by a goon defenseman on the opposing team.

In the locker room after our W, I'm a bit slow getting dressed due to a jarring hit to the shoulder I took in the second period.

"You good?" Ryder says, noticing me gingerly pulling on my hoodie.

"All good. Just gonna ice it when I'm home. And then get Diana to kiss it and make it better."

He snorts.

I grab my phone from my stall and find an alarming number of missed calls from my mother.

Worry instantly jolts into me. One call, maybe two, wouldn't be a major cause for concern. But she's called four times—when she knows I'm playing a game this afternoon and likely wouldn't be able to call back.

"Hey, I'll meet you out there," I tell Ryder and Beckett. "Gotta call my mom."

I click Mom's name to return the call, and she picks up on the first ring.

"Hey," I say apprehensively. "Is everything okay?"

There's a slight pause.

"No, it's not."

"What's wrong?"

"Shane..." Mom's voice trembles. She pauses again, clearing her throat. "You need to come home."

Fear runs up my spine. "Why? What's going on?"

"Your father's in the hospital."

CHAPTER FORTY-NINE
SHANE

Helpless

I MAKE THE DRIVE TO VERMONT IN UNDER THREE HOURS. DAD ISN'T IN the small hospital outside of Heartsong. Mom told me to come to the bigger one in the city. She refused to give any other details, so I have no idea what the hell is going on. Was he in a car accident?

She doesn't answer any of my calls for the three hours I'm in the car. I'm forced to sit behind the wheel in a state of total panic. The Briar football team is playing Thanksgiving weekend too, and I wish I had the forethought of swinging by the stadium and dragging Diana off the field so she could come with me. But this isn't her family. Not her responsibility.

I'm a jittery mess by the time I park in the visitor lot in front of the hospital. Mom finally decides to acknowledge my existence, answering my last text to say she'll meet me in the lobby.

The wind hisses past my ears as I hurry toward the entrance. It's nippy out, so I shove my hands in the front pocket of my hoodie. I didn't bring gloves. Or a coat. I just ran out of the rink with my keys and phone, leaving everything behind like an idiot.

I enter the lobby, searching, and when I see my mother's familiar face, I stalk toward her. "What the hell? I've been calling you for three hours."

"I'm sorry. We were talking to your father's doctors."

"About what? What's going on?"

I notice the deep lines cutting into her features, digging around her mouth, wrinkling her eyes. She looks…old. Haggard. I think back to the last few months, the small arguments they were having, the moments of tension I caught between them. I examine her face now, and it hits me like a freight train. This wasn't a car accident.

"He's sick, isn't he?" I say flatly.

"Yes."

"What is it? What does he have?"

Mom bites her lip.

"*Mom,*" I thunder, then take a breath when she flinches. I rub the bridge of my nose. "I'm sorry. I didn't mean to snap." My voice shakes. "Just tell me what he has, okay? Actually, forget it. Just take me up to see him. Where is he?"

I start marching to the elevator, but she grabs my hand, tugging me backward.

"Not yet," she says quietly. "I need to prepare you."

"Prepare me?" Fear pummels into me with a thousand times more force than the hit I took tonight. The bruise on my shoulder is nothing. A pinprick compared to the stab of agony I feel now. "How bad is it?"

"Bad."

She leads me down the hall toward an empty bench, urging me to sit. She takes my hand, and her fingers are ice-cold against my skin.

"He has pancreatic cancer."

I stare at her, not quite comprehending. "What? How?" I can't stop the sarcasm. "You don't suddenly come down with a case of pancreatic cancer—" Horror hitches my breath as it dawns on me. "How long have you known?"

"Six months."

I don't get scared often, so everything I'm feeling at the moment is foreign to me. And it's beyond fear. It's terror. It's agony I've never known. It's rage as I stare at my mother.

"Six months?" I push her hand off me, unable to fathom what she's saying. How she could do this to me. "You knew about this for six months and didn't say a word?"

"It was his decision." Mom sounds tired. Defeated. "He didn't want you to know. He didn't want either of you to know."

I suddenly remember my little sister. "Where's Maryanne?"

"She's upstairs in the waiting room with your aunt."

"Has she seen him? Does she know what's going on?"

"Yes. We told her this morning when we had to admit him."

I bite the inside of my cheek, hard enough to draw blood. The coppery flavor fills my mouth. "Why was he admitted? Does he need surgery?"

Mom shakes her head. "It's inoperable."

I swallow. "Okay. So, chemo? Radiation?"

"It's untreatable."

My forehead creases. "Is he dying?"

"Yes."

"Why the *fuck* didn't you—" I quickly stop when several heads swing in our direction. A nurse in green scrubs frowns at me as she walks past us.

I bury my face in my hands and release a silent scream. Then I lift my head and look at my mom. Helpless.

"What the hell is going on?" I sound defeated too now.

In a quiet voice, she describes everything they've been dealing with these past six months. It started with some bloating, then abdominal pain. A stomachache that seemed to come out of nowhere. They assumed the resulting loss of appetite was due to the pain. And, of course, eating and drinking less means weight loss. And I want to slap myself, because I *noticed* him getting thinner. Christ, I thought he was working out. He had let himself go these last few years, too busy with work to hit the gym or go golfing with me.

Here I was, thinking my dad's looking good, *congratulating* him on the weight loss.

Jesus Christ.

My stupidity triggers a rush of frenetic laughter. Mom gives me a sharp look.

"I'm such an idiot," I wheeze out, unable to stop laughing. "I thought he was losing weight because he was exercising. Meanwhile, he's fucking dying of cancer."

Dying.

The word lingers in my head. It thuds inside it. Like a drum beat. *Dying, dying, dying.* My dad is dying.

Mom keeps talking. She says Dad went in for a checkup when the pain persisted. The doctors ran a bunch of tests, and then— surprise. Stage four pancreatic cancer. It's metastasized. Spread beyond Dad's pancreas.

"So what are we doing?" I ask hoarsely. "What can we do?"

"All we can do is manage the symptoms." She reaches for my hand again. Our fingers are frozen. We're like two ice cubes touching each other. "Sweetheart, we're talking end-of-life care here. We don't even have time to prep the house for home hospice, so he'll be here until…" She trails off.

"Hospice?" I echo with a strangled groan. "It's that serious?"

She nods.

How is this happening? And why is it happening to *him*? My father is the best man I know. He puts everyone else first. His kids. His wife. His employees. Even strangers he meets on the street.

Fuck cancer. Fuck this thing that's trying to steal my dad. I refuse to believe there's nothing that can be done.

"There has to be something," I say out loud.

"There isn't. It's in his organs. It's widespread." She lets out a ragged breath. "The oncologist gave him a few days."

I stare at her in shock. Anger rises up again.

"Why the hell didn't you tell us earlier?"

"Because he didn't want to," she maintains, her tone firm. "He didn't want his kids to know that he was dying. He didn't want you to treat him any differently. He didn't—"

"No, I've heard enough." I stand abruptly. "I want to go see my father."

CHAPTER FIFTY

SHANE

The bad stuff

MOM BRINGS ME UPSTAIRS TO THE CANCER WARD. WE STOP IN THE waiting room, briefly, so I can see my sister. Maryanne rushes up to me and hugs me tight. She's not crying, but she looks afraid as she tilts her head to peer at me.

"Daddy's going to die," she says, and I almost break down in tears.

"I know," I tell her, kneeling to hug her again. "I'll be right back, squirt, 'kay?"

Mom leads me down the corridor and stops in front of a closed door. "This is him. I'll give you some time alone."

Nodding, I push open the door. The room is white and sterile, filled with a hum of machines punctuated by occasional beeps and the muffled sounds of footsteps from the hall. The blinds are closed, and the fluorescent lighting instantly hurts my eyes.

I force myself to focus on the bed. On my father lying in it.

I can't believe I saw him only a few days ago. He has dark circles under his eyes now. The lines on his face, etched by years of laughter, appear deeper now. It looks like he's lost fifty pounds overnight.

How on earth did this happen? How did he deteriorate so fast?

"Hey, kid." His voice, although soft, doesn't waver. He sounds the way he always sounds. Like my dad.

"You should have told me," I say dully.

I stop at the foot of the bed. I can't bring myself to go to the chair at his bedside. I glance at his hands, his arms, the IVs, and the tubes. Mom said he's on a lot of painkillers, but his eyes are alert.

"I didn't want you to worry."

"How can I not? Look at you!" I shout before taking a breath. My pulse is out of control.

"Come sit down."

"No."

"Shane."

The helplessness lodged in my throat is suffocating. I'm seconds away from collapsing on the floor in tears. I don't know what to do, but I can't just submit to this. The second I accept it's happening, then that makes it true.

But he's pleading at me with his eyes. Those familiar hazel eyes. Without a word, I walk to the chair and sink into it. My whole body feels weak. I inhale the scent of antiseptic and battle the urge to throw up.

"I didn't want to tell you and your sister because then you would have spent the rest of our time together feeling sad and fussing and making yourself miserable. That's not how I wanted you to remember me. Hell, I wish you weren't even here right now."

"Oh, thanks."

"That's not what I mean. I mean…I wish it happened when I was asleep or something. Fast. Without warning. So I don't have to lie here while you guys watch me die." He twists his face away, and I see the curl of his lips. The anger. When he turns back, it's with resignation. "I wanted to spare you the pain."

"But you can't. You can't shield us from this."

"I've shielded you your entire life. That's what I do. I'm your dad. I try to make sure the bad stuff doesn't reach you."

A knife of pain twists into my heart. The bad stuff *has* reached us. My dad's lying there with sunken eyes and tubes in his arms. Inoperable and untreatable.

Unsavable.

Dead.

Pain clouds his expression for a moment, and I watch him breathe through it. I can't imagine what's happening in his body right now as the cancerous cells ravage him from the inside out. And I'm angry again. Because he's been fighting this valiant battle. He's been fighting it all alone and didn't ask me to fight beside him.

"These past six months have been so nice," he tells me. "I got to see you win the Frozen Four in the spring. I got to see you fall in love with a good woman. I got to see you be happy. That's really all I want."

"If you'd told me—"

"Then what?" he challenges. "It would just have been a longer death sentence for both of us. You would've been feeling six months of agony as opposed to the few days you'll suffer through now before this poison finally takes me from you."

I almost choke on the lump in my throat.

"I didn't say anything to you and Maryanne because I wanted her to enjoy her science camps and her school. I wanted you to enjoy hockey. I didn't want either of you to worry. And I don't want you to blame your mother or be upset with her after I'm gone because—"

"Stop talking like that," I hiss out. "Stop it."

I can't see anymore. The sheen of tears has rendered me blind.

"No, I have to say this. And you have to hear it. I know you've had it easy so far in life. Your mom and I wanted that for you. We've tried to make things as easy as we could for you to be able to meet your dreams. Let you pursue hockey, make sure you don't need to worry about rent or expenses, or struggle for anything. You still won't have to worry about money, but you will struggle now because I'm going to be gone, and your mom and your sister are going to need you."

"Stop it," I mumble.

"No. I need you to promise me that you'll always take care of them and you'll always be there for them, especially Maryanne."

I can't breathe.

"Can we please stop talking like you're about to die right this second? You're not dying right now. Just let me absorb this."

"No. Now is the time for me to say it." He weakly raises one arm. "Before this morphine turns my brain into mush. I can think clearly right now, and I can see you clearly, and I want you to know I couldn't be prouder of the man you've become. You are everything to me. You and your sister."

His voice is finally starting to shake, and the tears now run freely down my face.

"Please stop saying this," I beg.

"No, you're going to hear it. You're going to hear how much I love you. You're going to hear how proud I am of you. You're going to hear how sad I am that I can't be there for your rookie season, sitting at center ice for your first Blackhawks game."

I'm done for. That's it. I curl over onto his bed with my face pressed against his arm, unable to control the tears. I shake harder when I feel his hand gently stroking my hair and the nape of my neck.

"It's all right. It's okay, son."

"No, it's not okay," I mumble through the pain. "How could you keep this from us?"

But I understand it now. I do. As angry as I am, I think I would do the exact same thing in his situation. I wouldn't want people pitying me for six months, worrying and fussing. I suddenly remember how Mom didn't want him to go for a walk after Thanksgiving dinner, claiming there'd been too much activity already. I thought she'd been worried about Maryanne. Now I realize she was talking to Dad. She wanted *him* to take it easy.

I shut my eyes tight and breathe deep. My heartbeat is throbbing in my fingertips, and it's more adrenaline than I need right now. When my breathing slows down enough for me to open my eyes, the weight on my shoulders is heavier than ever.

I slowly lift my head, swiping at my tears with the sleeve of my hoodie. "You can't go," I say. Because there's simply no alternative. "You *can't* go."

"I'm going to have to, kid. But I promise you, you're going to be just fine."

"No, I won't." My eyes are burning.

"You will because you're the strongest man I know. I've loved you from the second you opened your eyes. The nurse handed me your tiny, slimy, little body—"

I choke out a laugh.

"And you peered up at me with this knowing look on your face. Your mom says I was imagining it, that there's no way you could have recognized me. She says babies aren't even able to focus their eyes right after they're born, but I *knew* you saw me. And that day you became my best friend."

I have to swallow the howl of pain that wants to escape.

"You're my best friend too," I say simply. "And you're the best father anyone could ever hope for. Like, you put other dads to shame. They ought to feel humiliated."

He cracks a smile. "Damn right." His breathing goes shallow again, as his voice trembles with emotion. "I want you to remember that no matter where I am, I'll always be with you. Watching out for you."

I squeeze his hand, feeling the unbearable crushing weight of this impending loss. I can't do this. I can't say goodbye to him. My heart aches with the knowledge that this might be one of the last conversations we ever have. This man shaped my life. Taught me the values that I live by. What the hell am I going to do without his wisdom? His guidance?

"And I need you to promise to stay on the path that we tried to help you create for yourself. You're going to go to Chicago and report to training camp. You're going to step onto that ice for your very first NHL game, and when you do, you're going to look up and I'm going to be looking down on you."

I start to cry again.

"Promise, Shane."

I manage a nod, squeezing his hand tighter. "I promise."

"Good." He chuckles softly. "Just one more and then I swear I'm done making demands."

I can't return the laugh. I'm in too much agony.

"I need to hear you say that you'll take care of your mom and your sister."

"Of course I will. I'll always take care of them."

"Good," he says again.

A short silence falls. I listen to his breathing. It sounds shallow again. Wispy. And his eyes are starting to get hazy.

"Are you okay?" I ask.

"Just tired. Maybe I'll take a nap."

"Do you want me to go get Mom?"

"Yeah."

I wipe my eyes and walk to the door, but his voice stops me before I can leave.

"I love you, kid," he says from the bed.

"I love you too, Dad."

Three days later, my father is dead.

CHAPTER FIFTY-ONE
SHANE

I don't want to be here

"ARE YOU OKAY?" DIANA FRETS.

It's Sunday. Five days after my dad passed in the hospital with me, my mom, and my sister at his bedside.

I don't know if he planned it that way. If he knew it was going to happen *that moment.* It was morning, and we were in his hospital room watching TV, me in the chair, Maryanne snuggled up against his chest. Mom was downstairs at the café doing some work on her laptop, when Dad suddenly said to Maryanne, "Why don't you go find your mom and bring her up here? Let's spend a little time together, the four of us."

Maryanne darted off, returned with Mom, and fifteen minutes later, he was gone.

I think he probably knew.

Now we're at the house in Heartsong. It's filled with well-wishers, grief hanging in the air like a thick canopy of stifling smoke. The occasional sniffle breaks the soft murmur of conversation. In the corner of the living room is a table draped in flowers and wreaths, with a large black-and-white photo of my father. I can't look at it without crying, so I've been staying far away from that part of the room.

The burial itself was only for immediate family. Dad's buried in Burlington next to his parents. They both died young too; I realized this when I was at the cemetery, staring at their headstones. Grandpa died in his early sixties, Grandma in her midfifties. Both got taken out by cardiac arrests. Dad, meanwhile, gets fuckin' cancer, which doesn't even run on his side of the family. The universe has a sick sense of humor.

Diana was waiting at the house for us when we got back from Burlington. She came early to help Mom's parents set up the house for the memorial. Now, she's beside me, wearing a black knee-length dress, searching my face with concern.

"What? Oh, I'm fine."

I look around, wondering how long we need to be here, how long these people are going to be in my house, coming up to me with their sad faces and rote condolences. There are faces everywhere, some familiar and others not, all blending together in a mosaic of sorrow.

I try to stay calm and collected, but sweat is forming on my neck. I lose focus of the room. I just want to escape before I'm drawn into another conversation with some distant relative I haven't seen in years, telling me how sorry they are that I don't have a father anymore. Everything fades slowly until a voice pulls me back to reality.

"Shane. You don't seem fine."

"I don't want to be here," I whisper to Diana.

"I know." She slips her hand in mine and squeezes.

Mom stands near the refreshment table with her twin sister, my aunt Ashley. Her eyes are red from the tears she shed at the burial. She clutches a tissue in her hand, absent-mindedly dabbing at her face as people walk up paying their final respects.

Across the room, Gigi and Ryder are talking to my sister.

God, my sister. She lost her dad. We both did. But she's still so young. At least I had him for almost twenty-two years. She's only ten years old.

Maryanne meets my eyes, the corners of her mouth lifting in a sad smile. My heart splinters. I squeeze Diana's hand harder.

Beckett is here, and some of the guys from the team. Even Coach Jensen made the drive. He's here with his wife, Iris; I saw them speaking to my mom for a long time. Lots of high school friends showed up too, a familiar one making her way over now.

Lynsey's dark eyes fill with sympathy as she approaches us. "Lindy," she says.

Diana releases my hand, and I step forward to hug my ex-girlfriend.

She presses her cheek against mine and whispers, "I'm so sorry. I loved your dad so much."

"I know. Thank you for being here." After I release her, she nods at Diana. "Diana. Hey."

"Hey," Diana replies.

It's not awkward or anything. Just depressing. Everything about this is depressing. So when my mom asks if she can speak to me alone, I welcome the respite. Except she takes me to the den, which is like entering a torture chamber.

Everywhere I look, I see my dad. I see our family photos. I see his books. I see those cardboard boxes he was sifting through on Thanksgiving.

"He wasn't randomly cleaning out the attic, was he?" I say quietly.

Mom shakes her head. "No. He was searching for his most important belongings to give to you and your sister."

A sob nearly cuts off my airway. The next thing I know, Mom hugs me fiercely, her arms wrapping around my waist.

This loss is…profound. I've never experienced anything like it. This gaping hole in my chest, as if someone ripped out something that makes up my core, a piece of me, and left nothing but pain and emptiness in its place.

"It's okay, baby," she says.

"No, it's not okay. He's gone."

"I know."

"So how is that okay?"

"It has to be. Otherwise, I'm going to drown," she whispers.

For the first time in days, I take a good look at her. I was so worried about myself, and Maryanne, and Dad lying in his hospital bed, that I neglected to really notice my mother. I realize now how utterly destroyed she is.

"You're not doing well." I take her hand and lead her to one of the armchairs, forcing her to sit.

"No," she admits. "I'm not. He was my high school sweetheart." Her voice is choked. "What are we going to do now, Shane? How am I supposed to live without him?"

I reach for her, but she stumbles off the chair and walks toward his desk.

"How can I live in this house?" She waves her arms around. "I can't stay in this house."

"You don't have to," I assure her. "We'll figure something out."

She keeps her back to me, and I see her shoulders rise as she takes a long, deep breath.

That's something I admire about my mom. I've seen her get emotional over the years, but she's able to regulate so fast, calm herself in the blink of an eye. I watch her arch her back, straighten her shoulders. She's in charge again. In control. She's the town manager of Heartsong, Vermont. She knows how to get shit done, and I love her for it.

"I need a favor from you," Mom says.

"Anything."

"Maryanne's not going back to school until January. There's no point, since the holiday break starts soon anyway. Can she stay with you for a couple of weeks while I deal with the estate stuff and search for a new house?"

"Oh wow. You're serious."

"I cannot be here," she repeats.

And I get it. He's everywhere. This is my childhood home and I'll miss it desperately, but the idea of being here without him is unbearable.

"I figured we'll do the holidays at your aunt's house. If that's all right with you, I'll let the rest of the family know."

I nod. Usually we have everyone here, but I understand why she doesn't want to.

"And of course Maryanne can come stay with me," I tell Mom. "I'll talk to my professors, see if I can bring her to some classes."

"I think she'll actually enjoy that."

"Me too. She's such a nerd."

It's the first genuine laugh we've shared in days.

"I'll check if Diana or one of my friends can hang out with her on the weekends when I have games."

"That sounds good. Thank you."

"Of course."

She gives me another hug. "We should go back out there."

"Do we really have to?"

Mom bites her lip. "Five more minutes?"

Without a word, we settle across from each other in Dad's armchairs. The coffee table, still laden with his books, sits between us. In here, we can almost pretend he's not gone. That he's simply out checking on one of his properties, that he'll be back soon, and we'll all eat dinner together. We sit there until eventually a knock interrupts the fantasy and forces us to return to grim reality.

CHAPTER FIFTY-TWO
DIANA

The chasm between us

DECEMBER

SHANE IS STRUGGLING. RIGHTFULLY SO, OF COURSE. HE JUST LOST A parent, and I'm doing everything I can to try to help him. Which at this point basically means playing Mom to Maryanne while Shane plays Dad.

It's not a bad job. She's one of the greatest kids ever. But she's also *Maryanne*. You can't plant a kid like her in front of a TV all day, not with a brain like hers; she needs the mental stimulation. So I've been trying to do fun activities with her whenever I can. Shane is too, but he still has hockey practice every day, and I have cheer practice every day. Since Maryanne can't stay home alone, we've been switching off on little-sister duties.

"I'll grab her from the gym before your practice," he says on Thursday morning, the week before winter semester ends. "What time? Four?"

"Yeah. Class lets out at three thirty, so we'll be there by four." Maryanne is sitting in on my physiology lecture. I have zero concerns about this senior kinesiology class going over that kid's head.

I walk forward and wrap my arms around him. After a beat, he hugs me back, dropping his chin on my shoulder.

"This is brutal," he says.

"I know."

My heart aches for him. I see the grief in his eyes every time they lock with mine. The only time it's not there is when we have sex. We've been doing quite a lot of that every night in my apartment while Maryanne sleeps in his. I think it helps him, the release. And it helps me because, well, Shane sex is the best sex I've ever had in my life.

"Should we grab dinner at the diner when you get home?" he asks.

I shake my head. "I'm meeting with Detective Wendt."

"Oh shit. That's today?" Regret ripples through his eyes. "I would go with you, but I don't think my mom would like it if I brought the kid to a police station."

"No, it's fine. We're just going over a few things in my statement. My lawyer will be there."

"What about your dad?"

"He can't make it, but like I said, it's really not that big of a deal."

I'm downplaying it. This meeting might not be a big deal, but the situation itself is. The prosecutor is going forward with the case against Percy since it's his second assault charge. I'm not even supposed to be involved anymore, but his lawyer has reached out to mine several times this past month. Percy's pissed about what I've set into motion. But even if I *wanted* to drop the charges, the cops aren't going to. And apparently Percy's being too stubborn and refuses to plead out.

"It's so annoying," I tell Shane. "He could just cut a deal and get probation. All he has to do is admit guilt and we don't have to waste time in court."

"I honestly thought he'd take a plea. But I guess a narcissist like him can't admit he did anything wrong. In his warped mind, you deserved it for what you did to him—breaking up with him, being with somebody new."

"Unacceptable," I say sarcastically. "How dare I try to live my life without him?"

Shane bends down to kiss me. "Text me if you need anything. I can always leave Maryanne at the diner and pay one of the waitresses to keep an eye on her while I run down the street to the station."

"I'll be fine, I promise. I love you."

I say those three words to him every day now, and part of me still curses myself for not saying them the night Percy was parked outside Meadow Hill. I felt it then, but I was still pissy that Shane went off with Lynsey. Now I realize how childish that was. If you love someone, you should *always* tell them. Life is too short, and you never know what tomorrow will bring. What if I kept my feelings to myself that night and something had happened to him the next morning? I can't even imagine living with that kind of regret.

"I love you too," Shane says before kissing me again.

He leaves for practice, and I return to the kitchen, where Maryanne sits at the counter drinking the smoothie I made her. She slurps loudly on the straw.

"You two are very mushy," she accuses.

"I know." I sigh. "It's disgusting."

Maryanne snickers. She laughs a lot more frequently than Shane. I don't know if it's because children are more resilient or if she's really good at masking her pain. But while she talks about missing her dad and has moments where she cries, she's not carrying the heavy weight that Shane's been struggling with for days.

"All right," I tell her. "Let's bundle up for the rock hunt. We have a few hours before we need to head to campus."

We're going for a walk, then lunch, then physiology, and then Shane and I will make the hostage exchange. It's going to be a busy day.

Shane's mom calls while we're at lunch, and I have to cut

Maryanne off midsentence. She's chattering on about the rocks we found on our walk.

"Hold on. It's your mom." I quickly answer the call. "Hi, April."

"Hey, sweetheart. Just wanted to check in. Make sure you guys are okay."

"We're great. Thank you." Shane's mother calls me every single day, which is about, oh, a million times more than my own mother. I'm lucky to hear from Mom once every few months.

"How is the house hunting going?" I ask April.

"Good. I think I found something. You can tell Shane I'll send him the listing later. Hopefully he'll have a chance to look at it. We can discuss over the holidays and also deal with all the estate stuff."

I can't even imagine how much "stuff" there is. Ryan ran several businesses, owned a ton of properties, and it all goes to Shane and Maryanne.

"Do you want to talk to your mom?" I ask, covering the mouthpiece.

She shakes her head. "I'll call her tonight."

"Maryanne says she'll call you tonight," I tell April.

"Sounds good. Thanks for helping out, Diana. It means the world, having you as part of our family."

Damned if that doesn't bring a lump to my throat. Yes, I have a family. I have my dad, Larissa, Thomas. But hearing those words from...a mother, I guess. It lands differently.

I'm still a bit raw from it later when Shane and I exchange Maryanne duties before cheer practice. And I'm still thinking about it after practice. As I'm leaving the locker room with Crystal and Brooke, I suddenly wonder if this rift with my mother, the chasm between us, is partially my fault. Because how often do I call *her*? What do *I* do to bridge the distance?

When I really reflect on it, I realize that somewhere along the line, I simply gave up because of her disinterest in me. The awareness that I'll never be smart enough for her took its toll and I stopped caring.

But I should care. I don't begrudge anyone who cuts off a family member; there are multiple reasons to do it, and I would never judge if someone said, *oh, I don't speak to my mother.* I wouldn't question it because I'd assume they had their reasons.

But, in the grand scheme of things, mine isn't so bad.

In the lobby of the athletic center, I walk toward an empty bench instead of the front door, waving the girls off. I sit down and dial Mom's number.

I'm prepared to leave a voice message, so I'm surprised to hear her voice. "Diana. Is everything okay?"

Like you care is my first thought, and when my brain catches it, it's all the confirmation I need. I *am* part of the problem. Maybe she does care. Why do I instantly decide she doesn't?

"Did something happen with Percival?" she asks in concern.

I suddenly realize I haven't spoken to her at all about what happened with Percy. I told Dad that I would contact her when I was ready to talk, and while I did touch base briefly, I never actually *talked* to her about it.

It's becoming more and more obvious that the failure of this relationship is two-sided.

"I'm an asshole," I blurt out.

"What?" She's startled.

"I never even called you to talk about what happened."

"No," she says tightly. "You didn't."

Despite my epiphany, a familiar note of accusation creeps in. "But you didn't call me either."

"You told your father you would discuss it when you were ready. I'm not the type to push."

Frustration tightens my throat. "But you should push, Mom. You should."

She doesn't respond.

"My ex-boyfriend punched me in the face. You should have been on the first plane out of New York to come see me." I sigh. "I'm not upset about it—"

"Really? Because it sounds like you're upset about it."

"No. I'm sorry. I'm having a thought explosion."

"A thought explosion." There's amusement in her voice.

"Yes, just…let me unjumble this." I take a breath. "I didn't want to talk to you about Percy because I was embarrassed. I thought that you would blame me."

She gasps. "Sweetheart. Do you truly believe that?"

"I did. But now I'm realizing it was my own insecurities making me believe that. I'm so used to thinking I'm a disappointment to you, I'm not smart enough for you, that when Percy snapped on me, I kept thinking how disappointed you would be or that you'd think I was dumb enough to let it happen—"

"Diana!" She sounds genuinely upset. "I would *never* think—"

"I know that now," I interrupt. "It was all coming from an irrational place. But…" I let out another breath. "My boyfriend's father died."

"Oh." She's startled by the abrupt subject change. "I'm sorry to hear that. This is the hockey player?"

"Yes, the hockey player. He's a lot more than that, though. But yeah, he just lost his dad. His sister has been staying with him this week, and her mom has been checking in every single day."

I hear a sigh on the other end. "Don't tell me you want me to call you every day, because that hasn't been the nature of our relationship your entire life."

"It hasn't," I agree. "And I'm not saying I want that, but a little interest in my life is not too much to ask for."

"I show interest."

"No, Mom, you don't. You criticize me when I talk to you about cheerleading or my dance competition. I understand you're not interested in it, but guess what. You can fake it." I start to laugh. "I fake it all the time. I'm not too interested in hockey, but I make the effort and listen to my boyfriend talk about it. Because it's his passion. And when Dad goes on about his stupid sausages and his butcher, I pretend to care. But guess what, I don't care about meat!"

Mom giggles. "Oh my God. Does he still go on about Gustav?"

"Yes, and it's obnoxious. But that's what you do when you love people. Support their interests. I'm not saying I want you to start coming to my cheer competitions. I know we're different. But I don't want to miss out on a relationship with you just because we're completely different people. Like, we must have *something* in common. Some common ground. I just don't think we've tried hard enough to find it."

"No," she says quietly. "I don't think we have either."

"Well, I'm willing to do it if you are. I'm willing to put in the effort."

"I would like that."

"Would you really?" I can never tell with my mother. She's so good at shielding her emotions.

"I would." Her voice catches. "It hurt me when you chose to live with your father after the divorce. I understood it, of course. He's the fun one. I'm the strict one. And even back then, like you said, we didn't have a lot of common ground. Our personalities are so diametrically opposed. But I felt like you didn't want to spend any time with me, and eventually I...you're right, I stopped trying. I speak to your brother all the time."

Hearing that brings a sting of hurt.

"And yet with my daughter, my firstborn, I barely pick up the phone. It's unacceptable."

"It's on both of us," I say.

"No, I'm the parent. I take ninety percent of the blame."

I snort into the phone. "All right. I'll accept the ten percent." My voice gets serious again. "Maybe I can come see you over the holiday break. I know you said you have a lot of work preparing your lectures for January, but—"

"I can set aside an hour or two for you." She's joking.

"Oh, thanks. So generous." I'm joking too.

"There's this excellent spa on the Upper East Side that I recently discovered. Should I book us a spa day?"

"Since when do you like spas?"

"Since always, Diana. You know I get monthly massages. What did you think that meant?"

"It didn't even occur to me that it might be a spa-type thing."

"Oh, it's a spa-type thing."

We say goodbye, and although my boyfriend still has a huge weight on him, I feel like one has been lifted off me.

CHAPTER FIFTY-THREE
SHANE

I'm not giving you up

I CAN'T DO THIS.

The odd, frantic thought first infiltrates when I'm dressing for tonight's game, my first one back since Dad died. I ignore that thought because it's inane. Of course I can do this. I've been doing this more than half my life. Hockey is in my blood.

So I push it away and go about my business. I throw on my pads, my uniform. I lace up my skates. I join my team on the Briar bench. And I play hockey.

I can't do this.

It pokes at me again halfway through the first period. As I weave through opponents and teammates alike, it gnaws at my insides like a dog chewing on a stick. And I can taste resentment in my mouth. It's not the first time I've experienced this bitterness since Dad died, but tonight it feels different. The cheers of the crowd, the adrenaline rush of the game, the familiar scent of the ice. Where it used to be freeing, it suddenly seems suffocating.

Maryanne is at home with Diana, and I'm here in this rink. I'm playing a stupid, pointless game when I should be taking care of my little sister.

I can't do this.

By the second period, it's a mantra in my head.

"Change it up," Jensen barks, and Beckett smacks my shoulder.

I bolt off the bench and heave myself onto the ice for my next shift. I'm not distracted. I'm not playing poorly. But I am operating partially on autopilot as I get checked into the boards, the cold surface biting through my jersey. The sounds of skates slicing through the ice and sticks clashing echo all around me. I gain control of the puck, surging toward the Harvard net. When the opposing defenseman lunges forward, I flick the puck backward to Austin, who slaps it into the net like a rocket.

Goal!

Our teammates roar their approval when we change lines again. Will slaps my arm, congratulating me on the assist.

I can't be here.

I barely hear the final buzzer over the incessant buzzing in my own brain. My mantra has evolved.

After the game, I hurriedly change into my street clothes and then track down Coach Jensen, asking to speak in private. I think he knows what I'm going to say before I even say it. He sees it in my eyes.

"I have to go home, Coach."

He's quiet for a beat. Then he sighs. "For how long?"

"I don't know."

"What do you mean you quit the team?" Diana's face is awash with worry as she follows me around my room, watching me throw items of clothing into a suitcase.

"I didn't quit. Well, I guess I did."

"Shane. You're not making any sense."

I walk to my dresser and open the top drawer, grabbing a handful of boxer shorts. My sister's stuff is scattered all over the bedroom, which she's been using since she came to stay. She'll need to pack too, but I wanted to speak to Diana about this first, so I planted Maryanne in front of the TV with a documentary about asteroids.

"I have to go home, Dixon. I can't be here right now."

"Okay." I hear her take a breath. "I get that. But…this is hockey. Hockey is your life. What if you make it to the playoffs? You can't desert your team."

Pain stabs into my chest. She's right. I can't.

But I am.

Exhaling a hiss of air, I drop the boxers in the suitcase and then sink onto the edge of my bed. Diana joins me, angling her body so she's facing me, searching my expression.

"What is this about?" she presses.

"I promised him I'd take care of them," I say gruffly.

"You are taking care of them."

"How? My mom is home alone struggling to sell the house before Christmas, so she doesn't have to spend the holidays with his ghost. Not to mention dealing with lawyers and accountants and executors to settle Dad's massive estate. And Maryanne is here, being passed around between you and Gigi while I'm at practice or in class or in the weight room. How am I taking care of either of them?"

Diana strokes my cheek. Her touch is so warm and comforting that I lean into it. I sag against my girlfriend, and she wraps her arms around me, holding me tight. Dixon has been my rock since the nightmare began. She's the only light in this pitch-black, claustrophobic tunnel I can't seem to find my way out of.

"I made him a promise." My voice is rough. "I can't keep that promise and stay on the team. I need to go back to Heartsong for a while."

"What's a while?"

I pull back and see the deep furrow in her forehead. I reach up and gently rub the crease away before pressing my forehead to hers.

"At least until after the holidays. Maybe longer. Maybe I'll have to take next semester off, depending on what my family needs from me."

Diana bites her lip. "You won't be able to graduate if you miss the semester."

"Then I'll come back in the fall." I take her hand, needing her warmth. She knows it and laces our fingers. "I won't be gone forever. Just until they no longer need me."

"I wish I could do more," she says with a sigh.

"You're already doing so much." I cup her cheek, leaning in to kiss her. It's a peck, a brush of reassurance. "You've gone above and beyond in helping me take care of Maryanne. But you have a life too. You have your own sport to focus on, and your own classes. It's not fair to ask you to do that."

Her throat bobs as she swallows. "Okay. I have to ask this. Are you breaking up with me?"

My jaw falls open. "What? Fuck no."

Relief floods her gaze. "All right. Good. Just making sure."

I chuckle softly. I've laughed very rarely these past few weeks, but Dixon always manages to bring some levity.

"I love you," I say in a strong, empathic tone. "I'm not giving you up. Ever."

"Ever, huh?"

"Well, as long as you'll have me."

She smiles at that.

"And if you're cool with it, I figured you could drive me home and then keep my car while I'm gone. I'll have my dad's—" My voice cracks. I can't think about him without breaking down. "My dad's truck. And Mom has her own car. The Mercedes will just be sitting in the driveway, so I figured you might as well use it here."

"Don't do this, Lindley. If you lend me that car, I'll never give it back."

"Oh, you're giving it back." I grin. "I love you, but not that much."

She crawls into my lap, locking her hands behind my neck. "Are you sure you want to go?"

I nod. "I have to."

She nods too. "Okay. I support whatever you decide. And now that football season is coming to an end, I'll be able to drive up every weekend to see you."

"I'm holding you to that."

THE BOYS ALL CAPS

BECKETT DUNNE:

> Miss you

LUKE RYDER:

> You doing ok?

SHANE LINDLEY:

> Yeah, all good

SHANE LINDLEY:

> We found a new place, so I've been busy packing up the house

LUKE RYDER:

> When are you coming back?

BECKETT DUNNE:

> Miss you

WILL LARSEN:

> Dude. Stop being weird

CHAPTER FIFTY-FOUR
DIANA

I didn't come here to hurt you

JANUARY

I MISS SHANE SOMETHING FIERCE. I DIDN'T GET TO SPEND THE HOLIDAYS with him because I needed to be with Dad and Larissa's family and then visited my mother in New York. I managed to squeeze in a four-day visit to Heartsong after New Year's, but it wasn't nearly long enough. Now I'm back in Meadow Hill and he's three hours away, and it sucks.

The new semester starts tomorrow, and I'm spending my Sunday night on the couch, watching old footage of cheer routines from past nationals. The Briar squad sailed through regionals, so once school's back, we need to kick it into a new gear to prep for nationals. I've been working with our coach, Nayesha, to fine-tune our routine. Nayesha and our choreographer handle the choreography itself, but they value my input, and the three of us are meeting tomorrow before practice.

Since my thermostat keeps shutting on and off for no reason—I definitely need to bring my dad in here, stat—I've got my heavy comforter curled up around my head, making me a human burrito. The muted glow of the TV casts shadows across Skip's fish tank.

I didn't even notice it had gotten dark out, but now I realize that the world has grown eerily quiet. Niall is probably in an orgasmic cocoon of silent bliss right now.

When a wailing meow suddenly cuts through the silence, I jump so hard that my blanket burrito nearly rolls over the couch.

Fuckin' Lucy. How did she get out again?

I don't want to unravel myself, but I always have Priya's back, even if it means dealing with her obstinate feline. I throw the blanket off and head for the entryway. When I hear footsteps beyond my door, I realize Priya is on top of this.

I'm already talking to her as I open my door. "Hey, I'll help you grab—"

I freeze.

Percy's standing in front of me.

Anxiety grips me like a vise, my breath catching in my throat.

"Diana," he starts, but I'm springing to action.

I slam the door, but Percy's equally quick. He wedges a black boot in before the door can latch.

"Just wait—"

"No," I say angrily. "Go away. You're not allowed to be here."

Oh my God, how did he even get on the property?

"I'm not going anywhere," Percy spits out. "We need to talk."

Only a sliver of his enraged face is visible, distorted by the doorway as I keep trying to close the door on him. He pushes at it, and my pulse races. I push back, and the wood rattles loudly as we both battle for door domination.

"Stop it," I order. I'm scared now. "You need to leave."

"Not until we talk."

He elbows the door again, the force causing it to shake on its hinges.

"No," I repeat, while my heart thunders against my ribs. Why is he here? And why is he vibrating with rage? When I saw Wendt and my lawyer, they assured me the case was moving along smoothly. Percy's first hearing is scheduled for this week, and Wendt said that when she spoke to him, he appeared resigned. Defeated, even.

Right now, he looks like a powder keg waiting for a spark.

"You need to go to the DA," Percy is saying. "You need to get this fucking case dropped, Diana."

"I couldn't even if I tried. The DA chose to go forward—"

He gives the door a hard shove, winning the battle and sending me stumbling backward.

He's in my apartment.

Pulse shrieking, I waste no time running to the living room. Maybe I'm overreacting, maybe he's just here to talk, but the last time he tried to talk, he punched me in the face. Fool me fucking once.

I dart to the coffee table, hands trembling as I fumble for my phone.

"Diana!" He storms inside, seething. "Stop it."

I snatch up the phone. The restraining order was my last defense, a fragile shield against the raging storm that is Percy, but tonight it's insufficient. He broke it. He's in my apartment, and I need him *out*.

"Put the phone away. You're going to sit down and listen to what I have to say. Because I'm not leaving here until we come up with a solution."

I ignore his desperate voice. My fingers frantically hit the number 9. Then 1.

"I'm calling the police, Percy, so you better get out of here before—"

The phone is batted out of my hand before I can hit the final 1. I cry out when it goes skidding across the living room.

Fear pummels into me. I look at his red face, then my discarded phone, and make a decision.

I burst forward, needing to get to the door.

Percy grabs me before I can make it past him. Pain jolts through my arm as it's nearly yanked out of the socket.

"Stop it. I didn't come here to hurt you. You're being ridiculous."

I don't care what he says. I don't feel safe. I *can't* be here. And although the restraining order failed, I know something that won't fail me.

Niall's ears.

"NIALL!" I scream, stomping hard on the floor. "Call the police! Percy Forsythe is in my apartment and he's—"

The first blow sends my head snapping to the side.

Pain jolts through my face. His knuckles got me right on the mouth, splitting my lip.

"You fucking bitch! This is all your fault! I only came here to talk, to sit down and discuss this like two reasonable adults, and you're treating me like some kind of criminal! Fuck you, Diana!"

As blood pours out of my lip, I throw up my forearms, instinctively protecting my face again. But he uses the defensive posture against me and punches me in the stomach. The heavy blow stuns me, a whoosh of air leaving my body. I nearly fall over but regain my balance at the last second.

"I got expelled from Briar," he fumes. "Did you know that? That's what your stunt with the cops did! The dean found out about the assault charges against me and kicked me out of my program this morning. Called me into his office on a fucking Sunday to tell me I was out. You cost me my fellowship. My career!"

He tries to grab me again, but this time I successfully sidestep him. I unleash a left jab that grazes his cheek, eliciting a grunt of pain. I'm not trying to fight him, only to distract him so I can sprint out of the apartment.

I want to scream for Shane but he's not here. He's in Vermont. So I cry out for Niall again, for Priya, even for the damned cat, as I race toward the door.

I make it five feet before my ex-boyfriend grabs me by the

ponytail, pulling me backward. He throws me on the floor. I land hard, the impact sending a streak of pain through my shoulder.

"You need to leave," I beg, feeling the blood from my lip dripping down my neck. "You don't want to do this, Percy. Please."

But he's lost to me. He's in a frenzy. He kicks me when I'm down, and I instinctively curl into a ball. He's undeterred. Tears flood my eyes when his boot stomps on my side. Agony blooms inside me.

"You ruined my life," he hisses. "I never meant to hurt you that night. You *know* it was an accident. But you still took that one mistake and used it to ruin my life."

When he kicks my shoulder, the heel of his boot grazes the side of my face, jolting my nose.

I whimper in pain. Blood now pours from my split lip and my nose. I don't know if it's broken, but it hurts like hell. A metallic taste burns my tongue as I try to crawl toward the door.

Percy stands over me, watching.

"You ruined my life," he says again.

I know I should keep my mouth shut, but my body is on fire. Agony ripples in every muscle. In my face. In my side.

I meet his wild eyes and say, "Good."

The last thing I remember is his foot kicking the side of my head.

CHAPTER FIFTY-FIVE
SHANE

You don't belong here

WHEN I WALK INTO THE FAMILY ROOM, MOM IS SITTING ON THE COUCH, back straight, gaze fixed on the crackling fireplace.

I've found her in this pose frequently during the month I've been home, stumbling upon these moments of numb silence. I get them too. There's been a weight on my shoulders since Dad died. It keeps pulling me down, anchoring me to this pit of endless grief. The only moment its grip on me lightens is when I see Diana, who's kept her promise to drive up on the weekends.

When she's not here, we're all keeping busy. Mom's back at work. Maryanne starts school again tomorrow. I've been dealing with the real estate agent and packing up the house. We found a place ten minutes away. That means Maryanne doesn't need to switch schools, so that's one less hassle.

The scene of tonight's dinner lingers in the air, a reminder of the countless hours I've spent helping Mom around the house. We take turns cooking. I do most of the cleaning, which is unheard of.

Maryanne seems to be doing okay, although she has her moments of sadness too, and she's thrown a few tantrums since I've been home. That's equally unheard of. She never used to be a tantrum kid. But Mom's sister is a child psychologist and maintains that this is normal, a healthy release of her grief.

"Hey," I say as I settle in the worn leather armchair, resting my beer on my knee. "Kitchen's spotless. No need to bring in the cleaner to check my work."

She shifts her gaze from the fire to me, cracking a smile. "I might have coddled you a little more than necessary with the cleaning lady, huh?"

I shrug. "Not complaining."

We chat about our plans for tomorrow. I plan on tackling the garage while Mom's at work. The shelving unit that makes up the entire back wall is full of random junk that we need to go through. We're discussing what items to keep and what to toss when a text lights up my phone screen. Ryder's been keeping me updated about the playoffs, and he just sent me the schedule.

"Shit," I exclaim as I read the message.

"What is it?" Mom asks.

"We're playing—" I quickly correct myself. "They're playing Yale in the semifinals. Briar hasn't faced Yale in the postseason in like, a decade."

I tamp down the excitement that tries to surface. Nope. I won't be on the ice next weekend. It's not my game to get excited about.

A prickle of discomfort itches my skin when I notice Mom watching me.

"What?" I say.

After a beat, she motions for me to join her on the couch. "Come sit here. We need to talk."

Uncertain, I set my phone and beer bottle on the coffee table and take a seat beside her. "What's up?"

"I've been doing a lot of thinking since you came home, and I want you to know I appreciate all the help you've given me. You've been a rock. Taking such good care of things around here since your dad passed. But I don't want you to lose sight of your dreams, and I think you might be."

I stare down at my hands, clasped tight on my lap. "I can't afford to think about dreams right now. You need me."

She reaches out and lifts my chin, meeting my eyes. "Shane. I'm grateful that you're here, more than you can imagine. But I don't want you to sacrifice your future for us. You deserve a chance to live the life you've always wanted."

"I made him a promise," I say gruffly.

"I know. He told me. But I don't think this is what he meant, sweetheart."

A rush of emotion closes my throat, making it hurt. "He asked me to be there for you and Maryanne. That's what I'm doing."

"Not at the expense of your own life," Mom says gently. "He wouldn't want you to quit the team. To leave school. In fact, he'd knock you upside the head for this decision. Because you're forgetting the other promise you made him."

My brow furrows.

"You promised you'd go to Chicago as planned. That you'd excel in your sport. You're a hockey player, not a babysitter or a box packer or an adequate chef. You need to go play hockey. *That's* the promise you should be keeping." She takes a deep breath, her gaze unwavering. "You don't belong here."

I frown at her. "Then why did you let me come home?"

She sighs. "Honestly? I thought you'd get bored after a week or two. Miss hockey and Diana, and go back to Briar. But you're not leaving. So you've forced my hand and now I have to kick you out."

A disbelieving laugh flies out. "Wow."

"Your sister and I are going to be fine. You've already done so much. Maryanne is back at school tomorrow. I've got work. The lawyers have a good grasp on your father's estate. And you've packed up nearly the entire house. There's nothing for you to do here. It's time for you to go."

A tentative smile lifts my lips. "I can't believe you're kicking me out."

Yet her actions—no, her permission, it lifts the weight off my shoulders, replacing it with a newfound sense of hope. I loved being home with my family, but I also hated it. It's been a long time since I've had to assume this much responsibility. Taking care of the house, driving Maryanne around everywhere, keeping her busy. I can't imagine doing all this while also playing professional hockey.

The longer I'm here, the more I realize how idealized my view of life has been. I've been injected with a dose of reality. My whole vision about being a young husband, a young dad, and believing I could still give equal focus to hockey, to intensive training and a grueling schedule... I've never considered myself to be naive. But... yeah. It's a challenging balance I'd never be able to strike right now.

Mom's right. I miss Briar. I miss my boys. And most of all, I miss Diana.

I scoot closer and hug her tightly, grateful for her support and encouragement. She and Dad were always good at that, letting me follow whatever path I wanted, rooting from the sidelines while I did it. They've almost got Diana beat in the cheerleading department.

"All right. I'll head back tomorrow," I tell her. "Hopefully Coach gives me my roster slot back and lets me play Yale this weekend."

"He's an idiot if he doesn't."

"Don't ever call Coach Jensen an idiot to his face. He'll destroy you."

"Not if I destroy him first."

I grin. I hail from a family of psychopaths.

"Do you want to put on a movie or something?" I suggest.

"Sure. I don't know if I'll make it through more than half before I fall asleep, but let's see what happens."

Chuckling, I reach for the remote, but my hand changes course when my phone lights up on the table. The caller ID displays an unfamiliar number. It's a Massachusetts area code. Usually I send unknowns to voicemail, but there's a funny feeling tickling my stomach, and for some reason I pick up the phone.

I answer with a leery, "Hello?"

"Shane, this is Priya. From Meadow Hill."

A chill runs down my spine. I clutch the phone tighter. "Priya, hey. What's up?"

"I'm calling from the hospital. An ambulance just brought Diana in. Niall and I rode here with her—"

The room spins for a moment. "What happened? Is she all right?"

"What's going on?" Mom touches my arm.

"Diana's in the hospital," I explain before refocusing on Priya. "Tell me what happened."

"She's hurt," Priya says, her shaky breathing betraying her calm tone. "You should get here as soon as you can."

I feel the world closing in on me. "Hurt how? Just tell me what happened."

"Her ex-boyfriend broke into her apartment and beat her pretty badly."

My entire body is frozen in place.

Beat her?

What the fuck does she mean, Percy *beat* her?

"What hospital?" I'm already shooting to my feet.

"St. Michael's in Hastings."

"I'm on my way."

CHAPTER FIFTY-SIX

DIANA

I want a sassy bitch

THE MOMENT SHANE WALKS INTO MY HOSPITAL ROOM, HE STARTS to cry.

"Don't," I beg from the bed. "Please. You'll make me cry too, and my nose is too congested right now. I want to be able to breathe."

But there's no stopping him. His broad shoulders shake from his tears. I can't even imagine how traumatic this must be for him—the last time he was in a hospital, he was clutching his father's hand, literally watching him die. His shell-shocked expression as he stumbles toward me confirms my suspicion that he's in the midst of a flashback.

"It's worse than it looks," I say wryly.

He doesn't answer. Just blinks back his tears as his frantic gaze runs up and down my body. I know what he's seeing. The bandage on my head, the split lip, swollen nose. It's not broken, thank God, but it still hurts like a bitch.

The real damage, unfortunately, is internal. My kidney took a good beating. The doctor is worried about internal bleeding, so she's keeping me here for observation for a few days. She warned me I have some bloody urine to look forward to.

Shane collapses in the chair that my dad was recently occupying.

Dad went to collect Shane from the lobby when he called to say he was downstairs, and I suspect he's in the waiting room now, giving us some privacy.

Uncertainty looms in Shane's eyes as his hand finds mine. He's shaking. "What happened?"

Shane's expression starts off angry, as I describe how Percy kicked the door in, and ends homicidal when I describe myself curled up on the floor while he stomped on me.

As I relate the evening's events, it's difficult to control the sick feeling in my stomach and the weak, fluttery sensations that keep trembling through me. The doctor gave me something for the anxiety, but I know a pill or two isn't going to fix what's wrong. As embarrassing as it felt to admit weakness, I remembered what my dad had told me about asking for help, and so I asked my doctor if she could arrange for a counselor to come see me. I've had anxiety attacks since the summer. I can't ignore them anymore. It's time to face them head-on, no matter how scary that might be.

The gravity of the situation keeps slicing into me out of nowhere. How close I came to being severely injured. Maybe even dead. If Niall hadn't called the cops the moment I screamed his name, if they hadn't shown up within seven minutes of the call, who knows what would've happened? As it is, I can't recall anything after that final kick. I just remember waking up in the ambulance, my head spinning.

"Oh, I also have a mild concussion," I tell Shane. "So don't turn on the big light." We're using the bedside lamp in the room, which offers an inoffensive pale glow that only slightly irritates my eyes.

He reaches up and touches the bandage on my temple. "What happened here?"

"I was lying in the front hall when he tried to leave. Bottom of the door clipped me and cut my head. Five stitches," I say with resignation. "I feel bad for my dad, though, because he has to go back there tonight and clean up all the blood. Did you know head wounds bleed like a bitch?"

"Don't make jokes. Please." His eyes are wet again.

"Hey, it's okay." I grip his hand. "I'm fine."

"I'm so sorry, baby. I should've been there."

I squeeze his hand tighter. "It's not your fault. You couldn't have known he'd show up tonight."

"I should've protected you."

"Stop it. You can't blame yourself." I adjust my position and wince when pain throbs in my side. Stupid kidney. "I don't want you feeling guilty."

He clasps my hand in both of his. When he speaks, it's through a fuck-ton of gravel. "Seeing you like this…it's killing me."

"I'm going to be okay. I promise. Might have to see a therapist for a while to help me sort through everything, but physically I'm going to bounce back soon. You'll see."

He leans in and places a tender kiss on my forehead. "I love you. I'm never leaving your side again. I hope you realize that."

That summons a smile. "I'm cool with it."

"Will the nurses throw me out if I get in bed with you?"

"I'll yell at them if they try. But come lie on this side. My left side is totally out of commission."

Shane stands up to remove his coat and kick off his shoes. Then he gingerly gets on the narrow bed. He's six one and stupidly muscular, so it's a tight fit, but he manages to settle beside me, propped up on one elbow while his hand gently strokes my hair.

"I'm coming back to Briar," he says. "Back to Meadow Hill."

"Don't you dare come back because of me. I'll be fine."

"Nah, not just because of you. My mom kicked me out."

I gasp, then instantly regret it when my side clenches in pain.

"For my own good," Shane adds. He presses his lips to my non-bandaged temple, and I feel him smiling. "She reminded me where I belong."

"In the rink," I confirm.

"And with you."

His hand drifts down my arm. I feel his fingers shaking. "I know it seems like I'm handling this really well on the outside—"

"Does it?" I say dryly.

"But I'm terrified right now. The fact that you're in the hospital is ripping me apart. Every time I think about him kicking in the door and hurting you…" Shane makes a strangled noise. "Don't let me leave this hospital tonight, Dixon."

"I won't."

"I'll fucking kill him."

"You won't."

We fall silent for a moment. I'm not hooked up to any machines, so the room is quiet. When Shane speaks again, his voice is trembling.

"You have no idea how much I love you. It's almost pathetic."

I can't help but laugh. This time the twinge of pain is worth it.

"Never saw it coming, Dixon. But you're everything to me. I don't know when it happened, but it's true. You're the heartbeat of my days. You're the reason I look forward to tomorrow. I honestly never thought I'd find someone who understands me so completely."

Oh my God. I can't believe these sappy words are leaving Shane Lindley's mouth. I'd tease him about it if he wasn't so damn earnest. Besides, I know exactly what he's saying. I feel the same way. I am unapologetically myself when I'm with him. Weirdness and all.

"Being away from you this last month was torture. I fucking left you and look what happened. He could have killed you."

"I'm all right," I say firmly.

"I wasn't joking before. I'm never leaving you again."

"You'll have to eventually," I tease. "What about when you're traveling with the Blackhawks on away games and I'm at home with the two children you expect me to pop out next year?"

He chuckles, his breath tickling my chin. "Yeah, about that… I may have changed my mind."

I'm startled. "You don't want marriage and kids anymore?"

"No, I do." He absently strokes my arm.

I wish I didn't have to wear this hospital gown. I asked my dad to grab me a cardigan or two when he goes back to my apartment tonight. But right now, I guess I don't mind it. My short sleeves let me enjoy the soft scrape of Shane's fingertips on my flesh.

"I definitely still want it," he continues. "But the kid thing... I think you're onto something with your waiting-until-your-thirties plan. Taking care of Maryanne when she was here and then being home with her this whole month..." He sighs. "It's a lot of work."

"No kidding."

"I don't think I'm ready for that."

"You could always find yourself a sweet little wife who will be fine doing it all herself."

"I don't want a sweet little wife." He kisses my shoulder. "I want a sassy bitch."

I snicker. "Did you just call me a bitch?"

"Mmm-hmmm."

A sense of contentment settles over me, which is ironic considering I experienced a beating at the hands of my ex-boyfriend tonight. I shouldn't be feeling content right now.

"Remember when you asked me if I would ever make sacrifices?" I say pensively. "If I could be the kind of partner who took on a larger load while you were in the NHL?" I purse my lips. "I think I could."

"Yeah?" he says thickly.

"I would make those sacrifices for you. Because you're everything to me too."

"Jesus, Dixon, you're so sappy. Have some more self-respect."

I snort against his shoulder.

"Anyway, congratulations," he says.

"For what?"

"I'm leaving you in charge of deciding when you birth our children."

My burst of laughter makes my side throb again. "Damn it, Lindley. Stop making me laugh." I snuggle closer to him. "But thank you. I appreciate you allowing me a say in our future."

"I like that."

"What?"

"Our future." He rests his cheek against the top of my head. "Do you mean that? You see a future for us?"

I reach for his hand and slowly lace our fingers. "Yes. I mean it."

I have no idea what that future will hold, but I do know one thing—when it comes to me and Shane, there's no doubt in my mind that the journey will be fun.

CHAPTER FIFTY-SEVEN
SHANE

Pretend your fingers are gently stirring soup

MY ENTIRE BODY IS BUZZING WITH ANTICIPATION AS I STEP THROUGH the heavy door into the locker room. The familiar scent of sweat and equipment greets my nostrils, but there's something else in the air. Faces light up when I enter, a few cheers erupting at the sight of me.

"Lindley!" Colson exclaims, coming up to greet me. "It's about fuckin' time."

Trager, Patrick, Austin, and a few others wander over, giving me manly side hugs and smacking my arm, welcoming me back. A lot of fanfare considering it's just a regular morning practice.

I grin, genuinely touched by the reception. I make my way to my locker, where I'm joined by Ryder and Beckett.

"Good to have you back," Ryder says gruffly.

"Glad to be back."

Beckett's already in his practice jersey and gear, so he sits on the bench while we get ready. "How's Diana?" he asks somberly.

"Better." My smile falters for a moment, because every time I think about my girlfriend lying in that hospital room, I feel sick to my stomach. "It's been tough, but we're getting through it."

My friends nod in understanding, a mixture of sympathy and support in their eyes.

"Let us know if she needs anything, mate," Beck says, his tone sincere.

"Thanks, man."

My chest is tight with emotion, so I twist toward my locker, pretending to search for something while I blink through my suddenly misty eyes. Jesus Christ. I'm not going to cry in front of a room full of hockey players. I've already cried enough in front of Diana since I returned to Hastings.

But knowing my friends are here for me is soul soothing. This locker room is a brotherhood, and I feel that bond every time I walk in here. I know I can always lean on these guys, even obnoxious Trager, when times get tough.

"She's dying to get home," I say.

"When is she being discharged?" Will asks from his locker.

"Tomorrow morning, I think. The doctors are finally satisfied her kidney isn't going to explode or something."

Ryder chuckles.

We finish dressing for practice, but before I can walk out into the tunnel, Coach Jensen intercepts me. He toys with the whistle dangling around his neck as he pulls me aside.

A mix of nerves and gratitude swirls in my gut as I wait for him to speak.

"Welcome back, Lindley," he says briskly. "I just wanted to check how your girl is doing."

"She's good. Thank you for asking."

"And the asshole who did that to her?"

"They arrested him the night it happened, but he's out on bail." Jensen's eyes flash.

"I know," I say with a sigh. "But he's in Indiana now. His parents came to get him, and he was given permission to leave the state with them so long as he wore an ankle bracelet. But he was booked for the latest assault. He almost killed her, Coach. Nobody's letting him off easy. The DA says he'll do time."

"They oughta throw away that key," Coach mutters. "Any man who raises his hand to a woman doesn't deserve to see daylight."

I nod in agreement.

"Anyway. Go join the men."

"Coach, wait. I just wanted to say..." I offer a sincere look. "I appreciate you giving me the time off to handle things."

To my shock, Jensen does something very un-Jensen-like. He places a hand on my shoulder in a comforting touch.

"Hockey's important, Lindley, but so is life. I'm here for you, and the team's here for you. You ever need to talk, come find me."

I swallow the lump in my throat, feeling the weight of my coach's words. As I make my way down the tunnel, listening to the familiar sounds of my teammates warming up, I feel a renewed sense of purpose, and I know that wherever he is, my dad is watching over me.

After practice, I drive right back to the hospital to see Diana. I come armed with snacks and my laptop, so we can watch something better than the hospital channels. I've stayed true to my word—I don't plan on leaving her side until she's home.

Her face lights up the moment I walk into her room. She's sitting up, wearing a white cardigan with green flowers, her blond hair around her shoulders. Despite the cut on her lip and the row of stitches on her temple, her cheeks have a healthy glow, and her eyes are bright.

Christ, I love this woman with all my heart. Being with Diana is like discovering a piece of myself that I never knew was missing. She makes me want to be the best version of myself, not because I feel like I have to impress her but because she inspires me to be better.

I don't regret my time with Lynsey. I needed it in order to grow into who I am today. But man, I see the difference now. I see the importance of picking the right woman to do life with. Preferably someone who can make you laugh your ass off.

"Hey," I say thickly.

She smiles. "Hey."

"Where's your mom?" I ask.

Diana's mom flew in from New York the morning after the assault and has spent the past three mornings at her daughter's bedside. Diana wasn't wrong about her mother's attitude—I definitely see the pretentious side. But I can also tell she truly loves her daughter and is genuinely trying to connect with her. That's all that matters.

"You won't believe this," Diana answers. "She went out for lunch with Dad and Larissa."

"Wow."

Even I know that's progress. Diana's parents have barely spent two hours in the same room since they divorced ten years ago. But I've seen them chatting in the hospital cafeteria more than once since Diana was admitted. Her brother wanted to fly in as well, but Diana put her foot down and ordered him to stay in Peru.

I drag my usual chair over to her bedside. She's allowed to leave tomorrow. Until then, I'm spending yet another night in this hospital room. The nurses know better than to kick me out. Although I do plan on getting Adeline and Marge a nice gift basket for their patience and kindness. And maybe an extra-large basket for Dr. Lamina, the psychiatrist who's been seeing Diana every morning to help her work through the lingering anxiety over the assault.

"How was practice?" Diana asks.

"It was good. Beckett was on fire. Can't wait to see him unleash his inner goon on Yale this weekend."

I open the bag of snacks, reaching in for the bag of plain potato chips she requested. I hand them to her, and she smiles happily.

"Any updates about him and Will?" she asks.

I roll my eyes. "Babe. Neither of them provides me with updates about their sex lives."

"Well, they should. I'm curious."

"I'll be sure to interrogate them tomorrow at practice about whether they've seen each other's penises lately," I promise.

"Thank you."

I steal a handful of potato chips. "How's your pee?"

"Barely pink!" She's jubilant.

I snicker.

"Hopefully the doctor clears me to return to practice soon."

That summons a grin.

"What?" she says defensively.

"My beautiful optimist."

"It can't take *that* long for a bruised kidney to recover," she argues. "Two weeks, max."

"Your doctor said a month to be safe," I remind her.

"I don't have a month. We're training for nationals. They're in April!"

"It's only January." I set the bag of chips aside and climb onto the bed, stretching out beside her. "Focus on recovery. The squad will be there next month. And in the meantime, we can focus on the next project. Wanna practice our Spanish?"

Yup, I've been recruited into learning it with her. So far, I know how to say, "I want to fuck you in the ass." Diana saw it in a Spanish porno once, so it was the first item on our vocab list. Which is ironic, considering we're not even into anal. Hell, I don't think she could handle my size even if we were.

"Later," Diana says, waving off the suggestion. "I want to give our other project another shot first."

I firmly shake my head. "No way. We tried last night, and it hurt you."

"Just don't be so vigorous this time."

It's true. I might have gotten a bit overexcited when I fingered her in this bed last night. I ended up jostling her side pretty hard, and her resulting pain forced us to stop.

"Pretend your fingers are gently stirring soup."

I howl with laughter.

"Quiet," Diana chides. "Otherwise, Marge will pop in and lecture us for being too loud. We already have one Niall in our lives. I can't deal with a second one."

"I still think we should set them up. Imagine the beautiful, silent life they'd lead."

"Do we have to talk about this right now? I want to come," she whines, twisting her head to kiss my neck.

I gently roll her onto her back. "Fine. I'll pretend I'm stirring soup. But only if I can grind against your leg and come in my pants."

"You're so romantic. Stop being so romantic."

I brush a kiss over her lips. "I'm obsessed with you, Dixon. I hope you know that. And not just because I've been sucked into your pussysand."

"My pussy is powerful," she agrees.

I bring my mouth to her neck and suck gently. She shivers in response.

"Wait, did you lock the door?"

"Shit, no. One second."

I hop up to take care of it, and I'm walking back to the bed when Diana's phone dings with an alert. She gasps the second she reads it.

"What's wrong?" I ask, instantly on guard.

"I have devastating news. Brace yourself, Lindley."

"I'm braced."

"According to this, Zoey and the Connor broke up."

My eyebrows fly up. "Wow. They only lasted, what, four months outside of the hacienda?"

"I know," Diana moans. "It's official. True love doesn't exist."

I lie down beside her and bring her hand to my lips, brushing a kiss on her knuckles. "You're wrong," I say, my voice thick with emotion. "It does."

EPILOGUE

DAVE HEBERT HAS ADDED SHANE LINDLEY TO THE GROUP
NEIGHBORS.

SHANE:

Thanks for the add!

SHANE:

Like we discussed in the meeting earlier,
I think the Valentine's Day party should
DEFINITELY include a secret Valentine
exchange. Also, my little sis is pretty crafty,
so she can help out with any decorations,
cards, etc etc.

VERONIKA:

I love secrets :D

DIANA DIXON HAS REMOVED SHANE LINDLEY FROM THE
GROUP NEIGHBORS.

BRENDA KOWALSKY HAS ADDED SHANE LINDLEY TO THE GROUP NEIGHBORS.

SHANE:

Glad to be back in the chat! Thanks, B.

DIANA:

Sorry, guys. Brenda accidentally added Red Birch resident 2B. She's asked me to correct the error.

DIANA DIXON HAS REMOVED SHANE LINDLEY FROM THE GROUP NEIGHBORS.

RALPH ROBARDS HAS ADDED SHANE LINDLEY TO THE GROUP NEIGHBORS.

RALPH:

Shane, not sure why you got removed before? Diana, not sure what the error was? Anyway, re-adding you.

SHANE:

Ralph, my man! Appreciate the add.

RALPH ROBARDS HAS BEEN REMOVED AS AN ADMIN OF THE GROUP NEIGHBORS.

DIANA DIXON HAS REMOVED SHANE LINDLEY FROM THE GROUP NEIGHBORS.

DIEGO GOMEZ HAS ADDED SHANE LINDLEY TO THE GROUP NEIGHBORS.

SHANE:

> Regarding the spring barbecue, Gustav says he's able to offer a deal if we go to him for all our sausage needs.

VERONIKA:

> Yum! You really know how to whet a girl's appetite :D

CELESTE:

> How tasty!

DIANA DIXON HAS REMOVED SHANE LINDLEY FROM THE GROUP NEIGHBORS.

NIALL GENTRY HAS ADDED SHANE LINDLEY TO THE GROUP NEIGHBORS.

DIANA:

> Niall, did Shane tell you about the drum set he just bought??

NIALL GENTRY HAS REMOVED SHANE LINDLEY FROM THE GROUP NEIGHBORS.

READ ON FOR A SNEAK PEEK AT BOOK
ONE IN THE CAMPUS DIARIES

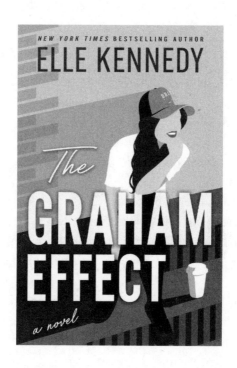

PROLOGUE
GIGI

Is he famous or something?

SIX YEARS AGO

When I was little, one of my dad's friends asked me what I wanted to be when I grew up.

I proudly replied, "Stanley Cup."

My four-year-old self thought the Cup was a person. In fact, what I gleaned from all those adult conversations going on around me is that my dad personally knew Stanley Cup (met him several times, actually), an honor bestowed to only the most elite group. Which meant Stanley, whoever this great man was, had to be some kind of legend. A phenom. A person one must aspire to be.

Forget turning out like my dad, a measly professional athlete. Or my mother, a mere award-winning songwriter.

I was going to be Stanley Cup and rule the fucking world.

I can't remember who burst my bubble. Probably my twin brother, Wyatt. He's an unrepentant bubble burster.

The damage was done, though. While Wyatt got a normal nickname from our dad when we were kids—the tried and true "champ"—I was dubbed Stanley. Or Stan, when they're feeling lazy. Even Mom, who pretends to be annoyed with all the obnoxious nicknames spawned in the hockey sphere, slips up sometimes. She asked Stanley to pass her the potatoes last week at dinner. Because she's a traitor.

This morning, another traitor is added to the list.

"Stan!" a voice calls from the other end of the corridor. "I'm popping out to pick up coffee for your dad and the other coaches. Want anything?"

I turn to glare at my father's assistant. "You promised you'd never call me that."

Tommy gives me the courtesy of appearing contrite. Then he throws that courtesy out the window. "Okay. Don't shoot the messenger, but it might be time to accept you're fighting a losing battle. You want my advice?"

"I do not."

"I say you embrace the nickname, my beautiful darling."

"Never," I grumble. "But I will embrace 'my beautiful darling.' Keep calling me that. It makes me feel dainty but powerful."

"You got it, Stan." Laughing at my outraged face, he prompts, "Coffee?"

"No, I'm good. But thanks."

Tommy bounds off, a bundle of unceasing energy. During the three years he's been my dad's personal assistant, I've never seen the man take so much as a five-minute break. His dreams probably all take place on a treadmill.

I continue down the hall toward the ladies' change rooms, where I quickly kick off my sneakers and throw on my skates. It's 7:30 a.m., which gives me plenty of time to get in a morning warm-up. Once camp gets underway, chaos will ensue. Until then, I have the rink all to myself. Just me and a fresh sheet of beautiful, clean ice, unmarred by all the blades that are about to scratch it up.

The Zamboni is wrapping up its final lap when I walk out. I inhale my favorite smells in the world: The cool bite of the air and the sharp odor of rubber-coated floors. The metallic scent of my freshly sharpened skates. It's hard to describe how good it feels breathing it all in.

I hit the ice and do a couple of slow, lazy laps. I'm not even participating in this juniors camp, but my body never lets me veer from my routine. For as long as I can remember I've woken up early for my own private practice. Sometimes I assign myself simple drills. Sometimes I just glide aimlessly. During the hockey season, when I have to attend actual practices, I take care not to overexert myself with these little solo skates. But this week I'm not here to play, only to help my dad. So there's nothing stopping me from doing a full sprint down the wall.

I skate hard and fast, then fly behind the net, make that tight turn, and accelerate hard toward the blue line. By the time I slow down, my heart is pounding so noisily that for a moment it drowns out the voice from the home bench.

"…to be here!"

I turn to see a guy about my age standing there.

The first thing I notice about him is the scowl.

The second thing I notice is that he's still astoundingly good-looking despite the scowl.

He has one of those attractive faces that can sport a scowl without a single aesthetic consequence. Like, it only makes him hotter. Gives him that rugged, bad-boy edge.

"Hey, did you hear me?" His voice is deeper than I expect. He sounds like he should be singing country ballads on a Tennessee porch.

He hops out the short door, his skates hitting the ice. He's tall, I realize. He towers over me. And I don't think I've ever seen eyes that shade of blue. They're impossibly dark. Steely sapphire.

"Sorry, what?" I ask, trying not to stare. How is it possible for someone to be this attractive?

His black hockey pants and gray jersey suit his tall frame. He's kind of lanky, but even at fifteen or sixteen, he's already built like a hockey player.

"I said you're not supposed to be here," he barks.

Just like that, I snap out of it. Oh, okay. This guy's a dick.

"And you're supposed to be?" I challenge. Camp doesn't start until nine. I know for a fact because I helped Tommy photocopy the schedules for everyone's welcome packages.

"Yes. It's the first day of hockey camp. I'm here to warm up."

Those magnetic eyes sweep over me. He takes in my tight jeans, purple sweatshirt, and bright pink leg warmers.

Lifting a brow, he adds, "You must have mixed up your dates. Figure skating camp is next week."

I narrow my eyes. Scratch that—this guy's a huge dick.

"Actually, I'm—"

"Seriously, prom queen," he interrupts, voice tight. "There's no reason for you to be here."

"Prom queen? Have you ever seen yourself in the mirror?" I retort. "You're the one who looks like he should be voted prom king."

The irritation in his expression sparks my own. Not to mention that smug gleam in his eyes. It's the latter that cements my decision to mess with him.

He thinks I don't belong here?

And he's calling me *prom queen*?

Yeah...kindly screw yourself in the butt, dickface.

With an innocent look, I tuck my hands in my back pockets. "Sorry, but I'm not going anywhere. I really need to work on my spins and loop jumps, and from what I can see"—I wave a hand around the massive empty rink—"there's plenty of room for both of us to practice. Now if you'll excuse me, this prom queen really needs to get back to it."

He scowls again. "I only called you that because I don't know your name."

"Ever consider just asking my name then?"

"Fine." He grumbles out a noise. "What's your name?"

"None of your business."

He throws his hands up. "Whatever. You want to stay? Stay.

Knock yourself out with your loops. Just don't come crawling to me when the coaches show up and kick your ass out."

With that, he skates off, sullying my pristine ice with the heavy marks of his blades. He goes clockwise, so out of spite I move counterclockwise. When we pass each other on the lap, he glares at me. I smile back. Then, just because I'm a jerk, I bust out a series of sit spins. In my one-legged crouch, I hold my free leg in front of me, which means it's directly in his path on his second lap. I hear a loud sigh before he cuts in the other direction to avoid me.

Truth is, I did indulge in some figure skating as a kid. I wasn't good enough—or interested enough—to keep at it, but Dad insisted I'd benefit from the lessons. He wasn't wrong. Hockey is all about physical plays, but figure skating requires more finesse. After only a month of learning the basics, I could already see major improvements in my balance, speed, and body positioning. The edge work I honed during those lessons made me a better skater. A better hockey player.

"Okay, seriously, get out of the way." He slices to a stop, ice shavings ricocheting off his skates. "It's bad enough I'm stuck sharing the ice with you. At least have some fucking respect for personal space, prom queen."

I rise out of the spin and cross my arms. "Don't call me that. My name is Gigi."

He snorts. "Of course it is. That's such a figure skater name. Let me guess. Short for something girly and whimsical like…Georgia. No. Gisele."

"It's not short for anything," I reply coolly.

"Seriously? It's just Gigi?"

"Are you really judging my name right now? Because what's your name? I'm thinking something real bro-ey. You're totally a Braden or a Carter."

"Ryder," he mutters.

"Of course it is," I mimic, starting to laugh.

His expression is thunderous for a moment before dissolving into aggravation. "Just stay out of my way."

When his back is to me, I grin and stick my tongue out at him. If this jerk is going to intrude on my precious early morning ice time, the least I can do is get on his very last nerve. So I make myself as invasive as possible. I pick up speed, arms extended to my sides, before executing another series of spins.

Damn, figure skating is fun. I forgot how fun.

"Here we go, now you're about to get it," comes Ryder's snide voice. A note of satisfaction there too.

I slow down, registering the loud echo of footsteps beyond the double doors at the end of the rink.

"Better skedaddle, Gisele, before you piss off Garrett Graham."

I skate over to Ryder, playing dumb. "Garrett who?"

"Are you shitting me right now? You don't know who Garrett Graham is?"

"Is he famous or something?"

Ryder stares at me. "He's hockey royalty. This is his camp."

ACKNOWLEDGMENTS

This book was a joy to write. From the first page, I was obsessed with Diana and Shane. I am so lucky to be able to do what I do for a living. I get to create fake reality shows and make my characters ballroom dance, which is honestly the coolest job of all time. And it wouldn't be possible without an entire support system of awesome people:

My editor, Christa Desir, for letting me live-text my reaction to the latest Fast and Furious movie as I watch it on an airplane when I'm supposed to be writing. (Oh, right, and for loving this book and letting me run wild with it). #family

The entire team at Bloom Books/Sourcebooks, and Raincoast in Canada, from the marketing and publicity department to the art team. Special shoutout to Madison for indulging my Love Island obsession.

My agent Kimberly, publicist Ann-Marie, and assistants Nicole, Natasha, Lori, and Erica. I'd honestly forget my own name if you guys weren't around to remind me.

Eagle/Aquila Editing for always dropping everything to proof-read for me, and a very big shoutout to my sensitivity readers who made sure the heavier subject matter and characterizations in the story were handled with care.

My sister and fellow puzzler for literally everything. You are the funniest person I know and my bestest friend ever.

Fellow authors, friends, and overall terrific people, especially Vi, Kathleen, Sarina, and Natasha.

And as always, you. My readers, the most supportive people on the planet. Thank you for reading, reviewing, raving, making me laugh, and always being there.

Finally, a quick note about some of the hockey plot points in this book—I usually fudge certain details, such as NCAA practice or game schedules, to create a fictionalized hockey world so that certain plot elements can line up better. All errors are my own (and often intentional).

Best,
Elle

ABOUT THE AUTHOR

A *New York Times*, *USA Today* and *Wall Street Journal* bestselling author, Elle Kennedy grew up in the suburbs of Toronto, Ontario, and holds a B.A. in English from York University. From an early age, she knew she wanted to be a writer, and actively began pursuing that dream when she was a teenager.

Elle currently writes for various publishers. She is the author of more than 50 titles of contemporary romance and romantic suspense novels, including the global sensation *Off-Campus* series.

Website: ellekennedy.com
Facebook: ElleKennedyAuthor
Instagram: @ElleKennedy33
TikTok: @ElleKennedyAuthor